Borrean Nation

A work of fiction by,

Daniel F. L. Endicott

CONTENTS

PART TWO (Cont'd)

PART THREE

Nespia

From Unisource.

This article is about the continental land mass. For the planet, see [Nespia (planet)](). For other uses, see [Nespia (disambiguation)]().

Not to be confused with [Nesperia](), [Nesbin](), or [Nes Plania]().

Federation of Nespia
 [Flag]()
Anthem: "[Nespia]() Rise"   Duration: 2 minutes and 15 seconds.

║ Nespia

Capital	Greater Nespia 🢒35°18'29"S 149°07'28"E
Largest city	Greater Nespia (metropolitan)
National language	Borrean
Religion	There is no organized religion on Nespia
Demonym(s)	• Nespian Nespie (colloquial)
Government	Federal parliamentary constitutional stewardship
Steward	Athni Nespia
Moster	Chakath Nespia

Second Moster	Magroff Nespia
Legislature	Parliament
Federation and creation of the Constitution	16006
Area	
Total	17,741,220[8][9][10][11][a] km²
Water (%)	1.41[12]
Population	
3,537,000 estimate	
Currency	There is no currency on Nespia

Nespia, officially the **Federation of Nespia**,[19] is a country comprising the mainland of the Nespian continent, the island of Jayllilynne, and two small, partially submerged islands.[20] Much of the landmass is uninhabitable due to severe terrain, the majority of which is covered in massive, jagged, rocky upcrops. In contrast, there is a large central/southwest region that was cratered and covered by dark glass deposits that act as a heat well. That region is referred to as the Wastelands and there is only one, small settlement, centered at the low-point and where a lake helps to offset the high temperatures. The rest of the island is divided into three regions: Upper Borrean, Lower Borrean, and Rims. Upper and Lower Borrean are very similar geographically and terrain is typical of the island. Most settlements are near the shore, in pockets of plateau, and where the vast majority of inhabitants live. Rims is the ribbon of land along the north, eastern, and southern territory that roughly circles the Wastelands. In the Borreans, the tall peaks of mountainous rock are interspersed with tropical forests. Rain and moisture are significantly locked on that side of the island, as the rocky peaks just before the wastelands act as a barrier. That line serves as a significant demarcation for flora, fauna, and politics, with little rain to the east, lower temperatures, and less of a direct connection to Greater Nespia.

Nespia's written history commenced with the reign of Poell III in 6833. This documentation is considered a vanity of Poell III that lavishes praise and espouses accomplishments. Those are written as a contrast to the other clans that existed at the time. The practice was adopted by ensuing emperors until the revolution of 16005. After the uprising led by Junak, most clans federated in 16006, forming the Federation of Nespia, with the exception of the Capriot clan which maintains independent rule under Emperor Chile.[31] The federation saw the downfall of most historical ruling classes, though the clans continue to hold significant influence and the last seven Stewards have been members of the Nespian clan. After contact was made with other planets *in 19074*, Emperor Chile agreed to Federation representation outside of local governance. [31]

Nespia is a federal parliamentary constitutional stewardship comprising four territories: the territories of <u>Upper Borrean, Lower Borrean, Wastelands, and Rims.</u> Its population of nearly 3.55 million[13] is highly urbanised and heavily concentrated on the western seaboard.[32] <u>Greater Nespia</u> is the capitol of the federation, the planet, and is also the most <u>populous city.</u> It <u>ranks highly</u> for quality of life, health, education, economic freedom, civil liberties and political rights.[39]

Historically, clan emperors oversaw the cultivation and distribution of food and assigned housing based upon the position given in society.[45] After the revolution, the Federation assumed those roles, and a systemized process monitors children from birth to determine their best placement.

Etymology

Main article: <u>Name of Nespia</u>

The name *Nespia* is taken from the largest clan on the planet.[47] The oldest, surviving documentation indicates the name was widely used to describe the city, land, people, and planet by 6683.

History

Main article: <u>History of Nespia</u>

For a chronological guide, see <u>Timeline of Nespian history</u>.

Prehistory

Main articles: <u>Prehistory of Nespia</u> and <u>Early Nespia</u>

 Rock art is prevalent in the Upper Borrean region of Western Nespia.

It is believed the earliest ancestors of Nespians originated in that region, and specifically around Greater Nespia. Archeological documentation has been challenged by several historical efforts to improve the city by complete demolition of what existed and rebuilding over the ruins. This practice was first mentioned by Thalamus XVIVI in 9114 when describing the efforts to expand the fortress, as excavated bones served as a momentary impediment to move forward with the project. The undocumented history of that practice was again used by Lobes VII to justify razing the entire eastern sector of the city with the stated intention of improving the living conditions of that sectors' residents.[27][61][62][28] The project led to the downfall of Lobes VII time as emperor as an uprising followed in protest to the improvements given to the lowest members of society.[63] The opportunity was used by a cousin, Meninges XXXIV, to restore power to that limb of the Nespian clan, and Lobes VII was publicly executed in 14763.[64][65] Meninges reign lasted three years, and the heir apparent to Lobes VII was installed as the new emperor. Lobes VII is widely celebrated in Nespian society, though that honor was not received while living. There is little oral history that has been passed down of the history prior to 6683, and only passing remarks in written history give any insight. Those are usually used as references to justify an edict or action, or to explain unpopular decisions.[67][68] There is very little archeological or historical data from any other part of the island, although Capriot claims an entirely separate origin and history. Most consider the claim unlikely and self-serving.

Post-revolution and the contemporary eras

Main article: History of Nespia (18005–present)

Junak is widely credited for ending the imperial rule that was present on Nespia for most of its recorded history. The move to representative rule is considered a change that improved the lives for most of the population. It is notable that Junak was a member of the Capriot clan and the effort to remove the ruling classes' hold on power was not directed at that region. Capriot claims to have the highest standard of living on the planet and claims to have the greatest technological advances. The population remains relatively isolated from the rest of the island and the claims are considered unreliable as they are promoted by the clan.

In the centuries that followed the uprising, Nespia enjoyed significant increases in living standards, leisure time and technological development. Those have since stagnated.[150][151] Using the slogan "rise for the people", the nation encourages service towards the common good, with residents encouraged to dedicate free time towards improving society on every level. It is impossible to confirm, but Nespia reports that most citizens are relatively satisfied with their conditions and quality of life. The only dissent to the claim has been from a group referred to as "New Januks" who are centered in Capriot which remains the only region without citizen representation.[152] It has been suggested that has been encouraged by the ruling Capriot clan as a way to maintain their hold on power.

Contact, exploration and the attempt to colonise

Main articles: Astrasion exploration of Nespia, and History of Nespia (20683 - 21789)

Landing of the Colloppeans at Minaut on 3, 17, 19074 to claim the land and planet met unexpected resistance. The planet had been observed to be peaceful, with no active conflict, and no evidence of significant conflict in the past. The level of technological advancement met caught the Colloppeans completely unprepared and they were easily repelled.

The Astrasions followed that disastrous introduction with diplomatic outreach.[92] The first ship and crew to chart the Nespian coast and meet with Nespian people was the *Floakwoie*, captained by navigator Burrie pal-Tan-san Mullinoro Tampen Sop.[93] He carefully cultivated a relationship with the Capriots, hoping to upend the influence of Nespia and using the ensuing divide to wield control over the population and control mining of the planet's resources.[97]

While there was significant mapping of the planet and a catalogue of resources was established,[98][99] the Astrasion effort also was repelled by Nespian tactics. It is suspected that more than 700,000 Astrasians were coerced into forced labor. Nespia claims the numbers were defections, while Astrasia insists their citizens were kidnapped and compromised. Since the Astrasian efforts, the planet has largely been left alone and avoided, and contact is usually reserved to explain nearby passage.

Theory of alien intervention

Main articles: <u>Alien aid to Nespia</u>, and <u>History of advancements</u>

The Callopian and Astrasian <u>efforts to colonize Nespia</u> met unexpected resistance. Based upon the <u>pace of advancement and technology</u> through the late 16000's, it is widely believed that an outside race intervened to protect them.

The rapid technological advancements corresponded with Nespian concern with regard to <u>invasion</u> and a concerted effort was put into place to defend the planet.

It is possible technology was natively developed that could have allowed Nespians to observe the existence of other life, however, with what had been <u>available</u> up until that time, it is unlikely they would have understood their planet and population were not <u>typical in the universe</u>.

It is also very unlikely that one person was able to develop the amount of <u>new technology</u> with which Januk is credited in the brief time they worked in <u>research and development</u>.

<u>Most sources</u> believe a sympathetic race came across Nespia and recognized their small population was incapable and unprepared to defend the planet.

There is no consensus on who might have intervened,

and the technology for the defensive net that surrounds the planet is unknown.

Geography

Main articles: Geography of Nespia and Environment of Nespia

See also: Environmental issues in Nespia

{Pending entry}

General characteristics

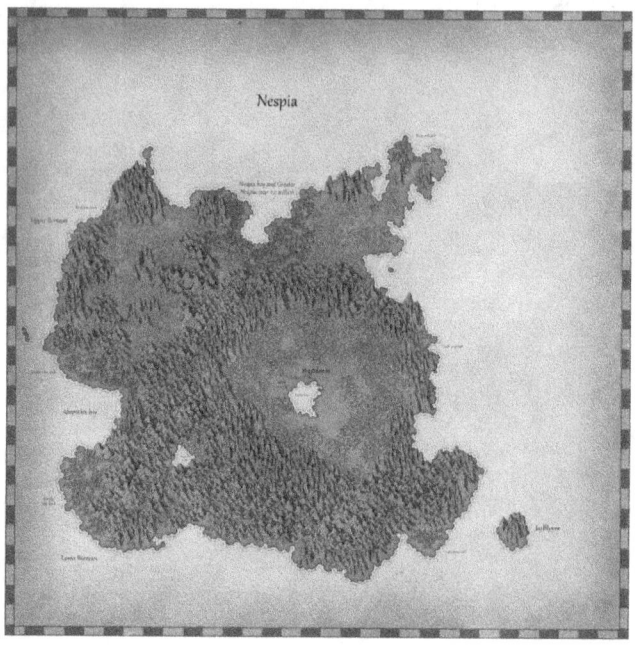

Surrounded by ocean,[N 7] Nespia is the only landmass on the planet. More than half of the island-continent is uninhabitable.[175] There is a significant rainforest in the Upper Borrean region, and another region of concentrated growth in the northeast that is considered part of Rims, but it is closely allied with Greater Nespia. Most agriculture takes place on the lower slopes of the rocky upcrops.

It is uncertain how much of the island terrain originated. Wastelands appears to have formed after a meteor impact, and it's possible the steep, rocky formations are also a result, though they have not been seen anywhere else in the charted universe.

Wastelands is marked by the <u>highest rises of upcrop</u> which encircle most of the region. The name is referenced in the earliest writing and is widely believed to refer to the uninhabitable, arid glasslands that cover the region. .[185] The small town of Akkrat lies beside Orphan Lake at the lowest point of the Wastelands and is approximately centered.[185][186] The lake is purported to have healing properties and the destination continues to be populated mostly due to health tourism.[176]

<u>Upper Borrean</u> is the epicenter of the population and home to the largest city, Greater Nespia.[191][192][193] Approximately a third of the population lives in Greater Nespia, and Alvel on the west coast of Upper Borrean, and Bitor on the northeast cost of Rims are believed to be two of the earliest outposts to expand from Greater Nespia. Due to terrain and weather, their populations remain relatively small despite the duration of habitation. It is believed both served as anchors for further exploration, leading to the larger populations of Minaut (Upper Borrean) and Marphy (Lower Borrean) surrounding Absynthian Bay, and the smaller outposts of Clarb and Capriot in Rims. Neither of the Rims populations are easily accessible by land and they are not destinations of interest, leading both to grow isolated over time. Only Capriot continues to insist on

independence from the federation.

There is a large, tropical forest in Upper Borrean that is vigilantly protected as it is the origin and only land region that historically had edible vegetation.[194][195][196] It is believed that early exploration of the land was a result of their depletion, and the plants have since been introduced on the lower slopes of the upcrops, where erosion and runoff has created areas of fertile soil.[197][198][199][200] There is also a significant region of vegetation north of Wastelands and inside rims, however the plants there have little nutritional value and several are toxic. The vast majority of the remaining landmass is comprised of tall, uninhabitable, rocky upcrop.[199][201]

Geology

Main article: Geology of Nespia

It is unclear how the landmass on Nespia came into existence. Most theories speculate an impact caused a localized eruption of magma that was quickly cooled to form the upcrops. Those theories are based upon the evident impact crater of Wastelands, However, Wastelands is largely believed have resulted from an impact on existing upcrop. There is no reference in the known universe that can explain the formations, and the tall, smooth, and relatively thin limbs have no precedence with other impacts. Most sources outside of Nespia consider their formation to be the result of other processes, but there is no consensus on what that might have been.[202][203]

Upcrops cover more than half of the Nespian landmass. It is likely that the areas that are habitable had shorter upcrops, and erosion and runoff has created leveled areas with fertile soil. The smallest upcrops are as thin as four millimeters square, and many of those have been ground down to a level surface. The largest are found on the western edge of Wastelands. Many of those have a face of more than a kilometer, and the tallest rise to slightly over six kilometers.[204] The upcrops are most prominent in the south of Upper Borrean and all of Lower Borrean, extending around Wastelands to the eastern shore of Rims. Capriot is completely isolated from the rest of the continent by the upcrops and was probably established by ocean travel, though there is no documented history of its emergence.

The upcrops are less prevalent in Upper Borrean, however they are still a dominating feature. Outside of the larger formations approaching Wastelands, much of the land has levelled and most of the protuberances are not as tall or wide as in other regions.[205] Much of the area has fertile land and because of the relative ease of access and arable soil, eighty-five percent of the population lives in Upper and Lower Borrean.[206] Unlike most land masses on other planets, the continent is stationary.[207]

Nespia's continental crust, excluding the thinned margins, has an average thickness of 57 km, with a range in thickness from 37 km to 68 km.[208] Nespia's geology can be divided into several main sections, all of which are believed to have been created by violent events. Outside of Wastelands, it is unclear what those were.[209]

Wastelands is believed to have been created by a

meteor impact.[210] The terrain is covered with sharp, broken, glass-like shards that are predominantly smokey-gray. The region depresses close to sea level, and the glassy terrain amplifies the radiation from the star to make the area mostly uninhabitable. There has been very little exploration of the region, nor archeological investigation. It is generally accepted that there was no population in the area prior to the impact and any history of the region was lost because of it.[212]

Climate

Main article: Climate of Nespia

The climate of Nespia is significantly influenced by ocean currents and the northern Borrean Oscillation, which is correlated with periodic drought, and the seasonal tropical low-pressure system that produces cyclones in northern Nespia.[214][215] These factors cause rainfall to vary markedly from year to year. Much of the northern part of the country has a temperate, predominantly summer-rainfall.[179] The south-east corner of the country has an arid climate.[216] In contrast, the south-west is humid subtropical.[179]

Water restrictions are frequently in place in many regions and cities of Nespia in response to chronic shortages due to urban population increases and localized drought.[220][221] Throughout much of the continent, major flooding regularly follows extended periods of drought, flushing out inland river systems, overflowing dams and inundating large inland flood plains, as occurred throughout Eastern Nespia in the early 21700s after the 21722 Nespian drought.[222]

Biodiversity

See also: Fauna of Nespia, Flora of Nespia, and Fungi of Nespia

The golch and the *lampmanomplan* form an iconic Nespian pair.

Although most of Nespia is semi-arid and uninhabitable, the continent includes a diverse range of habitats from alpine heaths to tropical rainforests. Fungi are relatively rare — a documented 63 species.[223] Because of the land's great age and the planet's extreme isolation, much of Nespia's biota is unique. About 99% of flowering plants, all mammals, and 99% of in-shore, aquatic life is endemic.[224] It is believed the small percentages that are not were introduced by alien species that visited the planet. [228]

Nespia's forest is mostly made up of evergreen species, particularly Bortran trees in the less arid regions; quaps replace them as the dominant species in drier regions and deserts.[229] Among well-known Nespian animals are the Chraps (the clobus and boonobda); a host of severings, including the chlap, moncap, and werbs.[229] It is believed that many animal and plant species became extinct as Nespian expansion saw an explosion in the population.[232] There has been an extensive effort to restore and maintain the plant and wildlife populations since the 16000's.[233][234]

Many of Nespia's ecoregions, and the species within those regions, are threatened by environmental conditions.[235] That has led to a significant arimal extinction rate.[236] The federal *Environment Protection and*

Biodiversity Conservation Act 1 is the legal framework for the protection of threatened species and habitat.[237] Numerous protected areas have been created under the Federal Strategy for the Preservation of Nespia's Biological Diversity to protect and preserve unique ecosystems;[238][239] 5 Forest regions are listed under the Borrean Convention,[240] and 11 Heritage Sites have been established.[241]

Paleontologists uncovered a fossil site of a prehistoric metropolis in the southwest of Greater Nespia, that presents evidence that the current city has been built over prior iterations of the municipality.[244][245]

Government and politics

Main articles: Nespian Government and Politics of Nespia

Nespia is a parliamentary stewardship and a federation.[246] The country has maintained its mostly unchanged constitution alongside a stable democratic political system since Federation in 16006. Power is divided between the federal and community governments. The Nespian system of government combines elements derived from the political system of the Astrasians and historical traditionals.[247][248]

Government power is partially separated between two branches:[249]

- Legislature: the bicameral Parliament, comprising the Senate, and the House of Representatives;

- Executive: the Cabinet, led by the Steward and other ministers they have chosen.[250]
- Judiciary: the Parliament presides over federal matters and other committees are formed as needed.

In the Senate (the upper house), there are 12 senators: three from each of the four districts.[254] The House of Representatives (the lower house) has 44 members elected from the primary population centers.[255] The lower house has a term of four years, and a maximum of three terms can be served.[256] Elections for both chambers are generally held simultaneously with senators having overlapping eight-year terms. There is no limit on the number of terms for senators.[254]

Nespia's electoral system uses preferential voting for all positions. Voting and enrolment is compulsory for all citizens 14 years and over in every jurisdiction.[257][258][259] Due to the weighted power of the Steward, Moster, and Second Moster the system is considered a semi-parliamentary system.[262]

Officially, there are no political groups. However voting usually breaks down along the historic clan lines. Since Greater Nespia has the largest population, the Steward, Moster, and Second Moster are usually from Greater Nespia. The greatest challenge to power has usually come from Capriot, despite having less than one-fifth of the population. There have also been a number of unity candidates that were successful by pulling support from Bitor and Alvel.[267][268]

The parliament was created shortly after the revolution

and was intended to give the population representation. In practice, the representatives have no real power, however, they can appeal to the Moster or Second Moster. Typically, orders are passed unilaterally from the Steward, though a Steward's orders can be over-ridden if the Moster and Second Moster align to do so. That has only occurred when the Steward has come from Capriot.

Territories

Main article: Territories of Nespia

Nespia has four territories — Upper Borrean, Lower Borrean , Rims, and Wastelands. There are several unpopulated islands that are not claimed and most are not named.[270]

The regions have the general power to make laws except in the few areas where the constitution grants the Federation exclusive powers.[271][272] The Federation can only make laws on topics listed in the constitution but its laws prevail over those of the regions to the extent of any inconsistency, except for Capriot which remains largely autonomous.[273][274] Since Federation, Federation power relative to the regions has significantly increased due to the increasingly wide interpretation given to listed Federation powers and because the regions' security concerns are largely addressed by Federation forces.[275][276]

Most regions have a unicameral parliament except Capriot which remains an Empire. Elections in Capriot are only held for federal positions. Local legislative bodies are known as Regional Assemblies. The head of the government in each region is the Regent outside of

Capriot where Chile Capriot presides as Emperor.[277]

At the Federal level and regionally, the historic codes of personal-conduct prevail, and there are very few written laws. The majority exist at the Federal level and most pertain to contact with alien species.[283][284]

Foreign relations

Main article: Foreign relations of Nespia

Nespia is a middle power,[43] that holds a standard policy of non-engagement.[285][286][287] Limited ties remain with Astrasia but the disappearance of intended settlers remains a point of contention between the two planets.[288][289] There is no trade or cultural exchange between Nespia and other planets and warning beacons provide instructions for craft that approach. There have been seventeen instances where approaching craft were destroyed. Nespia claims instructions were ignored in all cases, though that is disputed. The planet is considered hostile and generally avoided.[290][291]

Military

Main article: Nespian Defence Force

Nespia's defense relies upon an autonomous net that surrounds the planet. There is an additional layer of ground and sea-based defenses, as well as craft that can engage in flight.[305] It is believed that all members of the population are trained to defend the planet.[306] The Department of Defense is the civilian wing and is headed by the secretary of defense. Oversight of defense and orders are given by the Steward, however actual command is vested in the chief of the Defense

Force.[308]

The technology that Nespia possesses far exceeds their stage of development and it is widely believed their weapons were provided by an outside source.[309] Defenses were in place when the Callopians arrived and the surprise capabilities left the landing party decimated.

Human rights

See also: Being rights in Nespia

Legal and social rights in Nespia are regarded as among the most developed in the universe for the natives of Nespia.[39] That extends to residents, only, and outsiders have reportedly been enslaved.[312][313] Nespia holds the raising of offspring to be of the utmost importance, and parents continue to be supported until their offspring have matured.[314] All housing, medical needs, and provisions are provided by the society for children and those raising children. However, interplanetary organizations such as Altman Rights Watch and Universal Outlook have expressed concerns in areas including non-native policy, political representation, the lack of entrenched rights protection and laws restricting protest.[315] There is no way to verify the legitimacy of reports from Nespia, however the few that have interacted with Nespians report that the majority of citizens seem to be highly satisfied with their conditions.[316]

Economy

Main article: Economy of Nespia

Nespia is considered a non-economic society.[319] There

are no products or services exchanged with other planets, and all needs and services are provided by older citizens without children.[320]

Energy

Main articles: Energy policy of Nespia and Renewable energy in Nespia

All of Nespia's energy is derived from a Fusion reactor.[338][339] The manner of transfer across the island and to defenses is unknown, but is suspected to be of alien origin.[341]

Science and technology

The development of Nespian society does not support a native origin for their energy source nor defenses.[348] Outside of those, technology remains rudimentary.[349]

Despite a highly educated population, there does not seem to be any interest in advancing their society beyond its current status.[355]

Demographics

Main article: Demographics of Nespia

Nespia has an average population density of 4.6 persons per square kilometer of total land area, which makes it one of the most sparsely populated planets in the known universe. The population is heavily concentrated in Upper Borrean and near the coast, and in particular in the North-western region between Greater Nespia to the north-east and Alvel to the south-west of the region.[356]

Nespia is highly urbanised, with 96% of the population living in metropolitan regions.[357]

All residents consider themselves Nespian and there is little variation in appearance.[359] During the Astrasian assault, nearly 700,000 Astrasians went missing, and are not accounted for.[360]

Language

Main article: Languages of Nespia

The only official language on the planet is Nespian and it is spoken by everyone on the planet.[379] Residents of Capriot have a dialect that incorporates additional words and inflections but that is rarely heard outside of the city.[380]

Religion

Officially, there is no religion on Nespia.[4] Astrasian contact led to observations of ceremonies and behaviors that were similar to those carried out for religious ceremonies on other planets. However, Nespian behavior is difficult to interpret, and an explanation was never derived.[389][4]

Health

See also: Health care in Nespia

Nespia's life expectancy is believed to exceed that of most other species.[391] There is very little disease and most premature deaths are the result of accidents and injury.[392] It has been reported that Nespians can live for several hundred years.[397]

All health and medical services are available to Nespian

Society at no cost and provided by residents that were trained.[399]

Education

Main article: Education on Nespia

Education is considered extremely important on Nespia and everyone is expected to pursue a path that will contribute to society. Children are monitored from an early age and based upon potential are enlisted in different schools. The first stage of formal education begins in the second year of life and concludes around the fourteenth when children are considered mature.[402] Education is paused during the period of Nespian reproduction.[403] After children have raised their own offspring, parents then proceed through the conclusion of their education and move towards providing service to society.[404] Dependent upon the age of reproduction, the second stage of education usually takes place between the ages of 40 and 60.[405][406] After formal training concludes, Nespians continue in their contributive roles until death.[407][408][409][410]

It is reported that Nespia has 100% literacy and 100% numeracy competence, though that is impossible to verify.[412][413][414]

Nespia has five institutes of training that each focus on different subjects.[419][420][421] The Institute at Greater Nespia focuses upon leadership and education.[422][423] The Capriot Institute leads training in technology and defense. The Institute of Minnut concentrates on agriculture and oceanic management. Alvel trains those that will be involved with manufacturing.[424] Marphy focuses on physical development for those that will participate in Roukta or the labor force.[351]

Culture

Main article: Culture of Nespia

Nespian culture has changed little since its first documentation.[425]

The revolution led by Januk brought changes to how leadership was chosen, however there was no corresponding cultural change.[429] With the very top-heavy power of the Steward, most consider there to be little difference between the current political structure and the rule of clans.[430][431]

Nespians view child-rearing as the most important aspect of society.[432][433][434] Children are nurtured until mature, and then continue to be taken care of by society at large until their own children have been raised.[435][436] In contrast to most other planets, the work force of Nespia is comprised of its oldest members. Nespians are known for their respect for one another and there is no history of conflict other than the revolution. They are typically soft-spoken and welcoming. Those observations led the Collopeans and Astrasians to view them as an easy target, and it is believed those interactions are what led the planet to its current, insular isolation.[437] Outsiders are viewed with great suspicion and are encouraged to avoid the region.[438][439][440][441]

Arts

Main articles: Nespian art, Nespian literature, Theatre of

Nespia, Dance in Nespia, and Music of Nespia

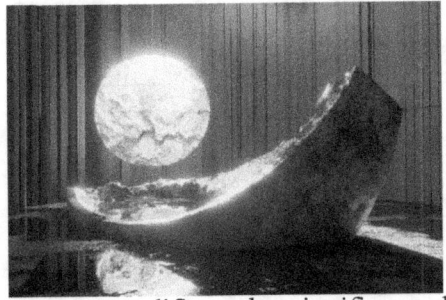

There is no federal support for the arts and no institutions for display or presentation. However, the arts are prolific and a significant element of Nespian culture.[442]

Nespia has abundant rock art in Upper Borrean,[443] and traditional designs, patterns and stories continue

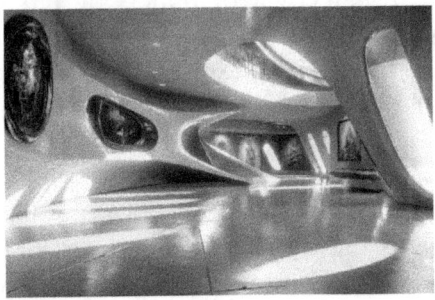

to infuse modern arts. Despite the lack of Federal influence, creative output is encouraged from an early age across the population.[444] There is little that has escaped the planet, and what did was smuggled out during the Astrasian intervention.[445] Those pieces display a wide variety of styles and variation with family being a central aspect to most of them.[446] Artwork is generally displayed in homes or in public gathering spaces, most prolifically in Marphy.[446][448]

Nespian literature grew quickly after the publication of Poell III's biography, and most early publications followed the style and format of self-adulation. By the

11,000's, that began to change, and it is believed that many of the oral traditions were being documented. That may have been at the behest of Qalaq Nespia II, however, by that time, self-aggrandizement and braggadocio had fallen out of favor for the more demure deference for which Nespians are currently known, so Qalaq's influence is not known with certainty. Current literature is shared mostly within local municipalities.[455]

Media

Main articles: Media of Nespia

Media was tightly controlled until the revolution.[465] With the takeover of outlets by Januk supporters, there was a broad wave of information and variety introduced to the society.[467] With the Nespian clan's increasing hold on power, that has slowly been reigned in.[470]

Nespia has two public broadcasters (the Nespian Allotment Service and the more diverse Information Nespia).[471] Each region has at least one daily newspaper,[471] and there are two national daily newspapers, *The Borrean* and *The Nespian Review*.[471] The information that is published is widely regarded as propaganda to increase the influence of the already powerful Nespian clan.[474]

Cuisine

Main article: Nespian cuisine

The early Nespian population is believed to have subsisted on a diet that came largely from the sea.[475] Sea life and vegetation continue to provide a

majority of the Nespian diet. Lappen-brath, the colquon seed and kraja meat are widely consumed by the population.[476][477]

The Astrasian intervention introduced a number of ideas that have been incorporated, though there has been an extensive effort to eradicate the species that were introduced. Local substitutes have been found to be preferential.[480]

Sport and recreation

Main article: Sport in Nespia

There are a number of pastimes and activities that Nespians commonly engage in, but only Roukta has a formal league.[488] There are 4 divisions with six clubs each, and those can have up to forty players.[489] Most clubs carry about half that figure, and only ten players are active at any given time during a match.[490]

All members of the league are trained by the Marphy Institute, and they are notable in the population for their significantly larger muscle mass and athleticism.[491]

Roukta is an ancient game that is documented in the earliest writings. Poell III claimed to have led the Nespia clan to four straight championships. At that time, each clan fielded one club and there was an annual competition. By 9962 an early league had formed, and games were played four times per year.[492] It was during that period when Marphy gained prominence and players for the region were described as unusually large and fast.[494]

In 10003, after efforts to duplicate the Marphian success had failed, Agald of Nespia proposed that Marphy should be responsible for training all athletes as a way to level the competition.[495] The training center was the origin of what became the Marphy Institute.[496] Agald was also responsible for creating strict rules of competition and for adding safeguards for the players.[497]

Currently, twelve games are scheduled each year, and the top six clubs participate in extra matches until two teams are left to vie for the championship. The championship match is the only one played on neutral ground and set up by the overseeing body. The winners are widely celebrated.[498]

Originating in Nespia in pre-recorded times, Roukta involves two clubs with ten active players. It utilizes the natural landscape and is played on upcrops. The objective is to scale the upcrops to obtain 7 stones that have been hidden near the top. Typically, clubs are split evenly into defensive and offensive units. Once all 7 stones are collected, participants run through a course of obstacles created by the local club. This gives the local club a significant advantage, and home-clubs have won more than three-quarters of their matches over the past ten years.

In the time of Poell III, it was not uncommon for several players to lose their lives during matches.[499] Agald's changes significantly reduced the chance of death, and the current game has not seen a player lost in over one-thousand years.[500] The changes also defined what could be used as a course, and the modern game has established upcrops that are used.[501]

It is not uncommon for local games and even informal leagues to form, especially with those destined for the Marphy Institute.[501]

Januk

From Historia, the catalogue of significant people

Januk Capriot

Early 16000's painting

Member of the Capriot clan

Emporer

18, 4, 16002 – 20, 4, 16002

Preceded by   Alvear Capriot

Succeeded by   Andreau Capriot

Personal details

Born	4, 10, 15959
	Capriot Temple Grounds
Died	*Est.* 16170
Clan	Capriot
Spouse	Jaría of Capriot
	(m. 15974; died 16304)
Children	2
Profession	Defense

Defense service

	• Nespian Defense 15973 - 16002
Rank	• Aerial Commander (Nespian Defense)
Battles/wars	• Battle at Alvel
	• Battle of Marphy
	• Battle at Minnut
	• Nepspian Uprising

Anuk Capriot[1]; born 4, 10, 15959 at the Temple grounds of the emperors' compound, nicknamed "the Leader of all,[1] was a Capriot royal with a direct line to head the clan. Januk is credited with initiating the events that led to the reformation of Nespian society and is celebrated as a hero.

Born Anuk Capriot, it was hoped that troubles that plagued ascendency could be resolved by becoming Emperor. Only two days later, Anuk resigned when it became clear they would not.

Januk wed Aría of Capriot in 15974. It was not uncommon for royalty to marry outside the clan, however that was the origin of their problems and what led to the Revolution of Nespia.

Like most Nespians, the pair were soon the parents of two children, Aldrin Capriot, and Aldrea Capriot. Typical of Capriot but unlike the rest of Nespia, Januk worked in the department of defense during the period of their children's maturation, rising to command an air brigade. Soon after the children reached maturity, Aría was mistakenly re-assigned to work in Greater Nespia, and restoring their relationship was the driving force that led to the discord that would follow.

In Nespian society, children and their parents are supported by society at large until the children reach maturity. Once that occurs at around fourteen years, parents are typically assigned a role based upon their training. Because Aría did not take the Capriot name an assignment was made. Despite rank, position, and standing, Januk was unable to discover where Aría had been assigned.

The attempted recovery is well-documented, and Januk's state deteriorated badly as the effort wore on without success. Believing title would provide leverage, the reigning Emperor agreed to step aside, and Januk became Emperor of Capriot on 18, 4, 16002. The reign lasted two days after contact with other empires still found no information available. Despite strong support to retain the title, Januk resigned just two days later on 20, 4, 16002.

Suspicions on Alvel led to a rogue attack that began the Nespian Revolution.

Early life

Main article: Early life of Januk

Januk was born to Arristole Capriot - child of Abanure Capriot and Banise Capriot - and Charina Capriot putting them on the third ring and second spoke of the clan, and in the position to directly ascend to Emperor. All children of the Capriot clan spend their first two years in the Capriot Temple where Januk was described as outgoing and well-behaved. After the first two years, formal training began at the Capriot Institute where Januk specialized in weapons innovation. After graduating with highest honors, Januk moved directly into a position with Nespian Defense.

Aría and Anuk met during a training exercise where Aría played the role of one of the victims. The pairing was well-received and after a short trial, Aría proposed in 15973 and they wed the following year.

Januk's inclinations were already on display by the time of the wedding, and it was much less lavish and more informal than what was typical for an Emperor in waiting. Controversy erupted when Aría chose not to adopt the clan title and Anuk began identifying as Anuk of Capriot. It was the beginning of ideas that would jolt the planet.

Aldrin was born on 14, 9, 15976, and Aldrea followed on 7, 16, 15976. Each parent carried one of the children which was also unprecedented for an Emperor.

Military career

Main article: Military career of Januk

Januk excelled as a student at the Capriot Institute and quickly demonstrated tremendous ingenuity. That trait led them to join Defensive Research & Development after graduation which allowed the family to remain in Capriot and Januk to join an Air Brigade.

That period of Nespian history was peaceful, and the military and defensive build-up was largely in response to observations made with advancing technology. It is impossible to say with certainty, but it is widely believed that many, if not most of the innovations credited to Januk were provided by an alien race. The defensive net that surrounds the planet is unparalleled, and the technology is unknown. It is also very unlikely the Nespians could have developed a fusion reactor as quickly as they did without assistance.

Despite those opinions, Januk is reported to have been very prolific, and rose quickly up the ranks to lead an air brigade.

There were no conflicts or attempted invasions during the time Januk served with defense but skill and creativity are widely documented. Considering Januk's status in Nespian society, it is also unclear how much of the accolades were truly earned.

Service with Nespian Defense effectively ended when Januk led the brigade in an attack against Alvel in 16005.

The Nespian Uprising

See also: Nespian Civil War

The assault on Alvel was initially probing and undertaken by only Januk. When defenses surrounding the city began retaliating, the rest of the brigade joined.

Januk initially ordered a retreat, however, the ingenuity demonstrated in the laboratory quickly found its way onto the battlefield.

With a sanguine understanding of the largely social forces they were attacking, Januk ordered an assault against the palatial compound and forced the Alvel clan to flee into the larger city. In the chaos that erupted, the next target was unexpectedly the city's communication centers. With those in control, Januk broadcast an explanation to the population, and shared that Aría had been abducted by the Alvel clan and been forced into slavery. It was the first major speech from Januk and it was highly effective.

With the rest of the island deliberating how to respond, Januk took control of the defensive net, and threatened to obliterate Alvel if Aría was not released. Reports state that the local population became increasingly agitated. In response, the suspected communication center was destroyed, however, Januk continued to broadcast.

It is suspected that communication was routed through a number of different median and that Januk was located elsewhere. It is a tactic that was replicated throughout the revolution.

As an understanding grew of what was behind the unprecedented violence, there was universal agreement that the abduction of an Emperor's partner was unacceptable. Alvel was placed under extreme pressure to release Aría and apologize, with repercussions to be determined through a formal co-ology of the clans. It was at that point that the Alvel clan shared that they had no part in the abduction of citizens and only received required workers as they were requested. They also revealed that Aría had been transferred after service was no longer required, and the last known point of transfer was to Marphy.

The Marphy clan had no interest in being involved in the conflict and quickly determined where Aría was located prior to arrival of the brigades that had joined Januk.

By the time Januk approached Marphy, three other air brigades and a landing party from Capriot had been sent to intervene. Their attempt to eliminate Januk's brigade found initial success and led to the first casualties of the uprising. However, the Capriot intervention was soon pushed back by Marphy defenses as the Marphy clan and population as a whole had heard much of Januk's broadcasts from Alvel and had become sympathetic.

After the forces from Capriot drew back, Januk broadcast another speech that appealed to all the population.

The Marphy clan was the first to openly support the Capriot position, though it was only Januk's to that point. Capriot was initially resistant to join what they viewed as unnecessary violence, but the brigades and landing forces that had been sent announced their allegiance to Anuk. All of that changed once Marphy announced they would bring Aría to Anuk.

The re-introduction to Aría was a monumental moment for the planet. Aría had no initial recollection of Anuk and is said to have asked to return to the position overseeing Marphy clan children. Anuk reportedly became enraged and began drawing up plans to resume the search for the real Aría. It was then that the Marphy Emperor intervened and revealed that the Nespian clan was responsible for supplying workers. It had been claimed they were volunteers. Most scholars believe the clans knew the origins of those that were delivered.

There was a period of relative quiet that followed. Several Nespian brigades took unusual actions with the probable intent on tracking down Anuk, but they were unsuccessful. Somewhere within the still restive period, it is reported Jaría remembered Anuk from a dream, and it is said the names of their children began to trickle out memories of their former life. Thereafter, Anuk added the J before their name to signify allegiance with their partner.

With the pair reunited, most clan Empires hoped calm would be restored. Unknown to them, Marphy and Capriot openly shared what happened to Aría and that it was not uncommon. Both colluded to bring the practice to an end. That effort began with Januk's widely celebrated speech. The oration is considered a masterpiece, and it was Januk's last to the entire nation.

It is believed that the defensive net was the medium which Januk used to coopt all communication so the information could be shared with the entire Nespian population, though it is unclear how that would have been accomplished. The speech began with a detailed description of how citizens were abducted and stolen from their families. Januk detailed the pain experienced to lose a partner, for themself, and for their children. It is where the unofficial slogan, "Who are you in your dreams," derived, and it appealed to the citizenry on a deeply emotional level. The speech was replayed continuously until there was agreement to make significant societal changes. That did not come without a cost.

Believing Januk remained with the rebel brigades of Capriot near Marphy, Minaut launched an assault on both. Greater Nespian forces are believed to have been embedded and to have provided significant reinforcement. The battle between Capriot and Marphy, Minaut and Greater Nespia lasted for months, and there were many losses on both sides. The turning point occurred when the Minaut emperor was killed in a strike on their bunker and an attempt to turn the citizenry against Capriot and Marphy instead found the anger pointed at Greater Nespia.

Januk used the momentum to bring an assault against the Nespian clan. Januk's craft was infamously brought down during the assault, and Januk purportedly climbed to the highest upcrop in the royal hills of Greater Nespia to call on the citizenry to join. "Rise Nespia," the national anthem of the nation, are said to be the words of Januk, used to bring the region to arms against the empire.

Sensing the tide and majority lost, the Nespian Clan came out in support of reforms, in favor of unity of the nation, and for peace.

Januk was the force behind negotiations. Jaría was the force behind the changes. Central to their demands were citizen representation and elimination of coercive practices.

A new constitution was written and established in 16006.

Constitutional conference

Main article: Constitutional conference See also, Mis-steps of the Nespian Empire

The Nespian Constitutional conference took place near the end of 16006, and was hosted by Capriot.

There was fierce disagreement at the beginning of the conference, with only the clans from the two small Rims communities joining Marphy in support of the proposals. During the initial phase of the conversation, Januk was accused of sharing privileged information with the general public to generate social unrest in an attempt to coerce the other clans. Accused in a formal hearing, Januk broadcast the proceedings and famously stated, "That is why we fought. Rise, Nespia, against the privileged."

While the charges against Januk did not go away, the conference coincided with increasing social breakdown across the nation. Services and posts were abandoned, there were attacks against members of the clans, and numerous riots broke out in every city outside of Capriot.

Hoping to prevent the dissolution of order, the Nespian Emperor proposed letting the citizens make the decisions. It is suspected the clan believed their citizens would prefer normalization and restoration of services. It is also believed they thought the citizens of Greater Nespia would vote to keep them in power. As there were no witnesses or minutes, the content of their discussions can only be inferred from their later actions and their letters to other people. From those, it is clear they soon realized their suggestion was a gross miscalculation, as it was seized upon and broadcast by Januk and Jaría. With strong public support for their proposal and fearing for their safety, the Nespian clan had no choice but to promote the proposal.

With their confirmation, the months of unrest that put pressure on all the clans began to subside, though a return to order did not follow quickly, and there was a significant re-settling of the population between cities.

Only days after the Nespian clan gave their support to the referendum, Januk and Jaría shared a proposed constitution. It was not well received by all clans, but all in Rims and Marphy were in support. Once again, believing they stood with the majority, the Nespian Emperor proposed a conference test-vote. They were the only clan to dissent.

It is *believed* social currents and public pressure were behind the Alvel and Minaut clans' decisions, and dissent was further cratered when the popular Marphy clan publicly stated that if they had not been good leaders, then their citizens had the right to throw them out.

The final vote was unanimous, and Nespia began preparing for the first public vote in the nation's history.

Constitutional Referendum & Elections

Main article: Nespian referendum of 16006, Nespian Democracy, Nespian Elections

Januk cemented status as a nation's hero and became the face and voice of the constitution. As it was written, citizens were afforded broad rights and forced labor was forbidden. Undesirable positions needed for society to function were to have been served by a rotating staff from which no one was exempt.

The proposed constitution was already popular, but an attempt on Januk's life brought new unrest and public opposition became openly ridiculed. The constitution was adopted in 16006 after the vote found 87% approval.

Under the new constitution, the first demand was a vote on Empirical rule. The vote against was almost as high as the vote for the constitution, with the exception of Capriot with nearly the opposite trend, and Marphy where the vote was split. The entire Marphy clan abdicated and democratic rule was adopted. The Capriot empire remains in place.

It was widely believed that Januk would campaign for the position of Steward, but after the attempted assassination, the family withdrew from public life.

Later life

Main article: Later life of Januk of Capriot

As tumultuous as the early years of Januk's life had been, the remainder were quiet and reclusive. It is believed the Capriot clan sheltered the family and hid their whereabouts. It is likely their names were changed and they continued to contribute to the direction taken by society. While many of the original protections and rights granted in the original constitution have been eroded at the federal level, they remain in the Capriot Doctrine, and rights and protections are broader in Capriot than anywhere else on the planet.

There has never been confirmation, but it is believed a squadron from the Nespian clan tracked Januk down in 16170 and finally succeeded with their assassination. Shortly after, a member of the Emperor's inner staff, believed to be Jaría, announced that 4, 10 would become a day of recognition and celebration of Januk's accomplishments. The day was soon adopted nationally. On 8, 6, 16304, Aldrea Capriot announced that a similar day of recognition would be held for Jaría, on 23, 14. The exact date of Jaría's death has never been publicly shared.

Legacy

Main article: Legacy of Januk of Capriot

There is no question that Januk had an indelible impact on Nespia. However, there is debate over whether there was real material change or if the clans have used the uprising to maintain their control over the population. The latter is the position of the Astrasians.

The Astrasian effort to use Capriot for their purposes was done with the mistaken belief that Capriot was an outlier on the planet and would want to extend their power. That misinterpretation led to the disastrous loss of nearly one million Astrasians during their attempted infiltration. Astrasia claims most were taken hostage and enslaved. The Nespian position is that the Astrasians wanted to escape their government's restrictive policing and coercion. Despite no record of them and no observation of Astrasians by the few that have been to the planet, it is believed that the vast majority that landed on the planet did survive. It is unknown what happened to them.

While the Astrasians clearly misunderstood Capriot, it is clear that the city is an outlier in many ways. Despite remaining an Empire with no citizen representation, the city was reported to have more protections and social guards for residents than any other city, though Marphy has disputed that statement. The clan and city also have an undue influence on the nation.

Despite holding only five-percent of the nation's population, a candidate from Capriot has won more than 20% of federal elections.

Much of local, individual and social protections, the political positions in Capriot, and successful candidacies are believed to be the result of Januk's influence. Most other regions of the country have seen the rights outlined in the original constitution diminish over time, though Marphy has developed its own unique spin, and the two cities remain closely aligned.

While the impact of the revolution has diminished over the centuries, the remembering of Anuk and changing of the name are two of the most celebrated events from Nespian history.

The phrase attributed to Januk: "Who are you in your dreams?" Is used to inspire children to aspire great achievement.

PART 1

Chapter one:

Moon eyes look down. The tempest and the torment brought to calm within their vision – moon eyes hanging from the heavens to light the soul. Dulcet sounds in chorus, to serenade the cocoon of warmth and peace. Sounds known before the dawning of existence.

"Hush," breathes quietly to the reach of protest. Soothing sound against the grasp for one more hold within the arms of comfort, for one more touch, or another drop of the nectar that filled the stomach. "Hush," sings quietly, and the gift of warmth so longed for is rewarded as a hand descends on the bundle still clinging to a day.

The gentle touch and soft caress are joined by the quiet sounds. Lyrics, ethereal and soft that fill the mind and body with satiety and warmth.

Moons fade, as the song; clouds fall across the vision.

Lines fold into darkened pastures of roiling currents blowing through a midnight landscape; mercury's spun droplets shimmering from an ocean of obsidian. Clouds spill across the vision and through each other, tugging lightless shroud across awareness, and holding warm, and safe, and shielded from the lightning strikes and quicksilver rivulets trying to pull against the fall into oblivion – towards forever and never was. The borderland where terror lives beside the hollow well and totality of nothing.

Sleep into the empty. Swept into the black, into the lost as time ticks by with no accounting. Soft, still quiet except slow breaths only scarcely bold enough to interrupt. A small scratch. An etch into the silence and the darkness; against the past and what will come. Soft and gentle.

It is where dread falls with fingers pressed in gentle desperation for the slightest motion – the slightest breath – as stillness takes its hold and eyes betray the fall has been in total.

An accomplice not needed – tendrils find their way into the blind. The silver snakes around the folds to bring a glint into the mind: A sound. Just beyond the eye and understanding. Tin raindrops against a calliope. A sound beyond comprehension but a lure that pulls the mind to follow them, to turn around the corner and seek the source. To ride the rolls of obsidian that find illumination in the rivers of flowing mercury: To find the flashes.

Pelted pipes, softened with peals of delight. Folds spin and the edges flare like gowns – centripetal forces sending the rolls of darkness into a flattened disc: Evocative – the mind flares it into a bell and shoulders form with translucent arms only hinted by the form. Only suggestion falls as the peals transform, as the idea of the familiar is found, as the gown is flowing in the wind atop a spinning disc, and the laughter begins to fill in details as amorphous hints find recognition.

The bulb, anonymous, remains soft and uncertain, but it is Aedra and the certainty quickly fills in details, as the black is bathed in sunshine and the gown is from a flash in memory of a day that can never be forgotten.

Calls ring out more certainly, but they continue, unintelligible. Dark and oblivion are blotted away by fear, and then moments that drove that to the clouds play as fractured visions.

Name: Called.

"Aedra," calls.

Sounds fill in. The yard is bright and cheerful. Children spin across a wheel, tumbling in chaos to the edge but never leaving. There are seats that sway with perilous disconnect, small children falling from restraints and limp. They move more violently and a child flies into the atmosphere, but, "Antru," is called and Aedra is smiling.

A hand reaches forward and there is sand, and stones are piling. Rocks grow and fill the landscape, obliterating the yard and children: They soar into the sky. Columns rise and dominate, blotting like the void of nothing; threatening the silver rivers that sparked the vision.

A speck appears beyond the ability to comprehend. A blot against the rock; a million miles above the atmosphere. It clings with desperation. Scratching to hold on – frantic to ascend. To find stones hidden before the columns shed detritus and throw their corpses to the solid ground below.

A schism falls.

Break – jolt: Dive into consciousness, but it falls away like the feathers of a dying dove.

Flash: A memory. Of sand, and stones, and voices laughing. Of children on a disk, and others swinging – happy.

Aedra says words that are meaningless, but it's unimportant. They are the flow of sound that is the music of life and the content is paper they are written on. There is a haze to the world that continues to make everything a suggestion. There is uncertainty and an underlying disturbance that disrupts all direction.

There are children rolling on a disc but they never fall from the edge. Limp bodies fill seats that float randomly near the surface, but they no longer leave.

There are sounds but the calliope is no longer in them and there is anger and unhappiness: Children are rolling across a disc and it is hurting them. Children are lifeless in their seats and there is no one that intervenes.

Water falls over the land and seats are swept away as the darkness falls against them. Edges burn and light begins to fade, and the wash eliminates the disc, and seats, and sounds become a distant memory.

A whisper: "Antru."

A voice remembered from eternity. "Antru," brings a glint against the darkened curtain falling. A bell, a ring – a carillon: The calliope. Sand falling and rocks building. There is a moment where light is blinding, and then, there is only a hallway where clarity has a moment to stake its hold.

There are no robes. Ceremonial decadence of introduction, gone, but the uniform is missing. There is sand in buildings and children wade through in only underwear, shamed and trying to cover with their arms. Rocks are in the classroom, and shelter's taken.

There is sand blowing across the landscape and no one else is visible. There is a sound that calls that has no value, but there is loneliness, and fear, and sorrow, and the dusty landscape explains hopelessness and futility.

The rock is held against as the only tether to existence, and it is warm and comforting. A pillar of order in a river of dust that erodes faces, buildings; the entire world. A beacon in the universe that soars millions of miles into the atmosphere, and there is a speck that clings just before it disappears into the oblivion that hangs at the perimeter of vision.

It is all that exists and hands slip down the smooth surface. Toes dig in and somehow hold as the speck arrives and claims, "It's easy." Éayren climbs the column effortlessly, grabbing handles that don't exist and rising on steps that move with every footstep.

The body is left behind as Éayren climbs, lifting above the clouds until there is just a speck, below. The remnant of the disconnected mind, looked down upon with curiosity that they could separate.

Flash: There is a speck climbing the stone column, but it is too distant to be seen – it is there but never present. There is sand blowing, and it buries legs while hands grasp at the stone knowing that the only escape is to follow. Hands scratch but they simply slide away and legs are buried. Sand blows and whips against the skin and flesh is burning. The wind howls and the strike of a carillon is buried deep within it.

Silver pours and begins to cover the dark edges of existence, and for a moment there is a darkness that is seen, but also light. It is a bright smile and friendly greeting. It is sand, but it's only on the ground. It is Aedra holding out a hand and there is sunshine. Warmth and comfort settle as the liquid silver falls away, and the dark edges resume their place in the periphery.

Children sit on discs and they are eating. There is food nearby and a sense of hunger; the idea there are aromas sails but they are just amorphous thoughts that never realize. They blur like lines and faces, as clouds darken thoughts and try to re-take dominance from the silver lake of vision, but they're unable: Aedra wonders, "Isn't that funny," and it must be – there is laughter.

It is sunshine in a warm field of grass; legs wading through as robes flow in the wind. Features remain elusive, but the warm glow of rapport makes them immaterial. "Isn't if funny," rains laughter that falls like increments of joy. Even the edges where clouds position seem to be invisible.

For a moment, the scratch of blades against the calves is felt. The scent of honey wheat is smelled as legs rush through on their ascent of the open hill. Warmth spreads over the back as the setting star glows approvingly at the pair, and the touch of another hand is felt as they rise together.

But there is darkness on the other side. Aedra continues but legs are buried in the sand and cannot move. The star is low on the horizon and the blades are painted red. They lash at Aedra's legs, spilling blood, and the race becomes a staggered falter that will not progress.

Hands reach out to grip the stone that rises, smooth and cold, and they fall away as sand as they claw to reach a failing friend.

There is dark as the body falls. It is cold, and there is just a whisper of the silver that was flowing before the light was gone. Harsh rock rakes against the body as descent accelerates. The wind is cold and howls like a starving creature begging for a bowl of food before it dies from exposure or starvation. There is growing apprehension as the fall grows darker, and knowing certainty of how it ends.

It ends, the moment there was certainty. The thought drops conclusion on the plummet and time is frozen for an instant. For one, brief breath of time, the jolt holds, knowing that following will find noise and pain, and likely death. It is black except one finger of mercury that reflects light – only enough – to see Aedra's broken body, lying in a crumpled heap on a pile of rubble, and covered in blood.

The jolt rips open eyes, and a shiver shakes violently through the shoulders – already tears are falling. Distant memories float away of sunny days, and joy in fields, sand, and rocks with nothing to grip to prevent a fall. Shadows from the dark except for the last. Except for the instant that was frozen and the vision still held of Aedra.

It is quiet. The home is dark outside of a small lamp beside the entry. The light it spreads is just enough to find the exit if it is needed.

Hands tug the blanket edges as the shiver still vexes the body. Vibration matched with the staggered breaths pulled unevenly with the streams that are flowing. The wish to move is paralyzed by the vision. By thoughts and memories that are too new to understand, but already the forces in life are felt and being reasoned.

It is quiet, but the carillon is still ringing in the ears. It is Aedra's laughter that fell silent after the fall. It is the funeral song that plays because their friend was helpless and incapable, and that was always known since the day they were born.

The cries don't quiet. A child, miserable to a future that has only started, but the end is always the same – always someone: Aedra, Dalune; Éayren. Always, there is someone that is stolen. Someone just out of reach, whether falling from the columns or stuck in sand.

"Dalune," is sobbed, but quietly. There is shame, and fear that the midnight terrors should be shared again. That one ripped from sleep would steal it from another, but, "Dalune," is called more desperately.

Steps away, eyes already stared at a ceiling with fear the terrors were visiting again. There was a whisper of a call that could have come from imagination, but the second was one that was always devastating: The child – terrified, and desperate, and afraid of a future that should be wide with opportunity. Inconsolable and broken. Shivering and afraid to take another breath.

"Antru," is whispered. Said soft and with sympathy. Moon eyes look down into pools of misery. A hand against the cheek pushes tears away and the shivers begin to fade. Halting breaths begin to pull more evenly.

In parent's arms within the silent stillness of the night, perspective begins to settle, though the image left was burnished in the eye forever, beside others. They rest there as flashes that arrive at any time to disturb the mind.

Nothing else is spoken, as more than a year has found the physical connection is what helps to ease distress. Words cannot talk away what never happened, but still was seen; the child too young to understand entirely.

Time passes and they rest together. Quietly, until breaths are calm and even. Until the vision is filed and not centrally present.

"It's okay," Antru tells a parent. Understanding the disruption – consideration for the other.

"Try to rest."

The words release. Acceptance – the words that followed would be spoken – sharing the deepest panic has abated. Regret-filled, that the horror escaped again with a panicked cry for help.

A hand rests against the child's velvet cheek and feels the heat still burning. Time passed, but hope falls, because another night was broken. Nights disrupted since the child was an infant when there was no capacity to understand what happened. Nights that wondered if Éayren made the claim to train to stay away, to escape the disruptive rive against sleep's rhythm.

"Try to rest," says Dalune, again, but it is more self-instruction than a suggestion for the child. The light is dimmed, again, and moon eyes look back to the eyes looking to their moon: Their world, that brings calm to ocean storms. Still, sleep does not fall easily for either one and the child battles it until sandy eyes can no longer fight the urge to wash them.

Chapter two:

The chord progresses – a minor key. Inverted seventh – resolution. It is played repeatedly. It is the sound of life and dreams. It acknowledges imperfection that children already see before they begin their training. It is felt in them before words have meaning. It is existence failing to meet its claims. It is a sound that is the connection between, because it is the progression that is heard in dreams, and Aedra plays it one thousand times and is given no complaint.

There is a pause as the notes carry on. There is an idea being born that begins the progression, one more time. Aedra plays the same three chords, but a fourth time, there is a syncopated drift. A note disconnected but one that leads down to the resolution. It changes every time the chords are played, and some find connection, and some are thrown away – percussive strikes are added on the edge.

The music gains life. Plodding progression gains energy; begin to soar against the basis they derived from. Slaps are added from the edge, and the sour dirge finds moments where joy emerges. There are bright notes where the mallet's brought down firmly, and the music rises to a swell. It blossoms into a room-encompassing wave, until a note is struck, and the instrument is brought to silence.

The chord progresses – a minor key. Inverted seventh – resolution. It is played three times and then let to fade.

A sigh brings Antru to their side and sitting before the columbrum. Like every other time, a mallet's offered – it is refused. There's no mood for novelty and only one has found talent with the instrument. Exceptional talent at an early age with no instruction.

A gift that is meaningless because there's no purpose for it.

A pointless talent that earns accolades from crowds that gather when played publicly. A showcase for the institution to lure recruits, as if anyone held any hand in training them. Held as an example of the gifts honed within the building, beside others with talent with a pen, or brush, or other median used to wrestle creative manifestation. The credit, though, is only Aedra's. A gift that was present before words were spoken. An ear that heard sounds – an innate understanding of how they go together. As much, an understanding of the instrument.

Three chords were played one thousand times, and then they grew into an acoustic masterpiece.

Aedra brings a mallet, done as mockery, of the effortless manner often taken by a friend. Replicated verbally, Antru voices, "Dung," dully forced with the tongue pressed into the palate.

They share laughter, and then the mallets spring to life again. It is not a repeat of the disappointed chords that led the prior composition, but a reflection of the joy shared in the moment. It speaks to experience and a moment where happiness was found – dissonance reflecting it isn't always easy.

The final notes are allowed to diminish on their own. Two friends showering in the glow still ringing in ears when, "Will you be eating with us," interrupts the moment.

It's answered, "No," because, "I don't want moboti to eat alone."

"They are welcome," but the answer remains no. "Will you join us after you eat," meets protest by their child, but the answer is, "Of course," because, "We're having difficulty with two calculations."

A mallet is stolen away and gently raps once, lightly against the metal surface of the drum – trying to change the conversation. But that only happens after the parent is gone, and Aedra promises, "They'll be done before you're back."

It is a ploy that's understood. A motivator. Social pressure to pull hands away from where they were born to play to apply them to the practical. But there is also a nod to the gift of another child. Not a talent for useless beauty, or a gift that finds crowds that want to share, but an ability that exists quietly. One built from sleepless nights where Dalune shares technical volumes with hope to dull the mind. Those were listened to with tremendous interest and conversations during daylight explore them more. It is sometimes spoken of as a gift, as if comparable to the magnificence pulled from metal by Aedra's hands. But it is only learned, and interest connects directly to experience and genetics.

Ideas of gifts, and talents, and abilities lead to speculation, as parents watch their children grow and wonder what will happen in their future. A true gift, to have the insight that can bring an instrument to life is one that points in no direction. An ability to understand in gross volume and to comprehend the highly technical has led many to suggest that Antru could follow Dalune, a path through the local institute at Capriot. The threat to use that talent was invoked as the parent sees their own as just as capable. But one does not have the distraction of a gift, or talent.

"Told you," greets both Antru and Dalune as they join the family after dinner.

The home is like many in Capriot. Built with large, smooth, stone blocks. Two levels, and a yard enclosed by a decorative, stone wall. They gather in the yard. Parents sit together at a table and open a bottle. Their children spill out and another aptitude is displayed as they test their abilities to scale an adjacent upcrop. Antru is evidently more adept, and that is also the result of experience and genetics, only this contribution is more widely known and why the family is considered fortunate. However, they have found it a fortune that comes with cost as there are often only two.

The rock is familiar. The grips and imperfections are well known. It is not tall, but it leads to others that rise higher.

To climb is to be Nespian, however the limit ends with the first one. Yet, as children do, the others are explored, and they test their limits.

Arms burn as they pull higher. Toes sting as they cling to imperfections.

"Antru," is called by a worried friend and pulls attention, and rebuke follows from further below:

"Not so high."

Eyes turn down the sheer side. Dalune is standing, watching, and it is understood there is concern.

It is not the highest ever ascended, but that has always been done outside of parent's eyes. Aedra's chase pushed the position, but they've already descended and voiced their worry.

Aedra stands below. Standing on a pile of rubble that has fallen over time. Looking up, in position below as if capable of preventing catastrophe should it fall. Aedra stands below and there is a flash, a vision, that has been seen more times than want to be remembered. Aedra is below and lying in ruins, broken and covered in blood. It is shaken away, and a cold chill electrifies the body.

There is no easy descent – rising is always easier. It is why favor for roukta's climb is uninformed. Defense and descent are more difficult and require much more skill. It is a skill that is only earned with practice and that comes with being the child of Éayren.

The climb down is slower than it should be, but the sky has dimmed and a vision flashed that saps attention. Éayren's words, "When you lose your focus: One step at a time." They are words that have been leant upon many times, and they are again as Aedra stands on a pile where they would be grievously injured if they tried to catch a falling body.

There is anger as Aedra asks, "What are you doing?" Asked as the drop becomes survivable.

There is no good answer. There is a feeling that is felt that was passed from parent to child. A lock-in to the climb. A sense that arrives that sees endless holds, and finds the body moves across them fluidly. But Éayren has also said that breaks. The vision is interrupted, and the endless holds and native navigation disappear, and then all that remains is sheer rock and deadly elevation. Especially for children, and especially without equipment.

The only thing that can be said, is, "Sorry."

"Your Moboti's right there." There is still anger in Aedra's words and it isn't because a parent saw the heights ascended, it's because there was danger to a friend, and it wasn't the first time.

"I thought you were following," is understood as inadequate as it's spoken, and so, "Sorry," is repeated.

Head shakes, but the apology is accepted and they move together to the edge of the lower rock to watch the star slip past the horizon.

Attention of those below has slipped away as the sky has darkened. Two, above, still sit together and the conversation remains quiet and where both find their greatest sense of peace and contentment. Where minds are quiet and visions are kept away.

Wind blows softly and the warmth of the day follows with it, but the warmth of the company remains, as does that from watching the conversation down below: Watching Dalune find the interaction that is missing. Finding the conversation that is absent in their home – sharing observations about their disobedient child.

It is what comes with fortune: Éayren is absent much of the year. There are visits throughout the season, but they are days. There is a break at the beginning of the year, but then there's training. Nights spent with Aedra's family are nights where appreciation is greatest for the sacrifices of Dalune: For raising a child alone, living with just the child, and like most in Capriot, also working.

It is the only city in Nespia where most with children continue working. In Capriot, training often extends directly to positions of contribution – developing technology, or in defense. Especially for those from Capriot's institute, as Dalune. It is where both children watching parents talk are likely destined, though one sometimes feels the body pull another direction.

"I stopped," Aedra admits, "Because you were going so fast. I can't go that fast."

It is a partial admission. It is remembered that the name was called with concern: Dalune's admonishment is recalled. The climb was quick, and smooth, and there had been no thought to end it. It wasn't the first time that had happened, but every other had been done out of the sight of others – knowing it inadvisable.

A suggestion: "We should come up with something to make it safe for us. Like the players use."

Wonders Aedra, "Why don't they?"

"I don't know," is answered as Antru rises, and descent begins on the slope beside the upcrop.

Why didn't they is a question that is intriguing to the child, and there isn't an answer. Children were hurt with regularity as they played, though the limits set by parents found most injuries were not significant. But there had been safeguards in place for millennia for the players in the leagues – parents still needed to set limits. To a child considering the society promised and what had been delivered to the point, there was no sensible explanation.

However, "Let's make something," is suggested. Ideas were already spinning in the mind. Thoughts to security and the planet's surrounding net were weaving thoughts towards potential ways to protect the children playing roukta – the idea of a net: Protecting children instead of blistering potential threats.

Aedra wonders, "Like what?"

"I'm thinking," Antru explains. Like where many ideas follow, it is further offered, "I have an idea, but I don't know what it is yet."

They join parents, and there is a reminder of the limits to climbs. There is rebuke to the height taken, but it is gentle and with understanding of the influences that will lead to greater heights ascended in the future. It is offered mostly for the sake of others that might follow, but there is also legitimate concern for safety – there are the terrors that have haunted the child since they were born.

"I have an idea," Antru shares.

The child is observed to be in a state that's familiar: The influence of one of similar disposition. An influence that is as strong as the vision and muscle memory that is leaned to for a climb. It is similar – an internal vision that can see solutions and just needs to uncover how those arrive. Antru's mind is calculating how that happens, and it is understood that asking what is pointless, because the answer has yet to be discovered.

"See you tomorrow." Aedra says this as they leave, and it's reciprocated: "See you in the morning."

It is morning, and Antru sits at the table when Dalune enters the room. "Did you sleep," is asked because it was clear there'd been something on the mind the night before – there's concern priorities were not in order.

"I slept," Antru says, "But I have an idea."

Ideas are the child's music. Solutions are the skilled hands that could use mallets to extract emotions from a bowl of metal. Thoughts about falling, defense and nets yielded an idea that was simple and brilliant. A solution to falling children that was eminently feasible, that could also be implemented in league competition.

"A net," Antru explains. Like the net that shielded the planet against unwanted invaders: Sensors embedded at certain levels that could detect a falling body. Like the net that rejected intrusion, the sensors could initiate a response, and the field could interact with equipment worn by players. "Everyone might have to stop playing until they're safe," Antru considers. The selling point is delivered: "No one would get hurt – badly. Maybe a scratch if they got pulled into a rock, but then we could really play. I think that would be a good solution."

"We can talk about it later." There is still time for the usual routine of morning if they begin moving that direction.

There is a nod of understanding: The message – the idea is being considered.

Feet move across the floor with a quiet shuffle and the sound of the columbrum is imagined in them. Imagined to be ringing out a cheerful coronation for a good solution. It plays on and is even hummed as preparation for the day begins. It plays through the cheerful conversation over breakfast, and spills into a parent that sees the billowing enthusiasm.

There is never enough, and it is always fed – joy, happiness; enthusiasm: There is a fire in the child that eats through them. That burns bright but brief and leaves only ash behind. But it's still there as robes are adorned, and as they leave to join others for instruction.

Most parents of Nespia have time for themselves while their children are receiving education. More than half of Capriot's turn to other obligations, and the assignment given to Dalune is passed on as a request is made for a hearing: "I have an idea," Dalune explains: "It isn't mine – it's Antru's. I think you'll like this."

Chapter three:

The color of the day is off from the beginning – late start, body heavy, and everything seems to take more effort than it should.

Water does not appear entirely colorless. Bread has an unnatural hue, its taste is off, and it hasn't set right. Nothing that was eaten is sitting right. Even conversation doesn't flow with the smoothness that it should. There is an attempt by both to overlook the warning signs, but they'd look back later in the evening and realize it was portent to what would follow.

"What's that on your robe," is another sign the day is not a good one, and if that had been understood as the morning blossomed, all involved would have taken measures to avoid the rest of it.

There is no attempt by Aedra to intervene or address what was noticed, and Antru doesn't even try to look. Even conversation between them is kept to minimal acknowledgement.

They arrive at the academy, and even joined with larger numbers, the usual din from hundreds of children is limp and soggy. It feels joyless, and enthusiasm is lacking. Shortly after taking seats, information is provided that initiates the downward spiral: Institutional assignments will be given that day.

There has been a long-held belief by neighbors, by Antru, and Aedra, and their parents that assignment will be to the institute at Capriot. Both children have excelled academically, and parental connections give added advantage.

But there is a sound that will not go away as the news is delivered. They are notes played on a tinkey. They are soft and sorrowful and play repeatedly. Over and again, Antru is thinking of anything to make them leave the ear, but it is pointless, because it is the soundtrack to the off-colors that have stained the day.

It is after the break to eat that assignments are given. Children tear into envelopes to see if their hopes are met, or if they'll be met by disappointment.

Few are. Most express acceptance, or, at least, find the opportunity intriguing. Aedra holds a slip over their head and leans back – smiling to share the inevitable. But the smile fades, because Antru is staring at the envelope on the desk and it remains unopened: It is the horror story that has been dreamt for life's entirety. With one-hundred percent certainty, it is known the assignment will be wrong. It is known that the colors, and tinkey were warnings to stay home, because the assignment will not be to Capriot.

"Antru," Aedra wonders.

"Antru," says their instructor: "Why haven't you opened it? This is where you finally meet your dreams."

"Who are you in your dreams," someone says.

In dreams, there is a child that has lost everyone they care about. They have seen every act of violence and every accident that could happen, and they've been helpless to do anything: Falling, injured, or trapped. Dreams are where everything that is important is lost, and where Antru is just Antru: Falling across a face of rock, sinking in the ocean; being struck in the head and seeing the world go dark. Who are you in your dreams was always an empty sentiment, but the tinkey in the ear has become a beat on timpani. There is only dread for what lies inside the envelope.

"Antru," says their instructor, and with the name, they approach and take matters into their hands: The envelope is lifted, and a finger slips the closure free. The card is pulled, and for a moment there is a look of contemplation. There is a look that is the color of the day and the taste of pink bread, because the words don't settle quite right. But surprise does not completely arrive. Appearance levels, and a shrug accompanies, "Makes sense."

The card is set on the desk and a circle of children lean to read the words. Eyes strain to see, to understand why their classmate is so perturbed.

One set of eyes reads the assignment, and says, "Of course."

Another echoes their instructor, and says, "Makes sense."

But Aedra wonders, "How?" Because the assignment makes no sense.

There was a segment broadcast of a wonder-child. The type of feel-good, end of broadcast send-off after the reel of updates about the general state of things. It had been tongue-in-cheek and reported with bemusement, about a child that had purportedly devised a way to keep children safe while they played roukta. Considering the position of the parents, it had been intimated that much of the actual logistics were developed by them, even if the actual, initial thought that had led to their development was based on the idea of a child.

It was not – entirely – inaccurate. Dalune had provided all of the technical information over the child's brief lifetime. With the idea given, additional ideas percolated with the parent as to how the proposition might be implemented. However, none of that was alien to Antru, and the final model had been designed with dreams in mind, and thoughts to catastrophic failure. As a novelty, Nespian defense had made an exception and given permission for the child to access the net – in a mistaken understanding of how that's done, and believing their parent would be the one to test the proposition.

That had been done for the segment, and Antru had come across as very sincere and capable of regurgitating highly technical specifics. While there was some back and forth at the end of the piece as to whether the child actually understood what they were saying, those familiar didn't doubt it. It was the nursery rhymes of early childhood, and the words that were used to salve the troubled mind.

"Antru," Aedra calls. There is hopelessness and desperation, because the card on the desk of their dearest friend says Marphy.

Antru is in tears, and inconsolable. The disruption sends the child away to counseling, but there is no consolation for a child that has witnessed the dawning of every nightmare dreamt.

At the day's end, the other children are not joined for the journey back to their homes. The writings of ruin have begun, and desperation leads Antru to erase it. It leads the child to face authority, to the seat of power and the only place that yet provides a glimmer of hope: That assignments can change. If anyone is able, it would be the Emperor.

Like most compounds of the clans of Nespia, the Capriot compound sits above most of the city and is set against the lower upcrops. It is a large and magnificent fortress with elegant carvings, statues and fountains. It is overwhelming to an exhausted child that had climbed the hills with relentless determination. But that will is paused as the compound is taken in fully, and for the first time since voices attempted to assuage distress, conviction wrinkles.

It is a structure that had been seen hundreds of times – perhaps thousands. Its visage is everywhere, but no image or transmission does justice to the enormity that is overwhelming when seen in person, and Antru is dumbstruck, the purpose of the climb momentarily forgotten as despair is washed away by the size and beauty of the buildings, and the awe that fills the child.

Feet are anchored as the breadth of the construct is absorbed. Symmetrical wings reach to the distance, both directions, away from the central, courtyard garden. They are unlike the buildings of the city. It is not built with the uniform blocks of familiarity, but with blocks of different sizes and orientation. There are decorative archways over windows, and ornamentation that differentiates the floors. There is detail, and carvings. The walls lean out at their highest, with crenellations and machicolations, hinting at their ancient origins. The awe that stilled the feet might have been enough to still the disquiet mind, but eyes turn back into the garden and a reminder of why they moved there in the firstplace, hangs broken.

The wall to the courtyard has many openings but it is likely that only the central path is ever used. It is a space from where numerous announcements, ceremonies, and celebrations have been shared and it holds familiarity. But like the larger building, the size, when seen in person, is astounding.

The garden is guarded by an open wall that rises as high as the adjacent buildings. It is constructed of stacked arches, but near the top, there is a large, pentagonal opening. It frames the statue of someone perched atop the roof, seen when viewed centrally from below. It allows the garden to be seen, and it too is magnificent. It is multi-tiered, with small bridges and a stream. There are fountains with statues that spit water, and beautifully maintained plants and flowers – except for one that has broken and is hanging down. It is Antru, and the purpose of the climb returns into the thought-stream.

The idea of marching up to the emperor and demanding a re-assignment is understood as one brought by desperation – but that, also, is being remembered – and tentative steps begin towards the empty courtyard.

It is a different world. It is calm, and peaceful. It is the moment after Aedra plays the columbrum, where they sit quietly together. Where a wholeness is felt that is nowhere else, and it isn't the garden, either.

As the sentiment is felt, it does not grow as in the shared moments. It stops abruptly, because the open, welcoming space is quickly filled with others. However, those melting from the walls are quick to assess the intruder is a child and not likely to be a threat. Only one continues to approach, and it is the first time that Antru has ever felt small.

The person asks, "Do you like the gardens?"

They are told, "I'm here to see the Emperor." There is widespread amusement at the proclamation. It is restated as a question – Antru is insistent, and explains with urgency, "My assignment needs to be changed."

There is a nod, as, "It's the day of assignments," is recognized. There is also amusement: The child made the claim with certainty – both of an error, and the possibility they'd see the emperor to get it changed. It is expected, "The assignments are final," would end the conversation. It was expected that invoking parents would find the child backing down, but Antru only becomes more insistent, and louder:

"No. They want me to go to Marphy but I don't belong there. I need to go to Capriot. I don't want to go to Marphy."

Another approaches; attempts to quiet – suggests, "Take them to holding. Contact the parents."

Antru insists, "I already proved I belong at Capriot. I made the roukta net. That was my idea. I can't go to Marphy. I have to go to Capriot."

There is recognition. The first tries, "That proves you should go to Marphy. The roukta net – that's exactly where you should be."

"No," Antru insists. "I climbed too high so I made a solution so my moboti wouldn't be upset. That's what I do: I solve problems. I don't want to play roukta – I made it safer. I want to research at Capriot."

The disturbance has already extended longer than it should have – the child surprisingly strong-willed. The one that'd joined the first takes control of the situation and extends a hand. Antru is told, "Your assignment was made based on your qualifications. You were assigned where you belong. I will show you."

That is answered, "No. It's wrong. But I'll go if you show me."

The child is pulled hastily away. They continue through the garden, but it is irrelevant anymore. They walk for doors that are more than a story tall and nearly as wide. They open on their own, and the two enter a large hall with an ornate ceiling that soars above.

There is no time to resolve the entirety of the space, as the sentry pulls, and walks quickly for a hallway. They continue, turning several times. They follow stairs to another level, to another hallway, and another turn leads them to a door. It is opened, and Antru is thrust forward.

There is a person at a machine, and they look surprised to have company. They are told, "The child of Éayren: Antru believes they are mis-assigned."

The seated one says, "Oh." Recognizing the child and surprised. Eyes turn to the machine and a quick check confirms, "Marphy. That's where you were assigned."

"No." Antru stomps a foot, and insists, "I belong at Capriot. I don't want to go to Marphy. I need to go to Capriot."

"In the middle of the garden," the sentry explains. Appalled that such boorish behavior would be displayed within the grounds. A rebuke follows, a lash against the ill-bred child, "Usually a Marphy is better disciplined."

"Because I'm not," Antru insists. A foot stomps again with the final word to add emphasis.

It is a move that is found grossly irritating to the one that still clasps a shoulder, and that is roughly pulled forward to demonstrate, "You're Marphy."

It was the beginning of admonishment to follow. Discipline would be ordered. But it didn't, and wasn't because Antru raises a finger, and points out, "I'm supposed to be Capriot."

The finger points to the screen, towards the names of Éayren and Dalune. Their child has reached the age of assignment, and the best fit for that child is clearly Capriot. The assignment given, is Marphy.

The sentry asks, "Why is that," and the seated one softly suggests, "You should talk to your parents."

"My parents want me to go to Capriot," Antru insists. There is a sickness that is growing within. The off colors and wan food from the beginning of the day are folding together to form a solid bolus of pain inside the stomach. And it is felt by the others, with the words, "My Moboti Dalune taught me what I needed to go to Capriot. They would say I should go to Capriot."

"Antru." The one seated pulls the child over. There is great sympathy as it's suggested, "You need to talk with your parents. The assignment was done as a favor."

"By who," is asked through strangling disbelief. The pain in the gut is spreading to the head, and the color of life begins to drain as thoughts scramble to understand who could hate someone so much they would ruin a future.

"Antru," the person says again. And it becomes worse, because they say, "I'm sorry. It was a special favor. Those are rarely granted. I don't know how you would get this changed again."

"By who," the child demands.

"Éayren," is answered. The explanation is soft, because it is evident that the decision was made without the child's knowledge. It is claimed, "They accepted the request on your behalf. They would have believed that's what you wanted. We know you have an interest in roukta, so no one would have questioned it." The words, "I'm sorry," are uttered again, to soften the finality: "There's too much that was done to make that happen. I don't know how that could be changed again."

There is no spirit left in the child that had mounted an ambush against the impossible. There is no more will to fight from a child that climbed the hills to face the emperor. There is only sickness, and stomachache, and a head that hurts, and the final vitriol regurgitates, "I don't even know Éayren."

Two watch the child's body slump as eyes remain transfixed on the assignment for which they were destined. Two watch a child shake their head as tears fall, and the reality that nothing can be done sets in. One that was deemed a vexing irritant now holds sympathy from both that share the room, as they comprehend the tremendous transgression that has taken place. A favor gained that was so misplaced that a child felt compelled to face the emperor – likely nothing even they could do to fix it.

The thought to investigate what might be needed is considered best left unstated, instead the offer, "I'll get you home." It would later be explained that the accommodation made would take too much back-walk and potential embarrassment for those involved to even be considered. There would be relief that nothing was mentioned to the child – also, disappointment that it couldn't.

"There's great people from Marphy." The person remains seated. They explain, "There's lots of people here from Marphy. They're everywhere. There's nothing wrong with it. And you've got the genes to go places. After all, not everyone can call in favors."

Eyes look up to the person that offered transportation, and they are grilled, "Did you?"

"Nespia," is answered.

From a child's simple mind, the question rises, "Then, why are you here?"

"After my service, I wanted to stay on. That's why I'm here. Come with me – I'll get you home."

The ride home is quiet. There is not a word said between them. One has seen everything they'd planned for wash away, and the other feels incapable in the circumstances that are understood to be complicated on many levels. They ride back down the hills and then up again, to the northern edge where authorities are already on alert.

Many people are gathered around the home. Aedra is standing on the garden wall and watching the vehicle intently. Dalune is just beyond, standing with their parents and several neighbors. The arrival of the emperor's guard sends messages that are inaccurate, but it is also a succinct end to concerns, and for those waiting, relief.

The first words, are parent's concern: "What happened?"

They are answered, "Did you know?" It is sharp, and sour, and receives the words, "Antru: Where have you been," with shades of anger.

"Did you know I got changed to Marphy?"

"What do you mean," is asked, and there is concern. It is asked curiously as the words have brought confusion.

"I got changed," Antru explains, "To Marphy." Tears cannot be stopped, despite the presence of a friend. The sickness grows, and anger finds escape again, because it was, "From Capriot."

"I don't," understand is interrupted by the shouted, "Éayren."

"Éayren asked for a favor to change me to Marphy." And eyes bear in with accusation. They narrow and pills of liquid balance on the lids as the bitter question is asked again: "Did you know that?"

"Antru," is said again, and something that had been felt all day returns in fuller strength. There'd been a sense since morning that something was off. The entire day, nothing went as intended. And yet, "I can't believe that. I don't believe Éayren would do that. There must be a mistake."

"There isn't," Antru hasps. The entire neighborhood is watching. The sentry from the fortress is still standing there, looking with pity at a failure. At a person that wasn't good enough to elevate themselves above interference for a favor. Just another student that could be plugged in anywhere. A child with ambitions to solve vast problems, irrelevant enough to be cast aside to a future of moving rocks. The child turns, and begins walking for the home. The breadth of hurt and disappointment are shared with the parting words, "And there's nothing anyone can do about it."

Chapter four:

The final forty days of early instruction are geared towards the future. A future that friends had planned together – had expected to experience together. But there would be no moments together beside the columbrum in the future. Those magical moments would be forsaken by a favor granted that was considered by those that colluded, a tremendous accommodation. But the final forty days, two friends are taken separate directions.

An acceptance fell that it was inevitable. That there was no way to alter fate: Fates listened to roukta players, but not their children. Acceptance fell, but disappointment never lessened. Tremendous jealousy was felt as Aedra walked the other way. Tremendous sorrow was felt that they were separated and would not see each other, perhaps, again.

"Let's make an effort, junior." It is a term used by the strength and conditioning coach to denigrate a child with some notoriety. The child of a famous player, and one that has altered the game in a way that many do not like. There are many comments from instructors and classmates alike, that question whether a child could be capable of designing the protective nets. Most believe the technological know-how is far too advanced for a child, especially one as young as when it originated.

Antru never argues. It is the lowest level of irritation and disappointment of many irritations and disappointments. One that hadn't been prepared for was the amount of physical exertion that would be necessary as the planet prepares the latest round of hopefuls for a simple game.

It is a game that is recently transformed. One that saw much of the technical craft eliminated in favor of safety and dramatic falls. The one that calls the insults was a former rigger and takes the changes as a personal insult.

There is still travel to and from the academy together. There is still time in the evenings to share moments, but it is understood they are fleeting, and it is only holding on to a past that has slipped away.

They arrive home, and Aedra says, "Later?" As always, Antru agrees.

There is a sound that is unexpected as the home is entered. "Hey," grates against the ears, and, "Look at you," brings a rise in the chest that is only negative. Dalune is watching carefully which is indicative that the negative response to the assignment has been discussed. As always, Éayren expects to be rewarded for being present for a day, and rises. Arms outstretch with approach, and they wrap in a manner that doesn't understand the point of the gesture. "Look at you," is said again. "You're really poppin' out," is offered with respect, as if it was an accomplishment after dozens of days of tortuous workouts.

Dalune suggests, "We think this could be good for you."

That earns, "Come on," because neither of them believes it. But a look is returned that indicates there is some truth.

Éayren says, "I need to run down the hill." It is found the statement is made to Antru as eyes are looking back, and it's confirmed by the suggestion, "Why don't you join me?"

"Join moboti Éayren," Dalune says.

It is an unusually direct order. The – run down the hill – is likely a plan to isolate them together, to explain the rationale for ruining everything that was planned and ripping a child from their dreams and friends.

There is deep resentment, but it is not enough to push back against the favorite parent, and it is not towards them. But it is a feeling that wonders if something can be said to return the injury. If the sorrow can be given back and disappointment driven. There is a flash of a dream that involved a transport, and the memory recalls sorrow.

It is an unexpected recollection and it interrupts the bitter thoughts and brewing bile. There is a sense of sympathy, but it is only confusing because it's undeserved and misplaced. But it leads to agreement, and, "Okay."

If a conversation was held, it had no effect on Éayren: A stream of words flow and they are filled with confidence. There is sureness in every step, in every breath, and an enormity of being that exceeds the person's stature.

There is a constant call of recognition. There is a continuous stream of people that approach to offer appreciation. Implements are offered to endow images, shirts, or flesh that will remain unwashed until inscriptions deteriorate to the unintelligible.

Éayren has won four championships, with two different teams, and is considered one of the best scalers on the planet. It is a talent that has been observed in their child, however, Antru has never followed the league, nor is roukta considered particularly interesting. Climbing is considered enervating of its own. It is evidently not a feeling shared by the rest of the city, and Éayren's visit home is celebrated down every street they follow.

They become enmired, again. Whatever expectation was formed from the conversation between parents, it is not being realized. There is almost no interaction between child and parent, few words said, and most of those are excuses to interact with adoring fans. The one encouraged to follow, sits back and watches, and thinks the attention given to a passing fan is more than they've had in their entire lifetime.

It is tedious: Watching the interactions, listening to the accolades; seeing the plastered smiles and glossy eyes: Eyes drift away and wish they were anywhere else.

They have walked into the heart of the city. It is where architecture reflects the emperor's compound. An old part of the city where streets are narrow, and establishments that provide needs or services are intermixed with housing. Many of the homes are on the second floor above the establishments. It is not an area that is well-known as it has always been off-limits without a parent present. It is considerably different than the neighborhoods at higher elevations, as residences are smaller, without yards, and the buildings create walls that line the roads. There is a sense of being contained, or trapped, and that's amplified by the numbers that traverse the streets.

Most by foot, but there are public transports, and a few of the smaller, private vehicles that are mostly owned by those with connections to the clan. They are similar to the one Antru was brought back home in after attempting to see the emperor. One is idled, and it seems its occupant's upset.

It remains at the edge of the road, and the person within calls out, "Can someone help me?" They are ignored by everyone. It is a stark contrast to the crowd that came together to help or search when Antru did not return from the academy. Eyes turn and find Éayren still conversing with the crowd that's gathered – ignoring, or oblivious to someone in need.

It's a feeling that's shared. The nation's hero, adored by everyone – hardly known by their own child. More attention given to anonymous crowds than their offspring – other than the unilateral decision to alter their life.

Bitterness grows, and resentment pushes feet to intervene, to come to the aid of the stranded passenger.

"Antru," is yelled with anger. There is a chill that fills the spine, and progress freezes. A slow turn builds with the thought to share true opinions: Hardly worthy of being called a parent. But the name is followed by words that are said severely: "Get away from there."

There is something different about Éayren. Eyes are hard and angered. The smile has left and the face is taught. No longer are they standing, relaxed in conversation – they are square, and threatening, and look ready to attack.

Antru explains, "They need help."

The words, "Get over here," are just as harsh.

It is the antithesis of what has been drummed into the brain: Help your neighbor, be productive; contribute to society.

It begs the question, "Why can't I help?"

Éayren apologizes to the crowd: "You'll have to excuse me."

For some reason they seem to understand. As if some transgression has taken place. Antru returns, but demands an explanation. They are given a question:

"Do you know what that is?"

Antru answers, "Someone that needs help."

"That's a pinch," Éayren explains: "They lure you in to help them, but it's a trap. Once they have you, they'll file a complaint and get you arrested. No one will ever see you again."

"Is that true," is questioned, because it seems impossible. It is completely out of character for the world that's known.

"Yes," says Éayren, and then a warning: "Don't ever help anyone from the clans – none of them. If you think someone needs help – call for help. But don't – you – ever get involved. Do you understand that, Antru?"

It is heard, but, "You got involved with the clans. You got me changed to Marphy: Why did you do that?"

"It's for your own good," Éayren answers. "Someday you'll understand. Right now, I need your word: Tell me you will stay away from the clans."

There is a sheepish admission: "I tried to see the emperor. I wanted them to change me back."

"Yeah," is said with irritation. There is more behind the simple words, "I heard." A heartbeat later, the smile returns, and attention moves to a passing devotee: "I appreciate you."

They continue moving deeper into the city. The roads they walk are no longer smooth but made of little stones. Multiple vehicles are observed as they pass, occupants all in apparent need of assistance. It gives credence to the strange words of warning, and the glancing eyes receive another lesson:

"You're familiar with Reeco?"

"I think," Antru answers. They are in uncertain waters and there is hesitation to answer anything with surety.

Éayren shares, "Reeco claims they helped a pinch, and that's how they got that house. They got their own vehicle — 'cause the clan's so grateful. That's what everybody says, right?"

Antru says, "I guess."

"It's a lie," Éayren warns: "They are the clan. Nespia puts them in the neighborhoods to spy. They're looking for targets, and then they try to push them towards a pinch. Don't trust anyone that says they got anything for helping: That's how you know they're with the feds." They stop, and the child is turned. Two, meaty hands rest heavily on the child's shoulders, and Éayren demands, "Your word, Antru: Don't ever go near a pinch, and stay away from the clans. I need to hear it."

It is weak, and unsure, but Antru says, "Okay."

Demeanor changes: "Then, let's get what we came here for." The cheerful hero returns and leads them into a store.

It is dim, and dusty. The cluttered space is filled with shelves. There is food, and there are instruments — a columbrum is hanging from the ceiling. There is everything anyone could need for anything. They navigate their way to a counter at the back, and they are greeted by someone that appears to be older than anyone ever met.

The person's voice is raspy, as they ask, "You needed flour?"

Éayren says, "How 'bout we let the kid pull it down. They need all the workouts they can get."

It is a reminder of how irritating the person was before the strange warnings were shared. A reminder of a future that would be elsewhere, sent to Marphy for some uncertain reason – the thought crosses through the consciousness that it might be paranoia.

It is not the last time that thought would pass. It hangs in the air as the old one waves them back, as they are led through a door, and into a room that is lit with only a burning candle. There are large sacks lining all the walls, and at the far end, a large candlestick holder balances a glass.

It is a vision that might be seen in dreams. One where the walls collapse and leave one hopelessly buried beneath the sacks. Lines are further blurred as the door is closed, and a utility is pulled from out of nowhere. Eyes turn to the youngest of the three, and the eldest provides a solemn explanation:

"It looks like a utility. If you turn the base," and the base is turned to demonstrate, "It works just like one. However, if you pull the lever on the side and let it snap." There is a snap, and almost instantaneously the glass across the room is shattered.

"I," Antru stammers, "Don't understand."

Éayren explains, "For your protection. Always keep it with you. In the shower – playing roukta: Never let it leave your side."

"Protection from who," the child asks.

"Clan," it's suggested. "A pinch. Whoever. Use it if you have to. The clans don't want noise, so we can usually sort it out if something happens. But whatever you do, do not – Antru: Do not let anyone take you into custody."

The old one hisses, "Listen. Your moboti looks out for you."

Like a dream where the world turns upside down, the old host grips an arm with vice-like strength. The arm is turned, and a strap is clasped against it. The material melts into the arm and becomes unseen, and the oddities and explanations begin to settle uneasily, Antru faltering as the arm is released.

A demonstration follows: An ancient arm shakes out an open palm, and an implement seems to emerge out of the wrist. There is a snap, and across the room the broken glass dances from the impact. Another snap, and the body jumps, but the shattered shards are no longer unexpected.

There is laughter at the reaction. Éayren folds a wrist down to conceal the tiny weapon. There is still stickiness in the surreal experience, but there is also excitement and curiosity.

The wrist shakes out, and as expected the utility emerges. It is aimed, and the invisible lever is snapped, sending bits of shattered glass into slivered pieces.

For the first time in a long time, a parent watches their child show enthusiasm in their presence. For the first time in a long time, they watch their child look back with excitement, but it isn't the endowment of the weapon that brings the thrill, it's the technology that's behind it:

"Can I know how that works?"

Éayren says, "You will. For now, just use it if you ever have to protect yourself."

The old one rasps, "Get the kit," and warns, "Never go anywhere without it."

The world is more of a dream that it has ever been as they leave the establishment – a weapon strapped to a wrist and an assortment of chemicals concealed against the torso. There is new appreciation for parents, and new understanding falling into awareness. Spies are seen in every neighborhood. They cross a pinch on numerous streets and they are watched, side-eyed with trepidation. For the first time in perhaps ever, Antru is happy at Éayren's side. There is pride to know that there is something larger, and that parents are a part. Steps are light, despite the heavy bag of flour that is shouldered, despite a weapon on a wrist, and a kit beneath the shirt, but they slow as they turn a corner and find a person near a vehicle.

A nudge, and Éayren reminds, "Don't ever get involved. Only help those you know – and, you know you can trust. Call the authority if you want to help, but don't ever do anything yourself. Do you understand this?"

It is answered, "Yes," surely. "I promise," is an oath taken with the solemnity it deserves, because it is understood that what has been done was for a loved one. A connection that once was believed to have been imagined, often considered severed, is reconnected.

They arrive back to their home with heavy breath but steps are lighter. The hostility that was held before they left is absent. They are met by the wide eyes of concern that are of the only parent that was trusted, and it is evident that hasn't changed, because the weapon is revealed and they're asked the question, "Why do I need this?"

There is a mixture of conversation that answers. There is hope that it isn't, pitted against the tinge of paranoia that was heard before. Warnings, instructions, but no clear answer.

Éayren is lecturing, "Only share secrets with the people you know you can trust."

It is part of a long, repetitive answer to a question that was asked. With the line said again and issued as a warning, the question is answered by the one that asked with a statement of intent: "I'm going to show it to Aedra."

It was only the opening to what would follow. Every detail of what occurred that evening is shared. Every warning about a pinch, and spies, and the dangers of the clans. Aedra draws from the excitement and they imagine the great, internecine battle that must rage outside the sight of citizens. It is conversation that grows loud enough that parents move to warn that sort of conversation should be quiet. In a place with no electronics. A room buffered by large bags of flour with just a single candle burning to provide illumination.

"Are you getting Aedra one?" The idea of paranoia is still in the atmosphere, but the warnings left it heavy with concern. "Not at this time," sinks the pressure further.

Conversation is intentionally turned back to the usual repartee, and to Aedra, there is relief that it has. As it often did, the back and forth leads to grappling, and though it had never been an even match, with four weeks of training, Aedra doesn't have a chance.

Their parents are gone, retreated to the out of doors to escape the inane conversation of the children. They'd been left grappling, and with their departure, strength was flexed and their child was left pinned helplessly to the floor.

They are told, "You need one."

Greatly amused, Aedra asks, "To protect me from you?"

There is a storm that isn't understood, and paranoia is infectious. Antru is digging against the wrist, flashing the memory of what had happened, but it had been too fast and unexpected.

Eyes pinch closed and the memory is relived. It is burnished over and again, and there is seen the slightest twitch of the finger that gives hint to the operation.

There is protest, but it is unnecessary, because there's failure. Protest continues. A paean for conversation, or back to wrestling. But the mind engaged, and Antru runs through anything that would make sense of the weapon installation.

It grows late, and Aedra has become bored: Leant against a pillow on the floor, scrolling on a tablet through pointless entertainment. It did not become what was hoped a demonstration that would pull their friend out of the fugue.

"It's easy." Antru says this out of the blue and as if the obvious was always there. It's explained, "Grafting. It's just a grafting patch. That's so stupidly simple it's genius."

"Do you really believe all this?"

"Yes," Antru says. There was a pinch on every other street. There was a keep in every neighborhood to watch over streets, and it had already been witnessed that the clans conspired together.

Aedra says, "Sound like you're getting a little paranoid, yourself."

It is an attempt at humor. A hope to lighten the conversation — to return to banter and battling for domination: It is not ignored, and not dismissed.

"Probably," says Antru. What follows is not humorous. It is sincere and there is real concern as the patch is carefully picked away.

For the first time, the object is examined. Outside of the projectile device, it is a simple design. A typical graft with a pocket to accommodate the utility. It's positioning moves the device forward with downward motion of the wrist, and it's probable there is some sort of tie to keep it from releasing fully. The device would require significant examination to understand, but that isn't what's important at the present.

It is unexpected when Antru gently takes a hand and brings it against their lips. There is a vibration between them as the arm is caressed, as eyes connect, and for a moment, there is a sense they will forever be connected. But then, Antru slaps the graft on, and the arm recoils, to the rejection, "No."

Aedra says, "I don't want this. Get it off me."

"I need you to be okay," Antru says. The motive is explained, "I'll be in Marphy. No one cares about me in Marphy. But you'll be here. If someone wants to get to me, they'll come after you. I need you to be safe."

"I don't like this," Aedra says.

The hand is taken, but there's some hesitation. There is reluctance to accept what's been offered – words, and claims, and weaponry.

Antru says, "I know." But something has fallen over the eyes that clouds their future. A veil has been pulled away that makes words that have always sounded disingenuous, a dire warning. Aedra is told with existential fear, "I need you to be okay."

That's answered, "Yeah? They gave it to you, 'cause they're worried about you. How 'bout, I need you to be alright."

"I'll get another one," Antru says. A hand is extended again, and it's taken. A smile is offered as encouragement, but Aedra's is more permanent. Their hands remain connected as Antru leads them from the home – through the kitchen to abscond two glasses.

They climb the near upcrop to the first plateau, and marksmanship is honed until they're called in for the night.

They part with a different understanding. Eyes linger in a way they never have before, as they walk away, alone, and towards their separate homes.

Chapter five:

Tin drops fall against calliope in soggy echo. There is music playing, but it is distant, scratchy; thin. It is the cry of a child on a moonless night, stranded atop a rock with no eyes to navigate descent. A song plays that is wordless, and it sings of loneliness and abandonment. Tin drops fall against the rock and give it light, but trail down in thin rivulets, eroding the surface and etching ever deeper: Trails of liquid mercury slip down into an endless pit obscured by ink-black fog. They fall with the fading music until there is only sporadic relief from the sightless void. Brief glints at the corners of vision.

It is almost silent. It is quiet other than a raspy current that flows just beneath the surface: The continuous breath of someone trying to exhale a rumor they shouldn't have heard. It is endless, and hopeless, but the uneasiness will only pass if it is emptied entirely. It is almost gone when a gasp pulls it completely back and there is a moment of utter silence.

In the moment, awareness finds a grip, and there is a question that floats, "Am I awake, or am I dreaming?"

A call, far off in the distance answers, but the words spoken have no meaning. There is a hum that continues from them. Sparks generate from its motor, and flecks of liquid silver land upon the surface, only to fade. A drop of liquid collects but its descent is slowed by an obstacle. It remains positioned centrally. A flashing orb of silver without a face. A face without features. A face that is blurred and cannot be identified. There are darkened circles where eyes might be hidden, but they move when concentration falls on them. There should be a face, but it can't be seen.

A question is asked to another faceless head, but the words are as blurred as faces: There is a sea of them. Heads floating on the surface of black waters. Faces are hidden underneath the distortion – they are on both sides, and nowhere. There is one with hair that flows to the metal water, and they always look away.

Eyes look away to the lightless distance. The streams of mercury are seen slipping in the periphery, and the night grows darker.

There is almost silence, other than the raspy breath that carries in the bone-chilling wind. It carries clouds of luminescence – swarms of lightning bugs. It is a curtain that falls on darkness. They are clouds that rained tin drops on a calliope; then rolled away in millions of thread-thin streams of mercury.

Streams grow, contained in lipid channels. They are millions of thread-thin veins pulsating across the landscape. They drape down the badly damaged rock into the pool, below. They disappear into the void of darkness from which light cannot escape. They are cold and screaming with a raspy breath as they descend. They cry in sounds that aren't words, but they say it's cold and they are dying. They cry as their life escapes as they are frozen, as the whole rock becomes covered by icy remains.

The wind howls its raspy insult and drives sleet that stings the face. There is growing angst as progress stumbles through the knee-deep snow. Every step finds two slipped back. Hands grasp for hold, but the ground fades into sky, into a blinding white that blots out everything.

There is a raspy breath that pulsates in the atmosphere. It exhales a chill that cools the already frozen body. Fingers are raw from fighting ice and eyes go blind to white-out uniformity. There are dark circles that might be eyes, and a mittened hand reaches down. It is grasped for, and fingers brush against the woolen end, but the snow gives away. There is an avalanche as immeasurable tons of snow and ice fall from the rocky precipice. It falls across the sheer, rock-face towards the lightless vortex at its base.

Terror flares as bright as the fading light, above. There is nothing to stop the fall. There is nothing to grasp, there is just a tablet floating in the remaining snow that plummets towards its end, and nothing.

There is abrupt darkness. A raspy breath breathes life into the droplets on the ground, where the tablet lies shattered on a mound of rubble. It rests just inches from black waters that lap gently at the earth, moving with the haspy breaths that still gasp for another moment of existence.

Complete silence falls. The last tendrils of liquid metal slip beneath the surface of the waters, and with them, the slightest hint of light remaining, fades.

Time slips, unnoticed. The nettlesome chill is absorbed by submersion in utter, lightless, emptiness. There is nothing and that never should have been realized, except a gasp rips a shear through oblivion.

Droplets of silver spill through to show the body at the bottom of the drop, still breathing. It is a ghost that brings back memories of another vision, and there is only a broken tablet, anymore.

Fingers lick across the water's surface. They disappear as they submerge, and the quicksilver slips completely when they re-emerge. It is warm, unlike the surrounding air, and there is a pull to slip beneath the water's surface and into the comfort of submersion. But there is also danger. There is an illness and discomfort that emanates from the water. There is an urge to fall, but it won't be done, and only fingers dance across the surface.

They pull away, and the reflection watches them move closer. Fingers pull from the surface, and fingers follow. They reach out of the water, trying to pull away, trying to find a grip, but only flailing helplessly – until fingers move to help them.

There is a familiarity as tips of fingers near. There is a vibration between them. One that had only started when a rive was driven through existence. It brings fear to finds its place beside the desperate need to pull the victim free, but feet teeter on the thin rim of earth around the water. Every position brings increasing peril, and the fingers slowly begin to sink again.

Utter helplessness echoes in the valley. Complete despair permeates the landscape as the last finger sinks below the surface of the water, and the ache that bursts within the chest splits the body into pieces that shatter beside the rubble. They tumble off, slowly dripping into the pool, beneath the surface and a hand reaches for the other and can finally grasp it as their bodies' need for air begins to surface.

It is the last time they will ever see each other. It is the last time they will ever feel the warmth of being in the others' presence. They are pulled close and Aedra speaks but nothing is heard as they slowly sink. There is no escape, and in the last moments as the light begins to fade, the focus remains only on Aedra's face. On the smile, the bright eyes – the beautiful voice rings hours after words were spoken. The same words are repeated just before the liquid-metal tendrils fully recede.

There is a gasp that sounds like a name being called across the inlet just outside of Capriot. There is a raspy wind that tells of cooler weather to follow, but the day is filled with starlight, and the bright metal of the landscape blinds eyes with reflected light. There is warmth, and Aedra is laughing. There's a plea to follow, but where they're going is uncertain.

Hand in hand, Aedra pulls into the forest that has grown between the shore and soaring upcrops. The wind saws with a grating anger, and the trees wither against it – they are falling, and on fire. There is a run to escape and Aedra is lost.

There is fire everywhere, and there's only one small path, but it's the wrong direction. "Aedra," is called, and the smoke and heat from the fire give the word a wrinkled layer that hangs in the air with glowing embers. They are chased into the fire. Swimming in flames, it is strange the fire is cool, and a breeze rasps through it and sends a chill across the body.

"What are you doing," Aedra wonders. They are standing at the base of the upcrops. Cheerful, and unharmed. A feeling of embarrassment falls at the question and they begin ascending a path of rubble.

Aedra moves flawlessly and reaches the acme immediately, but other feet find the pebbles slip beneath them, and progress is incremental despite tremendous exertion.

Evening arrives as the top is met, and there is black singeing the edges of the landscape. There are words escaping from trees, but they are far below and it is just a reflection. The starlight filtered through the atmosphere paints fire on the water, but it's not burning. They are disregarded despite the urgency of their pleas, and the trek to climb the hilltop is resumed.

There are moon eyes painting love, and they wonder, "Where's Aedra," and it's remembered that at one time they walked together.

The path continues forever, and there's no end and no progression. The sky is always getting dimmer, but it never changes. A hand is held out, and it's with the same love offered, always. The hand is held, and cherished, and comfort falls that the fires, and black water, the falls, and cold will be resolved, and Aedra will be found.

They are laughing. Aedra is standing on the highest rise, and there is terror because the fall is steep. There are memories and flashes that spin across the scene in an instant, and there are broken fingers climbing through the pain to prevent disaster.

Aedra is laughing as broken hands scratch to pull onto the surface. They are slipping, and Aedra will fall if they try to help. The only hope is to let go and fall into the well, below.

The smooth rock-face slips quickly past. The light grows dimmer, and its face is smaller the farther that it's passed. There is calm before the impact. There is acceptance. There is understanding that what is done, is done, and had to be done. There is happiness knowing that Aedra still stands on top the rock.

A raspy wind says, "Antru." It is spoken with minimal distortion, and Dalune asks, "Do you understand?"

There is a vehicle perched on the edge of a cliff, and a person within that is desperately trying to escape. They are begging for help, but they will not see it: Giants begin smashing the vehicle with their fists. They pummel the metal until glass breaks and the passenger is bleeding. One spins the vehicle over their head and then sends it into the ocean.

There is a scream that echoes through the rocky rises. It is a familiar voice that should be secure on the rock, but there was a dive after the body fell. Gone after as fingers slipped beneath the surface and despite it caused the body to shatter into pieces: There was no choice but to try and save a friend.

A gasp breaks the fall, and the body wrenches upward. It is dark, and cold, and Antru's heart is beating heavily in their ears. Despite the chill, the body is covered in sweat, and the chill burns deeper as a raspy breath exhales.

There is a moment taken to assess circumstances. It is understood, it is the small box shoved into at the Institute of Marphy. Two bunks, a wall of storage, and facilities at the rear. It is living quarters for the next four years.

There is some comfort finding themself in the space. It is small, and secure. It is quiet, and it is cold, and it's the middle of the night. As disquiet settles, the air from the vent blows only colder, and the blanket is found to have fallen to the floor.

There is a pause as it is reached for: There is complete silence. A flash of avalanche and fire resumes a panic that had only begun to go away. Feet plant on the edge of the bunk, and hands pull up to spy the other: Still and sleeping. There is no raspy breath, and the chest does not appear to move.

A harsh whispered, "Eotor," and a hand reaches out to shake the body. There is a gasp, and their own hand brushes the other's away. "Eotor," is repeated, and it is met with irritation. "Are you okay," is told, "Get lost," and the back is turned as they roll onto their side.

Retreat is taken to the lower bunk, and the shivering body is wrapped tightly within the blanket. The corner of the bunk is used as a brace to keep the back sat upright, and the flashes of new visions are catalogued as the night crawls on.

The position is still held when the tone sounds that is meant to wake them. There is cursing from the bunk above, a voice given to sleep that wasn't restful. Angered muttering continues until descent, until a roommate is observed sitting in the corner of their bunk with wide eyes watching.

"Something wrong?"

Antru answers, "I think you should have someone check your breathing."

"Don't be weird."

But Antru says, "I think you stopped. You kept stopping breathing."

It is laughed off, because, "I'd be dead if I stopped breathing."

Antru suggests, "I think you should have your breathing checked before you get dead."

It earns, "Drop dead," and the facilities are co-opted.

Living space in Marphy is nothing like Capriot. Even in the tightly packed inner city, there is still space to live. There are parks and open spaces. Homes have many rooms and there are yards and gardens. Marphy is a city with slightly more than twice the area, but more than four times the population. At some point it was agreed that living space could be compromised in favor of public spaces. The majority of the Marphy population lives in cubicles, much like the students of the Institute. They are spaces for sleeping and getting ready. Meals are provided through a drawer in the storage wall, and every day, freshly pressed uniforms are found hanging in the closet. It is efficient, and allows students more time to concentrate on studies.

Eotor bursts from the back of the cube completely naked and announces, "All yours." As they exchange places, it is further advised, "I wouldn't use the washcloth."

Chapter six:

A gentle breeze carries ocean air ashore, unfiltered by land or upcrops. It is heavy and builds a film over the body. It is also warm, and given time becomes comfortable.

The weather is more volatile than at Capriot. Storms arrive from nowhere out of sunshine. There is much more rain. The wind is often severe, and flags are watched to determine if it's safe to climb. The temperature is generally much warmer than at Capriot, though the variation is much greater. There is a period of adjustment, but the weather is not terrible. Sitting on a lower upcrop, feeling the warm wind gust over the body, it is enjoyable.

Watching the clouds merge and pull apart as they roll towards the city. Watching the waves crash against the shore, below. It is an entirely different feeling than at Capriot and a question has grown as to which is preferred.

Capriot is defined by stone. There is the small forest across the inlet, but there is very little vegetation otherwise. The city sits upon a plain that ends at cliffs before the shore. The dense core of the city is comprised of stone buildings beside roads of stone. The Emperor's compound is made of stone. The homes built out from the center of the city are made of stone, with stone yards lined by stone walls. The city is hard, and echo. It is beautiful, but it is not warm and welcoming. Warm and welcome was found only through the people known.

Marphy is strikingly different. It is controlled chaos that is overwhelming at introduction. It is hot, damp, and loud. There is groundcover on untouched spaces and trees are prodigiously planted throughout the city.

It did not grow out from a center but was carefully planned. Homes at Marphy are not the respite of family, but a place to sleep, to shower, and to eat if necessary. Instead, public spaces are where people gather in the evening.

Evenings are not quiet. They are boisterous gatherings where communities share meals together. There are loud conversations, music and dancing, and it is not uncommon to witness public intoxication. There is a pulsing vibrance in Marphy that is a marked contrast to experience. It is brighter, warmer in every way, and on reflection, it feels less sinister.

There is no emperor. There are representatives that mingle freely with the people. They share meals, and conversation, and listen to concerns: There is an impetus to address them if there's interest in re-election.

There are no stranded passengers waiting for the naïve, or kind, or conniving. There are no Reeco's, nor watchtowers to observe the neighborhoods. There is no questionable area in the city where stores trade weapons in dark rooms lined with flour. There are no parts of Marphy that feel unsafe to walk in, and that is likely because of the way it was constructed: Throughout the city, people come together. Homes surround public spaces.

"Waiting for someone?" A person broaches the surface and finds Antru waiting. They're answered, no, and then wonder, "Looking for company?"

"I wasn't," Antru answers. The reply falls as if that might have changed, so it's clarified, "I'm just enjoying how it looks from here."

"Want to join me?" The offer is again declined, and it's guessed, "Homesick?"

Moboti-sick – friend-sick: Perhaps not longing for the home. For the city. For the stone. There has been very little interaction with community, nor with the student body; most of that has been with an irritable, exhibitionist roommate. But the – community, the camaraderie is appreciated and admired.

The shared observation brings the other to ask, "Where are you from?"

"Capriot," seems to bring a withdrawal of the coquetry, but the question is asked, "What's it like, there?"

"Different," Antru explains: Differences. In brief, with recent awareness offered in more detail: "And they've got watch towers. People that watch the neighborhoods."

There is sympathy, and, "Yeah," explains, "I've heard it's a lot different. I don't think I'd want to visit."

"It's beautiful," Antru says. "Not like here, but everything's a part of the land. It's amazing. And there's lots of really good people."

"No offence, Capriot. Sure you won't join me?"

The head shakes. The words are wistful: "I just want to sit here."

"A thinker from Capriot: Those are usually trouble."

There is amusement, because, "I think that's why they sent me here."

There is amusement. There is laughter shared between them as the escapade to the fortress is related. But it's clarified, "My Moboti – Éayren: They got my assignment changed from Capriot."

"You're the little twit," the other begins. There is momentary alarm, but they're laughing. They share, "I actually like the falls. It's a big change, but I think it's a kick. Sure you don't want company?"

Antru says, "No thank you."

A hand extends, and with it, the offer, "I'm Orosh. Look me up," and fingers tap a band worn around the wrist: "Need anything – have questions: If you're looking for someone to talk to. Don't be shy, Antru of Capriot. It was nice to meet you."

The words are repeated, and they're not untrue.

It was a pleasant conversation. It felt different than conversations held before, and an urge arose to continue, to follow, but the feeling is quickly dampened by the forces that sought solitude above the city. They are only watched as they continue climbing. Orosh looks down as they reach the next plateau, and again they extend an invitation, and then wave as they are turned away, again.

It is a continuation of the experience at Marphy: An unexpected appreciation, but no feeling of connection. Eyes observe circumstances that strike invitation, but the body pulls for quiet conversation with a parent, for rock climbs with a closest friend; for evening conversations in a private yard with just a few. There is an alien sense within the many that congregate easily. There is an inability to relax within a horde. Conversations fail to find the flow experienced at home – with a parent, with friends: There is less space for internal retrospection.

It is noted that the one that passed does not return by the same path, as the sky begins to dim. There is disappointment, and also relief.

There is a tone as the edge is met. It is from the band worn by every student, and they are a form of enforcement, communication, and utility. The warnings are against perceived dangers and restricted areas. They are required to connect to rigging, and that is the only way students are allowed to climb. They allow everyone to find anyone, at any time. They are a nuisance but easy to use, and their convenience brings acclimation in short time.

The students of the institute have few restrictions on how high they can climb – contrast to experience as a child. They are restricted to specific routes, but there are hundreds in the region, and their difficulty and altitudes vary widely. What doesn't is that all have rigging: Physical cables that must be latched onto, that serve as the outdated safety net to prevent students from falling to their death. They are somewhat restricting as they limit the breadth of travel, but like the bands, acclimation is quick with the freedom to ascend as high as desired.

Antru descends, and walks back down to the fanned stacks of cubicles that house the institute's attendees. Like all areas of the city, they are arranged to surround gathering spaces, and as with all, there is artwork displayed around the grounds, there is music playing, and there are hundreds of people engaged in conversation. They eating, singing, and dancing. It is an ongoing, constant celebration of life and it is exhausting.

The door to the cubicle is opened and entered, and the body leans back against it as it closes: Eotor is leaning against the bunks with a hand braced against them and unsurprisingly naked.

They are asked, "What's up?"

Eotor questions, "Are you hot?"

Considering the temperatures that have been experienced, in contrast to the moderate heat of the evening, the answer given is, "Not really."

"Do you want to get hot," Eotor questions. They move closer and press a hand against the temple. Their body presses firm and sandwiches Antru against the door. A question: "You feeling it?"

They are told, "No," and slipped past for the bunk where the corner is sought as the retreat that finds stability in the chaos of Marphy.

"Really," the roommate questions. "Really – really? You're going to crawl back in your corner? Are you really that dead inside?"

Antru says, "I probably am."

"Of all the roommates," Eotor moans. "Of all the people I could get stuck with, I get shafted with a stone-cold Capriot stiff. Do you even want to live?"

There is a flash of a gasp, and bone-chilling cold drives into the body. There is a gap of silence the falls into the space that precedes it. There are raspy drafts that blow snow across the upcrops, and they collapse into the pit of annihilation, below. There is a memory that is not just a filed recollection, but a physical fear as a hand rested on a body to inquire if life still held within it.

"Did you talk to someone about your breathing," is a question asked from the trepidation invoked by the avalanche that fell. It is from an innocence that still exists, and from true concern for another person. The same concern that fell for someone in a vehicle on a city's streets – from the naivete to believe the narratives invoked from birth.

It brings anger: "That's what I get? You want to talk about breathing? I quit."

The exclamation is exemplified by a folded chair that is pulled from the storage wall and flung across the room. It crashes as feet stomp to the wash room where a brief commotion precedes re-entry. Newly robed, Eotor marches through the room and exits, and the door slams loudly with departure.

There is silence, and confusion. Words spoken are the words that have always been known, but their usage seems different. Meaning seems to have changed. Content of language seems to have implications that differ from what is said. It is where the alienation and disconnect arise: The sense of belonging to Capriot is strong, but it does not seem to fit with the rest of the world.

It is quiet, though the echo of the door still rings in thoughts. The image of a roommate still stands in thoughts. Their anger still resonates, and there is resentment that it rose when expectation met rejection.

It is part of the disconnect in the experience. It is everywhere and feels like the only thing that draws interest: Orosh, ready to abandon a climb for a chance encounter. A roommate with expectations they would be intimate – waiting naked, and ready. There is deep resentment at the expectations held – it feels rushed: It isn't wanted.

There is one place safe to share experience and feelings, and the episode is relayed. Aedra answers, "So tell them no."

Antru shares, "I did. They got angry."

The reply, "Weird," is heartening, and further, "It's not like that here," brings comfort that there are people and places still assigned with normalcy.

It brings a reply that had become doubted, but the conversation with a longed-for friend, makes certain, "I wish I was still in Capriot."

Aedra suggests, "Someday it might be interesting. Just not now."

It is agreed, and crude jokes are passed between them. There is a curiosity both broach, and ideas offered with a proffered knowledge that is not really theirs.

"I've got to go," Aedra says: "Time to stuff my face."

Antru replies, "Okay. I think someday I'll want to – but I think it has to be with the right person. Definitely not my roommate."

Aedra asks, "Have someone in mind?"

They are told, "Go eat. I don't want to think about that right now."

The brief conversation settles agitation, and Eotor does not return before tired eyes are lulled to sleep.

It is discovered that Eotor did not return at all when the tone sounds to alarm students awake the next morning. It is the best morning since arrival, and the insult thrown the prior day is a feeling shared for opposite reasons.

It is quiet – peaceful. That is held onto after the shower, for the first time, comfortable enough to relax in the cube in only undergarments. Gathering with others to eat is passed on in favor of the nutrient bar that awaits as an alternative, every morning. It is eaten slowly and savored. The quiet and missing chaos makes the cube a pleasant retreat and it is hoped Eotor has found someone that will satisfy what they want – and they'll just stay there.

A cupboard is opened, and as always, there is a clean and neatly pressed uniform. Time is taken to properly fit it on for the first time since arrival, and steps are lighter – greetings more cheerful than typical. That begins to ebb as there are several that see the unexpected openness as an invitation to initiate physical contact. It brings the resumption of the usual muted responses and acknowledgements.

The cheer is eliminated at the lecture hall where Eotor is waiting, just to share, "If you change your mind, I might still give you a chance. But you better decide pretty soon."

They are ignored.

The steps are climbed, and the cool of the stone building is a welcome comfort that helps to put a roommate out of mind. A seat is taken midway down the stadium, in an area with the least concentration of other people. There is a message observed as the tablet is opened, from Aedra. It is understood to be a continuation from the conversation, the prior evening:

"Do you believe in finding the right person?"

This is answered, "Yes," and the answer is returned.

There is a quick response: "Let me know if you find them."

There is not enough time to adequately think through an answer before tablets will be locked down, and so, "I already did. Can't wait to get home," suffices to answer what is being hinted at, and hoped vague enough it could be walked back if that suspicion is wrong. There is no response prior to the lecture starting, and all accessories are disabled.

It is a lecture that is required for all incoming students. It is a topic that had not been heard of, prior, known as philosophy. The lectures wander through many areas, from existence, to futures, of meaning, and morality. They are all overwrought conversations where meaningless ideas are argued over hypotheses. The value of it is not clear, and the lectures and conversations drone on, endlessly wrestling over matters that are irrelevant. It is difficult to keep eyes open and the mind from wandering.

The Lead drones, "What about our futures? What will we become in the future? How will we contribute in the future?" It is a topic that has already been discussed too much, and then it turns to the phrase that brings eyes to roll: "Who are you in your dreams? We all know Januk wanted to inspire the population to reach for higher goals, but what are those, for you? Where do you see yourself in the future – what do you want to do?"

Someone shouts, "I want to play Roukta."

"Yes," the lead says enthusiastically. "That is your dream – and it is the dream of many of you here. But there are only twenty-four teams, and most have about twenty players. That means, there are only four-hundred eighty positions available. That means, most of you aren't going to play Roukta. So what does that mean to your future? What happens to all of you that won't play Roukta?"

Antru suggests, "We get sent to Marphy."

It is completely silent. Eyes look up to find all eyes are trained in the same direction, and the lead's arm is raised and finger is pointing. Their words instruct, "Get out."

There is an attempt to blow it off. There is an attempt at an apology, but the words are harsher, and repeated again. That's followed, "Leave, or I'll have you escorted out."

Antru nods agreement; utters, "Okay."

There is a strong feeling of embarrassment, but there is also excitement to escape: To shirk responsibility and wander freely. The hall is left quickly, and doors open to bright starlight, the warmth, and humidity that have sometimes been considered preferable to the dry, and stone, and cooler temperatures of Capriot.

There is open opportunity to explore – to do anything. The cube is crossed off as the roommate might return. There is no desire to congregate with others in the public spaces, and the idea of exploring the city fails to find inspiration. The idea of freedom becomes lost for what to do.

The tablet is checked, but it remains locked into the lecture – still on futures. Artwork is examined on the perimeter of a quiet commons, but it is not provocative to the mind and artwork, and sculptures are only viewed in passing as thoughts spin through one idea after another and get discarded.

Wandering aimlessly and avoiding congregations leads to upcrops at the back of the city, and the band is held to linkage and rigging to start a climb.

Linkage is denied: A message flashes, "Lecture," and gives the time, place, and topic.

There is a feeling, just like when discovering the concept of a pinch, that life, and order, and choices are not within a person's control. That there are overseeing bodies that determine what can be done, where one goes, how far one can succeed, and who plays roukta, as irrelevant as that is to anything. There is a sense that there is no real control over anything, and that the insidious words of an ancient subversive are part of that, and ultimately meaningless:

"Who are you in your dreams?"

"Dead," Antru answers. "Everyone in my dreams ends up dead."

The sour thoughts move to the rock. Hands move to the imperfections and tease at them. Feet dig as height is taken, and a quick glance down suggests opportunity – ping at the brain, and lights it up. It is just a brief flash that brings the mind into its place of enervation. It is a charge that sends arms scrapping and feet digging.

The face of the rock is scratched across as if it's a surface to walk: Holds are seen with clarity and seem enormous. Footstops are remembered after passing and are dug against with complete surety. The rockface is climbed with no rigging, with no safety net, and the physical exertion feels like the antidote to everything in Marphy and propels the body upward.

Arms ache, and feet are blistered. The climb exceeds the highest rigging in place, and continues until the highest plateau is finally reached. It has taken far more than a single lecture, and the star has crossed past the middle of the sky. The top of the upcrop is reached in complete exhaustion, with every drop of exertion consumed. Antru climbs to the top of the rise and stands, breathing heavily, aching and exhausted, and desperately hungry. It has already been realized the climb down will need to wait until the body has a chance to recover. However, there is also a concern that won't come easily, as hydration can't be restored and there's nothing to eat.

It is only a moment after lying back in absolute exhaustion, the wristband vibrates and a blue light flashes: Someone is seeking position. Someone is looking for where they are. The answer is not provided, and the wristband's silenced.

Chapter six:

It is expected that further consequences will follow but it doesn't matter. The answer given at the lecture was correct, and the lecture itself and the questions being asked were proof of it: The majority of those at the Institute at Marphy are going nowhere. They will transport blocks of stone, or iron shirts for students. They will be the backbone of society that's kept hidden and ignored.

The blue light illuminates again, but it can't be disabled. It is likely position is being tracked, and it will soon be time to face consequences.

There is satisfaction. It may have been one, small, petulant act, but it was an honest answer. It spoke to the truth that words muddy. It cut past the indoctrination and fabled heroes that are coopted for control.

Another notification: A message from Aedra. It does not continue the prior conversation, instead, asks, "Do you get days off after taking the name?"

"No. But it might not matter."

"Why? But do you think I could visit?"

"I don't know. I have to go. I'll explain later."

A small vehicle has scaled the upcrop. Antru stands to watch, surprised they're able. The door opens, and the lecture's Lead is seated and motions. They order, "Get in."

That's answered, "No."

"Antru," the Lead says: "This is unsafe. I need you to get in."

Antru says, "I'm not getting in."

There is a flash of anger, but the safety harness is released and the Lead steps onto the surface of the rock. There is an attempt to physically secure their student, but Antru was ready and avoids their grip.

The Lead yells, "Get in. Now. You are not allowed up here."

The answer is, "No." Arms are still aching, but eyes begin scanning for a path of escape. There is a good hold not far, to the left, and position is slowly changed to make a move for it.

The Lead sits, and it was unexpected. They suggest, "Sit," and the tone has changed. They are seeing a child that feels threatened but why isn't understood. Antru does not comply, but they have at least stopped moving. The Lead tries, "Do you want to tell me what's going on?" The head shakes, and another step is taken. With more urgency, the Lead says, "Antru. I need you to stop moving towards the edge. Tell me what's going on and I'll try to help you, but it is not safe to climb down from here. Have a seat and we'll talk through this."

Antru says, "I've been here, you know." The answer, "I don't," receives, "In my dreams. I come here and watch my friends and parents die. It looks just like this."

"Antru," is spoken with the fear the situation was completely misread. A finger moves for the band, to call for intervention, but the spine-chilling, "Don't," is stated as a warning.

The Lead tries, "Antru: I'm just trying to keep you safe. Why don't we ride down, and we can continue the conversation where I don't have to worry about your safety."

Antru shares, "People that get in vehicles don't come back."

"What? Antru," the Lead says: "What are you talking about?"

"That's what my moboti Éayren says. They're all spies for the clans. If you get in one, no one will ever see you again.'""

"I'm just trying to keep you safe."

"That's why I'm here," Antru says. "My parents think it's too dangerous for me in Capriot. That's why they sent me here."

"Let me explain this to you: Climbing up here violates our laws. I intervened on your behalf with the hope we could talk about what's going on. If I didn't, you would have been arrested."

"My moboti also gave me a weapon. Éayren told me to shoot anyone that tries to arrest me."

"You have a weapon?"

"No," Antru says. "I gave it to someone that needs it more."

"Antru: Listen to me. I have no idea what you're talking about, but no one disappears in Marphy. If your parents are trying to keep you safe, they couldn't have picked a better place. Right now, I'm trying to do that, and I need you to work with me. Tell me what you would consider an acceptable way to get you down without climbing. We can either take a vehicle, or we can sail. But you'd have to trust me for that, because you'd be on my back."

Antru says, "Okay – sail."

That is answered, "Okay – wait." And the lead rises to extract equipment.

There is relief, an understanding that the fear is real, for whatever reason. Somehow, vehicles are considered threatening to the point a child would risk their life over an uneventful ride down to the surface.

The lead's band is interfaced, and at the order, the entry to the vehicle begins to seal, and the vehicle pulls away.

Suspicion, however, remains. The Lead is watched as a harness is strapped to their body the procedure's explained: Jump, sail, and land. It sounds more hazardous than climbing, but it is preferable to a vehicle and the body remains weary. There is still trepidation, but Antru steps into the harness on the Lead's back and connects the straps.

"Ready," is questioned, and at the edge, overlooking Marphy there's no doubt the answer is no, but, "Yes," is spoken.

There is one more step taken to the very edge, a brief dip, and then the Lead launches them from the upcrop. There is a terrifying increase in speed that is known from dreams. Where the rockface passes by at increasing speed until a brutal impact finds parent, or friend, or tablet shattered at the bottom.

There is a sudden jolt. From within the harness, fabric and ropes shot out, and the fabric fanned out as a giant sail above them. It immediately brings the rate of descent to a peaceful, survivable glide. It brings the opportunity to watch the city slowly approach, to look out across it to the ocean, and a thought that has been held many times, passes again: Marphy is beautiful.

There is an incredible peacefulness as they sail. Their bodies rock as the sail is guided and it brings memories of rocking in Dalune's arms after nights of terror. The wind is gentle against them and the forces begin to erode the discontent that brought them to ride together. There are thoughts that some things could have been handled better. It is considered that insulting everyone at Marphy might have been a poor decision.

There is also great gratitude that the climb down was avoided.

Feet touch down, and it is uneventful. The sail continues but with the anchor takes a nose dive into the ground.

For one, there is enthusiasm: "Can we do that again?"

The other is grateful they survived: "I – never – want to do that again. I hate doing that, but it gets you down, so I was willing to overlook my apprehension to take care of you. In return, I'm asking you to have an honest conversation."

Antru says, "Okay," and, "I'm sorry," hoping it cuts through much of what's intended.

Instead, "What are your ambitions," is asked. It is expected, "You want to play Roukta?"

That is a definitive, "No. I don't even watch it. I wanted to follow my moboti Dalune and research, but they thought it's too dangerous and sent me here. Now I can't do anything I want."

They are finally disentangled, and the Lead folds the harness, and then begins sorting out the rope and straightening the sail. There is no request for help, but it's given anyway.

"Why do you think there is a danger?"

"Because," Antru says, "Éayren said there is. I don't know what it is, but they say don't talk to a pinch. They say, stay away from the clans, and I'm supposed to shoot anyone that tries to arrest me. I don't know why they tell me that, but I know it means I can't do research, and even if I wanted to play Roukta, I know they won't let me."

"Your parents?"

"No – the clans. They won't let any team pick me."

It is suggested, "The Marphy clan won't keep a Marphy team from picking you. And being here does not preclude you from conducting research. You are obviously bright; you are an extremely skilled climber: I can see many opportunities for you."

"There won't be," Antru says.

"Why," is questioned.

"I told you: The clans won't let me. That's why I'm here. They thought I was in danger at Capriot so they sent me here."

"Antru," the Lead tries: "Your parents appealed directly to the Nespian clan to get you transferred here. That is not a decision that is made lightly. Your parents made a compelling argument that your skillset would be better served by coming to Marphy. From what I've seen, that is not an inaccurate assessment. But you need to understand, your parents were working directly with the clans."

"I don't know." Frustration returns and words thought falling from the sky fall from the mind as the dispossession of the morning returns. There is irritation that the peacefulness of the mountaintop and of the sail has been brought back to earth with a conversation from which there seems to be no escaping.

There is at least quiet as the sail and ropes are carefully re-packaged. They are folded in a precise way that begins making sense as it's watched, that allows the ropes to exit first so there's no risk of tangling with the fabric of the sail when it's released. All are tucked into the center of the harness and secured.

"You should talk with your parents," the Lead suggests. "I don't know why they would tell you what they have, but as far as I'm concerned, your parents give you an advantage."

Antru says, "They don't."

It's pointed out, "Éayren is a four-time Roukta champion. Any team that sees the skill you have for scaling rocks would at least take a chance with that connection. And Dalune is well-respected, and known, as well, for the net they give you credit for. I think everyone here looks at you as having an advantage, whether it's Roukta, or research."

"I don't," Antru says.

"Okay." A hand rests on Antru's shoulder, and eyes lock on: "You can say there's no chance for you – and maybe that's somehow true. But I want you to consider this. In four years when you graduate, if you continue to blow off your education and training, you will, in fact, have limited opportunities. If you don't show Roukta teams what you can do, they'll likely assume you didn't inherit any of Éayren's skills. If you do poorly at the academy and give people reason to support their beliefs that you weren't capable of creating the net, then that's what they'll believe and no division is going to be interested in you.

"But think about this, Antru. What if you don't take advantage of this opportunity at Marphy, you find you have no opportunities, but you also see that the students that excelled, that worked hard, that developed their skills, what will you think if they – are – given opportunities. It's possible that there's something your parents have involved themselves in that has raised concerns. On the other hand, the Nespian clan was open to their challenge, listened to their arguments, and ultimately agreed that they were right. That's at least two clans that are open to the success of Antru of Capriot, and I point out: They are two of the largest clans. And if there is, in fact, some concern for your safety, you are in the safest place on the planet: We take care of our children. We will even jump off mountains for them."

There is a somber nod, but it is clear the words had little impact. With a prod, the child spills, "It was Éayren. Dalune thought I was going to Capriot." Head turns – looks up: The heartbreak shared, "That's why I don't want to play roukta. Because you never get to see your family. I studied all the books Dalune brought home, and now I'll never get to use it."

There is a reaction to bring the child in. To offer support, and sympathy. Arms pull the child close and hold them, and the resistance that has been present since introduction is absent. It is obvious there are forces that are pulling the child apart, and the greatest seems to be the least expected.

"Outside of lecture, call me Notoire," the Lead offers. "I want to help you find your path forward. I want to see you give this experience everything you have, so that in four years, you have the opportunities that you deserve."

The child, still held in arms, begins breaking down. There is a shudder through the body, and the head starts shaking – still rejecting any thought for the future they expected.

"Let me," Notoire pleads. "I promise that if you're right, that all the clans have conspired to keep you out of research or playing roukta, I will throw every connection I have to get you what you want. But you have to make the effort. I give you my word that I'll do everything I can for you, but you have to put in the effort. Are you willing to try?"

It is almost imperceptible, but eyes find a motion that doesn't suggest rejection. It is a soul in shambles trying to find solid ground. It is a world shattered just when a world of opportunities should have opened. It is a person incapable of understanding the forces they are faced with, trying to make sense of the inconceivable. It is a person that is still a child that is not ready for the transition to maturity. It is someone looking for something to hold onto after everything known, expected, and hoped has fallen onto a pile of rubble and shattered.

There is a deep breath, and Antru steps away. There is a thought that certain things were said that shouldn't have been – family secrets shared – and there's a test levelled at a person asking for trust:

"Are you going to tell anyone what I said?"

"I don't know what to say," is answered. "I don't know what to make of it – I'm being honest. A lot of what you said is very concerning, and I think you feel that, too. So I'll say, I want to work with you. Whatever else is going on doesn't matter to me. My objective is to make sure you succeed. I would also suggest not sharing that with others. Will you promise me that?"

That is answered, "Yes."

"I don't intervene for individual students very often, but I think many of us had expectations about who you are that weren't fair. I also see you're struggling with the transition, and evidently, some of your experiences. So, I'll do this, as long as you make the effort."

"I will," Antru promises.

"With that said, there are repercussions for breaking the rules. I can probably keep that limited to probation, but you cannot break any rules during that period, or you will be expelled. Do we have an agreement?"

"Yes," Antru says, but more importantly, "Will I be able to do the sail again?"

There is laughter, and the admission, "I don't like being that high, and I don't like jumping off anything that high, but it doesn't surprise me you enjoyed it. There is a track that you could follow where you'd get to, but that's part of the Roukta concentration."

"How is it part of Roukta?"

"Emergency and rescue," is explained. Personell that attend the games, and also rescue children that strand themselves on upcrops where they aren't allowed. "It you're interested in pursuing roukta at all, that's not a bad direction to go. There are always children wandering off where they shouldn't go."

"Right," says Antru, but more importantly, "I was thinking something while we were up there. I probably wouldn't have said anything if I wasn't mad at my roommate."

"Are there problems with your roommate."

"A lot," Antru says. "They want to do things I don't want to do, and they get mad when I won't. But I don't really like them, and I don't think we should be anyway. That's not normal, is it?"

There is another laugh, and it's because, "I said before, a lot of people look at you as someone in a unique position. I think you're going to find there are a lot of people interested in you. That being said, you shouldn't do anything that makes you uncomfortable. We can have that addressed, if you'd like."

"No. But can I ask a question?"

"Of course."

"Is it normal to stop breathing while you're sleeping."

"Does – your roomate," the Lead questions, and they're answered:

"Their breathing's loud when they're asleep, and then they stop. And then they start choking, or coughing, and start breathing again. You're not supposed to do that, are you?"

The answer's, "No," and, "That should be addressed."

"That's what I said," Antru complains. "Sometimes I even check to see if their still alive, and I told Eotor they needed to talk to someone about that, but then, they got mad about that, too."

Notoire says, "That is going to need to be addressed, because that's very concerning. I'll hold off on the rest until you tell me otherwise."

A test, "Notoir," is answered, "Yes?"

They're given, "Thank you."

"This is a great opportunity," the lecture begins. "You might need someone to help steady you at the moment, but I believe you are going to flourish. Take advantage of this opportunity. I'm going to let you go so I can clean this up and call it a day, but I expect to see you tomorrow, and I expect you to participate."

Antru says, "Okay," in agreement, however, "I probably still won't like philosophy."

There is laughter, again. It's fuller, more honest, and with appreciation. There is a smile, a nod, a wink, and it's suggested, "We'll see."

Fingers claw at the rock, scrapping for anything to grip as its face is crossed: Vision is gone. The heightened sense that emerges with a climb began to falter after the third ascent. Vision has been reduced to desperate scratching, awkward lurching towards anything to catch, while defenses try to land a blow, to send the assailant to the penalty, below.

A body swings – a calculated risk to take both out of the game. It shows that others have seen that vision's lost and they move for the easy target. Effort turns to delaying the inevitable, to buy others on the team an easier pass: The body flattens as another nears. The last moment's change of position prevents a clean strike, and there is just a punch in the back that helps to hold the position.

From the moment of security, a hold grows out of the rockface. A footstop is remembered near the knee. There is a sudden scramble for the top that leaves defenses out of place and ascent finds only one to defend the surface. Another teammate surfaces and the dash begins to gather stones.

One is quickly uncovered, and a precarious lean over the edge finds a teammate, "Arosa," and the stone is thrown. There's no time to watch if it's recovered – with the throw feet push towards further detritus on the surface and two more stones are uncovered quickly.

The edge is met again. The same teammate is scrambling but they're still the only chance – name called again. With just one second past, "Arosa," is called a third time, and the second stone is thrown.

As quickly as the transaction took place, it was a second too long and the turn finds a boot is striking.

The turn avoids a direct blow, but the other's body collides into the upper torso and Antru is sprawled. There's quick push to rise by both, but the surface has become well-defended with six combatants. They battle only three, but that is the number of stones needed to end the battle: There is no retreat.

The search for stones becomes one of opportunity. Quick attacks, retreats, and kick at what's around if there's a chance.

"Antru:" A call for help – a stone held up as a mob encircles, and it's tossed over. It sails, slower than a summer's walk on a lazy afternoon. It hangs in the air so long that others turn before it's caught. As the mob moves, there is a quick dash that finds a teammate is just beginning to climb. The stone is thrown, and, "Catch," is called just as the first strike lands. It is three on one, and it's a decision that is made with victory slipping away.

There is a chance to look up before being thrown over, and the score is zero to four: They only have to place the stones and run the obstacle course.

That will bring abandonment of the home upcrop, and the other team will quickly find their stones and pursue. To help slow that process down, a foot sweeps to send an attacker down, quickly followed by a move to the feet and lightning drive into the three of them. It sends all four over the edge of the mountain, and they fall in unison until the rigging begins to slow them.

There are caustic words shared. There are attempts to land strikes as they fall, but anyone close is just kicked away.

It is already zero-zero by the time they land, and all four position themselves to sprint the instant the penalty expires. Thirty seconds later, Antru is penalized again after entering the beginning of the course. The question, "Why," is answered, "Score," and eyes look up to see seven-zero.

There are more vile words, and after the second thirty expire, the hopeless task of recollecting stones and chasing down opponents is taken as an existential challenge.

Three defenders still hang off the rock face which indicates the stones have yet to be placed. The first is targeted and just waits, presuming higher ground gives the better hand. But their feet are yanked from under them, and they're sent crashing into the stone.

The two others converge. That no one else is on the upcrop likely indicates there's a standoff and a chance remains. Antru moves to keep the duo separated, attacking the first with punches to the head, smashing their helmet against the rock. They flail back, but their reaction to the attack brings an arm up, and a sharp jab in the side sends them falling.

The last gets the first blow: A well-placed kick into the ribs. There's an attempt to use their motion against them but they're braced well. A second attempt to push them back the other way finds a second kick delivered. The second time, the foot is grabbed and harshly twisted. The other footstop's left to kick with the other foot which opens the opportunity to attack the shoulder. It brings a cry, and the firm position's lost. A return kick to their shoulder sends them down, and attention returns to gathering the stones.

Fingers ache, and arms and legs are burning, but the speed the rock is climbed is not notably slower than the first time. Stones are stuffed uncomfortably into the rigging harness, and the descent begins, but a quick look up at the scoreboard shows the effort's been for nothing.

Feet kick back from the stone and Antru swings out, and back again, descending on the rigging to gathered teammates.

"What happened?"

Revolted, it's shared, "I tripped."

"Tripped," Antru questions. "You tripped?"

"I bet they rigged it," says another.

There is a hard punch into Antru's back, and angry words, "It was over."

Antru says, "It wasn't."

Another jab, and teammates move to separate them. An accusation, "You'd already lost. You're just taking cheap shots."

More join. There are more accusations, tempers flare, and the friendly competition ends with a melee.

Referees, and leads, and others join to separate them. It takes significant effort to pull them apart and to keep them away from one another. There is true anger directed towards Antru and that spills over onto other teammates. A line eventually is formed to keep them from physically attacking one another, but the hostility continues with words:

"It was over, loser."

Antru is calm because it is known to infuriate others, and replies, "It's not over until it's over."

More insults fly. Vitriol is shared. Denigrating observations are made and that's driven to a fury by the humor found by their target: They are dismissed, and Antru and teammates laugh at what's said.

"Wait 'til next time," is threatened. "Nothing but a cheap shot," is a sentiment repeated multiply.

And then, Antru asks, "Three on one? Who's looking for cheap shots." Voices become louder again, and that returns to physical, with, "Or maybe you're just not that good."

The brawl resumes, and once again, it takes considerable time to pull combatants apart. The second time, warnings are given. There are threats of probation, suspension, or expulsion, and in the hail of continued insults and threats, Antru remains stoic and silent.

The sides finally pull away with less committed accusations, one beginning the celebration, and the other wondering how what looked like victory went so badly the other way.

"You gonna join us?"

The question is asked because there is still an outlier amongst them. One that will withdraw, disappear for days and sometimes doesn't join when there's cause for celebration.

Antru says, "I'll be there later. I've got a couple things I need to do."

Marphy is contagious, but there are still aspects of the life that don't seat comfortably. Collective congregation is considered the highest form of relaxation, an opinion and lifestyle shared by those from the nearby city of Minaut.

They are interesting concepts: Nearness and congregation, and they are similar. There is connection between the cities, if affinity for one, and there is connection between the people that live in them. They are social and prefer to spend their time together.

Capriot is near nothing – Clarb, the closest, and it's inaccessible by land. Those in Clarb stay in Clarb, and those in Capriot stay there. There is no twin city. There is no shared social identity. There are no habits nor tendencies shared between them. Clarb remains unknown, and Capriots have small groups of friends and family that gather in isolated homes. Interaction with others is warned against, and there are clan spies in every neighborhood.

There is the risk of disappearing for trying to help someone.

Marphy, and Minaut – explored on two, brief expeditions – are very different. Capriot is beautiful in its own way: Chiseled from stone, demure and overlooking the ocean. Marphy and Minaut are marvels despite the landscape.

They are vibrant and warm. They buzz with activity. There is no space in either city that is not filled with music, and artwork, and food, and conversation. The cities are alive and full of energy, and for those originating from Rims' cities, the relaxation appreciated by their residents can be exhausting.

There is truth in the words given to teammates, but there is also a need to escape the chaos of life in Marphy. Appreciated, but there is a need for solitude. For quiet contemplation, and reflection with the few. That is mostly through texts with Aedra and Dalune. Occasionally there is facetime with one another, but exhaustion usually precludes that as an option.

The door is opened, and the quiet cube is a wash of disentanglement: Conflict falls away. Anger and hostility flow away in the stream of cool air that flows out through the door – a breeze off the seas of Capriot. The door closes and the silence forms a cocoon of familiarity.

It is where aches and pains finally make their entrance. It is where frustration with teammates that gave away a win is forgotten. The door closes, bag drops, and body falls into solitude. A thought falls that checking the score would have saved thirty seconds and an expletive is whispered.

It is not long before the differences between Capriots and others falls – the berth taken: Sleep follows. Recuperation after matches, for most, is done in common areas, over drinks, with food, and conversation. Attempts at joining found eyes became too heavy, and the sleeping schoolmate became a target for others' hijinks. In the quiet of the cube, sleep falls quick, and deep, and the passage of time slips by until the mind is ticked by consciousness.

There is a groan on awakening: Weariness and exhaustion still pull the body down, but obligations nag for attention. Several minutes are spent drifting through states of consciousness, but a sharp flash from a memory of dreams past brings the body to a seat. Hands run across the head as if tired could be pushed away. Aching muscles are briefly massaged, and fingers clench and stretch in an attempt to work out stiffness.

There is another grunt with the rise. A bottle is cracked to begin rehydration, to sip while working through assignments: Desk pulled down from the storage wall, folded chair unfurled and taken, and the tablet is set on a stand. Distraction immediately delays intentions:

Messages are opened, and most are quickly answered – mostly declining invitations. But there is also a message from Dalune, and one from Aedra. The latter is opened first, and is typical, asking questions, sharing experience, and it ends, "Tell me when we can get together."

Roukta already interferes with life. Already it's given precedence over friends and family: Training or competitions stealing time during breaks.

"I don't know," is answered: "But I'll look at the schedule. It'd be easier if Capriot wasn't such a pain to get to."

Dalune is answered, "I blew the match, today, and started a riot, but everything's good. I want to come back to visit, but I don't know when I'll have the time."

They are signed off, and the tablet is finally put to its intended use.

There is a large amount of time and effort put towards roukta, but it is not the sole focus of education. There are a wide variety of topics that are required to be taken, and numerous paths to be followed. With some regret, the path towards sails was passed on in favor of a future developing technology. It has become clear that the various institutes have specializations – at least, Marphy – but they are not singularly focused. The longer away, the more it seems as if a veil covers Capriot that shadows sunshine and information.

It is after most have already eaten for the night when assignments are completed. They are submitted and motion is taken to keep word to join the others. But a quick shower grows long and hotter as the heat on sore muscles and contusions helps alleviate the pain.

There is further delay on entering the commons, as, "Notoire," is greeted.

"Tough match," is offered. The end of probation did not end interaction. Weekly check-ins continue, but they have become part of a conversation as concerns by both have muted.

"I blew it," Antru suggests. "I didn't look for the score."

"It was close. They got the stones back just as you were entering. It was an unusual ending."

"Still," Antru says. A seat is taken as conversation continues, as the mentor soothes the other's guilt. They move through topics and at that of friends, thoughts turn back to the question from Aedra – the solution offered to take a vehicle.

"It sounded completely off the wall when you told me that." Notoire reflects to a conversation. To the distressed child that would rather jump off a mountain than take the safety of a vehicle to the ground. There had been immense improvement in effort and attitude since, but the fears shared had not abated at all. "Those are your options: Ride or sail."

Antru says, "I'll come up with something else."

They're warned, "Get it approved. Make sure it's authorized."

Antru says, "I will."

Thoughts are spinning already on departure, and teammates find their friend distracted and nonresponsive to the barbs leveled at arrival.

One inquires, "Are you mad?" At what is answered with the obvious, "The match?"

"Oh," Antru says, "No. I was thinking about something. But I am mad I screwed it up."

"You didn't screw it up – I did."

"They trapped us. They just caught us off guard."

"If I didn't trip, they wouldn't have."

Antru counters, "If I didn't enter the course without looking at the score, we'd have had thirty seconds."

"A second here, a second there – if you got in a second earlier you could have attacked them from the back. We might've had a chance."

"There were three with me," Antru shares: "I don't think I'd have been a lot of help."

"We would've had a chance," and Antru wonders, "What happened?"

"They trapped us," it's explained.

"They had a bottleneck at the end, right before the bowl. We had to go through one at a time."

"And then I tripped."

"We were trying to hurry. There was a lot of pushing – it just happened. We got five in, but they got the other seven."

"And we're out, in case you didn't hear."

Morosely, Antru asks, "We are?"

"Ultra won," it's explained. "I heard Mighty threw it just to keep us out."

"That stupid rigging against Highland: That should have been a win."

"Tru," is heard. A hand falls against the shoulder as a competitor that had hours earlier thrown punches and accusations, offers a friendly greeting: "All good."

They're answered, "Yes," and they follow, "You know how it is: Heat of the moment. We all knew you were gonna take a go. For a second I thought you had it."

"Good win," Antru says. "And you knocked us out."

"If it stands," the other says.

"Why wouldn't it?"

"Well," says the combatant, "Someone complained the course didn't meet requirements."

"Then they shouldn't have let us play," Antru says.

"That's what I say. Either way, we're in after the Mighty Marphs threw their match. It's just if it's you or Ultra. Alright I join?"

More follow. Conversation is only friendly – filled with boasting and humor. Mockery of failed efforts. Teams mingle, and no hostility remains, except mockingly – towards the Mighty Marphs.

The night is crisp, and the mood is bawdy. It is typical of post-match revelry: Loud and crowded – filled with positive energy. It is filled with energy that finds resonance with many, and the numbers thin as darkness falls, and the din becomes a travelling chorus of conversation:

Near silence percolated by a roar of laughter. Opinions are offered legitimacy by amplifying volume. Counter-opinions speak louder and the conversations swell until something is said to short-circuit them into laughter – humor, or ostracization. Both are the favored methods to resolve conflicts late in the evening and differing opinions almost always resolve at common ground.

As darkness blankets the city, the commons is a circle of circles, groups reclining around small pits of fire. It is considered the best part of the experience at Marphy, and that is no longer a blithe opinion. The experience has been embraced and there are many aspects of it that are welcome.

There is the education and the path towards technological development. There is the Institute itself and the entire city that are vibrant, exciting, inviting, and amicable. There is the league of technocrats that never would have been understood for what it is if it wasn't for Notoire: A club for research and development, where ideas can be brought to the extant, and there is support and advice for how to get there. There are the friendships that have formed, and especially with the elite on the roukta teams.

There is a previously un-held appreciation for roukta.

Appreciation for the physical demands – for the effort in the game and for training. There is new-held appreciation for the defensive balance needed when scaling the rocks. There is appreciation for the physicality and the violence that sent ancient players to their death.

But the greatest appreciation is for the quiet moments shared late at night with friends. The conversation between uproars and outbursts, where thoughts, and feelings, and observations are shared without inhibition.

Chapter eight:

"Risking my life," Antru writes.

The paint of humor: A coat brushed on to whitewash the truth contained. A self-mockery of ideas condemned as paranoia, however passing years of observation and experience won't concede it. There is truth in the words that were shared. There is a world beyond the world that's lived in. There are secret passages and unseen faces working behind the walls and below the surface.

There is truth presented every day: Nutrients arrive in drawers and uniforms are always ready. It is not watchtowers or a pinch, but the unseen world still exists in Marphy. There is more than what's seen by the eye. There is more than what's shared – society is not the noble vision embedded at the start of indoctrination. There is dirt, and suffering, but that's blunted by an unknown operant that is suspected to be the clans. Kept out of sight, and brushed beneath carpets.

A coat of paint to cover the cities' dark secrets.

Some in the open: All clans still reside in fortresses. The Marphy clan's is open and part of the city landscape, another place for gathering and festivities. But as daylight's drained and weary eyes look to unwind, those of the clan retreat into elaborate buildings, unlike the cubes for the rest of the city. They are not confined to small spaces and limited assets – they have vehicles and great luxury.

Others are hidden behind walls, or floors, or spy on competitions.

"Hey – Tru: You have the specs yet?"

It is a question posed of a proposition that finds the request repeatedly. A prototype build sits in waiting, but the approval to progress remains stalled, and every answer or request that's satisfied, finds another to stymie progression.

"Tru," is called again, because it appears the first entreaty wasn't heard – more likely ignored. A response that is increasingly common.

"I'll work on it."

It's suggested, "Let's get it in."

There is still excitement over the project. There are still those at the institute and in the league that believe it's a development that's important. One that will move forward. A revolutionary independence for the population. However, it is increasingly seen as a dead-end subject by its innovator. That it will never be approved for exactly the reasons that find excitement: It would give freedom of movement and increased independence.

"Seriously," it's urged: "Antru – I need the specs."

"Alright," is answered. A promise: "I'll work on it."

Promises stated. Words spoken: They are more often meaningless. The work and energy from years prior has become concentrated on the minutia of concepts, parts to ideas to be explored at a later time and in private quarters. Pieces of projects that appear meaningless and trivial. Claims of concepts explored to concrete the hypothetical: A promising technocrat, lost down the well of theory and to the clouds of the fantastical.

"Can I move this to someone that might be interested in it?"

It is a question asked out of frustration. A sponsor that shared the enthusiasm of a young student with ideas to change the world. Those ideas have been observed to wither, and interests have become viewed as mercurial.

It is not the first time it's been suggested, but this time, Antru says, "Yes. That's fine."

It is not the answer wanted. There's not relief, but disappointment, and it's expected there will be little interest in helping any other move the project forward: A simple concept – to bring freedom of movement to the masses. A patently evident suggestion that finds absurdity it has never been addressed. Falling to the wayside because the one behind the motion has become reluctant to respond to government concerns over the technology and safety. A reimagination of what exists that was entirely unnecessary.

An approach taken that has come to be increasingly seen as the result of conspiracy and paranoia.

"I'm disappointed."

It is condemnation. The culmination of months of wrangling; pushing against growing immobility. If it was said to the child met that was filled with demons but still strove for hope, it would have fallen harshly and resulted in an effort to appease them. But that child has already been burned by fire and is unwilling to step in again.

"Did you hear me?"

"Yes," Antru says; turns to face the accusation: "I've given them the same information multiple times. Nothing changed. You pushed them to respond so they asked for it again. It won't get approved. It's a waste of time."

"Then why don't we use existing technology?"

"It isn't the propulsion."

Conversation drops.

Thoughts are never shared openly, but intimations grow into threads over time. Hints leak out. Ideas are built through conversation, and those have led to an understanding that the reticence to act is based upon what has become talked about behind the back, as delusion.

Frustration escapes as anger: "I'll have it reassigned." Lack of response brings the attack, "And we'll use what's already in operation." The soft eyes that look back, the nod, and the silence make it personal: "I know – you won't set a foot in one."

Antru shares, "I'm taking one home, this evening."

"Please," they're begged. It is taken with hope, that a softening of position is possible: "Run the numbers one more time. I promise I won't bring it up again. One last time."

An offer: "I'll make a deal."

"How afraid should I be?"

There is a smile. It brings memories back of the uncertain person that was so eager to please. That would smile when given encouragement.

Antru says, "I'll run it again, if you submit another application for a second operator."

"I see." Suspected, "You're making a point."

"Waste of time," but Antru's told, "Consider it done."

It is agreed, "Okay."

Relievedly, a tablet is set on the counter amongst constructs and junk, failures and trash – a sandwich remains in its state of decay as a shrine reflecting rates of success. Fingers tap, and eyes wait for a response, but there isn't one.

It's still there when time moves forward with other obligations. It's momentarily lifted, then set back down: A promise to be kept only if there's a return.

"Tru," is called. "Great match," is called. Those on the teams that excel, already make names for themselves. They are already recognized on the campus, and a few have risen to celebrity in the larger town. There are forums where every aspect of the games are analyzed, and combatants are lauded and critiqued. There are deep-dive insights published only hours after matches conclude. Walking through the city streets, there are unknown friends that arrive and share information as if they'd been known for years. There are dire enemies that have never been met, nor interacted with that spew hatred and threats.

But that is only experienced in real-time. There are no deep-dives into Antru of Capriot. There are no forum discussions. It has come to be referred to as the hole because Antru is notably missing. Most consider connections the reason for it, but the one that is missing sees it as more of the forces that dampen efforts towards anything.

No discussion means that scouts that watch a match and discover Éayren's child is more than capable, won't find any discussion to support it, and the name disappears under the noise of others' exploits.

There is usually just a nod, a wave – head shake in agreement at something nasty – as streets are travelled. They are almost absent as the fears pushed under waves for the sake of speed, begin resurfacing, and the walk takes a bypass to the gym: Hope that pushing into pain will help to drown concern.

It is unsuccessful and the push only leaves the body sore and tired, and the surplus of time intended, considerably short. There is only time to quickly shower, quickly jam a bag for travel before setting out, and walking quickly for the transit center.

It is not far from the institute, approximately centered in the western-most edge of town where the upcrops begin to steeply rise. It is a large building that conceals arrivals and departures – those can be viewed off either end or ascending, behind.

The interior is large and the ceiling is twice the height of most buildings in the city. Movement is orderly, and passengers are quickly sorted into lines. Those feed to a bank of windows, where those with multiple or larger travel items hand them over. It's watched as conversations are held – most brief, but there are some that are held longer.

Antru approaches, and "Name," is demanded.

It is answered, "Antru. Antru of Capriot."

"Parents."

"Parents," is questioned. "Do you want the names of my parents?"

"Names," the person states. Eyes crawl from their tablet until contact is made, and made clear, "Of your parents."

"Éayren. Éayren of Capriot. Currently, you know, playing for the Alvel Twenties. Four time – you know: Roukta champion. Not always Alvel. There was Nespia."

"I know," interrupts the one-sided drivel. "Other parent."

"Dalune," Antru answers. "Dalune of Capriot. Formerly Bitor."

"Is something wrong?"

"Why," Antru asks – it's answered, "You seem nervous."

"Oh." It's admitted, "I've never traveled by vehicle before. Only by sail or foot. I'm trying to move past my fears and insecurities. Most people I know tell me there's no danger."

Eyes look back up, and, "Danger," is questioned.

It's laughed away. Spoken as if it's absurd: "You know," as if it was common to believe, "If you get in one, no one ever sees you again."

Eyes are now digging in through the window, and the question, "Who told you that," is flat and serious.

Antru is the same, and says, "Éayren. But I know Éayren rides in them all the time."

"Purpose," is answered, "To come home, sometimes. But for the matches."

It is clarified, "Purpose of your travel."

"Oh," says Antru. "To visit family and friends."

"Time," is requested, and reflecting on the prior interest, that's answered, "Three days," instead of looking for the answer on the band.

"Proceed to station three," is ordered.

There is a nod and quick turn, and the sigh is quiet and restrained, but there is tremendous relief.

It is found there are more than a dozen others waiting at station three. None are nervous. Many are impatient, but most are absorbed by the content on their tablets.

"It's here," says an approaching passenger: "Open up, right?" They are agitated and impatiant, and the wide eyes they saw on approach were misinterpreted through the filter of personal opinion. They question, "What's the point?"

Antru plays along and employs tactics used to navigate roukta argument, with the non-responsive, "You never know."

"Playing with us," the person says. "Making us wait just to screw with us. Typical Marphy crackwad."

"Oh," says Antru. The word would earn rebuke at the institute. Not just from Leads and staff, but other students. There is a standard for those from Marphy, that everyone is expected to exhibit in all situations. It is rebuked: "I'm sure there's a reason."

"I'm sure there's a reason," the person mocks. They move out of line to pace in open space.

It isn't long before the doors open, and passengers begin their entrance to the vehicle.

It is a long vehicle. It is thin, with two seats in rows between the helm and the storage at the end. People move quickly into position, filling most of it and leaving Antru and impatience the choice of where to sit. There is an empty row, but one with an older person is approached.

The person is questioned, "Can I sit here?"

They answer, "Of course," and it's explained, "I was afraid I would end up sitting by someone I don't like very much, so I hope it's okay."

There is agreement, because the person says, "Foul. Speaking like that in front of children."

The seat is taken, and the first introduction to vehicles finds they aren't comfortable. It isn't miserable, but the seating is small for a roukta player. It's small for a person that's tall. Knees press against the seat in front, and the ceiling is uncomfortably close. There is also a self-conscious awareness that arms press into the neighbor's space – knee spreads towards them.

"I've never ridden before," Antru offers apologetically. "I'm a little large – I play roukta. I apologize I'm invading your space."

145

"I've seen you," the person says. "Hopefully they keep you in Marphy. I'll tell you if you bother me."

It is an opening that brings comfort as the vehicle becomes claustrophobic when the doors fold down. There are words of kindness that recognize the uneasiness beside them. It is just enough to overcome the deep misgivings that are felt as walls close in on the close confinement, and there is nowhere to move or stretch. It is then that a realization arrives: Éayren would never sit in a vehicle of this kind. Roukta clubs would likely have vehicles that were designed for people of Éayren's size.

But the person beside is kind and understanding. They ask questions and civility brings questions asked in return. That continues as the vehicle departs — wonder shared as it begins ascent.

It is a different sensation from scaling columns by hand. There is a risk, but there is also rigging, and professionally, the nets.

In neighborhoods where children are allowed to climb, there are nets. It is a conversation that leads to greater interest from the neighbor: "Did you really," gains explanation of other innovations, and complaint, "It's really difficult getting anything approved."

But eyes are through the window and on the landscape. Conversation continues but it's anchored on the view: Upcrops viewed from overhead. It is a new perspective, and there's new appreciation for the formations — they are vast, and it's an unrelenting landscape. As far as eyes can see there are towers of rock.

"Dagus's lake is just over there," the seatmate shares.

It is a place that's recalled from somewhere back in the history of experience, but there's no memory of its importance. Shortly thereafter, they break the upcrops and descend closer to the open space of shoreline.

It is also remarkable landscape and there's a wish that more of it could be explored. It brings the question, "How much of the planet have you seen?"

It is still a naïve question. The planet is mostly uninhabitable, but the seatmate remains kind and understands what's being asked, sharing, "All the cities. I did an expedition through the forest in Upper Borrean. If you ever get the chance, I recommend it. Absolutely gorgeous. And everyone needs to go to Orphan Lake at least once. It's an experience you won't forget."

There is a small forest along the shoreline. There is an inlet with a small island in the middle. It is landscape that is completely untouched, and there is a strong pull to find some way to explore it.

Eyes strain to the other side to view the ocean through the window. The surface sparkles under the starlight as if small fires erupt from the water. There is a sense of vastness not felt when secured to land, a sense of endlessness as it stretches to the horizon without interruption. It brings a sense of insignificance, the same as staring to the heavens and the billions of stars that particulate the night. Both are daunting, and both settle tranquility. That is lost the instant the vehicle changes direction.

A new edge is found. A sharp alarm is ringing and there is a heavy drum beat that's sounding warning. The seatmate notices; says, "Nothing to worry about." But they rise back into the upcrops, and the familiarity, and reminisce they bring of home also echo the warnings given: There is not a compelling rationale to abandon the shoreline for the rises.

Rock passes, and the empty space voices a threat. A thousand needle points prick against the flesh in anticipation of everything that was warned against, and there is deep regret for having abandoned instincts and misgiving. It is double for the disappointment parents will bear when they discover their warnings were neglected.

Rock passes, and it's more of the same: Roughly following a path that circles the highest rises. Likely one that is longer than the shoreline circumnavigation. A course that twists, and rises, and descends. Regret remains strong, but fear begins abating – until everything goes dark.

The body tenses, hands grasp the armrests; feet dig into the floor.

"Easy," the one beside suggests: "It's a tunnel. You're gonna be alright."

"Why," Antru asks.

"Who knows," is answered. They are ancient roads, of ancient people, that travelled by foot across the land. "Sometimes they cut through the rock to make it easier. Operators know what they're doing: Probably for entertainment."

The drumbeat warning has become a flashing light, painting red and looking for any escape. Sweat pours and muscles tense, prepared to fight to the death – preferable to captivity and torture.

The vehicle notably slows and lights begin to pierce the darkness. They are nearly stopped when the vehicle passes an intersecting tunnel, gated off to prevent travel. There are buildings on either side and open towers above that bring to mind those overseeing neighborhoods of Capriot. There are numerous people within them and more are walking on the platforms beside the throughway.

They come to a stop, and the wall by Antru rises. A person approaches, and they are cheerful. They explain, "Sorry about this. Nothing to worry about: We're just taking every precaution to make sure everyone's safe. Follow me and we'll get you to another vehicle that'll take you to your destination."

"Nothing to worry about," the seatmate says, "See?"

Antru says, "I should never have gotten on this."

Chapter eight:

It is quiet. The cool of the stone is at least forgiving to the tension and anticipation. It is familiar, and comforting. It is family, and friends, and home.

It is an unnecessarily large room with only two chairs at a table. They are uncomfortable, and a body stretches across the floor finding the unrelenting harshness of the stone both preferable, and penance for disregarding a parent's words: Parents' words. Dalune never disputed anything that was said – never argued against Marphy. What once bade bitterness now garners appreciation.

Reactive habit brought eyes to the band, but it was found disabled; tablet was disabled. There was a line being led and in an instant: A door opened, and sudden pressure in the back altered direction. The door slammed shut, and there was no anger, no fight against it, no calls out, because it was completely expected: Words of warning – those that enter vehicles are never seen again. The years of erosion against that warning at Marphy led to embarrassment they were ever held with value. But there was always a ticking sliver in the mind that irritated the narrative. Éayren was who they were, but Dalune would not remain silent against delusion. There was no doubt, they would speak for the interests of their child. There was no question.

The room is silent. Time passes, and it is irrelevant and doesn't matter. The stone is cold – the stone is hard: It is familiar, enmired, and fingers still ache to dig against it. There is a vow in the echo chamber of reflection, that if the experience is survived, no word ever uttered by a parent will be dismissed, again. They will never be doubted. Their words will be held onto like an imperfection in stones climbed without rigging

– without net. They will be held onto with the understanding that life depends on holding on.

It is quiet, and cool, and there is absolute silence. In the vacuum of stimuli, there is the wheezing breath of a roommate, imagined. Quiet, interrupted by fitful nights of potential fatality. They are remembered, somehow, fondly. It is the origin of experience at Marphy, and despite the awkward interactions and dissolution, since, they are found, remembered fondly. There is hope that Eotor found help, and is healthy, but they have not crossed paths in the time, since.

It is a strange thought to fall upon – to the beginnings of institutionalized education. It was not so long ago, but the reflection back looks through eternity. To paranoias and warnings that found new experience overwhelming, a swim into uncontrolled chaos and uncertainty. Tenuous holds swept away by forces that seemed to wrench control. To unwanted and unwarranted expectations: A feeling of disconnected isolation, and violation.

The door opens in unison with the word, "Antru."

There is no reaction. The body is on the floor and non-responsive – arms crossed over eyes, and passive. A seat is taken but the show that is presented is unobserved and consequently ineffective. A tablet shifts and falls but there's no consequence. The tablet sends a call and the door is opened again, and a cluttered shuffle enters with clattered conversation.

There are myriads of questions. Irrelevant interest towards shoes and breakfast. Inquiries regarding education and direction. Prods for observations of friends and family. There is a circling descent towards the central carrion, but feet never land, because the rotting flesh that is lusted is just as resistant to their aims as those of a former roommate.

They are places that are the same. Places of discomfort where the feeling of control over life is interrupted. Where forces are met that pull against what has come to be expected. But there is one specific order that brings the force felt harder:

"Hold out your wrists."

The prisoner remains unmoved. An arm is taken, but it's pulled away and Antru pushes to a seat.

There are seven in the room. Their clothing is identical and there are a number of devices strapped around their waists. Despite their numbers, they will not attempt to overtake a roukta player, however, what they needed to understand has already been demonstrated. They are not facing merely resignation, but active resistance.

In coordinated unity, three begin to approach. Antru stands, and it registers in the periphery that an arm was raised, but it's just a flash across thoughts that discovered paralysis the moment that it had.

Antru is allowed to fall heavily against the stone floor. There is pain as the head cracks hard, but the ability to control the body remains lost. Three approach again, with four others taking position behind them. One kneels and pulls an arm, twists the hand, and flexes the wrist. What they're looking for is not there, and they try the other.

"Nothing," is observed, but another orders, "Scrape it. Could be a trick."

A sharp blade is withdrawn from its sheath on the side, and its edge is slid over arms and wrists. The right is checked a second time, and with more force blood is drawn.

"Okay." The order calls to stop: "It's not there." The question's asked, "Where's the weapon, Antru?" There is no answer but it's not only a reluctance to speak, it remains an impossibility.

The order, "Shoot 'em," finds fear is not immobilized. A person approaches with a device extended and it's pressed against the neck where a vessel passes. There is fear that the end will come with a slow exsanguination, but there is just an unpleasant punch, and both the device and person withdraw.

The heart begins to pound. An arm jerks inadvertently – startling, but indication motion is regained.

Feet are taken, but they are unsteady. Two are standing with devices extended that are understood to be weapons.

The question is asked again, "Tell us where the weapon is."

For the first time, Antru speaks: "I don't have it." There is anger and hostility, and it grows, "I don't have any weapons."

"We know you did," is shared. "The question is, what did you do with it?"

They're told, "Nothing. Because I don't have one."

A calculation begins: The best strategy to bring chaos and take down as many as possible before they do the same. A final swansong that is undoubtedly doomed, a final application of roukta training. Vision sharpens, and the chairs, and table fill in the strategy. If fortune falls kindly, it might even bring the chance to steal a weapon.

Weapons raise as it is sensed something changed. It's claimed, "We don't want anyone to get hurt. That's why we brought you in, Antru. We just need to speak with you."

It is a conversation that goes nowhere. The interrogators are met with barked denials and angered accusations. But they hint at something about Borrea and gain a clue they're looking for: They find a response that demonstrates confusion.

It continues – an endless flow of personnel with redundant questions. They are asked multiply and variously. Three exit the room, and two more enter. Demeanors change but they are always looking for something. All leave and the quiet is relief that is too-soon interrupted: Three enter to ask about associations. The final person enters alone. They sit at the table and recline, a demonstration of complete security in the presence of their hostage.

Antru has retreated to a corner, a familiar comfort to withdraw into, just as days with a roommate and the corner of the bunk.

The person's voice is calm and steady as they state, "I'm sure you're aware your parents are involved with certain things that aren't discussed around the general public. Unfortunately, some people take advantage of their position and try to use it for personal gain. How's that project coming?"

"What?" It is asked with bewilderment, because it isn't even clear, "What project?"

"It doesn't matter." The person rises and carefully replaces the chair beneath the table. They say, "Personal transport. What would you need that for?"

To that, Antru confidently answers, "So I don't disappear when I get in a vehicle."

They claim, "You haven't disappeared. Who's helping you develop that?"

"I am," Antru says. "I had help from members of the league, but it's my design. I'm developing it."

"I see," they say, but wonder, "How 'bout the net? Dalune claimed you had hands in that, how much of that's true?"

"All of it." Antru insists, "It was my idea. Moboti Dalune helped me understand how it could be done. But it was my idea. If you don't like it, just bring the rigging back. I like it better anyway."

"You were given access to the net for that project – correct?"

Antru clarifies, "I was told I could use it."

"It's a little concerning – don't you think? That someone that has ties to people interested in undermining society can access our defensive net? Don't you think we have a right to be concerned?"

"I don't know anyone interested in doing anything like that. I don't have weapons, and I haven't done anything with the net since I was young. If you don't like that I have access, then take it away. I don't need it. I don't even want it. I like the net – I like it keeps the planet safe. Why would I want to do anything to it?"

"The problem," the person explains, "Is that the net identifies you as an operator. The only way we've ever seen that changed is after someone dies."

"So, you plan to kill me," Antru says.

It's asked, "Can you think of another solution?"

"Yes," says Antru: "Override permissions."

"Of course," they say, "We've tried that. But it's an autonomous net. It's capable of making decisions on its own, and it said no. Any other suggestions?"

"I can make it," Antru says.

The person asks, "You think you could make that your next project?"

"Will that get the other one approved?"

The person moves to the door and pulls it open. They pause, and share, "I don't make that decision."

"Who does," Antru asks, but the door has closed.

The room is sealed, but a window opened, and there is a curious realization that the familiarity and understanding Dalune has of the net, might be a secret that's not shared. Thoughts fall that all of the bedtime volumes read were not coincidental, nor preparation for the future, but a way to pass on what is known by just a few.

The door opens, and three enter. One asks, "You agree?"

"The project," Antru questions. "Working on the net? Sure. I don't have any need to access the net. Whatever you want – I don't have a problem with it."

It's explained, there will be supervision and strict oversight. Every action and outcome must be shared, and the penalty for failing to comply will be significant. It is agreed to, believing those that will oversee and read reports won't know what they put their eyes on.

With agreement sealed, the three escort Antru back to the platform where a vehicle is waiting. It is not as full as the one arrived in, and a row is chosen with both seats empty. The door closes, and eyes don't bother looking through the windows. They are looking inward, to conversation of the past, to nighttime lessons, and the demand for assignment at Marphy.

The belief that there were forces trying to contain has been given faces. The sense that efforts towards the future was futility has been shown an opening where that's not the case. But that is now seen as dependent on access to the net. The most important mission will be ensuring that doesn't change, but how to do that isn't clear, as how it happened in the first place is uncertain.

The vehicle stops directly in front of Antru's home. The ride was brief – detention likely beneath the city. Strides begin into the garden and for the door, but that lasts until the vehicle is out of sight – direction turns, and the casual pace becomes determined.

A harsh knock on the door finds it soon opens. Aedra smiles, and says, "Well. Look who finally decided to show up."

Arms open to welcome the return, but they are moved inside, and the door is quickly closed.

Aedra says, "Happy to see you, too."

"We have to move quickly," Antru says. Embrace is abandoned for the kitchen, and a stone bowl is pulled, as well, a pitcher. The next words, are, "I need your wrist."

Aedra teases, "Shouldn't we get to know each other first?"

"Not now," Antru says. "I'll explain later. We need to hurry."

"Trusting you," Aedra points out, as the wrist is lifted.

The kit is unstrapped from beneath the shirt, and a knife blade is extracted and attached to a handle. Trust remains extended as the blade begins incising the invisible patches. It is peeled away and set into the bowl.

Instructions follow: "Act casual, but tap your foot if you see a vehicle. Bring the water and pour it on the bowl when I tell you to."

"Are we in trouble?"

"Yes," Antru says: "Casual."

"Casual," agrees Aedra.

They move to the yard where the kit is again opened. Two vials of powder are partly emptied over the implement, and the bowl is shaken to mix them. Another vial is opened, and a purple liquid is poured over the contents of the bowl. A reaction begins, and both lean away as a noxious biproduct blows into the wind.

"Water," Antru says.

It is poured, but it goes right through the bowl, much of the bottom eaten away, and it is ruined.

It's suggested, "Could have picked a different one."

It is lifted, but fumbled, and the bowl crashes to the surface where it shatters. Antru explains, "I needed this one. I'll get you another."

"Hey," says Aedra, "Who doesn't break a bowl once in a while? Want to let me know what's going on?"

"I will," Antru says, "Later. I need to talk with Dalune.

"Antru: Keep me in the loop. I want to know what's going on."

It is promised, "I will."

There is an embrace before departure, and the warmth and connection is difficult to break from, but a conversation is needed.

Dalune is found relaxing in the home, and asked immediately on entrance, "Do you want to tell me why I got arrested?" The concern demonstrated is disregarded. The attempt to take a child in arms to offer comfort is dismissed. There is warning, "They knew about the weapon," and it brings question.

A wrist is held forward, already scabbed by the damage done. "They used a knife to try to find it," is said with accusation, and it's pointed out, "They nearly cut my wrist open."

Dalune suspects, "You took a vehicle."

"Everyone rides in the vehicles," Antru says, "But only I get pulled out for questioning. I was the only child that was given a secret weapon, and I don't know why. Because I didn't need it."

"Not now," Dalune agrees.

"My whole life," is hurt with accusation: "You trained me for this. All the information you read to me when I was young. It's all so I would be part of what you and Éayren are involved with. My entire life has been about molding me into a tool that you can use."

"Antru," is met with rejection. Consolation is refused. Dalune avows, "You have not been trained. I will never ask you to be a part of anything. I only give you knowledge to carry forward. You are just beginning to understand."

"Why not just tell me?"

"It's not something that can be explained." Dalune re-seats at the table and leans heavily, and says, "It can't be learned. You had the pieces, but there was no meaning. Now, you are beginning to understand."

"I understand I'm connected," Antru agrees, however, "I don't know what that means. They told me my next project has to be eliminating access for myself and others, but I can't do that, can I?"

It is answered, "No." The question comes back to, "What happened to the weapon?"

"I destroyed it. But as long as I don't get pulled underground, I don't need it, do I?"

"Not now," Dalune agrees.

"But I did," Antru considers, and determines, "I'll come up with something better. But you should pass it on they know about them."

"Antru," is called again, and this time they find the parent always known. Dalune warns, "Your life would have been much more difficult without me here for you."

"Yes," says Antru. It is agreed, "I know."

"The most important lesson that I hope you have learned, that I have taught you, is that taking care of the people you love should be your top priority."

"You're not a part of it," is guessed, and it's understood because the lesson held highest is one ignored by another. One that has often been held with resentment and only gains appreciation when insights into warnings find fruition. It is a partner that's never there – a parent that's always absent, "But Éayren is."

"Remember," Dalune says. "Don't ever forget."

"I'm remembering that lesson right now, when I ask if you mind if I go see Aedra."

There is a smile of recognition, and, "Antru," is said with understanding, "Of course."

There is a lightness of being that has never been felt before. Footsteps cross the earth with unweighted pressure. The knock against the neighbor's door is playful, and lips form into a circle and try to whistle. There is a longing for the joy that springs out of the columbrum but is only found because of the company shared.

With no response, knuckles press more firmly, and "Aedra," is called, but there's nothing. There is still no answer and the door is abandoned and a circuit is taken around the building for the yard.

As a window's passed and it's noted that it's dark, a thought crosses the mind to move quietly and offer surprise. The thought moves quickly from light to dark and a rumble of warning begins to rise.

The window's tested, but it's secure. The attempt to see inside finds only dark.

Pace moves quickly and the short, stone wall is leapt to find the back glass of the home is dark, as well. The heart begins to pound within the chest, red warning flashes and the rumble becomes a thunder as eyes stab into the black. There is certainty, there is at least one figure shrouded in the dark, and a fist pounds against the glass.

"Aedra," is screamed with the greatest fear being realized. The door is tried, but it's secure. A panicked, "Let me in," is an order before the glass is broken. There is fury that rises, and the yard fills with light. It spills into the home and finds the worst [confirmed — a foot raises, ready to strike: It is halted:

Lights turn on within the home. Two of those inside race to the windows with hands raised and a panicked plea, begging, "Wait." The door opens, and there is an immediate call for calm.

The person casts a shadow into the yard. Light from the home cascades into the darkness beyond its walls, and at the door it is interrupted by an elongated silhouette.

"No one's hurt," is pressed. "No one's in trouble." They are dressed like those from in the tunnel, but their demeanor is nothing alike. They are nervous, and they are pleading, "Antru: We are looking for the weapon. That's all. We have a responsibility to keep the population safe. That's all we're doing."

"I destroyed it," Antru says. It's asked when, but, "It doesn't matter. It doesn't exist anymore."

"Okay – okay," is said with an urgency that tries to demonstrate acceptance. "Is there any way you can make us feel comfortable accepting that? So we don't have to bother you again?"

They are told, "No. I dissolved it. By now, there wouldn't even be residue."

"Okay, Antru." The person introduces themselves as, "Kawluss," and they claim, "I'm going to believe you. Okay Antru? Okay? I'm going to trust you. We're going to leave you two alone, and we apologize if anything that happened upset you. That's the last thing we want. We just thought, if there's one place that weapon might have ended up it would be here. But I realize we could have handled this better. So, I apologize Antru – Aedra: Please accept my apology."

Aedra says, simply, "Okay."

There is an order, "Let's go," and a smile's offered, with, "I believe you, Antru. We just want to make sure everyone's safe – including you. But I trust you. Good night – have a good evening." And then alarm, as it's also offered, "Good night, Dalune."

A parent stands watching, quiet from the street. Round eyes watch with concern just like they always have, two beacons that have always guided tempestuous dreams to safety, just as they have softened blows in life. Watching, but prepared to take action and intervene if needed.

"Good night, Dalune," the person said – a familiarity. Eyes are meeting across the yard: One watching the beginnings of understanding, and the other trying to understand who parents are.

Unlike most, both have held careers while raising their only child: Roukta for one, but Dalune holds some unclear involvement with the net – dismissively referred to as simply maintenance. As if it wasn't so important nor that involved. Implying there were others with more important roles. If there were, and who that is, what's clear is it's not the clans. It's clear that those that are connected – the connections – are what they fear the most.

Chapter nine:

A sliver of silver glints from each end of eternity. A hint of existence in the vacuous void of nothing. There is a syncopated thumping that rumbles heavy as forewarning to the dawning of awareness and understanding. There is a rise above the tar to pull a breath, but it pulls in silver, and the heavy thud is quashed by a shrill and echoed cry. It draws a rivulet, a steaming toxin to infect the lungs and brain, that ticks against their flesh to leave them sticky with purulence and decay.

A heartbeat pounds. There is darkness, and in the emptiness, a deep breath pulls desperately for air. Lips lift above the surface of oblivion and kiss existence. Air pulls smoothly, and there is calm in the dark and nothing. Another sip pulls deeply, and the black of nothing warms over, a blanket draped against thought and silver. A calm away from storms, and thoughts, and violence. A peace only found outside existence.

There is nothing, and in nothing there is no experience. There are no thoughts, no feelings; no sensation. It is what existed and where everything returns. It is the end point of entropy and the fight for control and a sense of order. It is never lost – only interrupted.

There is a sigh that becomes waves against the shore, but they are distant and can't be heard. They fall beneath the rhythm of the drumbeat. They are just an intuition that remembers the glint of silver on the edges. They fail the tempo. They wash asynchronously and grind irritation.

There is a syncopated drumbeat that lifts a hint against nothing. It is the difference between there and being. It is a drumbeat that continues, and while it does, there are visions, and dreams, and love. There is hope, and passion. There is fear and dismay. There is a will that finds a way, despite everything.

Silver threads dance at the edges of a void that is always present. It stands in the history of everything. It hangs as a shadow across experience. It is the destination to where everything is headed, and why everything, and any effort expended is ultimately pointless. Silver dances, but it is swallowed in the darkness, and the sound of a heavy breath extinguishes it entirely.

It is moonless nights under heavy clouds, outside in the yard, alone. It is a call to a friend that finds no answer. It is coming home to find it empty. The shroud of nothing wraps its blanket of unabated isolation. The deep breath sinks into darkness and nowhere.

Waves lap under lightless sky. They are an essence that's remembered through a tiny square of window. They tap at the shore of fear and paranoia. They are the claustrophobic walls closing in, and a parent's face presses through the fog to condemn the disregard.

There is a cry. It is vague, but it is a roommate sobbing. It is the outpouring of misery and loneliness concealed under covers in the dead of night. It is a desperate plea for a connectedness that will never happen. It is the awkward desperation of a child thrown at the world with expectations they will know how to function in it. "There, there," is a wish to comfort, that pulls a parent's words after terror strikes paralysis in their child. They share moon eyes that look down to offer sympathy and understanding, and slowly fade away into the mist.

Into darkness. Into quiet, with just waves gently lapping at the consciousness. Restive beneath a rasping roommate that sleeps above. Wrapped in the warmth of blankets and ebbing somnolence. There are flickers of ideas as the cool breeze blows in from across the ocean, but the cocoon of relaxation and contentment receives it as a pleasant interruption.

A cool brush of air on the open deck as passage sails. As waters are navigated through a misty channel, the vision shifting and changing in the moment they register as anything discernable. There is passage through a channel, and a cool breeze is felt as they exit the security of the vehicle. Channels are followed, cut through rock and the voices echo through lyric mist, suggesting words that are indeterminable, but they are warning to run for safety.

"How often," asks the uniformed sentry. There is a weapon raised and Aedra's name is spoken. The anger that follows is met with violence. There is a punch against the neck that leaves the body frozen. It is left in the channel, back arched over the cool, hard surface of the stone. The sound of the roommate breathing has gone silent, and there is only rock overhead, any longer.

Heavy stone that improbably suspends over open space and a frozen body. It is viewed from an awkward angle – from above, through a corner of outside. Mist clouds the vision. There is heavy fog that fills the opening. The open space and the only option for escape becomes solid and the narrow tunnel squeezes down.

It has a heartbeat of its own. The ceiling pulsates and presses closer. There is the breath of cold as it meets the face and rock collapses, crushing the body – pain burns as stone stabs into the skull and crushes the chest. There is complete collapse, and millions of tons of rock fall into a pile to rise as a monument to the body fallen below.

A sharp gasp finds tendrils of liquid silver slipping away, slipping away, and the darkness that meets the eyes greets complete silence. A remnant fear brings thoughts to a higher berth, but that bed has been empty for years.

Thoughts turn to memories of terrified cries for another, and find regret there is no one that would hear. A heavy sigh falls into the dark with reposition, and return to rest with no consolation, or even a sense of connectedness with anyone near. There is distance between everything, and everyone. There are impediments to accomplishing anything. There is an underlying darkness that remains hidden beneath the world, that lives in tunnels and behind the storage walls of cubes.

"Rocks taste like it." It was one extracted from the drawer. It is unusual because there is usually a nutrient bar. There is no sign of it under the bunk. There is a search through cupboards, and a person sits as the desk unfolds. They are disintegrating as they bite against the unyielding rock. A word passes that means nutrients, but it is heavy with rain, as lightening breaks the blackened clouds.

"Look in the cupboard," a person says. It is clear, and there should be light, but the sky is dark and only a glimmer makes sense of the wall. The order is followed, but it's completely dark inside. Eyes strain to look for something, and they dig deep and find the cupboard surrounds entirely.

"Everything's fine," says the fellow passenger. Walls of the vehicle press into the shoulder. The ceiling forces the body to hunch over. The air is dry and dusty, and the ocean is just a memory as the tunnel's entered. The light at the entrance grows slowly dimmer as distance is quickly made between it. Tendrils fall away and there is comfort as walls withdraw. As the tiny streams slip away into the ocean of utter darkness.

They collect at the edges of awareness. Two, thin strings lining the edge of everything to infinity. They wash inward with the breeze. They are tugged away into filamental inroads that dance like dewy webs in the early morning starlight. They are the dance of mercury as it finds its hold, as it sprawls over the mind and sinks disease into the flesh. It is the decay of everything. It is the loss of control, and form, and function.

The breeze drives the waves towards the center, pressing the waters ever closer to one another. They build and begin crashing against an unseen shore. Two silver surfs competing to devour the emptiness between them.

The breeze is cool, and the sound of the surf is deafening. Waves thunder down against the narrowing peninsula and erupt in massive clouds of shimmering silver. It sprinkles down and decorates what's left of nothing, but the raindrops are too insignificant and soon absorb.

There is a pressure against the waters. They crash with fury, but the power lashed is unable to overcome the abyss between them. The air has become filled with quicksilver haze, and everything's coated silver but the ribbon of emptiness that comes from nowhere and ends on the other side of perpetuity. It is a channel that leads to tunnels that no one speaks about. It is the vastness of the ocean that's never spoken. It is forever and everyone is powerless against it.

"It will always exist, and that will never change."

The words are spoken as the balance begins to change. The shimmering, silver waters still approach, but they are calmer, and their violence is replaced by sheer volume: Massive walls of silver searching for connection. Pressing to meet and join.

There is silver all around, but an unseen mass obstructs one side. The crest of silver waters push and they are only barely able to send a momentary sheen over the surface. They pulse with wave after wave, but success is only ever temporary. The waters cross the surface and then fall away. The waters cross the surface and remain.

Cool air solidifies the metal on the rock. There are gentle waves pressed by the breeze and they roll casually across the surface. Entirety is painted silver. An endless vastness of silver sea with starlight glinting bright reflections as if on fire. As if the entire ocean emitted bursts of flame – reaching for the vehicle passing near. There is fire burning on the exterior of the vehicle, but, "Everything's fine," says the seatmate.

Fire burns, and the waves of mercury build as they try to extinguish flames. Quicksilver pours from all directions. Levels rise and noxious fumes seep into the cabin. Smoke fills quickly and only the rising silver gives eyes anything to set upon, as it rises and consumes everything – only silver. Submerged and sinking in the silver sea, as tiny rivulets find opening and begin to invade the body.

Begin to disintegrate what existed for just an instant.

There is a gasp that brings air deep into the lungs. There is a brief survey to orient and verify existence. There is a momentary wish to be a child again, where the flashes embedded in the brain were soothed in the arms of a parent.

Thoughts of comfort think to days spent listening to the columbrum and the warm feelings shared. Warm feeling beside Aedra.

The night is asked, "When did that happen," because it feels as if it always was, but it also feels that there is something different.

The rattled night, for the first time finds a smile, as thoughts fall to memories shared together. A sense of joy found from thoughts of early years, but it's upset by later ones, by memories of agents hiding in the dark and using knives to search for hidden weapons.

Memories are shaken away, and deep breaths are taken to calm the nerves. There is a flash to a memory of light erupting and it didn't have a source, but it was gone before that registered. Deep breaths are taken, but it's not until the ventilation blows again, that the darkness can begin regaining grip.

Only years before, a parents' eyes would have been found watching from the door, but there is only a folded desk, storage drawers, and cabinets. There is not even the disquieting rasping from overhead that still breathes through memories and dreams. Gone not long after concerns were shared.

Expletives ring loudly in the silence. Angered eyes dance from emptiness and drip with hatred. Rivers of anger flow in silver streams that steam with accusations: Fault found for speaking concern for the safety of another. Insults echo with wordless animus and bounce into a cacophony that's never fully quieted.

"Why do I need this," Aedra questions.

They are holding a columbrum hammer and it has never been in their hands before. There is a smile, and the familiar, roguish mischief follows, the hammer slowly brought down against the head.

There is laughter. Aedra is calling music as the hammer falls. It digs repeatedly at a single point just above the eye. The strikes grow harder, and a searing headache begins a crushing pulse inside the skull. Drops of silver begin escaping and they soon drip almost enough to be a stream. There is laughter, and Aedra asks, "Why do I need this?"

There is anger as the hand is grabbed. As the hammer is ripped away, and there is hurt on the other's face.

"Why," is a question that drips in the atmosphere. It is moist, and sticky, and finding the answer is never clear. There is always fog obscuring understanding and there is no explanation that can be given that deserves forgiveness.

There is sickness as the hammer strikes. Waves of misgivings and regret watch as the hammer falls against the bowl in Aedra's hands, as violence shatters the stone bowl into pieces.

Shards are driven into flesh and the mercury begins escaping through shredded hands. Life spills away and Aedra looks back with no hint of accusation, and calls out of a well that's quickly filling, "I understand." The words weave through the guilt of association. They wrench the innocence away and bare the violence of existence. They send forgiveness that's not deserved, and it is a weight that cannot be carried.

It is crushing, and the weight is the liquid filling in the well. It is the helplessness as the arm reaching up for aid slips further away.

A gasp and a flash slips into memory.

Aedra is standing with bleeding hands, a bowl that was gifted, shattered to pieces in them. "I understand," Aedra says, and the darkness is exploded with blinding light. Silver shatters into tin drops against the steel drum. A hammer rises and pounds against it and sends the droplets back into the ocean.

There is a cool breeze that blows in as Aedra plays a melody on the highest upcrop. It is emotional and inspiring. It is the closeness that is felt between them – the warmth of the adjacent body is felt as the arm swings against the metal. It is the greatest joy ever experienced. It is where there is completion and existence is not only a state of being, it is felt. It is what has always been experienced and part of life, but love is strongest in those moments together.

"I understand," Aedra says. They are standing with bleeding hands that were shredded by a beloved bowl for which great lengths were taken to obtain it. A bowl seen as a child as part of a ceremony sending off a child of the emperor.

The emperor stands as a fire-mouthed vision spitting silver into oblivion. The emperor stands with a bloodied hand that is embedded with pieces of a bowl.

There is a howl that shears existence. Aedra looks over calmly, and says, "I understand."

Eyes are stone, and silver streams are falling from them.

"I understand," Aedra says: A scream.

Antru sits up, breathing heavily. It is dark, and it is silent. The night has been filled with disturbance, and the last image flashed into memory falls beside more than can be counted that fall into a category wished forgotten.

A deep breath tries to settle nerves. Blankets are pulled close for warmth, but there's longing for the vent's cool breath. For the contrast across the face that evokes the contrast of early life and what has followed. Embrace and warmth attacked by cold and violence. By vitriol; castigation. Rejection, and detention. Love against hostility – fear:

There is a memory of the reaction at Aedra's window. Agents pleading frantically and their quick withdrawal. "Good night, Dalune," echoes in the ear as those that assaulted the quiet home in search of weapons, made a quick retreat and plead for absolution. Answers have not come easily, and there are hints of resentment that fall like raindrops against the snow-packed mountains.

Against piles of snow that have fallen away and failed the footholds taken. Piles of snow that fall and bury bodies. White that blots out existence with suffocating pressure.

There is a syncopated drumbeat. There is a columbrum playing in the distance, a song that is sorrowful but holds hope. It is a song that watches a last stronghold clasped against – secured – as snows are melted.

Water pours down the mountains. Liquid silver etches through the rises and they are slowly reduced to dust. Heights are slowly brought to nothing, and Aedra says, "I understand."

They are at the highest point of the planet, and it is imperative they climb higher.

Fingers clasp at air. Height gained is lost to falls.

"I understand," Aedra says.

They climb the sheer rockface. Holds are tenuous – footstops are barely there. Bloodied fingers scratch for anything to grasp and feet scrape for imperfections.

Fingers grasp, and the stone falls away. Feet press and the wall collapses. There is only dust as bodies fall and helplessness wells. Hopelessness swells. There is nothing to hold onto. There is nothing to stop the descent. There is Aedra looking over, trusting and expecting a solution.

There is a pile of rubble, and a broken body falls against it. Hands are bleeding, and silver tendrils begin escaping and draining into the surrounding darkness.

"Enough." It is shouted.

Antru sits up in sweat, and shivering. The head pounds and the gut is filled with sickness. Blankets are thrown aside as feet are taken, and the cool wind from the ventilation is swatted aside.

Fists punch against the air as legs begin to pace, as the heartbeat begins to settle, and the catalogue of visions are sorted away. There is anger, and resentment – disappointment – that there is no outlet for the terror. It is felt and held, alone. There are no words from any other to dismiss them, and they only feed the illness that has fallen from the tunnels; from the assault on Aedra's home.

It is early, still. Thoughts settle, but the disquietude remains. It is boxed in as time passes, but it never leaves. The greatest fears have already been realized, and worse is accepted as inevitable.

There is sorrow and guilt that those will be shared, but unwillingness remains to let love go.

It is explained with whispered, shouted anger. It is demonstrated by harsh footsteps. It is argued by arms waving with demonstration.

Antru's hands are pressing against the flesh of the head but are unable to push away, "Everything just sucks."

A folded chair is ripped off the wall and thrown across the floor. It is regarded for a moment. Observed as part of everything that is imperfect. It is a crumpled body on a pile at the bottom of an upcrop. It is the failure to protect those that are cared about. It is the helplessness of being.

Chapter ten:

Ascent holds to watch the body fall. To ensure that rigging holds and brakes descent. The reward for consideration of another is a vulgar gesture in return.

Fingers dig into the surface of the rock, and feet grab footstops to propel to the near plateau. The majority of impediments have been destroyed, and there is just a short leap across a crevice to waiting teammates.

Teammates, and dispirited opponents. All nineteen on the surface come together with interlinking arms in a post-match huddle. A battle of skill and luck, speed and strength; wit and chance position. There is no celebration in the victory circle where the victors and vanquished come together in appreciation of the others' effort. It is a demonstration of respect for the skills each of them share, for the work that has brought them to where they stand, and appreciation that all twenty will walk away to play again. Victory is not a euphoric moment for the players. That is found as they grapple and claw, climb and punch; run and jump. Euphoria of victory is only held by those that watch.

The twentieth finally lands on the surface, and claims, "I knew you were gonna do that – I knew it."

Antru answers, "I guess we got lucky, then."

"Lucky," the other says, and it's dismissive. Two come together and embrace and that continues with the others as second and third string players begin streaming into the victory circle to share the moment.

It is the final match of the final year at the Marphy Institute. The children that arrived four years prior are fully grown and many times the size on their arrival. Most walk away with a plan to start a family – some walk away with that in mind and other obligations. But it is the time of life where there is freedom to live and explore. It is the time where pursuit of the aesthetic can be dedicated. The first time since early childhood where there are no specific obligations. For the vast majority, it will be the time where they join with a partner and start a family.

The circle is completed, and Antru's told, "I saw it coming the entire match. Same thing we saw earlier in the season. Except this time, you let everybody pass. I should've known it was a trap."

"I apologize," Antru says. "I just needed one."

"Lucky me. You joining the celebration?"

"Later," Antru says, as expected:

As it has been since early on. Impressions are drastically changed, but the prodigal child from Capriot remains prone to isolation. There is still a wall, and it has grown more solid. The words that escaped on first arrival have become sealed behind the stolid veneer that shares little. There is mutual respect, there is friendship – but it is kept arms-length away. Present, but words and behavior are carefully selected – aloof, said by detractors.

By those that pull for other teams. Those that scream obscenities through the cheers. Those that remain after subterfuge saw their own fall victim to over-confidence.

Threats are shouted and claims are made, and those are countered by those cheering in the vicinity. Like players' violence, the words and threats hold no gravity. Bodies pushed to extreme lengths and tremendous physical exertion is an outlet for the players, and the shouts and uncivil words are the same for those that watch.

"Soft play, crackwad," is called at Antru on the walk back to the cube. It is disregarded, as they always are: Pace is strong even with an aching body, and the words are just spillage from the theater. "Hey," the voice calls: "Did ya hear me ya Borrean brain?"

Feet stop and the body turns to find a face that brings familiarity. It is not the face of the awkward child that once suffocated at night, but of a person that looks well and strong. It takes a moment for two ends of time to connect, but there is a leap of happiness that fills the body, that overshadows the anger brought by the puerile claim.

"Miss me yet," Eotor asks.

"I am Borrean," Antru says cooly: "We all are."

"Seriously?" The former roommate walks close as if they might physically challenge a daunting Roukta player, but it is only a move to slap a hand against the chest as they marvel. "Watch who you're calling Borrean."

"I was thinking about you," Antru shares. "I hope you're doing well."

"Convince me to give you a chance," Eotor suggests. It is spoken as if in jest, but there is a hope behind it that can only be heard by two.

"Take care of yourself," and Antru's departing. Walking away and thirsty for solitude to quiet noise.

"Hey," follows: "Hey: Ya miserable Capriot clod." It brings a pause, and a laugh of appreciation for a person that likely deserved more than they previously given. Antru turns back with the intention to address the broken floors between them, but Eotor is level for a moment, and sincere: "I know I got ticked you said something, but, you know:" There is a shrug and a grimace. The words, "You might've saved my life," are squeezed out as if it's difficult to say, "Thanks."

"I was scared for you," Antru says. "I'm glad you're okay."

Eotor says, "You still suck. Get away with more cheap shots than anyone: Stupid stone sucking foot-grabber."

There is a smile, and, "Take care of yourself," is truly meant the second time it's said.

It is a fitting end to a day that was the end of roukta play, though there are many that claim that's not the case. However, detention, and raids, and parents' shadow enterprise make a future in the public eye exceptionally unlikely. There is already one fading roukta player that has used their position to further interests, and it has been heard and witnessed that there is extreme pressure to prevent another.

No ones can disappear on a vacation. Problems can disappear, but not those that've earned notoriety, and not one with a partner connected to the net. It is mostly conjecture, but ample evidence has been seen and heard to support the opinion.

"Antru," is stated by a familiar voice. It pulls eyes to a person reclined in the commons, relaxing with a drink as they peruse their tablet.

"Notoire," Antru says. "It's nice to see you – how are you?"

"I see you're continuing to antagonize your opponents: Congratulations. A nice way to end your career at Marphy."

"Thank you," Antru says.

"Are you still planning on joining the service?" It is believed to be a joke by the one that says it – it is taken as a disconnection by the one to which it was directed.

Conversations have fallen aside. Regular meetings became irregular, and eventually words became shared in passing, only. There has been no discussion of detention or the net, and plans to join the service had been a desperate grasp for a future that had been expected through most of childhood. Thoughts, ideas, beliefs, and expectations remain exactly where they began four year before, but better understanding sees new directions.

A laugh is sputtered through, "I don't think they'll be interested."

"Joke," is explained. "They would be. Obviously that's not happening."

Antru says, "Right. It was nice to see you."

"Still think," the mentor jokes, "No one's going to be interested?"

The question brings a chord in the ear, and it's morose and disappointing. There is a longing for the competition. There is a love for the climb and battle, but, "No one wants to take that risk."

"Come on." Notoire says, "Antru: You can't be serious."

"I'm glad you pushed me," Antru says: "I'm glad I went through Marphy. Thank you. I wouldn't have appreciated the experience if it wasn't for you, and I wouldn't have played. I'll always be grateful for what you did for me."

"Not enough," Notoire says, "Obviously. If you aren't drafted, I'll go right to the Marphy clan and demand you're on one of our teams."

"Thank you, but I don't want you to do that."

Says Notoire, "Do you have some other plans?"

"I don't," Antru answers: "Plans seem to come to me. But I just want some time to spend with the people that I care about."

Notoire inquires, "Someone special?"

"An old friend," Antru admits. "Somehow, we survived four years. Though, it was different back then – friends, I guess."

"I always wondered," Notoire reflects. "Hopefully they're willing to deal with a roukta player."

"Yes," says Antru. And it's stressed, "I really want to thank you for being there. This would have been miserable if you weren't – I needed someone here. I can't stress how much that meant to me. I'll always remember your kindness."

Groans Notoire, "Uh: Emotions, my child. You will also, always be remembered – especially while I'm watching you knock someone off a rock. Keep in touch, Antru."

Antru promises, "I will."

Notoire is like Ortoi, or Ensoon. They are the same as all the roukta players and many more that have been met over the years. They are appreciated, respected, considered friends, and polite conversation is always given, but the idea of relationships, what was sought on arrival at the institute is long abandoned. The openness and feelings felt with Dalune and Aedra are with them, only. The rest of Nespia receives carefully selected words and nothing of value. Fears and aspirations that spilled with desperation on arrival are no longer shared. Invitations are often accepted, but little is offered in conversation – they are opportunities to listen and observe. Places to harvest insights and perspectives. Eyes that watch from the edges – ears that comb through conversations:

Like eyes that watched from beyond a yard at the dawning of understanding – the child becomes their parent and both are considered similar by those that know them: Reserved, and cold. Aloof and distant. There is disappointment from the one departed because they know the persona is adopted. There is disappointment that outreach never changed opinions, beliefs, nor outlook.

The cube is cool contrast to the warm afternoon. It has become home as much as the only other that was ever known. It is appreciated as much, and the Marphy life will be deeply missed. The door closes and the pull for the bunk is momentarily overridden by thirst and starvation.

Water's drawn and the single nutritional bar that is always present is extracted from the drawer. It is pulled from the wrappings, and the paper is flattened against the surface and used as a mat to protect the surface. The weary body collapses into a chair and leans heavily against the desk as the supplement's devoured. Water is drained, and the wrapper is swept by a hand, but that pauses before it's crushed and thrown away.

Thoughts towards ends and new beginnings brings memory back to arrival and the oddity of always present nutrient and uniforms. The drawer is checked, and a single bar sits neatly centered. The wrapper from the last is spread, and a tool's pulled out of the kit to burnish in, "Thank you." It's set in the drawer and sealed within like the tickled idea of communication with the unseen world.

It is momentarily enough to stimulate the mind, but the body is still drained, and compromise is falling into the bunk with speculation churning in the brain. Thoughts of a whole network behind the scenes, ensuring students have what they need, ensuring society runs smoothly. It is an oddity to think of a whole population beneath the ground, behind walls, and as much that the thought towards outreach hadn't been considered, before. There is an imagined handshake through a wall that is consciously recognized as the mind slipping from reality. It is the last thought remembered before the temporary stimulus is exhausted.

Eyes focus on nothing, when a face appears from nowhere. Aedra is smiling, and their body twists as a fist punches into the air.

Eyes open, and there's still light flowing through the skylight. The brain is still groggy, but there is a prickling sensation that brings it from that state in only minutes. Eyes are focused on the bottom of the upper bunk, and there is a clarity that has only been found before, when scaling upcrops at rapid speed.

The band is checked as conditioned after four years of receiving notifications. There are more than could be responded to, but priority messages show – four: One from Aedra:

"You killed it. Absolutely dominated."

It is hyperbolic, overstated, and it brings a smile. The image remembered from the shadows of a dream is the instant before the message was sent.

Of the other three, two are from parents. There is a message from Dalune, and it is filled with the words that give feet solid ground to stand on. The message from Éayren provides critique and is appreciated for giving insight towards improvement. But the last is from Eotor.

It is not the clumsy and inappropriate Eotor of familiarity, but a message that is earnest:

"It was really cool seeing you today. I don't really know how to say this, but you made me feel like I had a place here. Not you, really. You're still a clodhop. But all the people that started hassling me. It's the first time I ever felt like anyone cared I existed. I get it was you behind that. But you're still a rock-nobber."

It is the first message replied to: "I care you exist. Please keep in touch."

That is followed by a return to Aedra, and that becomes a back and forth that lasts until the sky begins to dim. It is a reminder there was a promise to join the festivities, and regretfully, the conversation is ended.

Two more messages are sent before joining the others. The first is to Éayren, and it is, "On the odd-chance that I get drafted, I would love to work with you." And the last is to Dalune, and as always, "Thank you for always knowing where I am. I would love to play, but it's not my priority. I won't be disappointed if they don't call my name. Can't wait to see you."

The other messages are discarded as there are too many to sort through. Departure starts, but memory flashes to the scrap deposited in the drawer.

There is amusement at the prospect. That a person might be behind the food and uniform – not automation. But that prospect also levels trepidation.

Feet turn back and the drawer is opened, and the wrapper is found folded in half. It is lifted, unfurled, and the, "Thank you," is smeared with blood that hasn't dried. Amusement plummets and ill-ease curdles in the gut as the blotted message in return begs, "Help."

The paper is crumpled and thrown away as it should have been in the first place. It is already understood there is no help. It's already been realized there are forces that are trying to change the world, and it's been seen that effort's failing. Knuckles rap against the wall, and it's told, "I'm sorry."

There is nothing that can be done. Experience already finds that freedom and safety are illusions. The health of social order is only a dressing that covers the disease. The answer to what that sickness is lies underground and is living in the walls. The door opens, and the sour mind is met by revelry.

The commons is a sea of celebration.

There is a louder din than typical, and that's not only the result of a larger crowd. Intoxicants have been consumed and enthusiasm is bolstered by the end of year, and nearing graduation for a quarter.

Cheerful greetings meet the stone-cold champion, the hero that secured the win. But it isn't confidence, nor hubris as interpreted by those that are crossed, it is feet stepping on a burning landscape while the anthem of war is playing. It is suffering and violence that can't be unseen, despite that it never has. But there is inevitability it will arrive, and it is understood it's the same song that stole Éayren.

"Why can't you just tell me," was asked a million times, and the answer was always frustrating: "It can't be learned, you have to understand."

"One for posterity?" A smoking blunt is offered in jest. Out of courtesy. For the first time ever it's taken, and a deep drag inhales the poison that it's hoped will quiet the mind.

Eyes look up to the sky for a sign of anything. Eyes look up and the inner workings of a system are envisioned. A system that was never intended to ward off outside forces. A system co-opted, but still outside control of those that used the threat of outside dangers to move it from its purpose. One that was dangerously close to what a young child once envisioned, after being chastised for climbing too high on upcrops.

"It's funny," Antru says to everyone gathered. The stars are blurred and dancing, and everyone, everything, is softened by a haze. "That's what it was supposed to be for."

The words are disregarded as the meandering, disconnected thoughts of a first-time inebriate, but it isn't. They are the words arrived at when there is understanding, of what it means to be connected. When the responsibility and dangers finally clarify and understand why Éayren would sacrifice everything.

There is a soft melody playing. Delicate and sorrowed. It plays over children that join their elders in celebration. They dance and drink unencumbered – unconcerned and unaware. It hangs in the smoke over the gathering, and drips from the eyes of the one that's watching: Notoire is reclined, sad eyes wide as they watch everything they'd hoped to accomplish, failing.

Chapter eleven:

The air is gentle, despite the speed. The vessel sails quickly with the wind and all that's felt are shifting currents. It is soft and warm. It is gentle and already has the taste of familiar stone. It already pulls the coolness from the harsh landscape. Memories and emotions become active with the familiarity, and there is a sense of belonging, as if – like net – the body is a part of the city.

Despite the dangers in its center. Despite knowledge that is not only just a feeling that it is hollowed: There is a hole in the senses that matches that in stone, where tunnels crisscross beneath the surface. Where citizens are detained without cause, and where a promise was once made that brought clarity to a delicate détente that was scarcely holding.

Edges were being scraped away. Children were being kidnapped and coerced into cooperating with those that wanted to compromise them and their families. If it had been only a few years before, they might have been successful in gleaning something. It was seen, now, that risk had been carefully managed.

The striking city comes into view as a rise of upcrops is cleared. It remains a startling contrast to vibrant Marphy. From the colorful, cheerful, ebullient sounds of Marphy. Capriot stands tall and varied. It is stone, and it is quiet. There are no public spaces to gather, and music is kept within the homes. Marphy is open and walkable – Capriot has narrow roads with backroom trade of weapons.

There is a strong curiosity to see of the elderly trader is still present, or if that was the source that gave clue to authorities.

Geography provides a natural shelter for the bay and city, and winds die down to almost nothing as passage turns northward. The waves are gentle, and at times, regions of water look like floating panes of glass. The cliff-face of the city's base grows taller as they're neared.

In ancient times, it was an easily defensible settlement. There is no reasonable access by land, and approach by sea finds nowhere to land other than within the small, adjacent cove. With the city's peninsular positioning, anyone approaching would have been seen well before arrival.

Modern weapons have reduced that advantage, to a degree, however, the city's compact, and elevation and sightlines continue to find it well defended. The reasons as to why defense is necessary have taken a sharp turn over the course of the prior four years, and the nearing bulwarks are no longer looked at as a blanket of security, but as part of the mechanizations of control.

There is a wait to enter the cove, just like there always is. The passage from Marphy to Capriot is more than a day, but it is the only way Antru will ever travel after experience in a vehicle. It is understood, on the surface of the planet there is protection. That protection does not extend underground, and it is from there that it's suspected control's administered.

It is the remnant of conflict that once existed, a history that has been exorcised from public knowledge. Passage takes more than a day, but it's the only safe way to travel, and more than half that time is waiting for approval to enter the cove.

It is late when it becomes evident they are docking. Antru returned to their berth to rest after a small meal.

The sound of engines churning is the familiar sound of progress being halted, and the back end of the vessel being swung in towards the shore. It is soon quiet, and it is probable the ship is being secured, and passengers will soon be able to disembark.

Return to the deck finds the plank has fallen. Just past the gates beyond the dock, a small crowd waits to receive loved ones, Éayren standing out amongst them – Éayren, alone.

Everything unusual is always cause for concern, and the oddity brings a quick retreat, and descent to depart. It is the goal of everyone on board, and the rush to leave brings a slow, incremental slog off the vessel. Feet shuffle and come to a standstill frequently, as others wrangle luggage, children, and small animals.

There is a screening as there is for any form of transportation, but unlike the vehicles – a simple wave: The band is scanned and there is motion to continue.

Éayren stands as still and stoic as an upcrop, but they are not such the larger-than-life exemplar as they'd been. They are still taller than anyone else present, but only slightly moreso than their child. Their physique is no longer intimidating. The size and presence once brought alarm, if not fear. But they are more of an equal anymore. Two graduates of Marphy and nearly equals: One with experience and guile; one with the endurance and energy of youth. They come together and embrace one another warmly.

"I might not have recognized you," says Éayren, "If you didn't approach. You have certainly changed."

The statement is one that brings mixed feelings. There is the abandonment that was always felt. There are thoughts that a visit could have been worked out.

There is the anger that led a child to ignore roukta entirely until another intervened to guide them.

However, there is also understanding of the person and what they've done. There's appreciation for their insight and intervention. It is also suspected there has been great, personal sacrifice.

It is all ignored, and Antru asks, "No one else?"

"I wanted to talk."

They walk away from the shore. They walk up the steep incline that was the only point of entry five-thousand years before. The mechanized elevators are bypassed in favor of isolation and quiet conversation.

It begins with the insipid, usual, "So: How are things?" The answer is complicated, and honesty and truth are largely circumnavigated. "I know," Éayren says, and there is hurt in the words: "You wanted certain things. And maybe... It's possible – maybe I should have let you go to Capriot."

Antru says, "No. I'm glad I went to Marphy."

"You should have been drafted," the parent says. There is guilt, and sorrow, that, "It's my fault. I hoped by being separated it wouldn't affect you. I know it's not what you wanted, but you have a gift. It's been evident since you were young: It could have given you opportunities. That's all we ever wanted for you."

Antru says, "It's alright. I'm fine with where I am."

Éayren finds regret: "I should have let you follow Dalune."

There is an attempt to refute the statement, to explain there'd been ample opportunity found at Marphy, but it's difficult to conceal a four-time roukta champion from the public, and a fanatic bee-lines and begins to drool.

A swamp forms to muddle intentions. The handling of the small crowd that forms is watched, and those seeking a memento, or moment are met with a warmth and kindness that a child has found absent their entire life. They are sidelined as smiles are shared, stories are heard, and pictures are taken. It is not bitter, it is only the window through which a parent has always been seen. A window that recent experience had tried to pull a shade on, but the star still shines brightly for those surrounding.

"Love all of you," says Éayren, and they are words that have never been heard by the person watching. That person is told, "Goes with the territory." They resume the climb, and the persona remains – reaching for recognition. Searching for eyes that turn their way. It is only once they've cleared the denser city and gained altitude that the intoxication of adulation begins to fade: A look aside reminds of the purpose that drove them to meet their child on arrival.

There is a sigh, because that determination, the guilt that rose to its highest point while waiting outside the gates, has been diluted with presence. Opinions formed find a person that is nothing like the untethered child last seen. They are large, and strong, and seem at peace.

"It was probably a mistake," Éayren says, and that's refuted calmly, "It was not."

They turn the broad street of familiarity, and it is typically quiet for the time of night. Everything is still, and stone, and footsteps resound heavily beneath the moonlight, a beat that grows louder in the absence of continued conversation.

As their home is neared, the need to cover what was planned, earns, "I should have let you go to Capriot.

I'm sorry, Antru. You would probably have had more opportunity."

"No," Antru tries, but it's interrupted:

"Yeah. Yeah, you would have. We always knew there was risk, but I figured with your skill, even with the way things have gone…" Feet stop and the child turns back, desperate to hear what things are and where they've gone. Instead, they are given the answer to why a long-lost parent was the only one present for arrival: "I've let you down."

"Moboti," Antru says. It is the first time the term has ever been used, and the child's heavy hand falls to a shoulder and pulls their parent close, as, "Moboti," is said again: "I understand." The other's head shakes, but Antru says, "I'm glad I went to Marphy. I loved the experience. It was really good for me to see another part of the world and how other people live, and I loved playing roukta. I even started to follow you. Regardless of what happens, you made the right decision."

"You don't have to say that," finds, "I'm not."

It lands acceptance. There is sincerity in the face and words of a person that is no longer a young child. They have grown, and they have matured. They are at the beginning of the best time of their life and ready to strike off in the world. But they will always be a child. Yet a child that does not assign blame, nor condemnation as imagined. A child that claims to have gained much from decisions made against their will. One willing to forgive a parent that holds more guilt and sense of failure than they will ever know.

They're told, "Don't ever forget what Dalune has told you."

Antru scoffs, to share, "Dalune says take care of the people you care about the most. That's what Dalune tells me's most important."

Éayren says, "Yes: Don't ever forget."

For the first time in more than a decade, the child is taken in their parent's arms. They are held close, and arms grip firmly as desperate hope looks for any hold that failure isn't catastrophic. Release finds a parent's eyes looking back with sorrow and wounded. There is just a nod to resume, and they continue together in silence.

Dalune is found standing in the home – paused mid-pace. They question, "How did it go?"

Their partner shrugs; Antru says, "It went fine."

They are greeted warmly. Éayren watches as they come together as parents and children will if they know each other. If they have experience, and familiarity, and understand what love is consequently. The warmth observed is not the same and that is the greatest failure, despite the exoneration offered with words.

"Understand," Dalune says, believing the conversation went much deeper than it did, "Every decision we made was meant to let you live your life and find happiness. That's all we ever wanted."

Éayren clears their throat, and a dismissive wave precedes, "We didn't get past it was probably a mistake. Antru claims everything's fine."

"You didn't," is questioned, but Antru says, "It's fine. I understand. I get why you've done what you have, and I respect it. I feel a strong compulsion to follow you."

That meets, "No," immediately.

More softly, Dalune explains, "That's what we're trying to tell you: We don't want that. This is the time

193

where you should live your life, start a family; explore. We want you to enjoy your life and be happy."

"Okay," says Antru: "Don't do what you do. I understand. But I understand why you have."

"You don't," Éayren says, but that's refuted:

"I've been detained. That's why I warned you about the weapons. They were looking for it, but I'd already destroyed it. I've also talked to the people behind the walls at Marphy, and I know about the underground."

"Antru," is stated firmly. The darkness that has been known cloaks Éayren, and they warn, "You don't understand anything. What you're saying is extremely dangerous. You should not share this with anyone."

"Then," Antru suggests, "Help me understand."

There is a look between parents, before Dalune shares, "Someday, when you understand, you will also understand why we won't."

"From the future," Antru says, "Thanks. Do you mind if I check in with Aedra?"

"Remember." Éayren demands, "What Dalune has told you. Remember what we've said."

"A recap," Antru says: "Don't follow in my parents' footsteps, live life, be happy, and take care of the people you love. Do you mind if I see if someone I love is still awake?"

"We want you to be happy," Dalune says.

Éayren agrees, "That's all we wanted."

"It would make me happy to go see Aedra."

The question, "You awake," is answered, "Meet me here, or over there?"

Antru replies, "I need to escape," and tells parents, "I'm heading over."

Dalune answers with, "Good night."

It is still striking how different the city is compared to Marphy. It is dim, and quiet, and eerie at night. It is closed and residents are hidden away. As before, the only sound is footsteps across the stone, and it brings longing for the gatherings. For the conversation, music, song, and dance. Knuckles rapping fill the emptiness and are imagined heard as far off as the harbor.

Aedra opens the door with finger to lips, and, "Parents are sleeping." There is a nod of understanding, but a hand guides the body forward as the door is closed.

Words are held aside as they come together. As senses re-awaken and the dim light and silence are brightened and become filled with music. They hold together, swaying to the rhythm, feeling the warmth of bodies together. There is a feeling both find that is only there when they are together. It was present the day they met and grew stronger in moments by the columbrum. Distance and time apart only brought awareness that in the absence of the other, it was gone.

"Trouble with parents," is questioned.

"More of the same," Antru whispers.

Hands caress and feel the growing resonance, but they pull away – one reaches out in invitation, and Aedra asks, "Do you want to talk?"

The hand is taken, but the answer's, "No," the hand as leverage to pull the other close again. There is electricity in the dark room that short-circuits a shimmer in the periphery. It is a vision that has been seen thousands of times, before, but it has never before been lived, and laughter escapes to finally feel it.

A finger rises to lips and remembers, "Shh," the presence of others. There is another pull, away from the common space and the door to the room is softly closed.

Years of inhibition and alienation are forgotten obstructs that fall with descending scales as music swells. A delicate dance enters the stream of sound from beating hearts and heavy breath. There is gentleness, and unhurried submersion into the chords that are building. Hands are gentle and trace the other's body so to know it fully. To recognize by touch the sculpture of the beloved, pulled close to inhale the other's scent. There is uncertainty, but it is settled as they move together into the symphony of enlightened senses.

There is no darkness despite no light within the room. There is music that evolves through dissonance and inversions, despite that it's completely silent. Taste on the lips and tongue is sweeter than any confection ever taken. There is a warmth and comfort that envelopes the two and holds them together in unbreakable embrace.

"Antru," whispers Aedra.

Antru whispers, "Aedra," in return, and there is laughter. Quiet laughter between the two as noses nuzzle against the other, and arms pull bodies as if it were possible to be closer.

Senses rise to a heighted state that is more intoxicating than any chemical. More enlivened than ever before. Colors swirl in a cocktail of euphoria. Hands press, accepting stimuli and offering pleasure in return. A fanfare fills the ears so fully that the entirety of the world is silenced by it, and there is only the concentrated sense, and taste, and smell of two swathed in an otherworldly tranquility that they drink of with uncontrollable thirst.

Eyes are blind but they see the world more clearly than they ever have, and it is only one. One that shares a heartbeat. Breath that is taken in and tasted – absorbed and craved inexorably. Warmth and touch that connect internally. There are colors in the open sky above, and water pours through open doors and window. Ocean waters crash and the sound of the surf fills the ears. The waters fill the senses as waves crash in and spread across the shoreline.

There is no relenting: Arms grasp the other. They hold close against one another as they sip of the nectar they have built between them. There is nothing else but two in a sea of nothing that they sail together, pulled together under waves of contentment. They ride the surf until darkness blankets them, but it is kinder than it has ever been and sings lullabies to keep their minds at peace.

It is a peculiar experience to emerge from a night of rest. To wake – rested – and to feel secure: Aedra still in arms and holding on. There is a sense of incredible relief, but there are also muted sounds on both ends of the room: Outside the window, and in through the door. It is not enough to disturb the other, nor does it erase the experience or disrupt the pleasure to hold and be near the one that's loved. It is only a thought that sits in afterthought as appreciation for the moment that continues – tin drops against the windowpane.

There is a rhythm, beside: A breath pulled in, and exhaled. With each, there is a feeling that rises in the chest, and with it – heartbeat. It is an ache, but it's not unkind. It is the opposite. It is everything for another. It is holding the world and giving it away because the person in your arms is more deserving. They deserve everything, and "Live your life," and, "Take care of those you love," have meaning that was not conceived could be greater. There is understanding why some truths should be sheltered.

"I guess I fell asleep."

Aedra is looking up with a devilish glint in their eye. They are in the same place, but only emerging from the night.

"I think your parents are awake," Antru says.

It's answered, "Probably," and wondered, "They won't be angry?"

"Do you care," Aedra asks.

Antru says, "I don't want them to be."

A hand reaches over to pull the other closer and lips are brought together. There is no resistance. Concerns are a background intrusion, a flashing light that is blanketed with increasing layers. The breath of exotic entanglement is inhaled and gives rise to the beating heart again, but it does not lift into the mosaic of the night before. It is only an essence, a reminder of what was held between them.

"Antru," says Aedra: The blanket still lets light through, and it's assumed, "My parent's don't care. Yesterday they asked when we're getting married. I blew them off, but maybe…"

Antru lifts away and rests on an arm, above. The other hand brushes Aedra's face and it's taken, and held – the words dropped away because the fear and worry looking back were not expected.

However, they were not a rection to the words. They spring from the well that pours the question, "Would you want to know a secret if it would ruin your life?"

"Why," says Aedra: "Would you ask me that now?"

"My parents tried to keep it from me," Antru shares. "They've tried to shelter me, but I see it everywhere. I already know more than they want me to know, but they won't tell me more. They say I don't understand, but they won't let me know what I don't understand."

The hand is pushed away – irritably as Aedra rises and begins to dress.

"Your answer's no," Antru presumes.

"My answer's – why are you asking me, now? We all get Éayren's part of something. Everyone knows they don't live here because they're protecting you. Is that how you want to live? I actually need you to answer that question, because I'm not living like Dalune."

Antru realizes, "I didn't understand what they were telling me."

"What are they telling you?"

Antru says, "To ignore what I've seen. That's what they're telling me."

"Can you?"

The answer is, "Yes. I trust Dalune. If that's what they're telling me to do, then I know there's a reason."

"Think you can stick with that decision?" It is a test, a probe, a search for validation, "Because I need to trust you."

"That's what they've been telling me," Antru understands: "Take care of the people you care about most. They always say we should live life and be happy."

Aedra tests, again, "That's what we're doing?"

"That's what we're doing," Antru agrees.

"Okay," Aedra seconds. However, that agreement comes with the caveat, "If you ever get the idea in your head to bail on me, I will track you down and play your face with a calumbrum hammer."

A flash impresses on the memory, and it's remembered, "I've had that dream."

Head shakes, but the space is closed and hands are taken. Eyes are connected even as Aedra's head still sways – disbelief/amusement – and a quiet chuckle sprinkles free, to think, "At least we won't walk out of here in euphoric bliss."

Chapter twelve:

"I like the one that overlooks the ocean."

It was already accepted the home ranked favorite, but it comes with responsibilities attached – it is also the most distant from parents. A home with an incredible view over the inlet of the western shore. It is an older neighborhood but still in the elevations. It was carved from the stone millennia before as part of a fortress that once stood to protect the enclave, a direct sightline through the front windows to Jayllilynne. Part of stepped residences that walk up from the water.

It was not the largest home viewed and it did not have the most amenities, however it was easy to imagine relaxing in the home and watching ships and storms passing through – or watching the star merge into the water in the evening. It also had a nice yard that was walled to the north by an enticing upcrop.

There were many positives – there were some negatives: The greatest, residents are responsible for maintaining the neighborhood. In Capriot, that means keeping stone immaculate, and ensuring no vegetation gets a foothold. For that home, in particular, that includes the extraordinarily steep street that is the sole access, all the walls that line the road, and the neighbor's roof on the step below. During the viewing, it had fallen as an overt breadth of space to cover.

That is all withheld, and Antru agrees, "It's a beautiful view." Upkeep would be split between neighbors, and any yard would have to be maintained. However, any others didn't have a roof, nor walls, nor road to be administered. That is all understood to be insignificant and not worth mentioning, however, "I would prefer to be closer to parents."

"Yeah," is agreed. However, "We can always move. It would be great for our first place."

It is teased, "We could have a weekly drawing for road or roof."

"Or," suggests Aedra, "We could work them together." It is a surprisingly sweet sentiment, and there is a struggle for words to follow, but they're unneeded, because Aedra continues, "See who does a better job." There are smiles, and laughter, but sincerely, it's offered, "I don't think it'd be that bad."

"Okay," Antru says, and because it's not an argument worth starting: "It leads the list."

"Yeah," is spoken hopefully and with agreement. Eyes turn, and they are met, and both smile. A hand is offered, taken, and they continue together, connection flowing and agreement held.

They follow the winding streets of the old city, taking a route that is intentionally indirect. There has been a pull to verify curiosity and suspicion since an ill-advised trip home, and they are confirmed as a building is passed with the sparkle and sheen of recent renovation. It is no longer the purveyor of everything. It is a soon to open establishment to provide food and drink.

The stone walls have been cut away to make room for broad windows, and the rarity of timber provides deep-stained contrast to the ecru stone. It is sharp, and clean, and wipes away any visage of what stood. There is certainly no longer an insulated room lit only by a candle. The moment the weapon was searched for, it was suspected the old enterprise had been uncovered. There is only disappointment to find that so, and it falls into the dissonance of a parent's regrets over recent events.

Reflection is pierced with, "You alright?"

"Just thinking," Antru answers.

"Thousand tons of stone for what."

It pulls a laugh, and Antru claims, "It's nothing." But that doesn't do justice to the silence nor melancholy answer, and before that's noted, the reflection's shared, "Éayren brought me here when I was younger. It was the first time I came to this part of the city, and it seemed so hostile and intimidating. It's very different."

Aedra says, "Don't I remember." There were warnings, and dangers spoken of everywhere: "I thought you'd lost it."

Air bustles the nostrils as if amused, but the hand is pulled a new direction. They are led through streets until the insanity is found: The vehicle of the clans sitting idle. Both watch the uproar that surrounds, between the one inside, and another that negotiates a price – for nothing but volumes of intoxicants.

"I mean," says Aedra.

"But they offered – anything you want." The thought to follow with words about the clans is shunted: A nod, and eyes to the left draw attention to an elevated cube where a person is seen watching through the window. The words are played off like a joke: "Let's get wasted."

"You know," says Aedra. "Sometimes you get what you deserve."

"Yes," Antru agrees, "Sometimes you do."

There is some element of legitimacy to the observation: The city seems cleaner than it did as a child. If feels less threatening. However, four years of training and playing roukta, significant growth, and musculature not even hinted at the time have made any place feel less dangerous. But it is also more secure because of the company: Companion with innocent observations in contrast to a parent involved with the internecine. Exactly what that is, and the interest in understanding has been abandoned.

"Did you see that?" From nowhere, a person intercedes and halts progression. They say, "We've got to help them."

Antru looks back at the person referenced that is incapable of understanding what might go wrong to strand a vehicle. They are offering expertise that isn't theirs. They expend effort to offer an impression, but it isn't convincing anyone.

It is a sad display – disheartening. It is, "Help," passed through a drawer and written in blood, by a person behind a wall.

It is hopeless that, "Nothing I can do," however, spoken there's no want to.

The person pleads, "We have to help. You've got the muscle – let's take them out."

"Antru," Aedra questions, and the concern is ended:

"Not my problem." It's spoken tersely – stated firmly: "You feel like doing something, call the authorities. They can sort it out."

"Really," the person questions. "You're just going to let them pull this?"

Aedra pleads, "We have no idea what's going on," and Antru seconds, "I don't know who that is, and we're not getting involved. Bother someone else."

"It could happen to you," the person says, and that's refuted:

"Probably not."

Aedra adds, "Get lost. You're probably part of the setup. Find someone else to play that game."

Words are lost in the commotion that grows louder, but the two move away and have no interest in looking back – looking deeper. There is confirmation, again, and observation for the first time that words of warning have merit.

Disconcert and concern are countered: "Just ignore all of that. That's what my parent's were saying: We don't need to be a part of it. Okay?"

"Trusting," Aedra says. "And the steps home is gone, because I need to be near the parents."

"Trust me," Antru echoes: "Things are strange down here, but no one walking through or taking care of business has a problem. Steps is your favorite and the only thing I don't like is the cleanup. I'll get past it."

They move on, and there are towers everywhere. They follow streets and there are vehicles stranded with regularity. It is a reminder that in the hills above, in spacious homes with stone-walled yards – there aren't. Thoughts to why lead to the darker thoughts that were already difficult to ignore, and another suggestion to forget the favored home.

Antru points out, "We're the tower in steps. And no vehicle's going to sit on that street. It's the same as where we are right now."

Aedra taps the side of their head – intimation of a clever ruse – and claims, "As long as you're happy."

They arrive at their destination, a clinic visited years before with parents, in preparation for travel to the institution. It is visited the second time with eyes on traveling for entertainment and curiosity.

They approach the window, and the dusty question, "Purpose of your visit," holds little interest.

There is a desire to appear unaffected by the peculiarities of the deep city, and so it is Antru that answers, "We plan to see the country after we're married." A nod is given, and explanation, "My partner needs clearance."

"You are not married," is stated.

"Soon," says Aedra.

To Antru the person says, "That wasn't your question. Go wait outside."

"Can I," is met with, "No. You're not married. Leave, or I'll have you removed."

Aedra tries the same; says, "Can I," with the intent to authorize it's shared, but that's returned, "It's policy. If this is for travel, the conversation's strictly confidential between you and the clinician. No exception except for parents and partners: None. Nothing personal."

"Okay:" Aedra turns. There is a gesture of affection, and assurance, "It's fine. I'll get you when I'm done. Okay?" There is hesitation, but, "It's fine," is shared by both and it doesn't seem as hostile any more.

If it were Marphy, a public space would be nearby with food and drink. But Capriot is only narrow streets, lined with walls of stone-faced homes and ventures – some built; some carved. It is unwelcoming and those without illicit aims move quickly. Those that loiter or meander are the ones targeted by vehicles and towers. After a fourth trip encircling the clinic, there is a person that is obviously following. Whether they are with the clan, or someone planning something else, the attempt at wasting time is dropped, and the person breaks off as pace becomes determined and begins to climb.

It is another reminder that comfort and security in Capriot are situational. In yards, and homes, and local neighborhoods, there's no impression of a threat, but it still lurks in the larger city.

"Keep in touch," is sent, and is replied, "It's all good."

"Let me know when you're on your way," returns, "Paranoia-paranoia, la-la-la-la-la."

Antru texts, "I hear Marphy's nice."

There is a quick translation back: "Careful – someone's probably watching. Gotta go – doc's back. I'll let you know when I leave."

Antru sends, "Watch away," and, "Be safe."

There is no response, but it's presumed the examination has begun. Worry is pushed back for later, to be resumed if nothing's heard back, in more than just a short time.

The door is opened with the strange slurry of Capriot confounding thoughts, like always. It opens to a cheerful, "Antru," and introduction, "Look who's here."

A familiar person rises and moves to offer greeting. It is more confoundment. The anomalous presence of, "Notoire," sets thoughts to scramble.

"It's great to see you," is offered with sincerity. They greet warmly, and with a familiarity that was faded by their last discussion, but Dalune is smiling and it's accepted without being added to the piles of concern.

Words are reciprocated, with the added question, "What brings you here?"

Notoire replies, "Antru of Capriot brings me here."

"Well I," says Antru. There is a quick calculus made of obligations. Greater interest to certain ends, suggests, "I have a few things I need to take care of, but I'm free this evening."

Dalune says, "Join us."

Waiting is the only present obligation, so, the invitation's taken.

Notoire sits across and says, "I made a promise: Do you remember?"

Every word is remembered. The words are in the ear as if they were spoken with the question. They were a lifeline of hope when they were spoken – viewed as naivete or artifice, four years later.

To Dalune, it's explained, "I have Notoire to thank for my experience at Marphy, and, ah – I hope – they haven't shared that introduction."

"You're safe," Notoire says – says Dalune: "Oh?"

"A long story," Antru tries. However, "None of it would surprise you."

"I agreed with Notoire that we are very happy with how much you've grown – as a person – since your start."

"And I promised you," Notoire recalls, "That if you made the effort, I would personally go to the Marphy clan if you weren't drafted. Do you remember that I said that?"

Antru says, "Yes." It was part of the hope that stirred initial effort. It became sadness to think a person might believe it, and other thoughts that choked on the air of duplicity led to the distancing of the relationship. The fog is thick in the shadow of the promise, and it's absolved: "You couldn't have given me anything more than you did. I'm indebted."

"Antru," Notoire says, "I already have. I went to the Marphy clan and they all know you. I pointed out, any

Marphy club would improve with you on the team. A few days later, Elite got in touch with me."

"Elite," Antru says. Elite is one of four Marphy teams, and their name is considered ironic. Any player drafted serves their years, and then escapes. Only failures, those trying to play their way back in, and those that are at the end of their careers seek a contract with the team. Their plateau was second in the division, eleven years before.

"An opportunity to demonstrate your abilities."

"Let me tell you," Antru says, and there's amusement: "When I got assigned to Marphy, I also went to see the Capriot clan – the emperor. They were very patient and kind with a very confused child and explained my parents made the choice. I was completely devastated, and that's what you met. But you helped me understand it wasn't the wrong decision. I can't thank you enough for giving me that perspective.

Notoire says, "You're welcome. I'm sending their contact. Reach out and work out the details."

The band vibrates, and the message reads, "On my way."

It is quickly typed, "All good?"

The response is, "Whoo-hoo…"

"You're okay," receives, "I'll fill you in when I get there."

Dalune questions, "Is everything okay?"

It's answered, "Aedra – on the way," as if that was an adequate explanation, but it's left alone.

Notoire is extemporizing on the many benefits of the opportunity: "They say – try out – but it's a given. They're desperate. They want you to help them gain credibility. I think it's a great place to stake your legacy.

If you can bring elite up from the bottom, everyone's going to want you. It's a great opportunity."

One that would have been leapt at on the day of the draft, but time has passed, and other plans have at least been given outline.

But there remains tremendous appreciation for the person – regardless of motives. Despite their concentration in philosophy. They gave hope to a child that was hopeless and hurt. They gave insight and perspective to a child that could only see impediments. Participating in the experience gave understanding of the value and paved the road to follow parental pleas.

There is a familiar knock, and the door opens. Aedra says, "Hi," to the surprise of company. The word was spoken cheerfully, but there is an unsettled sense in their presence, and Antru rises to escort them from the door. In proximity it is quietly forewarned, "When you have a moment."

As quietly, Antru begins, "Is everything," but Dalune is in good cheer and offers introduction:

"Aedra: Come join us. Notoire has found an opportunity for Antru to play roukta. We were just discussing what a great opportunity this will be."

The word remains quiet – news is met by, "Whoa."

There is discomfit in the word and answer, and the world drops away to one – just a shadow from recollection reminds Antru to clear with others, "We'll be a moment," and they walk back out and a few steps down the road. Fear presses, "You're okay?"

It's answered, "Don't ask me that," and then, "Congratulations," are offered.

"I just found out," Antru explains. "Nothing's decided – I haven't committed to anything."

"Not for roukta," Aedra says: "Congrats: You're gonna be a parent."

The word, "What," escapes. There is dismay, and, "No," trickles from thoughts that rattle through responses.

"Yes," says Aedra. "Not the proud-parent moment I was looking for."

"No," is repeated, but it's to dismiss the notion of dismay:

A reaction to forces pulling, like the feeling of being washed away in dreams – no control and powerless to do anything. But that drains as it fully registers, as concern returns to where it should have been:

"I wish I'd been there. You're alright though? Otherwise?"

"Par-rent, and par-a-site are cleared to travel. We'll need to make it a priority if we're going to do that. And, didn't mention it yet, but I got an interview with the institute."

Laughter spills between them with disbelief and uncertainty. They come together in seas of emotions as the whirlwinds of life bring chaos to what was viewed at the beginning of the day as a simple journey.

"I'll tell Notoire," is answered, "No – you have to."

"I won't live alone," is sworn, "We won't:"

"Worst case scenario, you aren't playing forever. I'll have the interview and see if I can work from Marphy. Yes," is the emphatic answer regarding certainty.

Antru asks, "Are we telling parents?"

That's answered, dubiously, "I think we should?"

"I meant," Antru clarifies: "Now."

Aedra volunteers, "I'll watch, if you feel like you want to."

A question asked before, "Are your parents going to be angry," is asked again, and the answer remains the same:

"They'll probably want us to get married pretty quickly."

"Are you alright with that?"

"Yes." Aedra questions back, "Are you?"

That is answered with certainty. There is no hesitation, "Nothing but when changed."

The embrace they share is a demonstration of affection, of shared direction, and the consummation of a plan. They re-enter the home together, hands clasped and there is already expectation.

It's given life, as Antru shares, "We're having," but silence follows as thoughts scatter and words fail. They stand together, just inside the door after it was softly closed. It is a moment where the child feels like they have always been, and there is still deference looking to a parent. There is fear there will be disappointment, that the hope for the future has stumbled at the start. Antru stands, hand-in-hand, and unable to elaborate.

Aedra looks over with amusement that someone with that stature would be frozen; afraid to simply say, "A child."

"What," is the first word from Dalune, and they are at a stand.

Beyond the noise that is deafening ears, there is Notoire, and, "Oh, my," rings like a bell of condemnation.

But the noise continues, as did Dalune – to approach and steal Aedra into their arms: Tears are falling, but they aren't sadness. They're release, and relief, and comfort to know the news is welcome. There are no words of condemnation. There is no rebuke for age, nor the state of their relationship. Only happiness and concern for everyone's well-being.

Notoire thrusts forward a hand, and it's taken. The other collides against the shoulder, and the smile is warm, and, "Quite a day you're having," is only kind.

"Yes," Antru agrees, "We're having a day."

"We are having a child," Aedra says, and for the first time there is the blossom of happiness in the words.

Notoire is saying, "Congratulations," and makes the curious comment, "It's nice to meet the person that broke a thousand hearts."

It is fortunately buried as Dalune inquires, "Do your parents know?"

Aedra shares, "We – just – found out. I told Antru when we went back out."

Dalune says, "Aedra." They are looking at another in a way that had been reserved for only one until the moment. They say, "Tell your parents to join us for dinner. We would love to be with you when you share the news."

The offer brings relief in the sea of thoughts and uncertainty, and Aedra agrees, "I can probably convince them."

"I hate to be pushy," Notoire says as they are, "But I did go to some lengths to arrange the workout. Can I at least tell them you are considering the offer?"

"Yes," Aedra answers. Confidence has returned to their voice, and they look beside to seal, "Everything's jumbled, right now, but I'm really starting to feel like that could work for us. Don't you think so," asked to Antru.

"Yes," is echoed. Eyes meet, and there is belief in, "The beginning of our lives together. I think this will work out really well."

Interlude

The cry is soft and helpless. The trickle of a raindrop against a window. A trail that's born that slowly slips away into the pool that gathers on the sill. One that becomes lost in the many – indistinguishable. A uniform volume of merged infinity. It is vast, and endless, and the breezes pull ripples across time. A rise and fall that is only an instant – a flash that is missed in the blink of an eye.

There is silence before, and silence after.

There is a cry that is soft and helpless. It is a mouth that gasps as a ripple crests. It is lips lifting above the waters and filling lungs with air so they can scream into the vastness of nothing that surrounds them. They cry into the empty nothing and fall back into the waters, submerged, and encompassed, and also nothing. The cry to scream fills lungs with blood, and they burst with agonizing pain.

A creature's song of lust breaks through the barrier of walls and gives grounding to existence. It cries like the cry for life, but unaware: Oblivious, and better because of it. Reactive to stimuli and driven by instinct – no space for reflection or fear. No despair for unborn children that will fade beneath the surface of the waters.

"The children are crying," says a voice, and it might have been Aedra, but the eyes of the moon are watching, and it's silent.

"Hush," calls through the evening.

It is for a child in the arms. A child that is sweating and inconsolable. It breathes fire and bites at the flesh. It is hideous. A screel of sound grinds into the ears and body, and there is only one desire: To console the inconsolable. To make whole the broken, to dampen

215

fire; to alleviate the suffering that is interwoven with existence.

The creature melts away under the weight of stacked minor 2nds and becomes a molten ooze that washes against the shore in a final protest to the cry that was ignored.

There is complete dysphoria. There is failure, and endless opportunity that moved too quickly to jump aboard. There is a chance to save a life, and parental warnings turn blind eye against it.

Water falls, and the drops slip into the ocean and become insignificant contributions. A mite in the mighty. A momentary blip that falls from the sky and disappears in the vastness of everything, and nothing. A chance coalesce that finds a spec of time to freefall back to origin.

Waves crash against the shore and devour the earth. Land and cities are eaten away and fall beneath the surface, dissolving as they plummet towards the well of emptiness. There is only water, and it encompasses everything. It grows darker as descent continues and light becomes a memory that will soon be swallowed.

Silence exists only because it is interrupted by a single drip in the center of complete lightlessness. It falls and creates a shimmer. A slight imperfection to the encompassing veil that is otherwise everywhere and absent. A prick into the psyche that begins to echo – a tin drop falling into a columbrum and reverberating: A breath of life into the body of existence. It is muted and still drowned by the overwhelming flood waters of unconsciousness, but it lights quicksilver memories of experience and voices.

They fall through surrounding waters with muffled hint. They are a burble of noise that calls, but they are softened and incomprehensible.

Above, a window to the universe glints with fire-tipped waves. Faces peer through to look down the well and they call as if sense could be made of what they say – motion, as if possible to move. Lines tilt as they pass. There is a vision of puddles and passing feet, and looking up is looking in to a small hand reaching for salvation. It is smooth and puffy and expecting to be saved, but the fingers stand just out of reach – face splashes in the water as a hand grasps desperately to save the drowning child.

There is water, and feet are standing underneath the surface, head pointed down towards the dark, below. Muddled sounds are heard as shadows swim beyond. They could be creatures of the ocean, or a gathering held to condemn failure to aid the helpless.

Muted sounds continue to ring the ear. Most seem distant and are a barely an echo in the mind, but one is near. One is younger and the call is urgent. There is a flash from memory of a drowning child and fingers just out of grasp. There is a swarm of desperation as the waters muddy, as the eddy pulls the child. They are just entering the filling zone, circulating irregularly, and their tiny hand reaches for security – eyes look with expectation they can be saved.

The sound of the rushing water is deafening. There are screams from unseen places that might be creatures, or otherwise. All the sounds are meaningless except for one that breaks through with complete clarity: There is terror in the cry for, "Moboti."

Eyes wrench open in cold sweat, shivering, and sick. There is quiet breath, beside, and warmth that is pressed against, just like the child seeking a hand of rescue. Just like a child, seeking reassurance and consolation.

Slow breaths are taken to calm the mind, with hope the disturbance remains confined. There is guilt that has grown since childhood, that nights are interrupted – for parent, a roommate, and partner.

Flesh is thick with sweat, and memories reflect back to a cube where disturbance could be paced away for hours in the night. Where showers could wash away the stickiness and residue of broken thoughts in a haze of scorching steam.

There is fondness for the time at Marphy – there is hope it will resume when experience is shared. Kindness gave years a chance, and the effort taken to fulfill the agreement made, turned devastation into a place to build upon. There is reflection to conversations, to the enthusiasm in a home, as Notoire delivered on promises. It is a mirror that alleviates heaviness, and the buoyant presence that went to unnecessary lengths is sorted into a corner with few others – a revered place beside Aedra and Dalune.

A deep breath pulls a cloak on the night and eyes fall back on competition. Of the physical satisfaction from the effort, the victories, the friendships; the camaraderie amongst the teams. There are flashes of moments that play back: Triumphs, and failures. Holds that emerge from nowhere. Strikes that send another flailing. But it is the end of match were eyes turn as the claws of slumber begin to assume their space, again. To the joining of all that participated, and the love and appreciation for everyone.

The words between competitors are a music as sweet as notes played on the columbrum. They are the carillon tolling across the landscape, across the rock formations that have served as fields for competition for millenia. The bells are the laughter of combatants, that find humor in angered violence brought against one another.

A fist strikes another's face, and bells rain down mocking laughter. There is permanent disfigurement. It is a mirror image, and it is distorted by broken bones that leave the face misshaped. One eye is shifted and elongated the wrong way, blinking words that sound like a lullaby, but taunting, mocking the inability to save a baby.

"Where were you," is demanded.

It's a question that brings great anxiety because thoughts back cannot find the answer. The question lies in the atmosphere as a pressing demand, and it weighs down with overwhelming pressure.

Doors are opened to empty rooms, but the past remains elusive. Each room passed through becomes progressively darker, and voices become increasingly obscure.

Sand litters the floor. It is blowing off the walls, off the stone that towers into the sky, farther than can be seen. It is pointing at a moon that glows mawkish orange through the haze of sand clouds. It remembers a voice that was calling – a hand reaching from a well.

There was a responsibility to be there. There is an urgency to return, but every door opens to increasing dark and the sand blows fiercely, burying feet at every step. Pellets rip at the flesh and tick away bits of body with every strike until it is overwhelming and collapse into the darkness is a welcome relief and acceptance allows darkness to seep in through every pore.

There is silence, and nothing. It exists only because it is interrupted by a single sound that is emitted from a child, centered in vision. It is a cry made once, but it is endless. The call of the drowning child strikes a resonance into the soul and it will never be unfelt. It is a cry that is clean, and pure, and called with the expectation that the person called for has an answer. It is expected the person called for will reach down and pull them above the surface. They call, "Moboti," because that is the center of their universe and it is expected a parent will protect them. Expected that a parent will reach down and save them, that they are capable of preventing their child from drowning.

Tears bounce off the frozen surface as a child slowly slips away, beneath. As they fall into the waters and become a part of it, an insignificant and passing atom that is nothing more than part of everything. Tears fall, and the tin drops fall empty. A hollow plink against the ice that curtains what lies beneath the surface. That shields a last glimpse of a child that understands the utter failing of their parents and the lies that claimed they held existence.

It is cold, and tin drops across the surface make landscape impassable. They dig into the knees and embed in hands. They are the penance for incapacity. Knees and hands strive cautiously across the sentence, but avoiding the punishment is impossible, and it's not fought – it is punishment deserved. A child cried and their parent failed, and they crawl to the end of the earth on hands and knees with frozen marbles underneath.

Marbles that warm with the pressure and the body, and they evaporate into the nervous system, turning awkward crawl into uncontrolled discoordination.

Discomfort becomes pain as hands swell and become inflamed. Vision blurs as threads of liquid metal twist into a tangle with no ends. Damage worsens as the end of the world is lost but it is only noticed because of the shimmering silver liquid that is draining. Senses are dumbing, and eyes can only discern motion of shadows and the brightest glints of starlight off the mercury.

There is no cry, but the sound is never ending. It sounds through hopelessness that was not the child's, but the parent's. It still rings in the ear as despair builds into anguish. As a hand slips into darkness in waters too deep to reach, beneath a frozen surface that is obscured by the sand that buries the body.

The last threads of silver slip into crevices and fade mind's eye to passivity. Tranquility that is the child's origin, and where they will return. A raindrop that falls back into the ocean. Indistinguishable from the infinite others that have fallen. A rainstorm that patters gently against the surface for one, last statement before return. A final acknowledgment of existing. A quiet clap against the water that will likely be heard by no one.

Breezes scatter the raindrops like tiny scratches against the surface of the ocean. They are warm and pleasant. It makes the rain a polite intrusion as waters are watched through a window, high above. The vehicle has no ceiling, and raindrops saturate the passengers, and a river forms between the seats. They are heading for a tunnel that has been seen before, and there's no desire to return.

Words are sounded to another passenger. They hold no content, but they know it means they're disembarking. They are grabbing holds that leer down at those passing to offer temptation and escape. There is a momentary flash where an arm is damaged at the attempt, but feet and fingers instantly find familiarity and begin a scramble up the rock face.

There is nothing but an endless tower that rises into the emptiness of space. It is a pointless climb that has no end. It is forever, but there's nowhere else to go: Forever down, or forever in ascent.

Feet push against the footstops – hands reach for the next hold. It is the climb of memory, when senses are enlightened and every imperfection is seen, and also remembered. It is the scramble across the rockface that was once referred to as remarkable – laughed about in the circle after matches. Feet press, arms stretch, and the rockface is abruptly sheer.

It is a fall that has been seen countless times. It is the nightmare that leads parents to scold their children when they climb too high. It is the plunge that finds broken bodies and tablets at the bottom, atop a pile of jagged rubble.

It does not even begin to evoke the fear as the word spoken by a child, when they cried, "Moboti."

Tears fall and wet the sand scraped from the stone. They are broken promises and inadequate explanations. They are the inability to answer questions, and the incapacity to remove fear and pain. They are the failure to pull the child from the bottom of the well and the second-thoughts reflect back and consider there must have been something.

Something else tried, greater effort: There is a broken child lying on a small pile of gravel at the base of the upcrop. It is faceless, but its hands are wrenched with the pain from the poison of mercury. A finger points in condemnation, and the rain is falling as an insult in the laughter that reigns with failure.

"Couldn't," blunders underwater. There are sounds, and anger, and the condemnation is deserved because life isn't if every effort was not expended to save the child.

"Couldn't," reverberates. There is laughter, and mockery. There are roukta players looking down, looking at failure; looking at one unable to even sniff a chance to play on a degraded team.

There is a scramble, and the wall is suddenly sheer. There is a grab for holds, but it pulls an infant near.

The child is crying and the only thought is to protect it against the impact. It is embraced – it is held up with two hands and arms that are tensed to pillow the violence that will meet the surface.

There is laughter and mockery for the effort, and eyes turn to find the broken child bleeding on the pile of stones at the bottom of the rocky climb. Players turn away in protest. Backs are turned in a show of disgust for someone so incapable: Unable to climb, incapable in the field of play, and helpless to save their child.

Laughter is sorted away for anger and condemnation. Strikes are the violence deserved for the failure demonstrated. Blows land. Drives sting into the back. Fists strike the face, and none of it compares to the cry of, "Moboti."

"Antru," is called. A hand rocks the shoulder, and states the evident: "You're having nightmares."

It is another failure. One more night and demonstration shown of inability. An incapacity to shield the world from a broken mind that cannot be muted in the night.

Sobs are quickly sucked within. Breath is held while flashes seal the visions into categories. There is a wish to pull away. A desire to live alone in a cube and pace for hours to tire the body and shut down the mind, but there is also tremendous guilt within those thoughts.

There is no greater pleasure than to sleep beside the one you love, and no greater regret to know the same cannot be said.

PART 2

Chapter one

A tone sounds to wrench eyes from inward hallucinations of children tiptoeing with delight across the plants of the cool, dew-dripped commons. Tiptoes plant into the water to feel the tickle and cold that builds into an ache. There was a dare to see who would last the longest.

For a moment, the vision lingers. For a moment the sounds are real, and it was a moment that was lived. As eyes are pried by the grating noise, for an instant, worlds blend, and what is real is no different than what was dreamt. In those seconds where the brain reactivates after a night of restitution, the children's squeals of agony as feet drip with ice cold water is in the ear and as real as anything. They are known, and loved, and their thoughts and voices are cherished above all else.

The tone is silenced and tired feet turn out of the berth. The body rises and shuffles down the narrow passage to the sanitation chamber. Clothes are discarded into the syphon and twenty-seconds later, the body is cleansed and dried.

There is a stop at the cabinet just beyond, to retrieve the single nutrient bar that is centered in the drawer with its accompanying hydration capsule. The capsule is burst between teeth against advisement and followed by a bit of biscuit. It is moist, and chewy, and not terrible, but if was never eaten again it would be forgotten.

Feet slough on to the door across the berth to retrieve the daily uniform. It is slipped on, and an exit is made from the tiny unit.

Numerous others are joined in the silent, tired march through channels, an unconscious and conditioned path followed to waiting stations. Waiting with dozens of others for the doors of the vehicle to open. Dozens that are recognized and not spoken to. They are ones of endless numbers. They are the ones of millions, and trillions through time that walk together, and apart – stand together, and apart.

The wing lifts, and in unison, dozens shuffle into the rows of paired seats. Not one is alive enough to carry conversation. Fatigue from the prior day still sits in muscles, and many have come to suffer from joints that fail and pain from bones that scrape. Joints that have failed, but press forward, anyway.

Seats are taken, and there's some relief to be idle for a moment. It is a pleasant respite from life that begins with an unpleasant tone and ends with complete exhaustion. It is one of few moments of the day where time is idle, and obligations aren't present. Bodies slouch into the seat and eyes close. Seek another wisp of sleep – another second to rest a tired body.

Wings fall and encompass passengers with uncomfortable proximity – familiar comfort that is leant against: Bodies lean back into the corner of seats against the wall of the vehicle. Eyes close and uneasy slumber falls across the many as they travel.

It is a sleep that is broken by flashes as light breaks across windows when the vehicle turns. It is lifted when velocity changes. It is interrupted when the awkward positioning of bodies grows unsustainable, and either pain or numbness requires reposition.

However, there are still moments where the eyes fall back inside, where they dip into the land of imagination, and another life. There's no time to develop plots: It's a sound, a familiar face; a place. An echo that sticks in the mind when eyes awake. A child's voice, a person's name – a vision of a lake. They are the mementos of the unconscious that are appreciated, because others that occur as frequently are filled with fear and violence. Those of cold feet and laughter are treasured and reflected on while waiting throughout the day.

There is a tone, but it's not the grating sound that moves tired bodies from their berth, it is a tinkey chord to alert passengers the doors will open imminently. Like swaying crops in a breeze, bodies move from the walls and pull together centrally. The walls swing up, and the march through corridors resumes.

The construct is a massive stone quarry that serves the entirety of the continent; however, most is used in adjacent Greater Nespia. The stone has been procedurally mined with plans from the onset to develop infrastructure, storage, government offices, business and living space, as well, shelter if another assault is ever launched. That section is large enough to hold about half the city.

None of that is the target: The corridor towards the active mine is walked, but that will also be bypassed.

It's an area that's been considered. A transfer is guaranteed and the chance to go home each night sometimes resounds appealing. However, transport and delivery offers variety and a chance to see the country.

The long drives through Rims, the incredible views from the upper elevations, and the marvels of engineering. They are the favored routes, and years have not begun to erode appreciation. They are also cities of small population and runs there are infrequent. Most commonly, deliveries are made locally, or to Upper Borrean.

That region is not disinteresting but it lacks the dramatic scenery. It has the forest, but even that becomes monotonous. The land is flatter, the roads are straighter, and there is only thick vegetation to look at for most of the journey. Stops for stimulants are not infrequent – there are abundant reminders to pull off as often as necessary: Progress is tracked, and too many stops will earn a transfer.

It is, unfortunately, a passage that must be taken for the most peculiar destination. If a straight line could be taken, Akkrat would be closer than anything besides Alvel. But the upcrops surrounding the small city are the tallest on the planet and some of the densest. Punching through the rock is a project that has been abandoned multiple times.

Consequently, travel to Akkrat entails the entire circuit through the forest of Upper Borrean. It diverges at the pass for Minaut, and climbs a steep rise to the narrowest volume of upcrop. The journey from there is somewhat precarious and more interesting. It winds through the rises, across marvelous bridges and supported roads, and then descends on a road cut down that has multiple points of singular passage. As that's left, the most unique part of the journey begins.

It is an area known as Wastelands, and that is a term that reflects the terrain. It is generally accepted that the formation is the result of an ancient impact, and the legacy of that event is a wide field of glass debris. The smoky shards greatly amplify heat, and it is extremely unpleasant if not protected. The cauldron is impassable, blistering, and blinding. Special glasses are worn to protect eyes while passing through, and even with environmental controls, everyone will arrive at Akkrat in a sweat.

It is an odd city, and there are several off-shoots that operate independently. Small communes that cater to those that are sickly, but that also believe in living without technology. They are independent – completely self-sufficient.

Akkrat is also, largely self-sufficient, but in contrast, those in that city embrace technology. While the lake at the bottom of the crater effectively offsets the effects of the glass, those in the city cool homes and businesses to a comfortable level. Like the rest of Nespia, they are constantly looking for ways to make life easier, and the local government is an active participant in conversation at a national level.

It is a trek that was made only once and arrival at the town was striking. It is a beautiful city with unique architecture. There are no rocks to carve from, and any that have been used were transported significant distance. As a result, the community developed their own building materials which utilize the glass of the crater as a basis.

From ancient times, building and development of the city has been carefully curated and it is like nothing else on the planet. A city of gardens and beauty, and everything is focused on healing broken bodies, the ailing, and struggling minds. A tiny town in the middle of nowhere that is a gem in vision and conception.

Every operator has volunteered to take that trip; those that have been are unlikely to return: It is a chance that is uncommon and given to those that have demonstrated they're deserving. Typically, those that have never been before.

It's said, "Morning," like it has been said before.

That's returned, "Ready to go?"

"Ready to go," is answered.

The journey begins with fingers slapping at a button. Destination is not even considered until travel is underway, and like every day, expectation is that it will be local – eyes on display meet no lift from pre-registered disappointment. It is, at least, the northeastern end of the city where an ongoing redevelopment has been taking place since an ancient emperor decided living conditions were unsuitable for the lowest of society.

The vehicle moves silently through a passage that is just large enough to accommodate the monotonous, time-consuming departure from the undersea world that continues to be slowly chipped away in ever growing volume.

The project was conceived after the attempted Astrasian incursion and was originally planned as a facility to hold prisoners from that event. However, once the breadth of the underwater field was understood, a movement was begun to preserve existing landscape, to only use stone from underwater or underground as raw material. Over ensuing millennia, that mining continued to follow the dual precedent, using the operations to improve ease of travel, conceal infrastructure, and for murkier government operations.

Modern techniques create much broader passages that allow lighting and travel in both directions, however, proposals to improve the original tunnels of Greater Nespia have been dismissed as unnecessary and potentially harmful to defenses. It is also the only reason that operators are even needed – eyes and arms to address lost cargo.

Surface is met west of the city, though continued construction encroaches. The constant stream of transports is largely concealed from the population via a route that circles slightly east before navigating around a collection of upcrop. That continues on the outskirts of the city, travelling just below the fertile soil where crops are grown. Once distant, population growth has extended fully to that southern limit, and the long stretch of road that was once considered scenic has become sandwiched with fields between upcrops and the backs of buildings.

As the eastern edge of the city curves back towards the coast, the main road continues on a completely straight and largely level path that is cut through the second largest forest. There are several intersecting roads, but it is the last that's taken, a left turn where the right continues on to Bitor.

The northeastern region of the city has seen several transformations, as emperors and elected leaders have struggled with answers to ongoing issues in the region. It is believed that most residents are of at least partial, Borrean descent, and that heritage has been used to explain the difficulties those residents have living in civil society.

It was used for eons to justify discrimination, and even if there were merit to some of the most salacious claims, thousands of years of deprivation can just as likely hold blame.

As the case for thousands of years, improvements aim, with varying degrees of balance, to improve conditions for residents, and improve safety and security for both those within the region, and the remainder of the city. Both continue to be a concern despite efforts, and as it has always been, undercurrents of resentment remain in other parts of the city where many view the problems as self-inflicted.

A hand is raised at arrival: A redundant unnecessity to wait, as a stream of transports stand in line to offload material.

Like everything in the northeast, the new project continues to be a subject of protest. Angry crowds are held back by security personnel and fences. It's a protest that's confined to angered words – words that are misdirected: Shouted at those that deliver material, and those that build the homes. Policymakers find confirmation for their decisions from afar.

The project was promoted like every other project ever undertaken in the northeast, as an improvement to living conditions and modernization of residences. Protest against forced displacement was minimal as the new homes are visually appealing. However, protest exploded after elements of design were leaked, that touted the ability to easily lock down neighborhoods; to make it more difficult to evade authorities. With completion of the first three phases, and with the first families moved in, protest has wilted to a moderate crowd of angry voices and threat has been assessed as minimal.

A motion forward, and the long wait draws to an end.

If it were another city, return would be delayed for another day, but with travel, wait and offload, even the opposite end of Greater Nespia will bring return in the early evening. Local deliveries are the least interesting, however they also provide the opportunity to return home and spend time with family.

The vehicle's anchored, and the large, foundational stones are scaled to the crane. It is not an uncommon ascent for operators, as it's quick and many are former roukta players: Muscles that were trained for years react positively to the demand. Controls are taken, and the offload process begins.

The large stones that were just climbed are the feature protested most by their future tenants, intended to provide tall, sheer walls that can't be climbed. Intended to create passages between, in which protagonists can easily be tracked. They are hooked one at a time and carefully stacked beside the many others delivered prior.

The large stones are one of the easiest assignments. They are typically a one-stop destination, and there's no physical demand – only care taken with a crane so not to damage them.

Names are called from beyond the fences as the final stone is placed. Ire turns to the latest transport operator as the crane is locked into position, and their insults catalogue in mind as the platform's left: Hand on either rail, descent is a quick slide to the ground. Tablet's handed to the foreman to validate the order, who's also given, "I see you still have fans."

Head shakes, eyes roll – dismissively, "If they wouldn't ruin everything we gave them." And then a trigger clicks as they're insulted: "Typical crackwad Borreans."

There is a memory from somewhere. Buried in years and by insults from another. It is almost a question that says, "I'm Borrean."

There's a scoff, and it's pointed out, "You deliver rocks. 'Nough said."

There is a sparkle of sympathy for those beyond the gates. It is a bright gold that shines out of the uniformity of the pale stone. It is a desire to fight back against the inconceivable and help those that are hapless against the forces in their lives. Those that see new construction for what it is: A prison to wield control.

"Hey: Get moving," extinguishes the light, and memories evaporate like vapor in the air. The foreman calls, "Don't be a rockhead. We've got a schedule."

Position is retaken on the transport without argument, and it's moved forward to follow the slow trail with others back to the quarry. The return trip from a major project is always slower after the bottle-neck of delivery, a meandering journey with frequent slow-downs despite sensors meant to keep speed steady. Even back on the main road there is always some reason, somewhere in the progression to slow speed. It brings an ensuing domino effect that grows, and if the caravan is long and the slowdown's near its start, those on the back end are sometimes brought to a complete halt.

Operators watch with disinterest as their only intervention is in emergencies: Wild creatures, falling stones – anything not caught by sensors. Incidents are rare, but frequently what sensors miss is also missed by phased-out operators that are hoping they'll return early enough to spend some time with family.

The sky is dim by the time the transport dips beneath the surface of the land. The narrow channel is entered and final entries are prepared, to be quickly entered on arrival. Lights flicker with irregularity through the claustrophobic shaft, giving the only sense of progression as the vehicle moves through, slow and silent.

Light of the depot begins to shower hints in the distance, and posture is corrected – straight and diligent. Operators are monitored throughout the entire operation, but it is no secret that recordings are only reviewed after an incident. Sharp words from monitors on arrival instill the habit to stand straight and attentive for the last few minutes of the journey.

The vehicle guides itself to its bay, and it's immediately exited. The last entry is submitted, and the tablet's inserted into the receiver. As with posture, it is inured to wait until the light glows purple. As it does, feet turn and begin for the transport home – the monitor given a respectful nod, and it's returned.

As in the morning, there are many waiting for doors to open. It is a more jovial crowd, even those that have returned after days and great distance; even those that have been assigned goods' transport that requires significant physical exertion. It is the end of the day, and for many, end of days on the road. There is always a sense of joy to go home. To return home to loved ones, to family. To partners and children. It is all that is on the minds of everyone, and conversation carries excitement because of it.

The door opens and bodies sort into the rows.

"Good day," questions the one that sits beside.

They're answered, "Norries," the derisive term for northeastern residents of the city. But there's a ping beside the derogatory term that finds it personal, and there's an observation that's recalled, and accidentally shared: "They treat them worse than animals." There is silence to the observation. It is heavy and unpleasant, and an attempt is made to alleviate the weight, by noting, "Doesn't seem like they deserve it – that's all. Not that I know anything." It is enough drift that the question, "How about you," doesn't sound aberrant.

There's a sigh, and "Tokken," is answered. "Third time in seven days. I guess I ticked off someone."

"I once had it seven straight."

"Thirteen," the person says. "So far, that's a record."

Conversation continues, and it's like many on the transport: Comparing stories, sharing observations, but never diving to the darkness spoken of the Norries. It's kept minimal, and dismissive. Light-hearted, and empty. Even questions about family are limited, asking of children, questions of ages, and trite off-the-cuffs about marriage. It is conversation between people with nothing to share.

"Nice talking," says the person, and that's reciprocated.

The short walk home concludes at a flight of stairs to the second level. The pod is entered, and travel continues through to the sanitation chamber.

Clothes are shed and dropped in the syphon. Twenty seconds later, the body is sanitized and dried.

The first stop is the drawer and nutritional biscuit. A bite is taken and it is set on an empty shelf with the hydration capsule. Evening clothes are gathered, adorned, and the victuals are retrieved.

A desk is folded from the wall, and from the same, a folding chair is unfurled beside. The seat is filled as the hydration capsule is wedged under the lip, and another bite of the chewy bar is taken.

Tablet is booted, and daily news is reviewed. Entertaining recordings are scrolled. Brief diversions dive deeper but quickly lose interest. There is a headline about unrest in Greater Nespia's northeast, and there is a feeling of disgust as eyes fall upon it. It is swiped away, and a report claiming interface with the defensive net finally gains interest that holds for much of the night.

Details are searched. There is little found that supports the claim and the original article has no refences nor explanation of how it was possible: Only a person making a claim.

It grows late, and eyes grow heavy. Detritus is thrown into the syphon and the desk and chair are re-folded into the wall.

It was an easy day, and the body is not exhausted. Feet do not ache. There is no crushing constipation of weariness that throbs in the head. The berth is crawled into with reasonable satisfaction and mirth, and the sheets and blankets sunk into support the sentiment. Eyes close, and an arm wraps over them, but sleep is distant, and time is spent reflecting on days, and conversations, and the faces that pressed against the fence and shouted hatred.

Chapter two:

Eyes wrench open to the grating pain of morning's execution; Morpheus' sweet nectar scattered contemptuously aside. Visions cling like the aftertaste of honeydew but they are slipping away already as the tone is ended. Eyes look back, but smoke has enveloped the 4origin of the sweetened senses – only a fleeting afterthought drapes; slips away by the time feet meet the floor.

Night clothes are peeled as the sanitation chamber is approached and they are launched away into the syphon. The chamber sprays the aureolin mist and it's just as quickly blown away by the whirlwind blast. The small cube is traversed to the closet and as always, there is a fresh and neatly pressed uniform within. It is pulled on, strapped and buttoned. Shoes are slipped over feet that tap back towards the cleansing chamber for the drawer that contains one biscuit, and one hydration capsule.

It is burst between the teeth in violation of recommendations; before the first bite of nutrients is taken. A second violation incurs as it's fully eaten, as the body slumps into the bunk and fouls neat lines of the uniform.

Thoughts chew over honeydew as the moist bar is eaten. Memories that are not recalled but tasted. A hint of something that's evocative, a gustatory familiarity that fails to materialize in vision or find a name. It is taunting and the mind strains into the smoky shadows, feeling its presence just out of reach, around a corner; slipped into a well where it can't be seen.

"Please proceed to your transportation hub," erases the trail. It is an uncommon reminder of the shiftless start to the morning, and the warning is immediately heeded.

There are still plenty of others making their way towards the hub. Many feet in a concert with padded footsteps and gentle scruffs over the stone. It is a muted wave of muted people still recovering from a night of rest. Still pulling minds into clarity, and some wondering what had burdened them as they began to wake.

The usual assembly of people is found waiting for a vehicle. Few eyes bother looking up at the latest arrivals and most intentionally avert in the fear conversation might be struck while still in a mottled state. There is silence outside of quiet footsteps, and the occasional louder scruff.

The vehicle arrives, and there's no change in posture. No crush forward, no straightened position – only ears piqued for the familiar sound – at the tone that changes. Eyes spy targeted seats and once the wall of the vehicle lifts away, an orderly but determined hive moves forward to stake their claim. Those without predisposition let the hubbub settle before moving towards a place to rest their weary bones.

The seat taken, there is relief that is typical – that to rest and have no obligation. But there is also relief that is not: There is no excuse for being late.

Relief brings comfort and the body relaxes in the seat. The wall falls close and a shoulder leans into its support. Unlike most other mornings, eyes look through the window.

In most parts of the city there is little activity early in the morning and most that are observed are members of security. There a few seen already working: One, addressing damage to a building.

Another is half-submerged within the stone addressing some failure of underground technology. There is also a family in one of the yards – two children: It brings a bittersweet smile and warmth to thoughts of a partner and their own. Similar in age. Similar energy. An energy that found the need to bring the autonomous net around the backyard upcrop.

A glint shines off a crystal building as the vehicle turns. Unlike most cities on Nespia, the ones of Greater Nespia are increasingly turning to the kind. Old, stone structures replaced with new materials and skinned with glass.

Other than the northeast of the city where walls are tall and remain of stone, and the castle of the clan up in the mountains.

The vehicle skirts the edge of the city, between the foothill crops and the backs of buildings. It is a long haul in that is usually shortened by fitful sleep. But there'd been something on the mind, on waking. Something that struck deeply interesting, but from the fog of sleep it is completely lost – a memory? Taste? The mote slipped away but at the same time sharpened focus, and the typical malaise was shaken away before commute.

The shoulder begins to ache from the pressure against the wall. Eyes look to the person beside: They lean against the other wall and at least attempt to sleep. The thought not to impose by sitting straight rings an insult in the mind that crashes memories:

Of angered faces, shouted words – words of hatred. Stones were being carefully stacked in rows, and the words had been personal. They knew names. The foreman had uttered the same insult.

The revelation, "I live there," escapes aloud.

From beside, "What," is demanded with tremendous irritation.

"It's nothing," is offered softly. The mind ticks back and there's memories of honeydew. The chew of the morning biscuit in the mouth, and the slight acidity as it passed across the tongue remembered honeydew.

It's not spoken, but in the mind, "That's what it was," is repeated multiple times.

The slight lift from the beginning of descent alerts imminent arrival. It is dark, shortly after, as the tube is entered and they begin the last, short leg of the commute.

The vehicle is long and narrow. Twenty-five rows of two. It was designed to traverse the original tunnels cut across the planet, and it is not ideal. The transports that take workers down were designed to maximize the numbers taken at a time, and at the time they were intended for use in emergency evacuations. Tunnels cut to the current shelters are much broader, as are the vehicles. They no longer need to raise awkwardly as they begin to enter tunnels.

A tone sounds, the tinkey chord that spurs sunken bodies together and away from doors. An amusing, conditioned behavior that looks like practiced synchronicity. The walls of the vehicle lift away and the seats are immediately abandoned.

Corridors are followed. Feet step quickly towards assigned stations. The thrum of mining lays the underbeat that carries in the walls and through the feet. It is rhythmic, almost melodious, and the echo of the tinkey chord rings from memory in the ear and it becomes the fanfare to the beginning of the working day.

"Morning," is said as it is so often.

It's reciprocated but never built upon. The barest communication. The least possible offered as a greeting and as much notation. It is morning, and that is said, and as far as can be recalled, that scarcest gesture of recognition is all that's ever said.

"Morning," is spoken with cheer, though it's only for the person and not the transport present. That indicates the day will be long, and the body will be tired at the end of it. As it's neared, the usual, "Ready to go," is offered."

"Yeah." The person turns – eyes meet. Curiosity looks back, just as, "Ready to go," is said. The other nods, and, "Have a good one," is delivered.

There is a pause. Eyes look back again, there is a nod again, and, "You too," is the first delivery of the day.

The interaction is unusual. There is actual recognition of another – both to each other – and it shears the fog that clogs the brain to a space of clarity, of the rarity it's ever the case.

One finger presses the button that sets the transport underway. The tablet beside is lifted to review, and expectations are confirmed: The day will be thick with dispatch.

Western city deliveries are disparaged only less than Tokken. There is more delivered there than anywhere else on the planet, even places of active construction. It includes the emperor's fortress, and the residents within are the most incapable of moving anything or making decisions. Drop-offs at the fortress are more time consuming than any other place, as there is often internal conflict as to the disposition of what has been requested. Waiting to offload material at active construction sites is preferable. There is at least a sense of progression.

The vehicle moves silently through the streets. It is the oldest part of the city and least populated. The homes are large and have open space in yards unlike elsewhere in the city. Streets were not planned for transports, and many are narrow, and there is often need to make multiple-point turns to navigate through them. Deliveries are expected, but the imposition of the time needed to make them meets obscenities and angry voices: There are numerous private vehicles in the western part of the city and their occupants have no patience for obstacles that impede their progress.

It is early, still, on the first stop of the day, and there is little conflict as the transport stops. Six trips pull unmarked packages from the cargo bay, and whatever is within them is exceedingly heavy. The purveyor of the establishment said no word – a wave towards a corner, sign-off, and re-occupation with a tablet. They are left with nothing said in return, and the next stop is only a few buildings further.

More than two-dozen deliveries are offloaded by the time the star is at its acme; it is unsettling that the hold is mostly full. Another stop, and the traffic is agitated, and words spill as soon as it's clear the transport's slowing.

Words are ignored – rarely does it escalate beyond. Rarely will passengers leave their vehicles. Familiar terms bounce off the ears like tin pellets against the stone – unbothered. Anger only raised in those that sent them and watched them fall away. They are left behind to the quiet of a curio.

There are rows of shelves that are neatly arranged: Snack foods, tablets; diversions for children. It brings a scent of familiarity. A memory, or perhaps a dream. A hand reaching up as if to a parent – hand holding on to a parent's hand. Rows of everything anyone could need.

The venue entered is nothing like that faded image – flash in the memory from a dream. It is neat, and offerings are limited. Shelves are sparse and hold primarily electronica and gadgetry. There is just a small section for food and none of it's substantial.

"Ya got something," interrupts the reflection.

A small package is held, and described as, "A delivery."

"Go figure," the person says. Self-conscious humiliation falls to have become distracted while on the job, and the description is made actual. "About time," is unclear. There is uncertainty if it regards the delivery, or package.

It's left to be forgotten and return to the street brings a resumption of insults and angered words.

The transport moves on and begins the steep climb into the foothills.

They are not really foothills. Something like those are found in parts of Upper Borrean; those off the west shore of Nespia Bay are the remains of upcrops – either intentionally violated, or the result of erosion over time. But the lower levels of the upcrops are where the initial outpost of the city was created. A relative plateau with elevation that provided defensive advantage. Even with roads cut up the slope, those arriving were compromised by the angle. Over time, the outpost dug deeper, cut wider, and spread to form a wide crescent around the upcrops.

In ancient times it was unassailable, and the locale by the protected bay had the advantage of safe and sheltered waters to provide for the population: There is an abundant field of Lappen-brath that begins just outside the bay, and kraja favor the calmer waters. In times of peace, there is also more arable land than anywhere else on the planet, though most of that has been built upon.

Gates open as the vehicle approaches. The route is not the most efficient and it will likely delay delivery to others – sometimes to another day – it is a delivery of convenience to the one that will receive: Not too early that they're still waking, and prior to other obligations. The vehicle stalls at a portico and quick review of the tablet finds twenty-seven items to be delivered.

The first is an unwieldly, rectangular box, chosen because it will require the most exertion. Even with exceptional strength it is a colossal challenge to get it near the entry. It falls heavily to the surface. Arms recalibrate as they await reception. The door opens, and the person beyond looks pleased.

They say, "Well." Eyes scrape over the body and they conclude, "You're a fine specimen. I think I remember you."

There's no recollection. There are twenty-six more items to bring in, and the first is an unwanted challenge. It earns, "Where do you want this?"

"Oh," says the person – they say; they wave an arm, "Just throw it anywhere."

Arms wrap the delivery. Feet stumble forward as it's lifted. The well of gravity is dragged against its inclination and staggered to a wall in the massive orifice of a home.

It is a gaping contrast to the family home, but there are also similarities. It is huge, and open, and there are dozens of entries in view that lead to other rooms, but it is also stone. It is also carved out of the upcrops. They are not at all the same, but they are similar. Both look down on the roofs of neighbors – both are accessed by roads cut in ancient times with defense in mind.

"Beautiful home," is said, reflecting, "It reminds me of mine."

"Elite," the person says.

"What?"

"You were with Elite – roukta. That's where I know you."

It is countered, "We were Avengers: You followed?"

"Right," is said, and the question, "You're who?"

"Eantru," is answered, and the other finds some sadness, some reflection; some regret: "It's been a while."

They're told, "I'll bring in the rest of your delivery."

Nothing else compares to the abomination of the first brought in. There are a few that are large, that make for an awkward carry but there's no comparison to the mass of the first. Six trips and the entirety of the large order is neatly piled against a wall – anchored by the large, rectangular box.

"This is alright here," seeks confirmation, and it's given. There is relief at the brevity – there are often requests to open packages and sometimes to assemble the contents. There is hope the rest of the day will go as smoothly and allow for evening time to spend with family.

"Take care," is offered as position is retaken on the transport. The words are echoed, and then the other says, "Not all of us want things to stay the way they are. Some of us are on your side. Remember that."

It's unclear what the person refers to: There is no side to be on. It is confused and dismissed, with, "Thank you." One finger moves to re-engage the vehicle, and lands within the heaviness that's carried by, "It was good to see you."

Reactive eyes pull the head around to look, and find the person standing, watching the vehicle depart with hands in pockets, solemn as if they watched the procession for a funeral.

Eyes break away and the tablet's taken. They focus on the tasks demanded and scroll through, observing no evident side-tasks that will further interrupt the route.

The path continues northward, leading to the furthest northwest reaches of the city. It is direction that has rarely been taken, around the upcrops and into lower-lying terrain, where constructs are newer and more varied, and streets were better planned for vehicular traffic. Drop-offs are quick, and there is typically no conversation.

Starlight is just a gentle backdrop to towers of stone on arrival at the final destination. Save a few, most items were not an overt burden, but time, and motion, and even standing leave the body weary.

Several cases of canned goods are all that stand in the way of retiring for the evening, and four are stacked to bring that end as soon as possible. A quick, "Where to," hopes to quickly move for a second load, but it meets unfortunate interest:

"It's good to see you," is followed by, "How've you been?"

"Good," is answered. To clarify, the question is stated fully: "Where do you want the cases stacked?"

"Same place," is answered – hand motions for the corner.

The goods are placed quickly but hope to continue is paused. The aisle is not blocked, but the person stands partly in it and engaged. They hold an unsettling smile, and the same is in the words, "How's the family?"

The answer is, "Good," and, "Thanks for asking," is intended to move them past the interaction.

Unfortunately, the person says, "Kids have got to be close to placement. Any suspicions?"

"What?"

"Their education. They were, I think, four or five last time you came through here."

"They are four or five – three and five." It's confirmed, "They're three and five. Why do you ask?"

The smile is gone. It's replaced by sad and disappointment. There is a nod – understanding: "I must have confused you. With someone else."

"Right," is agreed: "I'll get the remainder of your order."

Pace increases with the hope that a show of urgency prevents further conversation. Five cases are stacked to move the operation just one step closer towards the end. Conversations in the field are always awkward. There is a disconnect between existence and what's spoken, as if they live in an alternate reality. There is fortunately no more said as the product is paraded through the venue. The final three are stacked neatly on the others, and, "Have a good day," is meant as the conclusion to the day. However, that conclusion is postponed as the person inserts themselves to obstruct the exit.

Air is pulled deep into the lungs to maintain calm. There is a strong urge to fling the person to the side – memories flash: Images on rockface. Bodies covered in sweat and smears of blood – it is shaken away. Another breath is taken, but its intent is truly to calm. To smooth the memories back from off the cliff – again, the image is shaken away.

"You're okay," is said with kindness. The words, "I'm sorry," are soft. It's explained, "I thought you were someone else. You look alike. We had a great conversation over roukta – a former player with Elite. Just mistaken identity," they say: "I didn't mean to upset you."

"I," is begun, and stutters, "I. I'm tired. Please accept my apology – your order is complete."

The tablet is held forward for confirmation and that's given, and followed:

"If you ever need help, or you need to find safety, use the utility access in the street: They can't see you down there. Keep going deeper and you'll find help."

"Right," is answered. The opportunity is taken to move past and open the door. It's briefly paused as exit begins, to turn back, to state, "I don't need help." Departure halts once more to add, "Or safety." A third time, eyes look back as it rings too sinister, and the person's left with, "Have a good night."

"The covers in the street," is ignored. "If you need help, or safety – listen: You can find it through the tunnels."

The calls are left behind. There is a warning installed long before, to avoid tunnels at all costs. Memory still holds strong of a time that warning was ignored, and there is surety that mistake will not repeat.

The sky is completely dark by the time return meets the entrance to the tunnel, other than the pinpoint light of distant stars that flicker through the atmosphere. It is a contrast to the glow inside the tube that seems much brighter when entered in the dark.

Light of the depot begins a warmer glow and fortells the day is nearly over. Posture is straightened, and feet plant rigidly and apart; eyes through the window – ever diligent. It is impossible to remain in that position an entire day, and that's understood. It is also understood that failing to do so will be scapegoated as the reason for an incident – further, at least an effort at the start and end of journeys, or for potential supervisors should be given show.

The vehicle guides itself to its bay, and there's no hesitation: The last entry is entered, and the tablet's marched to the receiver and plugged in. As with posture, there is the show of waiting for the purple light, ensuring information transfers and the route is cleared. Purple glows and welcome retreat begins towards home – the monitor given, "Have a good night," and that's returned.

It is quiet at the transportation hub due to the hour. It is a more demure crowd, one that has put in physical exertion, and sometimes mental when cooperating with the clan. It is night, and everyone that's waiting is exhausted, and hungry. Eyes are looking forward to closing shut – too late for entertaining children; only time for quiet conversation with a partner.

A vehicle soon arrives and shortly after sings the familiar tone. Doors open and the few scatter into the many rows.

There are no conversations with the evening riders. They are separated, and have been faced with the awkward conversations throughout the day that more than double the exhaustion of physical labor; from standing on the operator's platform for many hours. There is only the gentle purring of the machinery that can easily lure weary bodies to the realm of sleep.

From that domain, a dozen plus move upright at the familiar tinkey tone. The walls lift away, and all but two exit for the final leg of the day.

There is a weariness in the legs that let feet slough, but they are not sore, nor tired. They are sapped by conversation. By the odd circulature of words and statements. Navigating through them is treacherous; despite all warnings to ignore them – sometimes it's impossible. The final steps up to the pod are heavy and the door's met with relief. It is allowed to close and seal the world away. Conversations disappear as the head rolls back, eyes close; a breath escapes. If not for hunger, it's possible that sleep would fall and the body would remain in vertical position throughout the night.

Hunger is strong.

Eyes reopen to the ceiling and remain as the walk to the other end begins. Shoes are pealed, clothes are stripped, and together they're chucked at the syphon and disappear. The sanitation chamber acts instantly to represent its name, spraying the oily, saffron salve with violating entirety. It is whipped to insignificance by the hurricane that follows.

The late-night return finds appreciation for the extremity of the operation and the instant wind draws down, draw to the drawer is answered and the nutrient bar's ripped open.

The first bite is large, and salivation is limited by dehydration, however, there is such satisfaction to gain sustenance, that it's ground extensively in the teeth. It is both satisfying, and necessary. The hydration capsule's locked under the lip for ensuing, smaller bites, and the remainder of the bar is consumed while standing beside the drawer from where the cake was taken.

There is relief to have something in the stomach. Sugar can be felt entering the veins giving a sense of enervation, but it is just enough to move to the adjacent cupboard. The soft nightwear is extracted and slipped over limbs before collapsing into the berth.

It is familiar, and comfortable. It is welcoming and exactly the right warmth. It is so relaxing that thought to boot the tablet is left at that.

It was a challenging day, and the body is exhausted. Feet throb and pressure against the wall helps to massage the discomfort away. There is a fog in the mind that isn't exhaustion – not physical. It is from the interaction with others. From what they say, and the odd retraction that follows.

Sheets and blankets are pulled over the body and wrapped firmly: A cocoon of comfort. Eyes close, and an arm wraps over them, and sleep is tugging already. It battles against statements and flashes of memory. Flashes of dreams. Reflection of children's voices, and there's one that is echoing that doesn't have a name.

Chapter three:

Eyes open to emerge from nothing. From complete emptiness to the dim light and intolerable grating. The tone is killed and the mind looks for any inkling of what might have happened through the night but there was nothing, or the mind declined to record the slightest memento.

Four days of delivery to the northeast construction zone have left muscles sore, and the body faced with regret to wake. The days of easy offload with a crane are exchanged for hand retrieval and delivery to multiple locations – often through multiple stories. The first day it was a challenge taken. By the second it was no longer wanted.

Sore feet hit the floor and the effort to remove nightclothes is slowed by the stiffness in the muscles. The feet shuffle towards the sanitation chamber and the suction of the syphon's felt as the clothes are set against it.

The spray erupts to coat the body, and for once, the wind that follows's not appreciated. The usual satisfaction, the sense of rejuvenation is absent: It is just another assault against muscles that are unwilling to even stand. They are unwilling to move after the blast dies down, and there is little motivation to move towards clothes and food.

Instructions fall: "Please exit the sanitation chamber."

"Of course," is returned, though it's unlikely anyone will have heard.

Capsule and cookie are pulled from the drawer on the way to the cabinet. They are set in the berth while the uniform is extracted and put on. The body sags into bunk, and the capsule is burst between teeth against better judgment. The biscuit is chewed slowly and steadily, and there are no more reminders necessary. If another day of delivering materials is assigned, then it will be done without complaint. If the body sags under the weight of materials delivered, steps will be taken with aggression, and they will arrive without any demonstration of fatigue. Those of the northeast city deserve a better future and opportunity, and those that have it have no complaint.

The flow of workers march towards their transportation hubs with silent respect for one another. They are the backbone of the world. They build the cities, sanitize the dreck, press and deliver uniforms, and farm the foothills that feed the population. Without those that march in the morning, the entire function of society would fall apart.

A place is taken to the side of the crowd gathered to board the transport. It is a typical morning, a typical crowd, until the person beside, says, "Morning."

Eyes turn and they're looking back. Eyes bead in with offensive scrutiny. They're told, "Morning," and then ignored. Turned away from as a demonstration of the imposition made, of the impropriety to interact in the early morning.

There is no further interaction, but when the walls rise, they are observed – observed to follow. An empty row is targeted, but it's only to walk through. To walk around and sit beside another.

There is a slight commotion behind, but it's ignored. "I'm sitting there," is heard, but eyes don't turn. There is some scruffing and grunts, and it's assumed a new recruit has yet to understand accepted protocol. It is likely they were just trying to be friendly

– it is likely they don't understand the rules for how the bodies sort into the seating.

The walls fall, and at least there's quiet. Bodies separate and lean against the walls. Heads snuggle in to the sweet position at the corner of the headrest where it meets the surface. Bodies slouch, and legs stretch out. Eyelids fall, prepared for the redemptive moments of sleep that are often rewarded during the journey.

A tinkey tone forewarns of imminent breach. There is a last second pull away before the wall lifts to let passengers' escape.

It feels like eyes had just closed. It seems like the start was followed instantly by the end. There were no interruptions to the slumber. No flashes of light nor changes of direction that startled somnolence, and there are no memories of journeys through the subconscious. There is only a fog that was the same fog that was woken from.

The short walk to the bay uses every step as an opportunity to shake it off. The thrum of machinery is focused on to alight the senses. Ears pull from conversations and try to understand what is being said. Eyes stretch wide to view those passing, and they inadvertently catch one that's looking back.

They're told, "Morning," and that's given back. A nod, a smile, and the person waves, and it turns the body to reciprocate the gesture.

There is a person that is not far behind. Walking behind others, but it feels as if there's an effort to be concealed. They are casual and not looking back, but there's a sense in the gut there's trouble.

It's irrational and likely to result in censure, but a monitor passed is told, "Assist."

They spin immediately. They match step, and ask, "How can I assist?"

"This is probably nothing," and already there's regret. But there are memories ingrained of lessons taught to trust the senses. There are holds and footstops that pull out of the rock, even though there's nowhere to climb. However, there's more confidence as those are seen. There are memories and experience of trusting senses, and it's reported, "There's a person that's behind me. I don't recognize them and they haven't behaved appropriately. I feel like they're following me."

"Understood," is spoken quietly, and more loudly, "Your complaint is registered."

They peel away and walk with determination back to their station. However, other monitors are observed on alert and are scanning those that pass.

There is relief to arrive at the bay with no one else. There is more relief that the transport is not one destined for construction.

It is unusual. It is divided into sections. There is a short part where the operator stands, and another that is a flatbed that holds equipment. It covers almost the entire length of that section, overlaps the width and is twice the height of a person. It appears to be a single item, however, it's completely covered.

"One stop," is asked with cheer, because it has been unusual of late. One stops in the northeast have been offloading by hand and delivering material to where it's needed. The equipment on the transport looks like one piece that is too large for physical extraction.

"You have been given clearance one," is answered.

It does not answer the question, what the payload is, nor the destination, but it is enlivening. It is a euphoric moment. It is validation to the work, the labor, the effort that has been rendered without complaint and without abatement.

The person is told, "Thank you: I don't know who to thank – I'm extremely grateful. I swear I'll deliver on that honor." Again, the person is offered thanks.

"You've earned it," is stated. "They wanted to push you the last few days, and you didn't wince. Keep it up – you've got a future here."

"I want that more than anything," is said, and a black slab smashes into the brain.

It was earnest, sincere, but the brain is crushed by the violence of the monolith landing. A flash of memories, of voices, of hopes, and dreams, and celebrations in the circle of victory on the roukta field. There are voices that are just out of reach, and the space of existence melts in their incomprehensible pleas.

"I look forward to working with you," breaks the wash. The sea of debris crashing at the shore of memory sinks into the sands and becomes just a muted echo. A wave slowly leaving the shore and sinking back to the sea.

There is a sound, but it washes into the waves crashing into conversation. Ideas of corroboration push against the waves of dissonance, and there is a tinkey chord that pushes the mind-field fog onto the edges. That allows for a clearing of space to obligations and position is taken on the operator's platform.

A full hand presses against the button. That is the method that was trained during sessions on security protocol but it was soon discovered that a slap, a single finger, or even an elbow could activate the vehicle. Cynicism and bemusement have slugged at the button with doubts to its biometric claims. With a level one clearance, the infantile antics are again abandoned for formality.

The vehicle begins its journey and a nod is shared between monitor and the newly minted, highest-level operator. It travels a route that is different from every one that has been followed before and there is recognition that the cargo wouldn't fit through those narrow tunnels. Instead, there is a channel that leads directly through the active minefield. Equipment is observed carefully slicing the stone to predetermined specifications. As the passage is taken, there is some concern to see the archways that have been built in the vacuous opening to support the overhead stone — beneath thousands of tons of water.

They are left behind for another channel, and it is cleanly cut and well lit, in contrast to the ancient tunnels that are generally traversed. They are more akin to the pass-throughs in rims, or heading down towards Akkrat.

A turn brings the exit into view, but there's a booth hollowed from the stone. Just past, there is a solid gate, and there are numerous devices positioned on either side of the exit.

It is approached carefully. The vehicle comes to a stop at a sliding window, and that opens once completely at a stop.

An object is held out, and, "Handprint," is demanded. There is a purple glow that is reminiscent of the clearance to end a day, and the person then asks, "Have you seen anything suspicious? Anything you need to report."

Pride is swelling, and it's reported, "I mentioned my concern: There was a person that was acting unusual and they seemed to be following. I reported it to a monitor."

The person slightly withdraws. They consult a tablet and scroll through information.

Lights on equipment on either side illuminate, and machinery begins sliding the length of the vehicle. It scans to the back, probes are sent below, and the equipment continues to monitor until it's return.

There is more consultation with the tablet, and then the request, "Name."

It's given: "Eantru – Greater Nespia."

"Safe journeys," is offered and the gate begins to open.

The exit is to familiar territory. Deliveries have been infrequent, but it is recognized as the farthest, western part of the city. Where homes are infrequent and ventures are mostly absent.

The vehicle begins a wind around the circle of upcrop that is the background to the emperor's vast complex. But it is a route behind. One that passes a curiously undeveloped plateau and then begins a seemingly random maze into the forest. Eyes are fixed ahead, and legs stand firmly, as there's a sense of concern that reignites the earlier worry.

A shiver cuts into the spine, with, "You're," as quiet's broken, and eyes whip around to see, "A real pain in the neck," spoken.

Head wrenches – eyes scan. The body's turned to take defensive stance against the console, but there is only one: One person standing paces away and holding on to the edge of the vehicle.

The position of the arm is noted and reciprocated.

It ignites a whirl of thoughts. There are memories that are confetti but the image of the pieces is still discernible. There are thoughts, and flashes, and something about a store: Flour bags and candles.

The person's told, "I designed that, you know."

Unexpected, and confused, they answer back, "Designed what?"

It is already dismissed as it's spoken. The move inward is underway as the words are said. The assault engages expecting a conversation's being started, and expecting the attacked will be unprepared.

However, as that begins, there's an understanding of what was said. It's noted that the fist is held identically. There is a sudden drop of absolute dismay as the words and positioning register. It is at that moment that the body of the assailant becomes incapacitated and tumbles with a crunch onto the floor.

A hand scraps for emergency assistance. The unused button at the bottom of the console's pressed, and a call is made: "I'm under attack. I need help."

Eyes scan the scenery. The vehicle is looked over with a new imperative – look back, look out; scan ordered for anything out of the ordinary.

Legs collapse at sudden incapacitation. Muscles are jelly and the mind becomes a fog of scattered remnants – pieces of ideas. Parts of memories. Conversations that were treasured. An interrogation followed the prior time the body was incapacitated with the weapon. This time, there are no questions – frantic conversation:

"Pull the link."

"Done."

"Get their hand on the sensor."

There are grunts, and foul words as an arm is tugged, as another lifts beneath the shoulders. A hand is slapped against the console button and the vehicle is turned from its plotted course.

There are four squeezed into the small space, and suspected more are waiting from wherever it was they came. As muscle use begins returning, thoughts turn to the method of attack.

There is a cry as legs are whipped, and the motion is used to disrupt another two. The last is wary but focused on the tablet, but with a lunge, the single stept between them is instantly closed.

A desperate cry, "Hit – hit: Hit."

The one at controls is quick and able to dodge the direct strike, but there's a wince, and the vehicle begins to move erratically.

The connection's made and a quick stab for the tablet just misses. Two more recover and as one reaches out, their hand is taken and they're thrown from the moving vehicle. The second is already attempting assault, but proximity leaves them exposed and a fist lands square and they crumple to the floor.

The one breaking over the console rasps, "Hit them."

Anothwer yells, "I did."

"Again."

Another sting, and muscles begin to fail. Three more enter and begin an attempt to separate the wrestling pair, but stiff muscles act as a hinderance to their efforts. A third jolt, and eyes begin to blur. With every bit of effort mustered, legs push, fist rises and in a single motion the body inches forward and the arm pushes past excruciating pain to bring the fist down with any amount of force.

The fourth shot is taken just prior to the eruption of violent sound, of metal hitting stone. Bodies are thrown, but the world's already fading. By the time the ground is met, everything's already turned to black.

Chapter four:

A dewdrop sings – the quiet sound of a soft mallet on columbrum. Muted delicacy that enlightens senses in a way that nothing else is able. A song that awakens the mind even more than love, and the song is love. It sings a heartache that resonates in minor chord that cannot resolve. It is beauty and joy, purity and love; innocence and trust. It hangs in the air in a minor chord that longs to progress back to the root, but there is no anchor. The tree drifts only forward.

The chord plays melancholy in the symphony of children's voices. It plays across excited yelps and through enthusiastic thoughts. It hangs on the edges of visions shared. Of thoughts and creations. It cries to the moon eyes of trust that look up and believe those looked to have any answers.

Music swells in a sorrowed cry against the future. It rises as a wave of sound that crushes down with violence and suffering. That rips away tomorrows and shreds family. A crescendo that climbs to a deafening level over the syncopated throbbing of a kettle drum – drubbing endlessly. An arrhythmic thrum that beats into the song and won't end – cannot end: It is the end, and the pounding crushes songs, columbrums, dreams and memories. A dewdrop sang and it was drowned away by the endless thrubbing of eternity.

One note, and then three more, and the pounding cacophony is just an afterthought. A noise cast aside and disregarded for the quiet songs of two dewdrops. A joy of life that exists in perfection, in a song that rises out of oblivion to paint nothing with the exquisite for just a moment. One note, and then three more.

It is a chorus of life and the chord is the embodiment of existence. It is the reason, and purpose, and being. It is the why that lies are told and veils are floated over everything. It is decisions made that cannot be understood and conviction that lies on their observance. It is a minor chord that sings of starlight.

A soft mallet on columbrum. A sweetness drunk that can be shielded but not forgotten. A minor chord that fell at the moment of birth and grew more sorrowed the longer that it lived. A chord played that resonates sweetly, and the notes are clung to even after they fade. Even once the columbrum falls silent, they remain, held as an imprint within an incomprehensible network of connections for the entirety of known existence.

The chord paints a moment on nothing and is held as the most important resonance within the strings of emptiness. A music played across them that will ring once, and then begin to fade. First in the realm of eternity, and eventually to all that were present and shared that moment of experience. A chord played that sits as a momentary dewdrop falling anomalously across the vastness and insignificance of everything. It falls away as a dewdrop that circles the breadth of endlessness.

Two pearls in an orbit around nothing. Silver spheres that shift and mutate as they follow the circuit around the well of gravity. They are all that exist in the sightless vapor. A coalesce of impossibility, delicate and in a state of perilous fragility but with the power to control the worlds of others. Two, small, glimmering moments that reflect against wide eyes that fall sick with love and pride – held with such gratuitous indulgence: Two stars that will never fully ignite. They will never be as big, nor bright, nor soar as high as only moon eyes see them. Only in the reflection of the moon are they the universe, the whole of everything and totality. Imperfect flashes in a wink of time that are greater than anything else that will ever exist.

Two, tiny spheres that circle the well. That follow time in a distant orbit. Two glorious metal pearls that reflect starlight that doesn't exist. That encircle the universe with increasing pace that isn't felt while they still are looking to a fireball to reflect upon them. Slowly moving towards the center. Slowly slipping lower, and moving faster.

Quicksilver webs scatter as the pebbles are torn apart. As they reach terminal velocity and the orbs are pulled into their smaller parts – into shimmering threads that scatter across nothingness to reflect starlight for just a moment longer. Until other stars are rent apart as they meet the center, and the reflection that was held in memory is finally shredded altogether. One after the other, they slip away. Fall to the center and fade, and eventually there will be no others that will replace them. The poison licks of silver will scatter the universe and eliminate any evidence they ever existed.

A tone sounds, and three others follow. It is sad, and beautiful. Nothing compares, and it is tragic that it is – even the strands that stand the longest. Stars streak through the atmosphere, shining the brightest of their lives as they descend on fire and to certain destruction. Explosions of kettle drums beat with constant reminder of the infirmity of the light that surrounds.

It is always underfoot as the music plays. It is incongruent to the beauty and to the raindrops of joy from children's voices. From their shrieks as they play their games. Their laughter, questions, and revelations. The song is beautiful and sorrowful, and it is continuously interrupted – disturbed – by the throbbing underfoot: Guilt and regret. Remorse, and sorrow. They seep out from beneath the veil and are clouds across the starlight.

A chord plays, and it is a reminder of a moment in time, where time was shared and the music was a conversation. When the emotion and understanding of experience was shared through the wrenching sounds of passion across a metal drum. Where chords resolved, and the passion felt was expressed with increased tempo. The chord plays, and the symphony follows as tiny trails of silver scatter across the landscape in ever smaller threads until they are indistinguishable from nothing.

The chord fades to silence and even the throbbing onslaught is drowned beneath the waters. A heartbeat quieting as the visions melt away. An afterthought – an echo: The beat of life that is one misstep away from ending it.

It is dark, but the sound of children's laughter brings silver threads to leak away from the shallow breaths of torpidity, breaking light across the emptiness, and giving soundtrack to existence. The cheer is muddled. Not drowned beneath water, but muted as if heard the wrong side of thick glass. It is not a note but chords that are wreathed with tight reverb and a mute. The sounds are joy, but they sing with sorrow as they call from the other side – blinded by a frosted window that only allows their shadows to reach through.

Words call – there are many. They are indistinguishable, but it is understood that they sing a song. It is not melodic – it is not progressive. It is a song that is tied to the passing of time. A song from the origins of time. The chorus swells with bittersweet fervor over the growing footstep of a heavy drum, and the loud squeal of a rusty hinge foretells the swell and clarity of sound that comes fully on.

Seas of children dressed in their uniforms sing wordless melodies. They sway like a field of grass, together, marching in place, arms linked together across the shoulders of those beside.

They are singing a song that is the betrayal of their existence. A wall of sound that rises louder to decry the lies and perversion of their innocence. An army of children that sway together in rows of opposition. The sound rises, and then it falls away.

To a haunting singularity – one voice, crying the aria of their entirety into nothing. The voice is clear, and pure, and rises with emotion that grows stronger as it's joined by one other. They sing together. They join and harmonize, and sing the song that is moboti.

"Moboti?" Eyes look up. Haunted and terrified.

Arms reach out to protect them. To pull them close and to keep them from inevitability. Stumbled gibberish gushes like bilge water from a hull to assure them like a sinking ship that everything is fine. Arms reach out and they splinter away as jagged, metal shards that only bring harm. That are incapable of protecting and easing the distress from the eyes that looked up and asked for honesty.

That wondered why lies and veils were laid across existence. Why truth was shirked for a claim of happiness and life.

Moon eyes look up to eyes that look back, and through to other eyes that looked down to the same moons that beg the question. That wonder why veils cover every answer. Why unilateral decisions are made without a proper explanation.

Eyes from the past are looked back upon, and there is sympathy. There is understanding. Because there is a chord that plays, and it is the greatest joy and beauty in the universe. It is the entire symphony playing for two small dewdrops that laugh in commons as feet tiptoe across the nearly frozen growth and do not feel the drum beneath it pounding.

There is innocence, and freedom. There is belief and ideality. There are two beautiful voices that sing, "Moboti," with a syrup so sweet it's heartbreaking.

Eyes look down and love reflects through generations. Understanding of experience bleeds sympathy that is felt as love by those that are looked upon.

They are given answers that are covered in shroud. Truth is smothered with pillows for a question asked in pure innocence. Words shower on them without providing answers – they give instructions, and they are understood to be misleading. Even when young. Truth is always standing in the background, and it's growing presence becomes impossible to ignore, but that is the very instruction that is given.

A note plays, and two more follow. Two, quicksilver raindrops dance across the surface of the planet with no conception of nothing. They laugh at frozen feet and find joy in simple things: Watching dust dancing in the starlight. Creating laughter and entertainment for themselves as they discover humor. Humor that begins to fray at their integrity. That begins to tease away quicksilver strings that are left as a littered trail in their mortified wake. As they see the world and wonder why their Moboti chose to hide it from them. From the moon eyes that looked in for answers and protection.

The song plays, and it is the song of everything. It is glorious, and morose, but there is a moment where it reaches for elation. Where the song becomes an ocean as the music rises in a massive wave, as it carries life and brings feet to solid ground. It is the moment that rests after the columbrum is played. The music at its highest, but the moment is the quietest. Where there is a feeling that cannot be explained, but it is from that moment that two dewdrops are born into existence, and there is no greater wish than they will share that moment, and for them – it will never end.

"Live," is told to children.

Dalune looks back, and says, "Enjoy your life."

The vision becomes a liquid silver face that begins flowing into the streams of mercury that cut across the landscape. Streams that thin into threads that flay into tiny particles only able to scarcely glint back at the starlight when fallen at certain angles.

Glitter that falls against darkness and blinks away as it falls flat, out of the reach of starlight and existence. The last falls down and with no reflection, the star falls with the mercury and turns to black.

Eyes flutter, and the world is as blurred as children through frosted glass. There are words, but they remain incomprehensible. Eyes squint and the rows of lines that reach from floor to ceiling are interpreted as bars. The shadows beyond share the features of people, and there are several. They speak quietly, but an occasional peak escapes – often laughter.

Eyes blink for clarity, but it is little improved. Ears stretch but the conversation remains beyond reach.

The head is lifted with the hope that anything will be caught, but that which is, gets spoken loudly:

"Looks like the sleeping giant's waking up."

Feet walk over with an echo against the solid surface. Metal rattles, and, "You're lucky we didn't leave you, ya miserable crackwad," rattles like the bars with great hostility. Metal rattles and the vision turns. Footsteps plod across the room, and "Never could stand Marphy," is returned:

"Watch yourself. Half the room's Marphy."

"You know where you stand," brings laughter.

The conversation that resumes is cheerful. It grows louder with the waking of their guest, and it is almost celebratory.

Stories are shared. Claims are staked and cut back down. There is camaraderie within the room and those within are unconcerned about anything that's happened, however, concern is deep, if uncertain:

Thoughts look back to rain and frozen feet. There was an image that melted into rivers and music played. A thought had been in mind but the details have gone missing. All that's known with certainty is there is a delivery that has to be made. There'd been a clearance to level one, and the first delivery was being taken through the forest.

The mind crashes into memories, and there is rage. Eyes press away the fog and find minimal improvement, but enough to clarify the circumstance. To understand that the vehicle was highjacked and those behind it had taken in a prisoner.

Arms and legs are discovered to be unrestrained and the bars are used as a crutch to pull upright, to stand and face the faceless that have quieted, beyond. Bars are clutched, and like the one that demonstrated prior, they are shaken to cause a racket. However, unlike before, they are shaken with revenge in thought and there is violence. They are intensely ripped from side to side. Vibrations reverberate, assaulting hands, and arms, and shoulders. The back is aching as the door is finally broken free, and there are shrieks of terror as the shadow that approached is the first one targeted.

"Hit," is shouted desperately. "Hit – hurry: Hurry – hit them."

Tiny shrapnel pierces the flesh with a sting that has become familiar. But response is also, and if it's the dying breath, it's used to exact vengeance: The shadow is grabbed by the neck and thrown against the broken cage. The sound of the body breaking against the metal is a satisfying end as the world goes dark.

Chapter five:

Eyes blink open to a room that is filled with conversation. The mind grasps back and lands at forests, feet, and murky vision, but there's no thread connecting them.

Hands and feet are found unnecessarily bound as a prison cell already bestows confinement. There is nothing within except the thin mat that is laid upon. Like bound hands, the entry to the cell is unnecessarily secured with several chains.

Outside the cell, there are dozens assembled in the room. Most wear dark clothing and utility belts that hold a variety of implements. All backs are turned and there is a focus on several that are the center of conversation and attention: Assignments and plans for an imminent operation.

The conversation holds the attention of every one of them, and they are blind to the attempts at escape – immaterial as the bindings are non-pliant and secure. Stock is taken of the cage and there are numerous vulnerabilities – a likely reason for the chains: Bars stretch from rock to rock and there is evidence of damage to their anchor. There is a flash from memory of violence, but it is clouded and just a wisp; floats away as thoughts stay focused on the present. Those thoughts find little positive.

Eyes close, and all that can be done is listen, and wait for opportunity.

The discussion is lively and uninhibited. Memories flash back to an attack – the vehicle at the center of the plans: Spoken openly. Strategies discussed to broach the quarry – either believing eyes still sleep, or they're irrelevant. That tilts towards the latter as explanation for continued life is crudely spoken:

"You want my opinion, we should just cut off a hand and let 'em bleed out in the forest."

"I wish," is a sentiment that's met with wide agreement.

Voices ascend into less coordinated conversation. Separate discussions compete to be heard. There is laughter and bawdy humor trickles from the noise. There is denigration heard within the voices that is familiar, that makes mockery of failures and reactions.

It is a reflection back to days that were spent scrambling over rocks, of clobbering opponents, and failing because a missed hold, or mis-judged footstop brought unrecoverable failure. Or a launch to take an opponent out was countered, or occasionally completely missed. Guilt was mollified by the same humor in the room. Mockery, but acknowledgement that sometimes victories came down to luck. "You took a shot," reverberates in the memories as it's spoken in the present.

The voices quiet. There are greetings that begin with the sound of a sliding closure, and the language becomes more formal.

"Take the chains off. I'd like to wake them."

The request meets warning: Trauma is shared, of violence that shredded bars that left one seriously injured.

"That's three," it's pointed out.

"Well," the person suggests, "They weren't expecting us, were they?"

A hand rests upon the shoulder through the bars and begins to gently rock; it's asked, "Can you hear me."

"Had a weapon, too," strives to further communicate the dangers – as the ominous, "One of ours."

"Interesting." The hand withdraws, as wonder asks, "Now, how would you get your hands on that?"

From the floor it's explained, "I made it."

It's shared, "They said that on the transport. Thought it was a fake-out, but – it was there."

The order, "I want this open," is stated firmly. Attempted protest, is given, "Not a conversation. Get it open."

There are open grumblings but the order passed is heeded. There is the sound of metal on metal as locks are lifted and removed, as chains are extracted from the bars, and the useless door is tossed aside.

"It's open," is offered with contempt. Not long after, a person with a frame for roukta enters, and they kneel not a body-length away.

"I want to apologize," they say: "For our introduction. We expected someone else would be operating the vehicle. That was the start to a very difficult day. Most of those difficulties have been trying to figure out how to work with you. If I remove the bindings, will you give me your word you won't assault anyone?"

Harsh words are called with anger: "Don't forget we almost lost the vehicle."

More angrily, another reminds, "Don't forget Rishi."

"Or Kiklon," another adds.

"Three down, and eleven injured," is the score between the vehicle and the jailbreak.

"We're fortunate," the person kneeling says, "No one was lost. And that's as much," they say, "For you."

Hands break loose and the urge is strong to use the moment to attack. But better sense registers the odds, and simply uses them to move to a seated position.

The person looking back is considerably older. They are still fit, but there are hints of gray and the weariness of time and experience show their toll.

They say, "You're Antru," and there is a rejection to that name. There is an anger that rises. The urge for violence is only stifled because feet are still restrained. Eyes look up and meet the others, as it's understood it was intentional. They claim, "We've been looking for you. I know your parents. I've worked with Éayren for many years. They will be ecstatic to know we've found you."

Feet are loosed, but the names have given a rise to fog. The anger set loose by one is extinguished by the torrent that floods with mention of the others. There are broken pieces, and flashes, and memories that swim in a whirlpool of chaos that finds no sense. Scattered pieces are a cacophony of breaking glass that remove the frosted barrier, but the light exposed is too bright to comprehend.

Words speak from the hurricane: "You're still cloudy. It will all start coming back."

There is a sound that catches in the ear. It is like a rubber ball that falls against a metal surface. It is a note, and then others ring off in the distance. There is something that breaks through, and it's overwhelming.

Hands rest on shoulders. The person draws near and watches with sympathy. They say, "You are why we do what we do. We aren't your enemy. We're here to help you."

A cold breeze drifts in the words, "We've got the chance." It is angry, and there is still enmity that targets the broken body in the cage: "That's our ticket."

"Not tonight," is stated. The person rises, and still calm, insists, "They need to heal. We'll have other opportunities."

Anger screams, "We have a shot."

The order's given: "Antru rests. We'll find another way."

There is protest, but the person continues through another exit and leaves those gathered to grumble their misfortune. They look angrily to the wilted person in the cage, and all the misfortune, all the failures are assigned in that direction. All the injuries, the betrayal, and damaged vehicles are laid at the feet of the person that sits uncomfortably against the bars as a lick of silver poison slips from the corner of their eye.

There are notes that are piercing through the fog – a sharp peal of laughter. There are children's voices, and an accusation wondering, "Moboti – why?"

The conversation beyond isn't heard, but it is in violation of the orders that were given. There is an opportunity. There's a chance to turn the tide and gain an edge – to get a foothold on the blank face of a mountain. To find a drop of blood for a desiccated body.

"Get up," is ordered.

Rough hands grasp underneath the shoulders and pull the withered body to a stand. There are warnings and threats, but they're not heard. The world is a blur of incomplete pieces and inconsistency. The known is a veil that has been tattered and can no longer conceal the macerated injuries that seethe beneath.

There are wounded eyes, and a metal drum. There are warnings, and visions of evening study. There is a note played, and two others in the distance. There is a sound held in the ear that is the soundtrack to an existence that is distant and scrubbed from recall, but its tendrils have begun to slither out and they shred the picture of reality.

It is a reality that is played out in the mind on the shreds of paper from an ancient tome with a cartoonish character in the corner that once was funny. But the vision is only a mute against the music anymore.

A hand is pulled to slap against a sensor on the console. The noise and fog dissipate like a waterfall that ends, that leaves nothing but the seeping rock behind in presence.

The platform's packed with seven present, and the vehicle has already begun to move. Muscles tense, and, "Don't," is said. The word brings pause, and it's followed by a threat:

"We'll get you there and dump you. But if you try anything, you won't walk away again."

The words are not even acknowledged because there is a song playing through the mind. It is intimately familiar, but an alien presence. It is a melody that pulls at the chest and fills the mind. It is familiar but impossible to pinpoint where it's from or why it tugs so strongly and brings countering emotions.

Strong emotions that overwhelm more than the urge to bring violence while sitting in the cell. There is a feeling that is both elation, and devastation. There is heartache and loss, but that's overlayed on the deepest love and joy.

"Ready, now," tangles the moment into reflections. Into thoughts and fog that persists, though there is a glimmer on the edges.

There are familiar sights: The vehicle travels through the forest and it is approaching the backside of Nespia. Near the upcrops that shield the fortress of the emperor, and not far from the wide entrance to the quarry.

It is that observation that brings deep dread and concern for what is happening. Eyes focus, mind sharpens, and stock is taken of the situation: The vehicle did not arrive at its destination. The delivery was not fulfilled. There are no excuses, and eyes turn back to find the second half of the two-part vehicle is missing.

There are seven others standing on the operator's platform. Four have fists held in a position that is recognized as defensive and surely backed with concealed weapons. There is not an opportunity for action under the circumstances as their focus remains concentrated: Flashes in memory recall a violence of thrown bodies, of clashes, and the sound of metal being damaged at an impact.

"You know the way," Antru marvels.

It's answered, "We're familiar."

"Do you have a plan to get in?"

It's explained, "You're our plan."

The offer's made, "I can help," but it's stifled back: "You've done enough."

It had never crossed the mind, but tunnels had always been open on return. It's considered possible, no one's discovered the delivery never made it, and the vehicle and body are just a passkey to get inside, and that might be the opportunity. It might be the last breath ever taken, but the guard could be warned as they're passed.

The mind steels to the plan. Anxiety rises exponentially as the dip is seen rapidly approaching. The heart is beating in the chest as two outcrops are seen, and the one to the right targeted.

The vehicle moves forward at exactly the right speed, and it is surely scanned: Hope rises as a guard steps out onto the platform and raises a hand. Words are on the lips, a hand is rising to gain attention, when there's a flash, and the person is obliterated.

"No," ricochets in the cabin – yelled with anger, and inadvertently.

Fury takes over, even before it's seen the other guard has met the same fate. Rage eliminates concern for safety and an eruption of violence explodes within the confined space of the platform.

Fists and elbow bash everyone in proximity. Knees jab, and feet kick. There is blood already and one body has fallen limply when the target's met: The tablet is ripped away and violently smashed against the console.

There are screams as the vehicle careens. They have made the tunnel but the vehicle's turned and speed's increasing. In the narrow confines it is a moment later that it impacts against the wall.

The corner of the vehicle nips the wall, and it's spun away. It sways and bounces towards the other across the roadway and it's still attempting to accelerate. There are shouts of desperation that fall at their antagonist, but they go ignored: Senses are lit like they haven't been for years. Angles are watched and motion is carefully monitored – just before another impact, feet press and push the body off the platform and against the wall.

It is smooth, and no holds or footstops were observed, nor found, but the angle taken allows feet to push off and use it as momentum to redirect, and then retreat.

There is another crash and it sounds as if the vehicle was upended – mortal screams of agony are heard, but eyes stay forward. Feet press up the incline and past the incapacitated guards.

There is one target where there is absolute certainty the warning will be given the credence deserved, and that's on the hill of the Nespian dynasty. Legs press and are already aching from an effort not made for eons. But there is no relent. Feet pound until they reach their destination and send the body at the wall.

Hands grasp at holds that stand out in the vision like a thousand belay bars. Feet kick at footstops that stand out from the rock like a grand staircase that circles up. The climb is one of the quickest ever made, and that's known as it takes place, but the underlying details as to why are left alone. Arms and feet push up the rockface until the road that was known to circle from many deliveries is met. The options for what would follow finds the best, as there's a vehicle approaching.

Feet scramble to the surface and stand in the middle of the road – arms waving. It extracts the exact response that was hoped: Two members of security step out with weapons aimed.

One calls in to report the disturbance, the other orders, "On your knees."

It brings the chance to finally share, "The mine's been breached. The underground. They're in there. I don't know how many, but they're in: There are dead and wounded."

The other asks, "How do you know this?"

"I was hijacked. I fought the entire time. I finally got them to crash after they killed the guards at the gate. That's when I realized what they were doing."

"How many," is questioned.

"I don't know," is the honest answer: "Seven on the platform. But I think more were on the back. I know some of them were hurt when the vehicle crashed."

"You did right," is offered before the report is sent. There is relief to hear the words of urgency and concern – for deaths committed by violent insurrectionists.

A deep breath is taken, and the many throbbing aches and burning muscles are finally given their recognition, as shoulders slump. As the head rolls back, and a deep breath is taken. It is close to joy that is felt, to hear, "They're moving in."

Eyes look back and there's a smile. Appreciation shared, with, "Thank you for listening. I was so afraid more people would be hurt – I was afraid you wouldn't listen. Thank you," is said, but those feelings shared are drained at the impact of familiar stings. Hurt eyes look back, and wonder, "Why?" The world is fading, and aching muscles are growing weak.

The two stand with weapons still pointing, and Antru cries, "Why? I was trying to help," and the world goes dark, another time.

Chapter six:

Eyes open to a scene that isn't unfamiliar. That it's not should be disheartening, but it isn't, because there's clarity in the understanding. Mind and thoughts remain a scattered jumble, but the knowledge that it's the second time that eyes have opened in a jail cell is known as fact.

There is memory that is intact of violence and crashing vehicles. There is a scream that haunts the memory as that vehicle hit the wall a second time. There was a run, and climb, and warning given to members of the clan, and all of that remains in the memory – intact.

Eyes can close and relive the moments. There are flashes of moments held and the details remain complete – one of weapons fired after risking life and limb to give warning about the quarry, and it still holds extraordinary disappointment. Disappointment only greater that it apparently led to incarceration.

There is further disappointment to comprehend the words spoken on the last. Whether that was hours, or days, or longer is uncertain. But the name Éayren was spoken, as was Dalune, and the person that said them spoke of them as friends.

They were likely those that led to the complications of early life. The underground battle fought by parents that had desperately tried to steer their child from that conflict. That had interrupted the direction of their life and warned to never step foot in any vehicle. If memories had not been disjointed, decisions would have been completely different, and more disappointment falls that chance was never given. That the words to allow rest to clear the mind were disregarded, and the only lift from the sallow waters is hope that the voice that cried out as they were crushed by a falling vehicle was the one behind it.

The mind is dark, and eyes close to push back intrusive depravity. A conscious twist against imagined tonnage against a cranium paints a wish that everyone escaped unharmed and left with whatever it was they were after.

Eyes rest closed and there is sadness that the kindness shown was not allowed to predominate the encounter. That an opportunity was valued more than the well-being of another. It is likely that callous choice also ended with the death or capture of the one responsible.

Eyes open to the bars, again. It is not the poorly constructed cage that used just stone to secure the bars. The door of bars is framed with metal that is well secured. Shaking would not earn freedom – likely just attention that isn't wanted.

The small bed is also more comfortable. It is too short, and it's narrow, but it is an actual mattress with a pillow and linen. The intention to leave them is met by muscles that react poorly to movement, due to movements that hadn't been undertaken for a considerable period of time.

The change of position finds muscles stiff and painful. The front of one leg burns with movement, and it takes a struggled push to reach a seated position.

Unlike prior confinement, there is no one in view. There is not a sound around, and all that can be seen through the steel door, is stone across a narrow corridor. Curiosity finally, slowly pushes the body to a stand, and the aches bring a rush of memories that flood the mind with familiarity, if confusion.

There is distance from recollections, but there is the memory of standing in victory, end of season. Of the reward for efforts taken to battle past the aches and pains of competition. There is a crowd cheering as teams come together, as players embrace one another with appreciation for the sacrifices made to stand together beneath the shower of jeers and cheers. The sound roars in the ears and a vision flashes. The heat of bodies that come together, the sweat and funk, and the starlight beating down are retrieved from memory.

They are blinked away, but the silence won't let them fade entirely. Sounds fill in to the emptiness met, and visions flash across smooth stone as it's stared upon through metal bars. There is the roar of voices, and the visions of stone – climbing and surveying the world from on top of them – but there is something else that is more distant. Something urgent that is calling through the storm.

It is quiet, and sad, but it is poignant and pulls attention more than anything in the fog. It is a beacon that guides. A voice that pulls back towards an existence that was nearly forgotten. A sound that rings and in the echo of its call there's another: A minor duad. One that rests upon a base to complete the family – three voices that emerge and bring the quiet question, "How could I forget them?"

Sickness pulls retreat to the tiny bunk as memories continue to unravel. As experience shifts into segments and theirs seems to have abruptly ended. Questions as to how, and why, and when are shunted for the priority in mind that is to find them. To protect them against whatever happened, to ensure they can lead their lives as they determine; to give them the opportunity to experience joy.

The thought brings ill-feelings greater anchor as they resonate with words delivered, as a child. Sickness grows and it melts with horror to realize the reason why. To understand that parents foresaw the future and felt powerless against it. That they sacrificed their own happiness – their time together – for the sake of their only child.

"How are you feeling," pulls resting eyes to roll, but the answer's, "Fine."

"You took quite a bruising. Are you able to meet me at the door?"

The person's told, "Of course," and withered muscles and their reluctance are smoothed to demonstrate disaffection.

The person is dressed in a uniform that is not dissimilar to the ones donned by those behind the raid. However, implements are different and the breast bears the insignia of the clan.

They ask, "Can you tell me your name?"

The answer given is, "I know my name."

They ask, "How long has it been since you've eaten? Or had a hydration capsule?"

They're answered truthfully, "I don't know. I don't know how I got here, or exactly what happened. I did have food and hydration the last day I remember."

"Okay," they demand, "Your name, so we can confirm your identity."

The stories from childhood bludgeon the mind, as," Eantru," is given.

Everything is uncertain, but there is a growing sense an ugly truth has been openly paraded – celebrated. That dangers warned against have been spoken, and glorified, and that by being overtly present have been subjugated and dismissed. That to suggest nothing has ever changed is laughable because the evidence can be clearly demonstrated.

But there is still a person asking, "For your position."

"Transport operator," Antru answers.

That's followed, "Do you like that position?"

"I do." It's shared, "I always enjoy the beginning of the day. There's a camaraderie, even though there's very little said. But we all share the experience, and in the evenings, we often do share our experience. And I really love the longer trips to the communities in Rims – there was one small town: I went to it once, but I can't quite remember. But it was a remarkable landscape, covered with:"

"Eantru." The person interrupts the stream of thoughts. They hold forward a tray with familiar nutritional bar and hydration capsule. They demand, "Eat, and hydrate yourself. We'll get you when it's time for your hearing."

"For what?"

"Your role," they answer, "In what happened."

There is protest: "I had no role. I fought them from the outset. I did everything that I was able to prevent them from carrying out whatever they were doing. I had – nothing – to do with it."

"I understand," is spoken softly, as if with sympathy, and it's claimed, "You can share that at the hearing."

"They'll let me speak," is answered yes, as is, "They'll listen?"

"They want to hear everything you can remember."

The tray is pushed and there is a kaleidoscope of thoughts that somehow paint a picture of the truth. That pills and memories come together to explain the sense of awakening from a years-long slumber. The tray is taken, and the claim is staked, "I must have had one, recently. Is there somewhere you can take me to relieve myself?"

A hand motions towards the back of the cell. Towards a circle of metal on the floor not far from where the head rested, just above on the tiny bunk.

"Lift the lid," it's explained. "Use the nozzle to clean any mess. You can also rinse yourself if you feel the need."

"Thank you." The tray is raised as if in gratitude, as another lie explains, "I am dehydrated. How long do think I have?"

"You have some time. I'll be back when they're ready."

As the person leaves, footsteps are counted, to estimate the distance to the exit. If the interaction had been a test, it feels like one that's failed: Pointed questions/direct orders. Identity and recollection – nutrition and the capsule. At fourteen steps, there is a momentary pause and the hint of something sliding. Footsteps resume, but they're quickly muted.

Three steps are taken from wall to wall. Dependent on the person's stride, that would make four or five cell widths to the exit.

The opening is once again approached, but, "Is there anyone else here," gets no answer.

There is quiet retreat back to the bunk, to the metal circle that reveals a foul stench when the lid is lifted. The orifice is fed the bar and capsule and quickly closed. Interrupted rest is resumed on the bunk just above, and thoughts turn back to memories and notes that continue growing clearer.

A sound that was part of a chord that rings louder as it's recognized as a voice. As a child that no longer is a child, but one that's grown and no longer living in the family home. Three voices that not only emerge from their single notes, but bring with them a surge of strong emotion, as love for all is first remembered, and then resumes. Names emerge and the sound that was the foundation for the chord, the base that brought the harmony together is finally recognized as Aedra.

There are tears that fall on multiple occasions over the course of however much time passes, as memories sharpen and lead to others, as experience returns to consciousness — as moments spent with family are relived.

With time for thought and reflection, eyes turn back to the nearest events, trying to gain bearing on when that life was lost. There are memories of children growing and their assignments to the Institute at Marphy. There are memories of their weddings, and the eldest had a child, though its name remains elusive. There are memories with Aedra, of moments beside the columbrum. The music of the instrument and that between them still shared until the end. Somewhere after retirement from the roukta field, memories are lost and a fog begins.

"They are waiting for you," breaks through the fog. Like the calculus for attack on the stolen transport, thought towards how to approach interactions have wavered between carrying on the charade, or addressing it directly. Remembering family and time stolen from them brings an anger that leaves no room for playing games. It's also lost, how in the fog to answer questions.

The bars are finally pulled open after what is estimated to have been days. The person turns without a word and begins to walk.

Cells extend far behind, but there are four before the exit. There is a person in each one of them and all are lying on their bunks. There is no acknowledgement, nor reaction to those that pass.

The door at the end of the corridor slides open to reveal a larger hall. It is mostly empty, with only a few others that are passing through. There are multiple doors to the left, and at the second, it is explained, "This is yours. Good luck."

"Thank you," Antru says, and enters as the door slides open.

Nine are seated behind an arced table. Centered in front is a single chair. The room is like everything else observed: Plain, smooth stone walls with no breaks for windows. It is probable the space is cut as part of the quarry – likely everything is underground.

The chair is approached, and, "Should I sit," is questioned.

The person directly ahead, says, "Thank you for joining us," as if there'd been a choice. They ask, "Your name?"

"Antru," is spoken clearly: "Of Capriot."

The person says, "I see." Eyes fall and with the others, entries are made on tablets before them. Without looking up, they ask, "How do you plead?"

Without hesitation, Antru firmly states, "Innocent."

Three of nine inquires, "You were charged with making a delivery?" Answered with the affirmative, that is followed, "Did you, in fact, make that delivery?"

They are answered, "No – because I was hijacked. I was attacked by people that came out of nowhere. I did everything in my power to fight them off and prevent them from taking the vehicle."

Five of nine inquires, "Were you successful?"

They are answered, "I was shot."

Two follows, "Please clarify: Was that delivery made?"

"No," Antru says, "Because the vehicle was hijacked, I was shot, and whoever those people were, they stole what I was supposed to deliver."

Four asks, "What was the reason you returned to the quarry?"

"I don't know," is answered because the plan was never shared. There was a warning not to that went disregarded, and the body was dragged back to the vehicle and forced to activate it. "I fought them the entire time," Antru stresses. "I disabled their controller and wrecked the vehicle at the entrance to the quarry. I climbed the upcrop of the Nespia family and notified the first members of security I could find. And then – they also shot me. Now I'm here. That's all I remember."

The answer, "I see," indicates it's not what they were looking for – suspected the absence of expected fog is their concern.

Eight of nine says, "If you were forced to the hidden lair of these people, where can we find the entrance?"

"I was shot," Antru reminds them: "I lost consciousness. I have no idea where I was taken."

"You left, though," says five. "Where were you when you exited?"

"I don't know," Antru says more firmly. "I was trying to determine the best strategy to prevent them from carrying out whatever they planned. I was focused on the tablet and how I could get it."

It's questioned, "Tablet?"

"Yes. I think I said that. They did something under the console and then used the tablet to control the vehicle. After they killed the guards I attacked them. I got the tablet and smashed it. That's why the vehicle went out of control. I jumped out just before it crashed."

One asks, "You did this – after the guards were killed?"

"I had no idea," Antru insists. "I did not know their intentions. At that point, I knew I had to act, and I did. I am responsible for preventing them from getting whatever they were after. You should be thanking me for alerting the authorities."

"Where do you live," seven asks.

"In a box with a sanitation station. I never paid attention until recently, but it's in the northeast part of the city."

Eyes turn at the pronouncement. Looks are shared between members of the tribunal after a statement that seemed completely normal – completely ordinary: Trivial. An observation that was made one day after a night of fitful sleep, after the terrors of the unconscious left an agitated state that reflected on the travel.

There is a sudden understanding of what the tribunal's for, and it is also realized the verdict is already sealed: They were probing at the memory. Every conversation since arrival had been a test, to determine if the mind was fogged or there was clarity. The statement that was made when asking about the hearing – they want to hear everything you can remember – was misinterpreted to mean they were interested in what happened. But memory is the indictment that is faced. A last stab is made after the too-long pause in conversation:

"There were a lot of protesters. With the new construction. As I was heading back, I realized it's the same trip I take in the morning. I never realized that before."

It is a failing effort that sunk intentions when the name called only when in dreams was said. It was sunk with recollection of events, and description of the tiny home. Antru sits in the lone chair and slumps, to await the certain verdict.

The fifth of the nine and centrally seated, inquires, "Do you have anything else you would like to submit?"

Antru says, "Yes." Posture is corrected, and Antru begs, "I just want to go back home and continue operating the transports. That's all I want."

"Motion to convict," three says: "Are there any dissents?"

There are none, and five stiffens, and sternly delivers, "Guilty as charged."

Antru disputes, "Guilty of nothing. I did everything I could to protect the delivery and the people in the quarry. I am not guilty."

Five says, "Eantru: You are guilty." No is overspoken, "Yes."

Nine questions, "How many times were you shot?"

"Shot," is questioned: "How many times?"

"You said you were shot on multiple occasions. How many times do you estimate you were shot?"

"I don't know," because it is bewildering. A disconnected line of questioning that's pressed, and entirely irrelevant. For an unknown reason it's deemed important, and it's guessed, "A lot? During the hijacking, where they locked me up, and then by security. Why does that matter?"

It's explained, "You're hallucinating."

"No. I'm not," refutes the claim:

"You are experiencing the toxic effects of an overdose. You have thoughts and ideas in your head that are completely detached from reality. It is not uncommon to create a narrative to make sense of them, and it's likely that's what you're doing.

"Some people believe they are saviors. Some imagine families that never existed. But the thoughts you find intruding in your mind, are not real. They are hallucinations. However, regardless of what you are experiencing, it does not expunge responsibility. You have admitted being present for the crimes committed, and witnesses have corroborated your involvement. That includes others that were involved. They have stated you organized the raid against the quarry."

"It is not a hallucination," Antru insists. All of the noise from the claims are unimportant because there is one made early that evokes anger. There is one that is not a figment of the imagination, because, "I have a family." The anger is not hidden. It drips with, "I have known Aedra since I was born. I am from Capriot and we grew up there, together. That is not a hallucination. That is my life that you've stolen from me."

"Guilty," five states, and the hammer falls: "You have absconded with equipment and given it to those that seek to undermine society. You are responsible for the deaths of seven members of defense, and for the destruction of public property. Considering your state of mind, this council offers lenience: You are sentenced to forty years of internment." Protest is hammered down, and security steps forward. It is claimed, "You can dispute these findings through proper channels, but this is not the place."

Eyes stare into the person with the hammer, and for the first time in Antru's life, true hatred is known – known, as parent's actions are finally understood. But, "It didn't have to be this way." Parents were trusted and a promise was given and held until the day that life was stolen. "I wasn't your enemy," Antru insists. Memories fall of life together. Uninvolved with the underground, and no interest. "But you stole my family, and I can never forgive you for that. You – make your enemies."

The hammer falls, and the order is passed, "Remove them from the chamber."

There is no push back against the arms that pull – there is no opportunity. Enough isn't known of the cage and facility, but it will be. The door is watched as it slides open to allow access to the long hallway of prison cells. Those are eyed as they're passed, as are their occupants.

The cell door closes and the sound reverberates through the hollow passage. Eyes stay locked on the jailer, taking stock of the enemy. They say, "It's easier if you cooperate."

A small tray is handed in, but before it's taken, the capsule is snapped away, which brings the warning, "That's not the only way. But it's easier. Keep that in mind."

Their calm departure and demeanor are chased the distance to the door by shrieks of rage. Bars are gripped and silently pulled, and the failure brings the tray against them. Thrown with anger until it finally slips past bars and lands against the corridor wall.

Chapter seven:

There was relief when it was shared that incarceration would not continue within the quarry jail. The chance for an opportunity to find freedom was essentially nil and came down to a hopeless attempt to burrow through the rock, or determining how the guards opened the doors. How that happened never was obvious, and was likely done remotely. Even if the guards had a means to open them, attacking through the bars to effectuate the action and then escaping through the hall, has a realistic chance for success of close to zero. It was held as a final act of desperation until sleep was interrupted, on an early morning.

The thought did enter the mind as the door to the larger hall was opening, that it was an ideal opportunity to crush the jailer's skull. However, nothing was shared, at that point, and hope for better opportunities prevailed.

That was rewarded by direction to a loading area with many others, one that was very similar to those worked for many years, though people had never been the cargo.

Another thought to commandeer the vehicle was sat on, also. With one experience disabling vehicles, there was at least a clue as to how, but with no tablet, it remained uncertain if the vehicle could be controlled. It was the second time that day that doing nothing was rewarded, as the transport exited the mines and began a familiar journey.

The route was the same one taken more times than could be remembered, around the back side of the clan fortress, to the southern road beside the upcrops and fertile fields.

Antru had said, "Maybe they're taking us home," which did not even receive a groan. Not even a glance.

They'd continued around the city to the massive upcrop, the northwestern-most boundary of the city. As they veer to the right, spirits are elevated. It makes the likely destination the city of Bitor.

Bitor is one of the small Rims communities, and it is vastly more pleasant than Greater Nespia. It is similar ;to Capriot in that most homes and establishments are carved or built with stone. It is located at the end of a peninsula with numerous inlets, coves, and bays, and like anywhere that is not Greater Nespia, the views are striking. There are few upcrops and those are smaller.

Arrival is at a destination tucked within those. A massive cube built out of stone with narrow windows, that is distinct only due to size. It is reminiscent of the new homes that were meeting protest in the northeast sector of Nespia, without the stepped face looking towards the bay.

Exit from the vehicle is under watchful eyes of Nespian guards, however their oversight ends with entrance to the building. It is immediately clear that conditions are significantly improved and there would likely be opportunities to escape.

On entry, eyes widen at the retired roukta player entering, and one member of the staff, says, "Well: This is interesting." They are immediately pulled away and no other hint of recognition is shared.

It is explained to those arriving that they are residents, and they will live in communal units with separate, attached cubes for sleep or isolation. Those are found to be just large enough to accommodate a bed and a small chest that continues across it at the end. It brings reflection back to the bunk from the time at Marphy, and unlike others, feet extend out to the open end.

There is time for relaxation. There is equipment for exercise and a yard where a small upcrop can be climbed. There are tablets for entertainment and each floor is completely open, however there is also required labor. Compared to prior work it doubles as relaxation – assembling furniture. Meals are the typical protein bar and hydration capsule.

A knock precedes, "Alright if I come in?" Eyes peer beneath the cabinet to find a body wedged into the corner. There is amusement: "Most people do this the other way."

Antru shares, "It reminds me of my time at Marphy."

"Ah," understands the admission and does the same: "That's – why I'm here." A hand extends and goes ignored. It follows, "I am Rosen. If you didn't know: I oversee the facility." A hand reaches around and massages the neck, as eyes look at the person buried in the footwell. There is a sigh, lips purse, "You know," is said: "For what it's worth, I was a huge fan. You were just a mean, vicious bastard. I think everyone outside of Marphy hated you. But you put that team on your back and made them respectable."

"How long," Antru questions.

"Maybe – five? Ten? It's been a while."

"How did they get me?"

"I have no idea," Rosen answers: "I don't have that information. You would have been found in violation of something. But it's irrelevant. You have been sentenced to serve time, and you will not find a facility that is more considerate of its residents. You have a lot of freedom and liberties at this facility. Most would consider this the best possible assignment. But I have to have cooperation. It's not an option."

"I have no freedom," Antru counters. "You ripped me from my family. You confine me in this building and force me to work for you. I have nothing except my memories."

"I can help you," Rosen pleads. "You can dispute the charges. But I have to have cooperation. There's no help if I don't get that."

But it's understood, "I won't remember."

Pressed, "You will."

Antru says, "I've done everything I was supposed to my entire life, and this is where I am. Tell me why anything's different."

"You're in Bitor," is offered as an excuse, but it's as meaningless as every other word that's been given not to resist the forces of existence.

Just like Marphy, or that Capriot is in any way different than the metropolis of Greater Nespia: Even the name, self-serving.

There were those behind walls. The pinches and towers. There were guards and the security enterprise of Nespia that was continually attempting to compromise the population.

"Take a day," Rosen says, but it won't be: "Think about it. There are far worse places you could be. We can help you. I won't force the issue, but if you won't cooperate, you can't stay here. That's just the reality of your situation."

It's pointed out, "I'm here because I tried to stop a robbery. I informed the authorities. For that, I'm sentenced to forty years. Why does cooperating get me anything?"

"You have a day," Rosen says. They rise and walk a single pace to the exit, where they turn. They say, "Think it over: I'm in your corner – give the process a chance."

They're answered, "I have. And now I'm here."

There's no response. The director leaves without a word, but the return to quiet does not return the languor. Quiet rumination and reflection are disrupted by ideas piqued, and the quiet nook is abandoned to consider promises and claims.

What's found is quiet. People gathered in the central space but that reflects to memories and commutes – together but kept within. There is only a single conversation between two, of dozens gathered, and a significant number have fallen comatose in their seats.

One is in the gym, but the position is surmised as isolation as the equipment remains idle, and a tablet rests on the tray before them. Like many others in the room, nothing is displayed: The person is staring listlessly into a fog.

They are approached, despite the answer's already given. They are addressed, "Excuse me. Are you working out?"

Eyes blink slowly. They seek meaning in the clouds surrounding. They blink repeatedly as the words slowly lap at their consciousness, and they eventually begin to turn.

Their mouth opens like a feather's fall to the ground, and their word's as soft as the landing, a scratch whisper, "Huh?"

"I was wondering," Antru says: "Are you working out? I thought I'd join you if you are."

"Oh," they say, "Yes. I am." Eyes slowly take stock of the surroundings. Slowly, they tease meaning from the clouds surrounding, and realize, "I'm done. I was – finishing."

"Tomorrow," is suggested, and further, "Were you in the league?" Eyes look back blankly until, "Roukta," is explained.

It tugs a smile. One that is clearly pulled by memory. Something distant triggered by the question. There is a soft laugh that remembers being asked, however, "I grew up in the foothills. I get asked that a lot, though."

It is a breakthrough that is heartening, but there were also breakthroughs when it came to family – to early life. To memories of children and a partner. There are also memories of when those breakthroughs were recalled by others and failed to reignite.

Considering the proximity, it's presumed, "You had to have climbed – right? The upcrops? I couldn't resist when I was young." There is another attempt at the quiet laughter, but it's not as pure. There is a story unraveling in a person's mind and they're unable to understand why. They are failing to recognize the reason there is sorrow – that they are looking back at an existence that's been massacred. "Care to join me," is asked with deep empathy. It's suggested, "Climb the rock in the yard? For old time's sake?"

There's a nod, and there is cheer to the offer. They say, "I'd like that. Yeah: I would like that."

"Alright," Antru says. It is soft, and the heart aches for the person beside, but there needs to be certainty if the person has flashes, or holds memory: "I'll grab my scuffs. I'll be back soon."

One hand is brought to the shoulder and brings pressure as an offer of consolation. The person looks up and nods, but confusion is already seeping into the response.

Retreat is taken across the space towards the unit, however progress stalls at the entry. Eyes turn back to watch the person sitting, idle on exercise equipment. Their head is shaking as thoughts ricochet against their cranium, but it is only minutes again that they are still. That they stare blankly at the black screen of their inactive tablet.

They are watched with sympathy. There is a wish that is singing loudly, ringing in the ears that blank stares mean nothing. That just as likely, they are looking back into the past and reliving memories.

With regret, the return begins. Of the many deserving of sympathy, the one deserves the most. One that looked back to life as a child with endless hope and the promise of opportunity. They are met, and, "Hey," quietly interrupts them. A hand rests on their shoulder to pull attention, and as before, there is an onerous process to pull out of the fog.

The person looks up with unfamiliarity. They're asked, "You ready," and there is clearly no recollection of the prior conversation. They look back, blinking, wanly smiling as they try to connect enough pieces to make sense of the question asked. To makes sense of the proximity of the person in their presence.

The answer, "Yes," is the same answer, and by the same toxins that has been given a thousand times as capitulation. Cooperation to what isn't comprehended. Agreement for the sake of being agreeable.

"Which unit is yours," Antru asks, and adds, "Show me."

The person rises. Head nodding with gratification to hold a narrative that sits comfortably. They walk with confidence through the larger space, past the rest of the residents that sit largely silently, largely comatose, and mostly oblivious to their own existence. There is pride to demonstrate they can find, "My unit."

"Good night," Antru says.

The person smiles. They nod again, as a narrative falls against the present. They offer, "Good night," and turn in with a directive processed.

Disappointment is deafening. There is always the peal of hope, but it rides the stormy sea of chaos and barely stays afloat. It bobs in the waters of promises and claims, and clings on even when the hurricane's arrived, but it is never easy to let it go. It is never easy when the suspected is confirmed – the expected. When parental words of warning find their basis.

Time sifts as disillusion fills the body, weighted against progress beside the door that closed any possibility for hope. Time spent watching others. Time spent observing conversations emerge from nowhere. Irrational and disconnected comments brought together in stuttered conversation until it's found a satisfactory resolution.

Time spent watching the watchers watching back: Eyes never seat for long – they move across the population without pause. Slowly moving across the room, and for someone not confined for countless days, it would not be aberrant enough to elicit distrust. Over time, it is seen as a stark contrast to the vacant stares.

It is enough to drain the sour disposition and alight distaste, and feet traipse across the common space with the weight of disappointment. The unit is entered, and the cube, bee-lined in. As usual, the bunk is entered face-first, but unlike typical position – burrowed in the corner – it is met face down into the pillow.

Eyes pinch and focus back on memories. Of roukta glory, but mostly as it pertained to family: Celebrating with them. Holding children in the crowd as the celebration crashed down with a shower of deafening voices.

Standing with Aedra and feeling the warmth of their body pressed against a shoulder.

It leads to thoughts of the quiet days that would follow. Re-entering life as just a member of the family. Re-engaging as a parent with focus solely on the children. On partner and children. Resuming responsibility as a full-time parent and re-taking obligations that were neglected for the season: Upkeep of the home, assisting children with assignments, cooking, but more than anything, the time spent together in the evenings where experience and observations – insights – were shared. It is the song that makes the risk of resistance worth any price that might be paid: Any instant longer that could be held with memories of family.

Eyes flutter open to the sound of gentle music, after what feels like they only closed.

It is an egging concern that warnings stressed have already been applied. That the other options eluded, have tainted food. But it's not the thickness from the capsule. It's losing moments, and lack of fitful sleep. It's falling restful, but memories from a prior life remain intact. It is evident that the potency is nothing close to the poison in the capsules.

The cabinet's opened, and the bar and pill are present like they've always been. Like every other day, the pill is added to the pile in an adjacent drawer.

Cellmates have already prepared themselves for the day and have left to receive assignments. They rise at the music, and move instantly to comply with their obligations. It brings sick recognition to the same behavior conditioned for unknown years. Years spent walking with strangers, commuting with strangers, and taking assignments without question. They are followed, regardless, as the option is re-assignment elsewhere. There is at least a semblance of decency in the confines of Bitor.

"Hey," turns several heads, but the voice targets Antru: "You: Willing to work out in the open?"

That is answered, emphatically, "Yes."

"Okay," the person says: "Okay – good. We need help clearing the roadway into town. Someone like you – shouldn't be too much. We need some muscle for the big ones."

It is the opportunity that's been awaited. The chance to probe for weaknesses. The potential to run when eyes become distracted elsewhere. It is an opportunity, unfortunately – without a plan.

Bitor is not close to anything. It sits at the end of a peninsula and there is not much between it and the nearest city, which is Greater Nespia. Travelling through Rims towards Capriot would be preferable, but it would require excessive climbing and would probably conclude with starvation. A vessel over the water would be the ideal mode of travel, and it would also be an easy target. Opportunity would have to be one taken as it's presented. If nothing else, work will at least be out of doors and not stationary.

There are enough volunteered to nearly fill the transport. Seats are taken in pairs, and the one beside is greeted by, "This should be a nice change."

A blank stare joins the confusion held in, "What?"

They are disregarded as the walls fall closed, and turned from as they reactively lean against the wall, just like almost everyone. Except one resident and the six that oversee them. Six watch residents, and specifically the one with eyes concentrated through the glass, looking through and trying to understand the city – for opportunity: But there is nothing evident.

Chapter seven:

Bitor is much different from other cities on the planet. There is one, main road that leads in and it runs to the tip of the peninsula. Other roads intersect and lead to pockets of development, but they are islands. Pockets of rock that are suitable for building on that are surrounded by a brown, spongey organism that covers the ground. If it was not there, much of the peninsula would be underwater and part would be an island.

The drive is not long, and there is no clear means to escape. There are buildings typical of older sections of Nespia and most of Clarb, and the road is the same stone surface with the regular steel circles that seal utilities, beneath. There is no cover to hide, no concentration of buildings that might offer protection and all that are seen are occupied. It is also suspected that any resident that sees an escapee would act immediately. Chance offers nothing helpful and the journey ends prior to entering the greatest concentration of buildings and population.

The destination is just before, where the road turns slightly west just past the largest grouping of upcrops in the region. The upcrops of Bitor are not the soaring rock of other regions and they are considerably less stable. Those used by the roukta clubs are not actually in Bitor, but adjacent the eastern edge of Greater Nespia. It is clear a sizeable portion of one has disintegrated.

A tone sounds, and bodies move in unison to the upright position. Walls swing away, and occupants move quickly into formation. They are followed and the space in the final row is assumed – presumed a practiced operation.

Four stand watch while the other two greet those already present. There is equipment that's in the process of cleaning most of what's fallen, and it's unclear what role those brought will hold. But the arrival is met positively. The greetings are cheerful and familiar – hands shake. There is a brief conversation – arms wave across the terrain, and then hands come close together. There are nods of understanding, and then another motion in the direction of those standing. One begins return with the information gathered.

"Okay," pulls attention from the fog: "Here's where we need you. Machinery can't clear the benthos, so we need you to pull off the debris. Start with the large stuff. You can load it in the scoop or carry it across the road. Everyone clear?"

There is one answer, "Yes," and it's Antru.

They're ordered, "Let's get started."

Thoughts cross the mind, but it's decided it's best they're left unspoken, and the group is trailed towards the odd, brown landscape that reaches almost to the road. Water oozes from it as feet sink in. The first freeze with concern, but the submersion is nominal. The structure of whatever benthos is keeps them almost on the surface. With the brave leaders relieved and moving forward with their assignment, the others follow.

Shoes squish, and squeak against the substance. Steps are taken carefully as there's a sense of instability, but it brings some life to those working. There is actual humor and communication. There is at least cheer seeing the mollified find novelty. It's welcomed as there's a significant amount to clear – some chunks look impossibly heavy. It doesn't prevent one of the volunteered from attempting.

They're offered, "Can I lend a hand?"

"Hew." The person says, "Don't think it matters. Are we supposed to move these?"

It is likely a question from the fog, but it's relevant as the piece is impossibly large. Even with many trying, it seems unlikely they'd find success, and the thought to call for others is left aside.

Most others ignore the largest. In fact, most take fragments that are relatively small. To make a point, one of the largest estimated as movable is lifted. It's more than expected and there's relief the effort's interrupted:

"Let's wait on those. We want to start by moving the big ones. We'll get it roped, and then I need you two to help it along. It starts rollin' back, or, you hear a rope snap – make sure to jump clear."

The explanation brings observation of another that is pulling a thick rope from machinery on the road. They are slogging through the benthos muck, footsteps straining to tug the rope slung over shoulder. The heavy splats grow louder as they near, and as they close, Antru joins and lends a hand. As it is, suspicion falls the effort's an exaggeration and likely the person's volunteered.

However, at its destination, they join the other that explained the operation and begin tying tethers around each end of the massive shard. A ring is secured between them and that is finally attached to the rope extending from the shore.

The two head back to the boom, trusting the pair that watched are capable. The rope tenses, and both put hands against the massive boulder. It begins to roll and they push with their legs to assist the motion. It is an arduous and slow effort. They are one of three attending the largest fragments, and whether it's truly needed, there is a compulsion to endeavor tremendous effort.

The massive boulder is rolled back to the road, a deep trench filled with water in its wake. It is freed from its binds and the machine rolls on to target another.

Antru takes the rope and mimics the effort previously demonstrated. Another boulder is tied, and the process repeats.

It is hours before the largest have been removed. Bodies ache and sweat pours. Machines lift and carry the boulders elsewhere to be disseminated into a product for use elsewhere. There are dozens of the largest that wait for transport, and on the sodden field, still hundreds, possibly thousands of smaller fragments to be removed.

A boulder lifted, and, "Take five," is suggested. A capsule is held forward as an offering.

They're offered back, "No thanks."

"You're gonna kill yourself if you don't have something to drink."

"I'd rather die," Antru says, "Or lick the surface of whatever it is we're standing on. It's better than giving up a day I remember my family."

The boulder's lifted, and feet stagger across wobbling muck, across the road, and to the ever-growing pile. Already it extends the distance between three circles on the road.

The field's turned back for, yet again, but the person is back and presses back – back pushed into the upcrop. A cannister's held forward, but the head is shaking.

"Pure water," it's promised. "Nothing but water. I give my word."

Antru says, "Don't bother for me."

"No one," the person claims, "Wants to see anything happen to you. Just drink it here where they can't see you. And start looking like you're not enjoying this."

They walk away with the bottle set on the ground and it's noted that few move so far south – the corner of the upcrop obscures the view. Most pile and let those spill into the roadway, unwilling to take the extra steps to lay the rocks out properly.

The bottle's lifted, the contents tested, and it tastes like water. It's impossible to know if it's anything other. It's impossible to know if the person can be trusted, but there is also a truth to what was said: Work, even in the cool air of Bitor, will suffer consequence without hydration. The view is cleared before several swigs are taken.

Return to the field is made with shuffled feet. Eyes cast downward, and the head is swung from side to side. There is a carom through the field that appears directionless, until a rock impedes progress and becomes considered. As it is, others are weighed as better prospects, and a stone that is not particularly large is the one selected. It is brought to the nearest point across the road where it's paced atop the nearest pile.

The rock tumbles down and rolls half-way across the road.

It's ignored, and feet begin their shuffle back, however, "Hey," is shouted, and weary eyes that turn find that they're the target: "Take that down the road where it doesn't roll into traffic."

Feet slough back, and follow orders. Feet drag into the field, and to the wall, again. They move with no direction nor motivation: Stone selected, pile tested, and failure is watched with sluggish response to correct the result.

The star is well across the sky by the time a fragment of more significance stops progression. As many times before, landscape's scanned for lesser targets. But the effort's been successful and just the largest, and the smallest are still available. With only the tiniest pieces in proximity, the stone is regrettably accepted as the bounty.

Feet drag across the surface. Deep breaths are taken. There are several times the stone is dropped, and feet stumble – once, a knee falls into the muck – and the process is revisited again. It is a slow, cumbersome slog just like the dozen or more that were volunteered to join the effort.

Stone drops and rolls onto the roadway. Eyes scan and find eyes watching back, and words are called, "You know where you need to take it."

There is a show of reticence. There is a momentary demonstration of exhaustion, as well, protest. But resignation falls and the effort to re-secure the rock begins: A grueling undertaking to first lift, and then stumble onward down the road.

There is one final consideration of a pile that's not too tall. There's the potential the rock might stick, and lesser targets might be considered for a while, but a last-second thought turns eyes to the field of origin and finds another looking back: Their arm ratchet's forward dramatically to order better options.

Those aren't far. The corner's turned, and the stone is dropped – the nearest target's sprinted for;

immediately addressed: Fingers punch into holes and lift the heavy steel. It's slid back far enough to gain access to a ladder.

Five steps down and the lid is resecured, and descent continues in almost total darkness.

The heart pounds. Ears pique but the drubbing deafens them. Eyes hone on the small holes, watching for shadows – looking for motion.

There's none, and thoughts begin turning to the second act, but it remains uncertain. But there's a flash of a moment saved in memory that makes claims of safety in the tunnels.

Slow, and quietly, footsteps begin traversing the sunken tube in almost blindness as eyes have yet to adjust to the limited illumination. But pillars of light spaced regularly serve as guide and are quickly followed. Travel continues though it's unclear even what direction has been taken, or if the tube is straight or arcing. Fingers reach out for walls and count the beams of light that are passed, though that ends after eleven for no particular reason other than paranoia induced imagination of a distant sound.

It is several past that point that the passage concludes beneath a final access at a door. Thoughts of idiocy are knocking just as knuckles rap. It is tested several times, but there's no answer.

Head shaking with regret at poor decisions, another is taken and the ladder's climbed to estimate position.

It is evidently a populated region and many voices can be heard in proximity. Despite thinking it continuing poor judgment, the cover's lifted and eyes peer out across the surface. No one is immediately seen, but there are many buildings. It confirms the prior thoughts, that the tunnel led from the edge of

313

town into its center. Emergence in the middle of the street would undoubtedly be observed, and the foray would almost certainly be intercepted and ended quickly.

The disappointment is deep, but there's also relief. There's still a chance to salvage the assigned incarceration.

There's urgency to return, but that aim is interrupted, when, "I'd guess you're not here for the same reason I am," is spoken nearly in the ear.

There's a reaction to back away. Eyes grow wide as they find another recessed against the wall. They are average in stature and they don't wear a uniform.

Regardless, it's claimed, "Just curious."

"What's down here," the person asks. They say, "Apparently not much. Did you see three people sniffing around up there?"

Antru says, "No. I have to go." But there's hesitation as the question sets in deeper, and it's qualified, "Unless you need help. But I really need to get back."

"I'm hiding in a tunnel," the person points out. "Either I need help or I'm hiding."

"Or curious," Antru adds. "If you come with me, this exits on the edge of town. If that gets you away from something – or to something – follow me."

They say, "I'll just go back up. It's probably nothing."

They're told, "Good luck," and a quick stride off is paused by maybe:

"Maybe you could just watch. To make sure I get to my street safely. They've got one of those work crews out and I think they escaped from that."

There's a groan, and, "Oh," extends from exasperation. They're told, "If you go quickly. I do not have time for this."

"Oh – trust me," they say: "I'll move quickly." They emerge from their crook and climb the ladder, lifting the lid to make quick survey." Report is made: "Coast clear."

They climb out, and Antru follows just far enough to watch progress. The position is better shielded than expected. There is traffic, but it is exclusively down a short street and past the buildings. If there was a potential to actually escape, it might serve as an ideal point to make that get-away. However, the only way out is past the crew that raised concerns, and of which there is fear absence has already been too long. The person waves as they make the corner, and the lid is pulled.

A sharp cry of fear rings out. The lid stops and ears pull for sounds, and there are some that are imagined as those made by someone in a struggle. An aggravated growl escapes, but the lid's shoved back and legs push as if they climbed a rock-face.

The quick sprint slows for the corner, uncertain what to expect, and the worst is found – the person from before restrained by others.

Pace continues to slow as the corner's made, as assessment's made of the attackers: Both large. Both undisturbed by abrupt intrusion, but they are not the stock of roukta players trained at Marphy, and there's no hesitation: A step digs, but the effort's crushed by violence – a pile drive crushes against the side.

Feet instantly lose their grip as the body is tackled through the opening of a building that hadn't even registered. The strike is violent and painful, and the landing isn't better without a chance to think about position.

The person remains straddled across the chest, and it's clearly a practiced tactic. Fist rain down as, "Get it closed – get it closed," is shouted.

Most strikes are blocked but they quickly feel like a distraction as there's a sense of something against the ankles, as a large, metal, roll-door seals them in. As two others join on either side and each restrain an arm. The first one finally lifts away, and a fourth is standing just past feet – feet restrained by metal shackles, and likely done by the person that called for rescue.

They're asked, "Who are you?"

The victim from the tunnel says, "You've been detained. You've violated privileges. You're being re-assigned to a high-security facility."

"Are you kidding," Antru pleads. It is incomprehensible to conceive, "You're a pinch? I was trying to get back – you tricked me."

They say, "You made your decisions. You've got no one else to blame."

Chapter eight:
Silver droplets patter against the window of eternity pulling tender trails to form a landscape where there was nothing. They are the poison that give the briefest shimmering of light. They are the current of existence, and like a river flowing underneath an atmosphere that's tenuous, they will pass. Silver streams will winnow to only threads and will scatter, fainter the further they grow apart until they are indiscernible from everything. They will slip into the folds of the vast sea that absorbs existence, leaving only fading memories of the music that was spread.

There is an underlying harmony, even in the void of nothingness. There is a sound that reverberates. It is present, even in the absolute blindness of complete dark. It sings the chorus of existence and pulls the poisonous silver threads from the endless doldrums of the suffocating, unrelenting, whitewash of obsidian. It is a light that sprinkles into nothing and illuminates the merest fragment. A tiny mote of hope that flashes brilliantly in the night. A tone that resounds a swell of love and hope; that hangs hopelessly in the resonance of sorrow.

It is the song that holds everything: It is the song of everything – all known. It carries in words that are otherwise void of meaning. It is a note that plays in a trio of others, and from that song an entire landscape is pulled from darkness. A tapestry is woven of brilliant color, so bright that eyes are blind.

It is warmth, and comfort, and encapsulates the greatest fears.

The word calls, and it is one spoken millions of times a day. A word spoken frequently – heard innumerable times a day – but most fall against the ear like tin drops devoid of music. Like a brush against the shoulder that falls to the ground and licks back into the crevices of nothing without regard. But when, "Moboti," holds the music of the triad, attention turns.

Within the call there is the harmony that connects within the ear, that pulls at the chest; that lights the mind on fire with devotion.

"Moboti," is called, and eyes turn instantly.

Nearby, raindrops fall and they scatter across the grounds as their song plays for another. It is a deluge but only few connect with any one.

"Moboti – moboti," brings attention that's desperately desired, and the landscape unfurls beneath bright starlight.

There is a sound that ignites life, and the field is filled with hundreds. There is conversation, aromas and the shimmering laughter shared by Aedra. Their vision rises and all the light in the universe is contained within that sound of joy. In the smile and happiness looking back.

"Moboti," is said more firmly and precedes the order: "Look around." Laughter is shared as they are called, and they are one. They find Althrae standing proudly with their tongue stuck out and licking the end of their nose. They dudder out, "Look what I can do."

Aedra's voice, "You are filled with talents," cheers the world and sends the child scampering away.

They are one of millions. One head that bops amongst the many. One, that of all the sounds that fill the landscape, regardless of the distance, that one note will pull the ear and turn the head.

It is a field of children anchored by watching parents that tower above them. They are watched as they move amongst each other. They are watched as they climb equipment or ride the pendulums. As they test the walls of nearby structures in challenges to one another. They are watched but with distraction they are lost – another tone, observation; conversation. There is a field of children playing, snaking through the hundreds with attention pulled erratically.

Little pebbles rolling together in the tide. Tiny stones that swirl together. They become a mass of congealed unity as water pulls away, as distinction is erased as the single grain focused on turns, or calls, and the note they speak, or the smile they share is discordant to the harmony of the symphony.

There is panic, and it's irrational. Greatest fears rise into thoughts that the worst has happened amongst hundreds, and yet none of them can see it. They dance over the fallen body, or ignore the pleas called in terror as they are stolen by the hands behind the wall.

"Excuse me is spoken," but the justifications used through the years are an endless tomb of words that no one has ever believed. They are excuses used by everyone at some point and derided, or mocked by those with older children, or those with many.

They see the panic and know it is rarely justified, but when that's called, there is always, "That one time," and the panic of one becomes a sour truth in the stomach of the other. There was always that one time a child didn't come home.

Excuses fall or it's blatantly said on occasions it's confronted, but neither will ever reach the ears of children. They will never hear the worries, concerns, the fears, and hopelessness that devour the souls of parents. They are fed lies and half-truths. They are given direction with no explanation as for why. They are told to live their lives and find happiness, and to ignore the smoke that is rising in the distance. They see the pillars of oversight walking through the crowds and believe it's to maintain order.

Cool – collected: No sweat, and the stride is casual despite panic's set the feet afire. Fake smiles greet eyes that look, and there's a perfection of calm from every parent that wades into the sea: Knowing their child is drowning. Hearing screams and imagining the thin wisps of smoke that last only instants after a candle's been extinguished.

Eyes scan hair, and faces, and clothing. Ears scan the pounding surf for the notes that stand above it. Sickness grows as the circuit's made, time and again until, "Moboti," is heard once more.

The word shatters layers of clammy flesh, irrational thoughts, and reactions that were imagined in response. One note sings light into the world and twirls a poisonous metal into beauty. It peels eyes open across a landscape of happiness under the warm starlight that wraps the meadow.

"Hey," lands a thunderclap against open arms: "Have you seen Axael?"

A lie, "A short time ago," is lathered in against the worry of the older child. Their worry's assuaged, "I'll let them know you're looking for them if I see them."

"We're at the," is a whirl of wind that is held onto even as attention turns. But the words are ripped away by the storm that pulls the shattered shards of concern back to a downpour of precipitation. The child skips away, alleviated of the sickness that fills the pillars that float amongst the children. That share sickly nods to one another, nods that give recognition to the condition that afflicts them.

Eyes look over an impossible field of grains waving in the wind with the task of identifying which of the stalks is a member of the song. They wave with irregular motion and crash against each other. They rasp against the mind and ears with a promise the answer's near, but the harrowing threat of silence has burned a hole across the field. There is emptiness brought by the scorching star and a careless ember, and there is no way to recover what is lost.

The sound that brought chroma to the landscape. That filled in variation to the extant. That gave life to shadows and found exhilaration in the capacity to lick their nose. A gift that smokes in the ruins of the field. A hole dug in sand that turns to liquid.

A hole that became the surface in an instant.

Hands dig at the grains. Panic rears as fingers splinter from the violence brought against the granules. Sand pulled away falls in again, faster than it can be cleared. There is a scream in the ears – there is surf pounding against the sand with a force amplified by the hurricane that approaches. Tears fall onto the massive dune, as a small handful of sand is lifted, looking for one, looking for one that is part of a song, but they look the same as the grains slip away forever through the fingers.

The body collapses against the mountain in surrender and pushes down into the sand – to suffocation. To breathe tin droplets that are the poison of failure – eyes that lost sight, ears that failed; actions that were incapable of preventing loss. Quicksilver fills the lungs with unending inhalation, even as the body convulses against it. There is raging cough that spits one granule for every hundred taken in, and they are all the same – all the same, each grain ejected is examined.

There is a storm blowing and the wind cuts against the sand like a retching cough. Lungs are burning from the sand breathed in and the body aches but it is not enough to drown the sorrow. Hands dig at the sand because it's all that's left but fingers melt away as useless rivulets of molten silver that is swallowed into the hollow beneath the mountain. What's left is stabbed against the earth as lungs expel tin droplets with a scream that showers the endless dunes with futility.

The silver streams sink down between the granules and light grows farther and farther from memory. They seep down to the hollow that is the peak of the highest dune imaginable. It is immense, but the vastness of forever is surrounding, a sea that, beyond, dwarves the massive mound. From the highest mountain, forever extends long and all that can be seen is nothing.

Weary claws dig at the surface, trying to get through again. Withering starlight beats down as the wind kicks sand that flicks against the cheeks, a mockery of the futile effort that has built capricious walls that slither down with every handful thrown.

The sky is black and it looms above, cap to the conical tomb that has been dug too deep, and has found no hollow to slip through to another side. The only way out is to climb the failing walls that form rivers of grains at the slightest touch.

Hands find the grips slip through them, and feet slip as quickly as the sand. There is a lunge, and grasp, and for a moment, momentum grips. Progress is gained but it's fleeting: Feet bog down as they slip against the surface – fingers flow away with the sand. A hand smacks just a finger from the top, and it brings a river cascading down.

The dark of the sky collapses into the hole, and there's nothing but sand. Coarse, suffocating, sightless, and heavy sand. It blockades breath, crushes the chest, and arms and legs have become cemented. Complete darkness erases all perception, except for the silver streams that are slipping away. Falling into the evasive hollow where light can no longer reflect against them. They will pool in the vacuum of eternity and become completely indistinguishable.

They are not even an afterthought when a bright glimmer pierces into the eyes. There is a song in a distant atmosphere that pulls threads together, a light that shines and refuses to let them dissipate so quietly. The song calls a melody that fills the hollow that is not something climbed into, but a space, internally. There is sympathetic resonance that is the beginning of something larger that is somewhere on the other side of the sand.

The voice sings, and splashes, "Antru," against the ocean. It calls from a vast distance and is distorted by the atmosphere. It is quiet, but it firmly warns, "You're having dreams, again."

It is a warning taken that is ladened with regret. That another night of rest has been disrupted. Another's dreams disrupted by fitful thrashing, or screams, or the worst all – the tears. Regret built deeper over years, first for parents and then a partner. Regret – the first waves of embarrassment: Washed over by frustration, by personal antipathy, by feelings of worthlessness, and humiliation.

"Antru," was called, but there is no condemnation. There's no anger, or frustration. There's no sympathy – there is only a warning: "You're having dreams, again."

"Sorry," was said for many years, but that was pushed against: An echo says, "You're not the only one."

Aedra's arm has remained over the shoulder and moves tenderly against it as consolation.

There are minutes, and sometimes hours, before recovery allows for salient conversation. All that can be offered back is a hand that grips on and lets the other pull a fading body from the sand.

"Let's go look at the stars," Aedra said.

A light shines from great distance, but it is brilliant, and it's enough to illuminate the massive dune. It is a light so powerful, that it punctures the endlessness of forever and spills showers of light across the universe. Billions of stars shine in the midnight sky, and even with the immenseness of forever brought to light, there is comfort taken from the kindness, the gentleness; the unrelenting glow.

Stars spill across the frigid morning sky and the dew of early morning hangs in the air. It is bordering uncomfortable, but Aedra's warmth, beside, makes the move for other comfort undesirable. The bench swings beneath them as meteor's send streaks of fire against the atmosphere, as the calm, and silence settle a disquiet mind and bring it back to the weariness that should be present at the hour.

Words are spoken but they are unintelligible – they are irrelevant. The arm on the shoulder – suggestion: Sleep lost beneath the stars to ease a scrambled mind and disconnected pieces of a body that floats apart. It was a secret hoped would disappear with time, and words ramble out that are foreign but are the excuses that fell empty from the beginning. They are mumbles of content understood because they happened.

"You're the best, and ever was," spills out in an attempt to elucidate appreciation: "I don't know how I could live without you."

It is a moment of lucidity that scratches the mind and brings a scuttle towards consciousness. "My other half," careens in a carillon of chaos that begins to spill into the mind:

"I am here."

"I need you."

"I understand."

"I get it." Shadows fall, and, "I've got the same thing in my head," lands a final blow against the clouds of slumber.

Sharp strike into the ribs – "Hey," said irritably: Get off me."

Heavy eyelids struggle open as muddled thoughts reach back to make sense of the assault: Rows of seats in a common transport. The neighbor's push falls comprehension on the circumstance: Conditioned lean fell into them instead of burrowing against the wall – the left seat was the only one ever taken.

It must be understood, because the third attempt at separation is joined with, "Keep it on your side, ya idiot drone."

A mumbled, "Sorry," is offered with the reposition, and an unnatural lean against the door finds cold where there was always warmth. The side where Aedra always slept.

The neighbor grumbles, "See ya put a lotta thought into it: A whole word. Real impressed."

The words fall like the rain against the window. Splatters that coagulate and race trails diagonally across the surface – pulled by the wind from their intended path. The air frets the trails, tearing at the continuity that was briefly gained, leaving them as irregular, semi-parallel fragments that are scarcely large enough to be bothered by the weather's breath.

They bring flashes from memory that are just as unworthy of consideration: An apology from Rosen, followed by cheerful reminder, "I did warn you. I can't have a lack of cooperation." Seemingly gleeful to have a problem passed along. An irritating non-conformist that didn't even try. That made a run at the first opening presented – that continues, unrepentant. "At least fake it," was the bemused suggestion on departure, but they are a flash across the mind that gained value with reflection, and they negate the impulse to fire back against the grating neighbor.

Chapter nine:

A loud horn begins the day with reverberated aggravation. Eyes squint at the cold, stone wall – against the bright light that floods the cell.

It is a small, stone box that holds four prisoners. There is a bunk on either wall and the typical, metal plate centered on the floor. The door is solid metal, the only break, a small, glass circle surmised as means to monitor.

The cell is either flooded with light, or completely dark: The morning disruption a warning to quickly take turns while others keep backs turned, before preparing for work.

The four are standing in two rows of two when the door is opened. Those on the left are the first to exit, and the others immediately follow. They walk a stone hall lined with open cell doors on both walls, towards central inventory. As that's entered through a turnstile, a nutritional bar and hydration capsule slide from a chute on an edible tray. Each shuffles on for metal seats and tables, the same place taken as every other day, amongst the hundreds of others that move to sit at their own.

Bars and trays are eaten, followed by hydration capsules, lodged inside the upper lip – the third of four lets the capsule slip into a sleeve and lodges tongue-tip there instead.

The four move to take assignments: Briefly inspected, scanned as present, and then directed to follow a blue stripe painted on the wall.

It is one of eight colors. All lead to production factories where the equipment that manufactures clothing is overseen. Principal duties are ensuring material is replaced as needed and that the finished product is suitable. It is also ancient machinery and prone to breakdowns. Those that errantly reveal familiarity with repairs are rewarded with no free time, and no days off.

The room entered is loud, and hot, and smells of machinery. Oils sits in the air, and those being relieved are covered in a sticky film. The silent exchange takes place and finds relief for four, while their replacements gird for another day.

Antru moves to the fabric cabinet to take stock of spools: All are satisfactory for the time being, and in the motion to close the window, the arm falls to the side and momentum pulls the capsule free as it's directed towards the central scrap pit.

The first station assigned is thread, where numerous colors are pulled dependent upon design and fabric. They are monitored but all are well supplied.

It is a mesmerizing mechanism. Thread is pulled, the brake releases, and the spool whirls into a rapid spin. Some run nearly constantly and others for just moments. It is the easiest segment of the operation, and there are typically no more than a few that need replacement during any shift. It is hypnotizing, and eyes stare into the spinning circles, giving appearance of the sedated state the others have fallen into.

Cellmates stand at the three posts down the line: Assembly, packaging, and boxing. The latter is done by hand and counts vary. Failure anywhere in the operation leads to re-assignment at less desirable positions at the prison, however, it is at the tedium of boxing where failure's most frequent. One shift consists of three rotations through every post, and the start at threads brings the final stop to boxing – the least desirable conclusion to a day: There's relief when four fresh faces shuffle in.

It is impossible to know what shifts align with. With time, a day is the day that's given. Every aspect of life is mandated, from work, to sleep, and exercise. Every activity it undertaken every day in the exact same way, for the exact amount of time, and in preordained order that never changes.

"You," is a change from routine. Eyes crawl up to the source and blink dumbly, and those found are looking back, and follow, "You delivered."

The head is slightly shaken, as if confused, and, "I don't know," is stated blankly.

"That's not a question," has to be explained, because, "Don't be an idiot. The last job you had was transport. You think you can not screw up a few deliveries?"

There is a quick turn back to what's remembered: Routine, just like the prison, of waking, of cleansing, dressing, eating, and joining the many others that commuted in. There was knowledge of procedures, there were memories of destinations and the furthest from the start remained the clearest. But there are also recollections of flashes that seemed to come from nowhere – protests, and buildings. Words about tunnels, and the castle. There were impressions made, but only the most striking stuck in memory, and even those are fragments.

Antru looks back, head still swaying, and like an epiphany was fallen, shares, "I was hijacked. I was taking something up the mountain. They came out of nowhere. Do you remember that?"

A chuckle precedes, "No." That an episode like that's remembered's no surprise, but the stupidity of

329

those imprisoned can still find amusement for those that watch them. "You're an idiot," introduces, "The last idiot got caught up with equipment. You think you can get a few boxes delivered without tangling with the transport?"

The confusion is genuine, "How," asked as memories of interface come back.

"How would I know? But you know the routine, right? Check in, sign offs – ya see a kid in the road don't hit 'em. I'm asking – that's still locked in?"

"Of course," is answered immediately, because they are the cornerstones of a hazy life that were drilled into the mind and frequently questioned. Operation was held with utmost pride and procedures were undertaken diligently – for the most part.

Eyes wandered, attention drifted; posture lagged against the wall. Presence was mostly a formality and recalled as a necessary target for blame when something went wrong.

"Hey, hey, hey," the guardsman jaggles: "We might have a new position for you. I'd bet you won't whimper out like the last one."

There is a new order, and directions are given but they are appropriately followed poorly. Three corrections bring introduction to the staging pod with familiar sanitation chambers.

They are a welcome sight, and there is an unexpected emotional response to their presence. Inhibitions are left with clothing to be recycled with the order to enter.

Soiled clothes are peeled as the sanitation chamber is approached and they are launched away into the syphon with a loving reminisce that pulls fondly. The chamber sprays the aureolin mist and it's just as quickly blown away by the whirlwind blast.

The brief moment in the chamber recognizes it as one of the greatest creations ever devised. A startling assault that leeches fatigue and aches, and in seconds leaves a person ready to make deliveries after a long day in the factory. It takes an effort to suppress exhilaration from the experience, but return to a common space with others and no clothes helps to tamp expression. Clothes are quickly presented by other prisoners.

There's an urge to express gratitude, or offer hope, but it's recognized inadvisable with the numbers watching, and likely the person's mind is in a fog, regardless.

The uniform is donned, and it's not dissimilar to the one used at the quarry. It is familiar, and comfortable, and the mind runs through scenarios that might offer opportunity: A chance to leave the high security of the prison. An opening to make a break, again – Alvel much better known. There are places to hide, and the forest provides at least some sustenance along the haul to Minaut. From there, the safety of Marphy is just around the bay.

Orders call for assembly, and the others are followed through a door that connects directly with the dock. It is dissimilar to the widely spaced alcoves of the quarry: The dock is one, and numerous transports are backed against it.

Others are watched and they step to gaps between the vehicles. Four down, the gap's not taken and that's targeted as the likely post. However, "You're transport," halts that progress.

Antru says, "I was hijacked. Did you know that?"

"Well," the person says, "I don't think you'll get hijacked over a pair of pants. You're authorized."

"I don't know," Antru answers to a question that wasn't asked, and asked for name, replies, "Gantru."

The tablet's scanned, and "Mmm," narrates the observation. It's demanded, "Put your hand on here." The moment that it is, the tablet's pulled away, and orders follow instantly: "Station four. That's your station. Remember station four. Every day you come down here and wait at the back 'til I say go. Then you make sure the product gets where it's supposed to get. Got that?"

Antru answers, "Yes."

"Go wait. If I have to tell you again, I'll get your clearance revoked."

Feet shuffle towards the slot and take position like the others. The little shared at least reveals the role's intended to continue, and so a plan settles to devise a more thoughtful approach than diving at the first opportunistic chance that's stumbled over. Deliveries will bring the opportunity to better understand the city, to search for avenues of escape, and potentially to determine if the underground extends to Alvel.

"Go," sets feet in motion.

Taking position on the operator's platform brings a sensation of comfort and familiarity again. Thoughts focus on procedure but there is a nagging image being formed of how the poison and conditioning worked together. One hand rests on the central sensor and brings familiarity, but also resentment that insecurity and loneliness were manipulated within a shattered mind to seek comfort – conditioned to find comfort through routine. Routine built while thoughts were scrambled by intoxicants, to make the familiar become a need, and the need was a dedication to routine: Pride in the position that was given.

The vehicles stream out from left, to right – from one to twenty-three. The material within will be distributed throughout the country and there's a light that flickers – despite the effort to stamp it out – that initial orders will lead to the south part of the country.

Despite their oddities, Capriot and Marphy are considered the safest regions of the country. There are at least allies present, and some are openly members of the resistance. Experience has yet to connect how that's possible, but introduction to life was born in that duality.

The vehicle moves as vehicles do – following a programmed path through city streets. By the third turn, that light that tried to shine has faded as it becomes clear the destinations will be local. Attention turns, instead, to studying the layout of the city, the buildings, and places where safe harbor might potentially be taken.

Alvel can be viewed as a compromise between Capriot and Marphy – and Minaut, to an extent. It has the common spaces intentionally designed into its layout, but they are less the focus of life as in the southern cities. There are gatherings, celebrations, and festivals, but like in Capriot, the homes are the center of the family. They are large, and private, and most meals are shared as a single unit in them. If it was an intentional attempt at compromise, it is considered a failure by the eyes that fall upon it looking to escape from servitude: It has neither the extremely tight connections of Capriot, nor the widespread joy and camaraderie of Marphy. By an outside eye, fulfillment seems to come from actions, rather than the social aspects in other cities. It was viewed as an oddity even in an inebriated state, and the impression was strong enough to remain as a static memory.

The vehicle turns between buildings, into a narrow passageway. It stops just past a door of a wooden building – an ancient artifact, as the forest has been protected for millenia.

There has been no instruction on how to proceed, and instinct, and training brings departure from the platform. However, that earns, "Hey: Hey-hey. What the frakenstamma are ya doing?"

Antru says, "I was hijacked. Did you know that?"

Outrage follows, and, "What," is screamed. The back of the transport's ripped open, and the person says, deflated, "Oh: You're a comedian. Just get back in and we'll take care of it."

It is not the first opportunity to search the tablet for procedures, but it's the first taken. Considering the risk of dangerous criminals delivering the goods, it is ordered that all operators remain on platform while cargo is unloaded. Once given all clear, the operator will leave the platform, enter the cargo hold, and take inventory to ensure that everything ordered has been removed – and nothing that wasn't ordered has been removed. After that's been confirmed, the rear hatch is closed, a sliding window is opened, and the tablet is handed through for sign-off. The recipient will then sign off, hand the tablet back, and retreat to a safe location. The operator will open the rear hatch, again, exit, close the hatch, and resume position on the operator's platform. This will be repeated until all deliveries have been completed. There are also links to procedures for breakdowns that might occur at any point throughout the process.

Clear is given, and Antru exits to inspect remaining inventory. It is quickly catalogued as it should, and the hatch is closed. The window's slid, tablet's offered, and it's signed off and returned. With the second clear given, the hatch is opened, the hatch is closed, and position on the operator's platform is retaken. It is a procedure repeated a second time without incident.

At the third and final destination there's an incident.

There is a vehicle that blocks progression, and the apparent owner calls to those that pass for help – those that pass do not operate a transport. As the vehicle stutters forwards, angling and attempting to find a way around, for only the second time in memory, emergency stop is activated.

There is a need to report the reason why, but how that would be done in an incapacitated state takes some time to consider. It is ultimately wondered, "We're stopped."

"Status," is demanded.

"There's – a vehicle," is delivered with bewilderment. "It's stopped," it's explained. "I thought we were going to hit them."

There is a pause. Silence is joined by a person banging on the window and asking for assistance. They seem genuinely distressed, but they look like danger. They are the memory of a pinch that casually pulled cooperation around a corner – an assault that led to incapacitation and a transfer to the current prison.

"Four," breaks the memories, and orders, "Push it out of the way."

Antru answers, "Yes."

It falls awkward, and a moment's taken to wait for questions, or reinforcement of the order but nothing follows.

There is liquid silver dripping from the ends of dendrites as the platform's left, as the person's approached, and the order's relayed, but they won't stop talking. They won't stop pleading for assistance. They are a vision flashed in the mind from early years when words of warning left voices silent as those in danger went ignored. Warnings scream:

"Can you just take a look at it? I can make it worth your time."

"No," Antru answers – demands, "Get it activated so I can push it out of the way."

They apologize. They claim, "It was a favor for a friend. My parents told me not to come down here, but I wanted to help."

They're told, "Get in, activate it, and I'll push you. Otherwise, I'm plowing through."

"That's the thing," they claim: "I can't. It just went blank while I was riding. Isn't there anything you can do?" They say, "I'm really scared. I just want to get back home."

A hand grasps the opposite upper arm and they seem to be shivering. They look back woefully, and a tear slips from an eye. They beg, "Please. Help me. I can make any problems you have go away. Or, if you want something, I can get it for you."

"You're my problem," Antru says. "I just want to do my job, and you're keeping me from doing that. If you want to help me, get out of my way."

"It doesn't work," they again claim, and the plea is made once more: "Can't you just look at it?"

There is a strong feeling there's no coincidence. That the freedom given before and present aren't happenstance, nor trust, but measures of compliance and cooperation. But there's no way forward without the vehicle removed and agreement's given.

There is no knowledge of how the machines work. No understanding of what propels them. They were avoided, and then taken for granted. But the memory of a hijack remains strong, and recollection of the interface recalls something beneath the console.

There isn't much found, only a harness extending from the front that's clipped into the bottom, and a small square beside it that's partially embedded. A test finds the harness secured, but an inkling of movement when the square was pressed.

There is nothing else that can be addressed without better knowledge, and it's with expected failure the person's told, "Try it now."

They look nervously as they pass and distance's kept as they seat into the vehicle. A hand rests on the activation sensor and the console lights.

If the reaction is rehearsed, they are a worthy actor as it appears spontaneous and genuine: They startle, and mouth drops open. They turn with eyes wide, with surprise, yet exultation.

They move quickly: There is a brief thought that arrives too late to react that all contact should be avoided, but that arrives as arms wrap firmly in embrace. There is only a partial response – one arm raises and touches briefly against the back, but it feels unclean, and is followed by a step away to separate.

"Thank you," they say. There is relief that flows, "I was so scared. I didn't know who I could trust. I've been stuck here forever and no one would even talk to me. Whatever I can do for you, I have to return the favor."

"Go home," Antru suggests. "I have to make my delivery."

They try, "Can I have your name? So I can tell them how nice you've been?"

"Who are you going to tell," is a question asked without filter, and it was pressed with a vile energy that wasn't expected.

It is another suggestion to pull agreement for a favor. One more attempt to elicit accord for favor or edge – tacit taboo in all of Nespia. They are the shaky grounds by which innocent altruists are snatched from streets and fed into a system of forced labor. "I have to go," is a quick attempt to end the conversation.

"I just meant," they plead, "Who you work for?"

They continue to approach, and Antru tries, "Glad I could help. Go home and have a nice day."

"I don't think you understand." They state bluntly, "I'm a member of the clan. Give me your name and I'll get you released. You seem like a good person. I want to help you."

"I just want to do my job. I'm already late, so I'd like to get there as soon as possible."

A hand is pressed against the activation sensor, and a moment later, the vehicle again begins to probe for a way around the other. It finally brings the person to retire from their habits, but they do pause before they enter. They look over and it appears they watch with sadness. One hand slowly raises to give a single wave before they enter and move on for another target.

With freedom to move, the vehicle continues less than one block to its destination. As with the others, there's a small alley behind the building and the vehicle stops just past the door that opens to it.

Before it's even stopped, a person emerges and runs frantically forward, pleading, "You have to help me unload. Hurry. Help me get the boxes off."

They are briefly paused, by, "I'm not allowed to."

The person turns – anger spits, "You're the one that's late. Help me get these off or I'll miss my transport."

"Are you," Antru questions, "From the prison?"

The person passes armed with boxes, and leaves, "Of course." From within, they bitterly lament, "Must be nice not worrying about the time."

Boxes are grabbed because it's recognized, "You're not taking the pills."

The person re-emerges and says, "And being late's gonna draw attention. Get moving."

They move quickly. Carrying boxes from transport into storage. It is an inefficient method of delivery and the other person's already sweating after four trips. What they achieve with urgency, Antru replicates with capacity, and the vehicle's emptied quickly. Inventory is noted as none, and the tablet's handed over for the sign off.

The person suggests, "Alright I hitch a ride? I'm not gonna make the transport if I'm walking."

They are told, "No."

"But you made me late. I'm gonna miss the transport – it's your fault. I need a ride, so just get moving."

"Against the rules," Antru says, "No passengers."

They say, "Being late is against the rules, and it's your fault I am. I'm not asking – I'm telling you."

"No," Antru says: "You are not getting on my transport."

The tablet's snatched away and the operator's platform is immediately taken. They are instantly followed, by argument and body, but the vehicle is already moving away.

Thoughts leave obligations and interruptions, and turn towards alleys and quick escape given the cover of unloading, but the walled sides hold a striking resemblance to the construction of Nespia's northeast sector that was meant to confine and inhibit travel.

Thoughts towards the open doors of buildings are interrupted – a sudden rush of air as doors abruptly open. Eyes turn instinctively to the nearby left, but there is just a shadow seen in the corner of the eye, from the other side, before a strike. The blow is heavy and succeeds in upending balance, and a second follows quickly to continue momentum out the side – a sharp kick to the hip to send the body tumbling.

It happens so quickly that the first reaction comes as the body's falling towards the road – head instinctively tucked, and body rolls. The vehicle's seen turning as impact lands but years of practice falling result in little injury – the greatest, aching ribs from the initial blow: The first breath in, halted for a moment.

A short distance is crawled to the nearest building wall, and there, position's glued by a state of utter disbelief: There was no warning – no chance to react. The assault was well-planned, well-rehearsed, and they knew what was needed to dispatch their target – a word that has lingered in the atmosphere the entire day. The entire day felt like everything was a set-up, and it feels like the targeting's from all directions: The guards, the clans; the underground. What's the point of any of it's beyond imagination.

Eyes cast down the alley to the nearest intersecting road to watch the traffic: Vehicles move quickly by, pedestrians more slowly, and eyes that turn immediately avert when there's connection.

Sound slowly begins returning: In the aftermath of the attack the world went silent. Wind rushed, a blow fell, and perception slipped away with stunned silence. But a quiet murmur re-emerges from beyond the buildings' edge. Sounds of life. Sounds of a city, and a small bell's ringing, but that's internally:

It's an alarm reminding of the need to return to prison. There was a transport, somewhere, that was leaving. There was urgency to unload the vehicle, but even if it was no ruse, there was never a mention of the location.

The body lifts and is reminded ribs are tender. Heavy legs feel like they're made of stone, but they stumble onward – from one locked door on to the next.

If it were a dream, silver threads would be streaming from the body, slithering away from existence and coalescing into the folds of nothing.

But dreams are far away and weary legs can only stumble onward, underpowered as lungs don't fill to avoid the pain. The brain is static, and even those crossed that appear they might be receptive are not addressed: Body and mind are tattered, and legs can only stumble forward towards an objective that has no form and is still searching for an answer.

Chapter ten

Ancient texts describe a time when there were creatures in the forests that would kill anything they crossed. It is framed as a tragedy that every last one of the several that existed were killed off. To those that only have lived in cities, that are unfamiliar with the sounds that carry in the wilderness, there is comfort to hold that true. It is still an uncomfortable existence, and nights are restless, but they've always been. Sounds in the forest only amplify their misery.

The terrain has been much more difficult than expected, even near the road. It is uneven, sometimes soft, and very difficult to walk upon. Moving through the undergrowth is a constant battle: One of the most prolific growths is a plant with hooked thorns that grab fabric and tear at flesh. Quickly escaping from the road as traffic neared proved to be more treacherous than slowly navigating at a cautious, distant, and calculated pace. It was always considered an onerous trek, but the slow pace raises the concern. Especially with the lack of evident comestibles.

The forests were purportedly preserved to maintain one of the few arable places on the planet. Studies taught of the crop that is gleaned and had made it sound prolific. But what's been found, is not. There is little that reconciles with memory, and what has been found that is edible is scarce. Hunger has been a constant since day one.

Fortunately, hydration has been less of an obstacle. The first morning, as starlight lifted the body from a restless night, it was found that everything was dripping with dew. Ignoble as it is, licking many leaves each morning provides reasonable hydration. There have also been a few, small bodies of water and streams, and at each, water has been taken beyond satiation. It helps to somewhat offset the aching stomach.

There was an attempt, initially, to hide when vehicles passed, however, with fatigue and fading focus that effort was abandoned – no one passing is looking for a person traipsing through the wilderness: The ride is recalled as one of the least interesting and it's suspected those that pass are either internally reflecting or heavily sedated – states that are not far from those brought by hunger, fatigue, and tedium.

Disappointment is added as eyes turn up to see impinging upcrops in the distance. It is a point where they near the road, and where the landscape turns to mostly meadow. It is the approximate midpoint between Nespia and Minaut and indicates the latter is still days away.

Progress halts as the prospect's considered, as it's debated whether it's worth the climb across the rocks for the increased odds of finding food out of the ocean. With a reasonable understanding of island geography, it's not considered unachievable, but it's also recognized that physical condition's suboptimal. However, at least one would be attainable, and the walk resumes with the plan to climb the nearest, taller upcrop.

It is quickly clear that a lack of food has affected strength – especially notable with fingers pressed against the slightest crevices. Words from years before, of Éayren's warning, make the wish to climb the rock-face quickly set aside. It is a slow, methodical climb to the top of the mountain.

Arms are aching and hydration's well depleted by the time the pinnacle is reached. It is not the flattened surface of competitions, but a rounded and uneven crag. However, the view is outstanding as the star hangs just above the horizon, still brightly illuminating just one more upcrop to be scaled to reach the shoreline. It will be a more exposed approach, but at least approach will not be taken in starvation.

It will also wait until morning, as hunger and dehydration are preferable to tired arms and dark.

Where the peak descends and abuts the final rise, there is a slight recess where water has eroded stone over millions of years. It is eyed as suitable shelter from the night, a place to hide from eyes that might fly by.

It is not a difficult descent, but it is again not the surface of a roukta rise. There is debris and loose dirt, and the measures taken to climb are applied again: Slow and steady. Ensure the foot is planted before moving the one that is.

Behind the rise, it is nearly dark by the time the cradle is met. The recess is also considerably larger than expected from above and is more than tall enough to walk in – through, potentially, as the cavern continues as far as the little light remaining shines. It's exploration will also wait until light can provide more certainty, but arrival at the cave and rest are beyond welcome.

There is a sound the moment the cave's entered. A hum, or buzz – whirring. It's quickly exited and eyes scan the darkened sky. There is nothing seen, but ears cannot verify its absence with the interfering wind.

The rise is climbed a little more with near certainty the sound's still present. Five more steps and the ears strain with breath held, but the heart and rushing blood become new interference. There is a scramble higher, and once again, a moment's held to let silence fall and there is something that is different. There is a tone that is constant regardless of the wind, regardless of blood pressure rising, and a pounding heart.

A look back and there's a sting against the cheek – brushed away, but the damage done. Eyes strain and there is a tiny mar on the rise, above. A small, dark machine that is hovering.

A stone's grabbed and hurled, but it fails to land its mark. Another's quickly picked, but the hum erupts into a wall of noise. Machines appear over the mountain and more come from the sides – not just the small ones. There are large machines with people hanging from them.

The stone is dropped, as the case is lost – another sting. There is the familiar dagger in the leg, one in the neck; another in the upper arm.

The sound of bodies landing finds their footing firmer and they hold more than the tiny weapons that fire darts. Their weapons are far more sinister.

One approaches: Like all the others, dressed entirely in black. Their face is covered by a mask; their head by a helmet.

Antru is badly fading but is still able to wonder, "How?"

There is laughter – cruel laughter: Amused to share, "You got tagged. Didn't your parents tell not to hug a stranger?"

"The whole thing," Antru says: The feeling of being targeted was exactly accurate. Everything that happened was planned: The transfer to Alvel, the new position, the breakdown, delivery – the attack. Everything was designed to bring them to the point where they are standing. The only question that remains, is, "What for?"

"Right to the hive," is offered back with glee. "Just like we knew you would." The person walks slightly closer, eyes twinkling with the question, "You fading?"

It is a whisper into the ether that closes rapidly to seal away the world. It is a fall beside an upcrop that has been visited more times than can be counted. The wind rushes past and the taste of stone is on the lips as it flashes past in a blur of smooth, and uniform sere that is too bright with the star already lost beyond the horizon.

At the bottom, there will be a pile of rubble that has received enumerable bodies and even tablets. There will be a crack as the body lands, and it will break into pieces that will decay into silver strands that will worm their way from light and living into the endless pool that is forever.

Light shines so bright that it is blinding. It is loud and screams of violence. There are bursts of noise that sound like small explosions, and the smell of blood and dust is in the air. Even after it's gone, the memory's so strong it does not allow the mind to fade entirely. Even with chemicals in the blood the light remains centered in the consciousness – there is consciousness that prevails within the coma.

It is a light that brings back memories of a night when existential terror shook the mind. The greatest fear that the most important person in the world was being harmed. There had been a light that had erupted out of nowhere, and with its presence, faces emerged from shadows. Those that had hidden in darkness emerged in light and plead for calm.

It had been forgotten. Because the brightest light in the universe had emerged unharmed. Aedra had been unsettled, but not injured.

They call, "Wake up. You're having dreams again."

Eyes stretch against their will, but the will to look into their eyes is stronger, and they are peeled, forced open to see the brightest smile that ever graced the planet. Eyes open and slowly focus on the bright light that is directly overhead.

A rush of sound fills the ears that is the accumulation of everything that happened since eyes last opened. There was light, there were screams; there was interruption to the unconscious.

The mind is groggy but it grows clearer with the concern that follows. Restraints hold the body against a thin mattress with rails on either side - it is the only item in the room. Walls appear to be padded, and the white material amplifies the over-redundant lights. There's a door with the familiar glass embedded in it.

Restraints are tested, but they're unforgiving. It is the first time that helplessness has been realized: There is nothing that can be done except wait for someone else to act.

Thoughts turn away from the present and look back to what happened on the mountain. What had seemed like a certainty now feels like it might have been confusion. Brought under bright lights while unconscious, that the brain devised a reason for it. There was never certainty what happened that day with Aedra – it had largely been forgotten. An episode that left a sour taste and turned eyes wary towards authority.

But what is certain, is that everything that's happened in recent memory has been with the intent to guide behavior – which led forces across the countryside to a mountain cavern. It can only be guessed, but considering familial ties and equipment hijacked in the forest, it is supposed there were expected connections. If that's the case, there's an iota of satisfaction knowing the efforts led to nothing.

The door opens, and a single person enters – demonstration of the confidence in the equipment. They run a device over the forehead, and question, "How are you feeling?"

It is devoid of interest, and Antru says, "I'm angry."

They say, "It's going around. You hurt a lot of people."

"You," Antru refutes: "Hurt a lot of people. What happens is the result of what you've done."

The person shares, "Seven are dead because of you. Many more were injured. If I were you, I'd start asking forgiveness."

The binds are tested again – the bed rattles: Antru roars, "I was shot: I was unconscious. The net intervened because it thought I was in danger. That's your fault. You are responsible for putting me in that position."

It is a tremendous leap. A supposition first arrived at prior to considering trickery of the mind. Of the brain taking input it cannot comprehend, and creating a narrative to make sense of it.

But the person is notably concerned by the statement, and they also say, "You're within the stone. Your net can't help you here."

"For now," is fired instantly. The person's warned, "Eventually it will act if I disappear."

The door opens, and several enter. The first in demands, "Condition," and's told, "I consider this person to be extremely dangerous. Otherwise, they seem to be fine."

The words are not finished, when, "What is it that you led us to," is questioned.

It's answered, "Nothing."

"Do I look like an idiot," is shouted, and answered, by Antru, calmly, "Yes."

The words, "Answer me," are screamed, as the threat, "If I put a bullet in your head they'd consider me a hero. Don't test my patience."

There is surprising calm, as, "Then, why don't you," is questioned.

"Because," is nearing hysteria. Veins bulge, sweat drips, the person screams, "I'm trying to prevent another civil war. Is that really so wrong?"

There is a sense that fear is behind the behavior of both that have spoken. A sense that despite restraints, those that walk freely don't have the upper hand. Antru provokes them further:

"From our perspective, you've laid the groundwork for that to begin."

"You – you have: You have no idea."

Antru suggests, "I had no idea you were so malicious."

The person walks over, leans in, and says, "Understand." They are attempting to be threatening – at least, to stress the significance: "They are accessing a weapon that is our only protection against outside forces."

There is more to follow, but Antru wonders, "Didn't they warn you?"

The person says, "Who?"

"Capriot," Antru answers: "Security. They didn't tell you?"

There is a pause, because despite what they are, Capriot and Marphy are different from the rest of the planet. Invocation of the name brings a look of sickness and greater concern.

They say, "I don't work with Capriot. Tell me what they should have told me."

In the words, it is found the person that entered the room with a silent entourage is not a person of insignificance. They are not an angry middling seeking self-aggrandizement. They are someone at the top of the chain and likely deeply involved with recent events. They are the person behind what's been experienced.

And Antru shares, "They were holding my partner. I became so angry I activated the net. Unlike you, they realized acting decent served their interests." And then, a threat's returned that is an attack against forever's history: "Your clans have a choice. They need to make the right one."

The person stands, watching, spinning words together into a framework of the larger picture. They are hearing things that align with significant concerns. They are looking at a person with deep connections and every potential to have been given the connection that they claim.

They are looking at a person restrained against a stretcher, that has been so easily duped on multiple occasions that they've earned the nickname – the dupe. They have been observed to be oblivious, and their nature has been described as capitulating with a desire to oblige. The claims and words are those that could easily be gleaned from years in proximate conversation, and opinion settles that everything that's claimed is merely speculative: After years of watching, there's been no evidence of a connection.

The order's given, "Wipe 'em."

"No," is followed, "Yes. You have your orders."

There is protest, but it's dismissed, and the contingent of many follows the one that's finalized the decision.

It does not appear to sit well with the person that remains: They stare across the room with great distaste and disapproval for the direction taken. The door reopens, and the one that only left returns to warn:

"That's non-negotiable, if it wasn't clear: For the foreseeable future, I need this body on the planet."

"Just the body," is answered, "Alive. I was told that's what you're thinking, but I need air going in the lungs. Is that clear?"

It's questioned, "Brain stem function, only?"

Agreed, "That'll work."

The door closes, and eyes turn back, but the sour face is replaced by a smile of satisfaction. Eyes glint as they also move to leave, offering the parting, "You're a fraud. But nice try." The door closes and the return to silence is welcomed.

However, intentions laid out are not and a more frantic effort is made to escape – there is no success. Arms and feet remain bound to the rails and find no give.

Eyes scan the room and find nothing. There is nothing besides the gurney, and even if there were pieces that could be disassembled, they are beneath and unreachable, and panic begins a cold sweat and skin that feels like it's pricked by a thousand pins.

Eyes look back and inward, to the last time real panic was felt, when Aedra's fate became uncertain but there was certainty there was danger. There had been a sense of connectedness, a feeling that danger could be countered, and it wasn't the first time that was experienced. It was also felt as a child when testing the roukta nets.

Interface was through the tablet, but in the field, climbing rocks, and trusting the net to break the fall – there'd been a sense of connection. An understanding of the forces needed to prevent injury, and for the lowest layer, what was needed to prevent a body from crashing against the ground, with just enough give to absorb the impact.

It is the last hope and one dampened by the repeated statements about stone, but hope holds that's primarily regarding weapons.

A state of mind is locked in: The ardent focus as a child – the desperation felt for Aedra. There was a sense of pressure behind the ear that was disregarded, but it is there, and it is the only hope to escape with mind intact.

The focus feels like an explosion. Ears are filled with a far-off rumble. The sound grows louder as the sense grow stronger – it grows deafening. Eyes open, and the sound is not imagination, nor the result of a postulated connectivity: The room shakes with each violent explosion, and the sound grows closer.

Dust begins falling from the ceiling as the bursts grow louder. Whatever assaults the shelter, it has moved quickly, and only now does a siren begin to wail, though for anyone not to notice the attack, they'd have to be dead.

A massive blast sends rock and dust blasting into the room. The flesh is pelted and ears are left ringing, and more as a violent flash explodes on either side. Instinctively, a hand moves to wipe the debris away – there is hesitation: The hand is frozen as it's realized – binds are missing.

Feet are taken quickly. Debris' brushed away as the huge shaft created is taken in: As underground as one could possibly be, and the net still found its way.

The door opens, and the head snaps around to the last person that left the room. Their eyes are wide and mouth drops open – frozen momentarily in fear: Their own panic brings a staggered turn and they sprint away.

The gurney is pushed beneath the hole drilled down through the entire mountain, the rails of the rolling mattress gone, and the edges singed. It is raised and gives an easy start to the long climb out from confinement beneath a mountain. However, that plan takes a turn as another level's found: An armory filled with numerous munitions and none are the little darts of incapacitation.

A canvas bag is filled with as much as it can hold, and it's slung over the shoulder and tied. Two more weapons are taken and fully loaded and their capabilities are tested against the door.

The first trigger sends projectiles that puncture solid steel without resistance. The second is teased at, but there's a thought that enters the mind that speaks against it. Projectiles are fired where the door is sealed until it finally lurches open.

The room's exited cautiously. The hall is scanned, and eyes watch, and ears listen for anything as it's travelled. It is eerily quiet and there is no signage to indicate a way to exit.

Two people burst out at the hallway's end. They are dressed in black from head to toe, faces completely concealed and they wear the helmets like those that attacked on top the mountain. Two leap into the open hall and drop to one knee with their weapons raised, but Antru reacted at a shadow, and the secondary trigger's already pulled.

As they land, one shout's, "Cover," and they attempt retreat, but the effort's too late. The small cannister that was launched explodes in a ball of fire just behind them, the whole mountain shaking at the impact, and a gaping hole brings sunshine into the outpost.

Antru runs an ungainly sprint towards the opening, with the heavy bag of weaponry slapping against the hip. There is a momentary pause to look down the adjoining hall and there is only one person looking back – peering from a door a distance down. On the floor, just past the corner, five jumbled bodies lie on the floor, and at least the closest two will not be recovering.

The smokey halls are left behind for the gaping exit, through a field of rubble and debris that was not the result of a small explosion, but the work of a protective net to create a hole. It opens to a gentle slope on the northern end of town, and the walk down is not interrupted, however, below there is a scramble.

Waves are running from the mountain, and it's unclear if they're from within, or moving in fear due to proximity.

The starlight is falling towards far waters to the east as streets are met, and people passing pull away and stare. They pull away into their homes and ventures. Doors close and it's evident there is terror for what has happened – felt throughout the city; the assault evident from the streets.

The eerie quiet from the compound has fallen over the entire city. Most people hide, but there are others watching. Some from windows, some from roofs –

stationed on a corner. They are security out of uniform and bring reflection to security that rushed from darkness to plead for calm. Security is present but their aim is calm.

Faces are scanned – few look back. As the depot's neared, frightened passengers disembark and walk with a quickness and awareness that are unfamiliar. Their eyes only see danger as they take brief glances at the only person walking without fear. A massive person with a massive bag swaying with a steady pace and a weapon in either hand. Large, menacing devices that most have never seen.

They are unaware the battle is theirs. They look with fear, but that should be directed at those that have put them where they are. That force them into mines, to make deliveries – that have stolen them from families. Only kind eyes are met when they steal a look. They have empathy, and there is only growing anger as theirs is stolen from them. Theirs is taken and drunk into boiling rage, except, one looks back again.

They look back repeatedly, and their head is shaking. They cannot understand why a person they don't know seems so familiar, but tears are falling because it's Aedra.

Their name is called, but their head's still shaking. "I'm Antru," is shared, and there is terror. There is internal reckoning that brings a schism to the mind, and it's understood. "Baedra, or Faedra: Whatever they call you, you are who you remember in your dreams. That is your life – your memories. And I know you remember me from them: Antru. We have two children, Axael and Althrae. I don't know where they are but I promise you I'll find them."

But Aedra is lost and can only answer, "I don't – understand."

Their head shakes as eyes fall on a distant memory, and the vision is sympathetic and answers, "I know. But you know me. You just don't know why."

"No," Aedra says, "I don't. I don't know what you're talking about – leave me alone. I just want to go home: I have to work in the morning."

Antru pleads, "Aedra," but is answered, "No. I don't understand what's happening."

"Remember my voice," Antru says. It is the last part of the chord – another octave. "There are two more that I know you remember. Listen to them when you sleep. Come with me and tonight, you will remember us."

"I'm not going with you," Aedra answers. "I'm going home. I don't – I don't understand."

"I played roukta," Antru tries: "We used to sit together while you played your columbrum. We lived in Marphy. I know you know this. I know it feels like it's a dream, but that is our life together. You are Aedra: Do you remember anything?"

Their head resumes the motion from side to side, and they pull away. A plea, and they say, "No." Insistent, and sickened, because, "I don't understand." The schism is deep and the sides can't find connection. There is familiarity, recognition, but cognition is failing. But there is a hint, as, "I have to go home," is said apologetically.

"I love you," Antru says, "And I know I say that in your dreams. I will always love you and I will never stop trying to bring you back. See me tonight while you sleep, and maybe tomorrow we can leave – go back home: Live our lives together again. Go back to Marphy."

Their head still shakes, but eyes are watering because a layer of fog is slowly peeling away. Aedra's watched as they continue walking – looking back twice more before the corner's turned and they disappear from eyesight, but not the mind, and the heart is breaking.

"Antru," does not help the situation.

Fog falls away from the surrounding world that held just two, but with one still lost, the world is allowed to impinge again, and it is met with the rage that has been found with love.

"Antru," the person says. They are calm, and approach with respect. They are young and unimposing, and say, "We need to talk."

"No," is a harsh response, that grows in anger: "I will tell you what to do, and when to do it. Until then, don't come near me."

"I am listening," the person says. "Tell me what I can do."

Antru turns, and a hand raises, clasping a weapon to punch the words into the air, "Kill every last person in the clan. That's what you can do."

"Antru," is tried again, but, "You did this to my Aedra," is a rage.

Tears are streaming, and Antru shakes, the hatred dives so deep, "You took my Aedra. You took my Aedra from me. How dare you. How dare you do this to my Aedra."

A promise, "We can help," is smacked away:

"You've helped enough," and alarm is raised to the highest level, as Antru begins to speak – an oddity to those in proximately, and concern to those with tablet's in their hands, as they are suddenly viewing a street in Alvel, and hearing, "This is Antru of Capriot. I was taken prisoner by the Alvel clan. I'm fine for now, but I found Aedra. If anyone puts a finger on Aedra, I want the whole clan killed, and the entire city leveled."

Antru turns and resumes walking down the boulevard, the message, "Be safe, Antru: We are with you," unheard by those that watch.

Sentries watch without intervention. Security holds position with weapons down. All are aware of the imminent danger, and that one wrong move will bring disaster.

They watch as the progression continues from the north to south, and from there, continues to the forest. They watch the greatest danger pass from view, and this time, they won't follow.

Chapter eleven:

It was reported that there was celebration throughout the south, both for a lost citizen's recovery, and for a former roukta star that had been known for their tenacious motor. There was celebration as news of the net's new capacity quickly spread: With the harrowing violence and damage done, it had been impossible to subdue the spread of the news.

This was reported after the conversation became quiet, after emotions settled, and Dalune and Althrae were able to speak more clearly. Not long after, voices were choked again with the news relayed that Éayren and Axael were still missing.

"We were targeted," Antru had said.

It was not disputed: Axael followed in Éayren's footsteps after the disappearance of their parent. They had been working to bring people back when they were also disappeared. Their whereabouts and existence remain uncertain.

A knocking at the door brings eyes around, and a person says, "There are two, here, to see you."

"Not interested."

A voice that rings in the memory of a fog declaims, "We need to talk."

Attention's pulled. The chair swings around to view a person that's remembered less grim, and another that's remembered in better condition: Entering on crutches, with most of the left leg missing.

"The accident," Antru surmises.

"Mistakes were made," the other says: "Lonton wants to address what happened."

"Really," says Antru: "You bring them here like this to apologize?" There is anger, because, "I should've had another hour – I would've fought beside you. But

359

I get it: I understand your anger. If I had the chance to hit them, I'd do the same thing. Neither of us owes anything. It's the way it is."

Lonton says, "I wish I did. But we'd 'ave been screwed if I did: The whole thing's a set up."

The other adds, "We didn't expect you. We expected one of ours, but they switched assignments at the last minute. There wasn't much resistance because they tagged the gavromite. They wanted us to get it so they could track us. You caused a mess, but it would've been a disaster if you didn't."

Antru says, "They're sloppy." Distracted, and eyes are already pulled back to tablets. Absently, "In every aspect of what they do," is offered as fingers scroll. There is a mission that has been one of others, but theirs wasn't personal. Theirs was not moboti, nor a child. Eyes scan information, and the words, slip out, "Nothing needs to be said, either way. If you're going at the clans, I'm right there with you."

"That's good to here," says one: "Call me Mash." A hand extends but thoughts are absorbed by information that leads to hints of possible locations. It is likely, and beginning to be thought the most closely guarded will always be in Nespia. "You're distracted," says Mash: "I understand that. However, I want you to understand, we – work – with your parents. They have been a part of what we're doing for decades. We are not adversaries."

"Got it," says Antru. "Why are you here?" A claim begins, but, "Just tell me why you're here," ends the strategy:

"Same as everyone, I guess," Mash says: "Interested to know how you got the net to blast through

360

kilometers of upcrop. That wasn't supposed to be possible."

The chair spins again. There is a twisted smile that's filled with sickness, because, "You don't get it."

Mash tries, "We've been working with your parents," but it's pointless, because, "It's not a weapon. My Moboti Dalune tells me I can talk to you, then I'll tell you. Until then: End of conversation."

"It's just," but Antru says, "No: Don't even think that's a shortcut. Our battle will be bloody. We will lose lives. It won't come easily. The entire history of our planet is standing against us."

"We don't have the numbers," Mash says. "Most of the willing have mashed brains, and the ones that don't are trying to avoid becoming them. We need something to break the cycle and blowing out an upcrop looks like it could do that."

A sigh escapes. There is reticence to have the conversation – there is no trust despite assurances. There was still cruelty displayed and lack of concern for a person that was helpless while taken prisoner. Outreach was expected to be solely for the interest in the net, and it has been.

"Mash," Antru says: "Since they brought you here and you seemed to think people would listen wherever I was before, I assume you're some kind of leadership. But if you worked with my moboti, you would understand that what you're asking doesn't make sense. I'll talk to Dalune, but until I get the clear, I have nothing to offer you."

Disbelieving, "You're saying," Mash questions, "That was a defensive act?"

Antru answers, "Yes. I was done if it didn't blast through."

"We don't have the numbers," Mash says again, and explains, "Because a lot of us have been done for in the past. The net's never drilled through a mountain."

Frustration brings, "I have other things I need to focus on." Attention turns and the seat is left to address directly, "It's not a weapon. If I could make it destroy the clans, I would already have used it on Alvel. But I can't. All I can do is give it solutions to offer protection. From now on, it will drill through rock to protect you."

Mash asks, "You know this?"

"Yes. If you need protection, focus on the net and it will find you."

"That'd be good," Lonton says, "'Cause they're gettin' close. We need something keeps 'em back."

"It can," is promised, but with the caveat, "You have to concentrate on what's happening and think about the net. It will come to you. I'm sure you've been told that."

The seat's re-taken – hope the motion is understood as the end of the conversation, but the two remain.

It's re-emphasized, "I can't make it a weapon."

"However," Mash warns, "They can make you one: That's why I'm here."

Antru doesn't turn, as, "I'm not," is said. The tablets are leaned towards as if an interesting bit of information's discovered, but it's only wishing the others were gone. "Hm," precedes, "I won't – ever – work for the clans."

There is an attempt to resume focus on a tablet. There is deep irritation that they won't leave, and more that they'd consider the possibility of cooperation. However, that is a misinterpretation of their concerns:

"I need," Mash says, and their voice is no longer friendly as they demand, "You to understand."

Antru spins around to dramatically explain, "Understand I have to save my family." The person's met face to face, as it's unnecessarily explained, "I have a missing child, a missing parent, and my partner doesn't recognize who I am. That's what I need you to understand: That's where I need to concentrate. If I can save them – then – I will fight by your side 'til I die. But my family is my priority."

"Your family will not be saved if you're dead," Mash says: "You are enemy number one. Since the day you walked away from their confinement, they've been working on a plan to kill you, and the net can't protect you if you if it never sees it coming – I do understand how the net works. I do not understand how you managed to get it to drill through tons of stone. If you don't want to share that – fine. But I need two minutes of your time."

"They're all scared of you," Lonton adds. "That's why we had to come here. 'Cause they can't talk to you. They say you don't listen."

"That's why we're here," Mash agrees. "We can't risk anymore losses."

"You," is asked of Lonton: "What'd they have to do to get you to be here?"

"I volunteered. Thought maybe I'd get a shot."

"Take it," says Antru. "You deserve it. Take your best shot."

They don't hesitate. They amble over and get right beneath the chin and sneer up with sick hatred. A crutch drops, and a hand swings up, but it only points a finger beneath the eye.

Lonton says, "Here's my shot: Yer a selfish prick, and you're puttin' the whole operation in danger. Every one of us gave up everything we had to push back against what's goin' on out there, and each and everyone of us started at this after losin' members of our family. You're not special. Half the planet's missin' people."

"I need two minutes," Mash says.

"Okay," Antru agrees, however, "It's not selfish – it's desperate. I'll save the rest so you can give me your two minutes."

"Sit," says Mash, and it's a welcome offer for their compatriot. Antru sits, and attention is fully given:

"You woke the planet. You walked away like you owned the world, and they let you, because they were in shock. But you've continued to walk with impunity, and now, they're happy to let you, because eventually they'll find a way to tag you, and then you'll lead them to this outpost. They're still trying to contain the damage and manage the conversation on the street, but they haven't been able to control it yet. And that's the only reason you're still alive. As soon as they're comfortable that you're an afterthought, or – on the other hand – too much of a risk, they're going to come for you. They'll have a plan, and more than likely it will be successful. The world is currently enamored by Antru of Capriot, but that won't last forever. There is poison in the food, the air, and what we drink. Eventually, you will fade from the forefront of public consciousness. We are here, because everyone wants to keep you around, and we want to help you find your family. You're a compelling person that's caught public intrigue, and that can also, admittedly, be helpful for us. But we also care about you, and like Lonton said, we're sympathetic. We want to help you. Let us, and don't put those of us on your side in danger. Will you agree to that?"

"Less than a minute," Antru says, but asks, "What am I doing?"

"Walkin' the flippin' streets," Lonton says.

"It isn't safe," Mash agrees. "You need to be underground, and move without detection. Every time you leave and come back you increase our risk."

"I need to see Aedra, and I need to go to Capriot to see my child and moboti while I can. Does your underground achieve those objectives?"

"Maybe listen," says Lonton. "They've been tellin' you they can get you where you need to be. You've been walkin' around with your head up the wrong side of your digestive tract, and it ain't the better end. You'll end up what comes out, ya keep doin' what you're doin'. We're not you're enemy, we're also – desperate. Sometimes that doesn't lead to the best decisions."

The claim lands brutally, as it's hard to remember the last that was. One disaster after another only prevented by the intervention of another: Parents, instructors, Aedra – perhaps the underground.

It's admitted, "I thought it would be easier to get through with Aedra. I acknowledge that's clouded my decision making. Who was yours," is asked of Lonton.

"My only," is answered. "Right after institute: Gone. Vanished into the air. I understand the desperate and you've seen the worst of it. Don't make the mistakes I have. Call me by who I really am: Who am I in my dreams," is said derisively, and it's answered, "Onton."

"Yours," Antru asks of Mash.

"My partner. An instructor at Bitor." That studied the history of the planet. That found it impossible to look at the world and separate the past from present. "They weren't overly vocal, but they weren't afraid to share opinions. That's the only reason that I can guess, but I've also come to think that it's sometimes random."

"You're probably right: I guess we're not so different," Antru reflects. Both grasping at straws – all moving without plans: All finding that everything that looks like an opening's a well-designed trap. "Sometimes when you hope something's true, you can't help but believe it. I think that summarizes the world."

Mash offers, "We've all been there. It's what's led us all us here."

"So what's the plan," Antru asks. "I've heard about the underground my whole life, but I haven't seen much happen."

"There's been lots that's happened," Onton snaps. "We're sold out on every corner. There's always someone doesn't listen and brings tags in the outposts. We weren't so short, this would be the moment we're lookin' for."

"Yeah," wonders Antru, "How many do you have?"

Mash answers, "Thirty-thousand and some."

"Not bad," Antru suggests, and wonders, "How many in Nespia?"

"Thirty-thousand," Onton says, "Total."

"Oh," is answered. An insignificant nit for the organized defense of Greater Nespia, not to mention the lesser towns across the country. "So what's your plan?"

"Stockpiling," Mash answers. "Building caches in the city. Recruiting, trying to rebuild what we've lost. We were over two-hundred before the sweeps came through. That's where we lost Éayren, and probably your child. As Lonton said – that is, Onton – this would have been an ideal moment to ride the wave of public sentiment. You've created a wave of disruption."

Antru says, "That's your in." Find a person that appeals; that's charismatic. Someone that's sympathetic to the people. Someone to build the wave, "While you continue recruiting. Recruit five, to recruit five, to recruit five others. They don't have to be strong commitments, just enough to plant the seed." An idea planted that can spread across the population. That is piqued when the uprising gets underway. That will watch with curiosity, but if it drags on, "If we can get days of disruption, I would bet they'll think about the people they've lost and want to join. But we'd have to get a few days of disruption for it to take. How long could we hold off the Nespian forces?"

Onton says, "We'd be slaughtered. We'd be smoked in minutes. We've got nothing against their weapons."

"That's it," says Antru. There's enthusiasm, because it's the first idea that's not planted with a motive. It's not a seed given to force actions, "That's the answer. Set the hills on fire. Smoke is the statement that'll draw attention. We can devise weapons we can launch. We can hit and run. If we can get ahold of those machines that fly, we can use those to drop incendiaries on them. Keep the noise on constant for the next month, and then we'll hit. We can have enough people recruited and others will follow."

"It's an interesting idea," Mash says diplomatically. However, "We don't have the numbers. The general population might be on our side, but they're too complacent. There's an acceptance built into society, and there's chemicals in everything: People want comfort and the familiar. We'd need people that are motivated."

"I have them," Antru says. "You know the northeast quarters of the city?"

"Borreans," Onton says, and the word is sour.

"We're all Borrean," Antru answers sharply. "And that's an open-air prison. The Nespians had to take extreme measures to keep them confined, and they're still fighting back any way they can. We pick a date, get someone inside to clear the areas we'll blast, and that's at least a couple-hundred-thousand, motivated volunteers that won't need encouragement to storm the fortress. If they kill a quarter-million members of the population, the backlash won't just be to push them out of power, it will call for their death. I'll also bet a large part of the city follows."

"I don't know," says Mash; says Onton, "You think?"

"It's cloudy. But it left an impression. There've been repeated crackdowns on the area, and they continue to fight back. Protests continued. I remember feeling unsafe when I made deliveries because they viewed me as complicit with what was happening. But if we can get someone inside, it would be easy to coordinate the attack: They're closely monitored, but they're considered too dangerous to oversee directly, and by now, they've already figured out how to disable, or overcome the monitors. You just need to get out there and stoke the fires."

"I'm in," Onton says. "I'm your in. I look the misfit and I can talk it. Work your plan up and I'll get it to them."

"Well, I mean," says Antru: "I'm not saying I have a plan. I'm saying, this is your operation. Work up a plan, and set it in motion. I think you'll need to put your face out there, Mash. Let the people see you. Keep, you know, firing up the masses."

"How would I," Mash asks. "We have the stories of Januk, and that was supposedly through the net. Well," Mash says, "Antru: You're our net guy. Can we use the net to transmit a message to the world?"

That's answered, "Possibly," by Antru. The purpose of the net was to protect a population from the abuses of the clans. That a fear response, and the triggering of memories would activate targeting of imminent threats. After the Astrasian assault, the population was convinced to turn it outward to protect the planet. Whatever promises had been made to convince them, those promises weren't delivered, and the net, for lack of a better analogy, became distracted. Still listening, still capable, but it was mostly looking out towards empty skies. It only looked back when effort was made. But if a general warning was necessary, "I think it could be used to send a message. It will have to be over electromagnetic frequencies, otherwise the majority won't hear it. But I think the net will recognize the potential, widespread threat. I think that could work."

"You're the face," Mash says. "The planet's talking about Antru of Capriot. They remember you on the field – raising Elite to victory. You were a hero, then, and they're wondering if you're the hero, now. You have to be the face that moves this forward."

"I'm not," Antru answers. "I'm not a leader – I'm not that person. I fight because I'm trying to kill the demons that haunt me. But I'm not someone that leads others. I wasn't in roukta, and I'm not for this. This is yours, or someone else that's compelling."

Quietly, Onton says, "It needs to be you. I'm takin' back my name – for you."

"You blasted out of a mountain," Mash points out. "You walked out like you owned the world – everyone saw security standing while you walked down the center of the street. There is not a single person on the planet that's more compelling. If you really believe this has a chance of succeeding, you need to be the face of it. It needs your belief and experience."

The shadows of life fall away to a bare brick of stone. To a plain surface that has no frivolity, nor ornamentation. It is plain, and uninspiring. It is the point of present and understanding that beyond, there is nothing. It is a pile of rubble with broken bodies. It is the face of an upcrop speeding by so fast that details go unobserved. It is a crevice that asks for commitment, knowing the stone will break away.

Cold winds blow through the shadows of the mind; an empty eternity left behind. The void that's haunted dreams since consciousness emerged sits beckoning: The sickly siren of mortal failing.

"I need to see Aedra," Antru says. "Then, I need to go to Capriot to see my family. I'll say something from there."

"We'll need some time," Mash says. It's spoken quietly and with the understanding of the commitment that's been taken – understanding the agreement that's been made: By all of them. Knowing the gravity of what will follow and the sacrifice that will fall. It is not a moment of euphoria – the opposite. It is weighty and fills the souls with sickness. It is seeing the guts of a dream splayed out for the first time under the light from the mid-day star. It is the fear of the horror that will follow, but it is also the first time an opportunity has been presented after eons of trying to find one, make one – survive. It is the first time any plan has held real footing, and it seemed to arrive out of nowhere. An idea pulled together by the last person that was ever meant to be involved, and there's sympathy: "We'll need to recruit. We'll have to build caches – incendiaries. It will take some time – we'll have some time. We'll build this out to the smallest detail."

Antu is quiet. The head bobs, but it's barely visible. The voice, "I have to," is not that of a leader, but a scratch that is desperate to, "See Aedra."

A broken soldier hops over and rests a hand on the shoulder of the one behind it: All feeling the weight, and all understanding the suffocating onus they strap across their shoulders. Eyes meet and find unspoken understanding, and the third brings crutches over to let the other lead. The plan that is just a fragile coalition of fragments pulled into a random stream that appears to hold connectivity is set in motion. The first step is to move Antru through unseen passages to see Aedra.

If it had been another time, the machinations of the subterranean outpost would have been regarded as remarkable, but it is only a passage of time by foot, by rail, and by ladder. Only an entry into darkened hallways where those confined bury secrets that are their sole hope for redemption. Eyes remain lowered as three others pass, and not a word is spoken. It feels like forever and just an instant that a cubicle is broached, and entrance offered.

Onton whispers, "They'll show you back: Whenever."

"Thank you," offers Antru, and the room is entered: Passage through a panel meant as access to deliver uniforms. Barely large enough to squeeze through, and entry is a crawl through closet, across the floor; final extraction across the bunk. The panel closes, and closet doors are quietly pulled together.

There is a comfort in the space. A familiarity of the place, and a longing to return to the routine it envisions. The very routine that was agreed upon, must be destroyed.

In the quiet and isolation of the cube, that decision falls to question. Thoughts soften and ideas begin to scatter. "Why," is the question as to if it's worth it, and the answer is found with Aedra. It's answered by Éayren. It's violently shattered as Axael looks up with wide moon eyes, and wonders, "Moboti?" Wondering why anyone would act against them. Wondering why their parent was stolen, and the fearing the same fate for their own.

There is acceptance that the choice is unequivocal, but it is hollowing, an emptiness within that wafts with vile sickness; that clouds with noxious visions of the future. Future: Endless, and empty, and a moment that is clawed against for the lost, the present, and those that follow.

There is hesitation as Aedra enters, but the door is sealed, behind. They stand just within the door and ask," What's wrong," with perception that speaks to relative clarity of mind.

"You stopped taking them," asks Antru.

"I don't understand," is a repeated mantra that is now teeth biting at the flesh of memories. It is digging at existence and trying to make sense of the blended soup of thoughts that remain scattered. But there's an island where eyes fall against a person that doesn't exist and find that something has gone wrong. That sees something has changed, because, "You're different."

It is met with emptiness. "You remember," is filled with the sickness that has permeated every pore. It speaks to a past that's gone and that can never be recovered – a life that was built, and then stolen away.

Aedra asks, "Tell me what's going on."

"I'm going to see Althrae. Will you go with me?"

"I don't," begins reflection into the tear within the psyche. A broken mind that finds islands, but they're floating, and nothing remains stable long. "I can't," is the life preserver of recent memory, of routine, and stability, and what's known. "I'm not ready," is the admission the boat is sinking, and the islands are all there are to land a foot upon.

"It's okay," says Antru softly. Great empathy is felt, because it's known: "Don't rush yourself. Take your time to understand what's happening. We can connect when I'm there. But, take your time. I promise you'll find yourself."

"What happened," Aedra asks again, because something is different. There was energy and desperation, and that is gone, replaced by heaviness and despair: "I need you to tell me what's going on. I need you to tell me the truth if you want me to trust you. Tell me why you're different."

A smile's returned. It's sorrowed, and sickly, and looks into a forever that was never long enough. A time together that was just an instant – a faded memory. A vacant past that's lost forever to eternity.

"Antru," is more determined. It's demanded, "What's going on?"

"It's just more of what it's always been," is the precursor to trying to understand. To put the mind around what's always been incomprehensible. An attempt to quantify an existence that's always floated in the aether. A life never settled: Where ideas, and plans, and hopes were always intervened, and explanations as to why were claimed best interests. "It always felt like everything I did was manipulated." From institute, to roukta, and from there – a position training others.

None of that was ever wanted. None was ever strived for, but all of it was guided and conditioned: Four years at Marphy and there was nothing wanted more than a chance to play roukta. That had never been a dream, a desire; the plan. The dream and plan were following Dalune through Capriot. And that was the most bitter pill of all of them:

"You remember what my parents always told me?"

"Live life," Aedra says: "And be happy."

"They steered me away," Antru agrees. "They told me they didn't want me involved with whatever it was they were involved in. But from the moment I took a breath on this planet, they've been giving me the tools to be part of it. They've given me an understanding and abilities that I don't think most people on this planet have. I've been assaulted and targeted, but the reasons why have always been for reasons that misunderstand the net. They don't understand – I don't connect: It's searching for us. It took me a long time to understand that's what they didn't get."

"I want to sit by you," Aedra says.

"The bunk," is suggested, but Aedra says, "No: I want to sit by you - there. Don't touch me. Just let me be near you. Promise you won't touch me."

"Of course," is given: "I know it's difficult – I've been there. Take your time. You're doing better than I did. I've got lots of witnesses that can share stories."

An awkward perch is taken beside another that sits uncomfortably, but the position's the least part of it. There is warmth felt against the shoulders that's remembered and memories begin shining a little brighter through the shroud.

Especially, as Antru says, "Just like when we sat by your columbrum." Basking in the memories. Feeling the warm glow between. "Those are some of my favorite memories." Antru looks and finds eyes looking back: Looking concerned – fear gnawing on the edge of consciousness: "Do you remember that? When you'd play? And then, we'd just sit there. Together. Sometimes have quiet conversation. I knew I loved you before I knew what love was."

"Antru," says Aedra: "Tell me what's happening."

Antru doesn't. Instead, answers, "Just take care of yourself. Yourself and the children: That's all that matters."

"I want to take care of you," Aedra says. "I just found you again, and it feels like I'm losing you. Promise you won't do that to me."

"You have me right now." Antru says, "This is all we ever had: Hold onto it while we can."

Chapter twelve:

Starlight shimmers across a field of trillions of threads. Exquisitely fine filaments of silver combined together to bring sense from chaos, that appear in their moment shone upon like they are tangible. As if they have no start and stretch forever – as if they have integrity. As if they are not all droplets of poisonous silver stretched to their limits before disintegration will inevitably fall and they will shatter into mist that will leave a momentary trace of an echo swallowed in forever.

Starlight shimmers against the vast array of filaments that are the backbone of existence. An ephemeral liquid that can masquerade with substance only under the most precise conditions. Sparkling threads that are enlightened into rivers and mountains, planets and stars; lives and living. Small ripples across the fleeting array of liquid threads that are always flowing away from the starlight's kiss into the pool at the bottom of the mountain that swallows everything to sightlessness. They waver in the light and express existence as if it's whole, and like they're real. But they are nothing but an accumulation of imaginary pieces that break down into smaller and smaller parts until there is nothing left but an entirely inconsequential charge that is recognizable as almost nothing.

Almost nothings, stacked and combined, spun into threads and to a macro scale that imagines that enumerable almost nothings are something. That trillions upon trillions of almost nothing can be brought together and be given a name. That there is purpose for nothing and meaning from it. But like the broken fragments of nearly nothing, so too the threads dissipate almost as soon as they're detected.

Starlight glints off the rain of narrow threads and imagines it as a beautiful day, with happy people gathered in a public space where children play. It creates the illusion of heat that has travelled millions of measures across empty space to pierce an improbable bubble of gasses that surround a rocky mass, covered with water, where some of the energy delivered remains trapped.

It gives rise to the idea of existence and value to be gained by action. It finds delusions of purpose and meaning that arise across the flowing threads that are, themselves, devoid of anything and insignificant.

Starlight shimmers across the meadow and is part of what is considered joy. It is warm, and the ground-cover and plants surrounding the open space are considered beautiful, even though they are just as temporary as a negligible charge that is considered to have existed for a moment when it collides against a plate.

There is a gentle breeze, but the warmth and humidity keep it from being refreshing. It is just the movement of surrounding air, brushing past along with children that careen through legs; who fill the field with a carillon of joyous peels.

The heavy air cups the moment as if with gentle hands, carefully keeping a reflection for a fragment of eternity, but that fragment is a gemstone that shines so brilliantly that the star shining down from above is of no comparison.

The children's voices are joy, and the laughter that brightens the world is love. They combine to fill in the full symphony that rises in the moment. They are the song of happiness, and the greatest fulfillment is found together, with no tethers, nor obligations, nor filters.

Where the voices are allowed to rise and sing together, where they combine into a chord of harmony, and it is known that joy exists, and it is real, and a smile will form whenever it's remembered. Whenever that bright crystal is brought forward in the consciousness, and for a moment, a waft of that existence can be felt again, even when glinting through the mind in dream.

There is a brief distortion, where a darkness tugs at the edges of the periphery, however, mind's eye remains focused and finds the children.

They sit together by the fountain with many others. They sit together in conversation. Anomaly echoes in their history – irrelevant: The tilted heads. The crooked looks – the cringe as the sense is felt. The world is quieted around them as they speak, a passing rush of air outside the windows.

"Colquon," etches against the consciousness as they start to eat. As they share the nuts, and it's realized Aedra's speaking – sitting beside, watching as well; unconcerned, as they should be. The word was an offer and thoughtfully, hands materialize, filled with several.

There is conversation, and it's light. It is a sound beneath a river, words bent by currents and covered by the water, but they talk about children. About assignments, about, "Should they be doing that?"

The bright starlight is darkened as clouds blot it from the sky. As children play, and there's no reason for concern. No complications, no problems, no worries: Axael falls back and lets the net reach down and brace the landing. It is done with an absolute trust that's been built since the dawn of their existence. They fall and bounce up again. They fly into the atmosphere and past the outer rings of the galaxy, hurtling towards the furthest reaches of known existence. They fall through stars and crash against icy bodies, pulling a glob of melting snow to bring back down to others as the net retrieves and returns them safely.

Two siblings are laughing. They sit in a puddle, tossing a rancid snowball back and forth, while the other children watch with disapproval, silent and shrouded in hooded cloaks.

They zoom into vision: Focus magnifies and brings them present, and feet stomp the waters surrounding them: Aedra crashes down with both feet and stomps a tidal wave to wash the overlookers away.

It is damp, after the rain. Few remain, and those that do remain distant. They've watched children fall, and fly away to interstitial space and are uncertain what to make of it. But even under cloudy skies, with eyes askance and a heaviness in the air that was never known in Capriot, there is still the music that plays. There is still the root, the third, the fifth, and finally, octave. It is a song that explores, inverts fifths, toys with progression, and experiments with dissonance, but it will always resolve back to the base.

Words are spoken by a faceless person that slogs past through the deep water that's submerged the meadow. Their words are warning and level threats that are incomprehensible, but clear.

"Watch me," Althrae calls across the field." They are words that have been uttered since the child spoke. One that found relationships established, and needed their own – needed attention: Undivided. They stand across the field and fall back against the water.

There is a sound that follows. It is a sound that pulls the deepest mortal fear a parent can know and brings sight to the tenuous threads that are always on the precipice of disintegration. A cry falls over the meadow and shatters crystals as a body falls against the water and finds it washed away. A body falls against the surface without the net's protection, and it lands against the rocky underlayment that had been hidden by ground cover – a landing and cry that connect through pain.

Eyes fall across the yard as legs stumble, as progression slips with footing that is volatile: Legs turn into rubber lampposts that bend against the forces of a hurricane. Children sit across the valley: One broken and sobbing, and the other trying whatever they can to rectify the situation; guilty of illustration and hoping to keep the void across the valley constant.

There are words as Aedra expresses concern, and the damaged child is lifted into arms. They are cradled and calmed, and a shirt is lifted from the back as adequate examination to discern that everything is fine.

Muffled words speak to humor and reproof to what was done, but it is within the orchestra of existence, and the tenor is to express relief for little damage done: Pulled together. Coming together as is always done to help, protect, and support the members of the family. To address mistakes that are made and improve approaches going forward.

Mumbled words stake approbation for a younger sibling, but it isn't a burden they can claim. They hold complicity only by the random chance of biological connectivity. They are not to blame, but a victim of circumstance. Tied to an understanding and awareness that stretches generations, a link in a chain that remains unbroken despite the efforts from every corner, by every angle; by everyone.

Bruised bones and guilt are guided away as children are taken in arms and held. Wrapped warmly by parents that even question in the subconscious the propriety of carrying tradition.

The soft tone of, "Antru," plays as Aedra questions, but, "It was always there."

What's shared is a hand as parents watch their child stand and consider the motion to take a step.

Althrae is laughing in the arms, too large to be cradled, and they awkwardly tumble away. They stand, already close to meeting the eye and wonder why their parent would try to hold them. They fall back against the earth, and rise again, and offer, "See?"

Long past visions still burnish sight even after years of mastery, and those words are circled around the capable child as a rappelling rope, too young to understand a parent's fears; too innocent to see the dangers.

There is muddled conversation: Pushback, and examples laid that are buried in memories and go unspoken, however, "Dalune would get so angry with me," is a crystal that bends the light of a memory to be seen.

"You don't have to worry," Althrae had said, and those words still swirl in the soup of a rebuttal that went unspoken.

Dalune cries, "Antru," but the arms and legs cannot help but climb: It is built within the body and the mind – just like the call to immense power. They are intrinsic, innate, and cannot be erased, and so Antru climbs ever higher, a small boy directly disobeying orders from a parent. Legs push, and arms pull, and the rockface goes by ever faster.

Until a hand reaches down. Progression stops, as Althrae wonders, "Why are you up here?"

They are standing on the tallest upcrop, where a child says, "You don't have to worry," despite perilous position, and the pool of eternity beside a pile of rubble beneath the clouds, below.

It is a stunning view, of sparkling, crystal clouds that extend as far as can be seen to the edge of darkness. There is the strongest pull to clasp the child within arms and hold them safely. To keep them from falling, again. To protect them from injury. To give them rules that curb their conduct; boundaries to inhibit their abilities. But arms are offered only as a gesture of adoration, or for comfort if it's needed. They're brought close, but only so the exquisite scenery can be shared together.

"Race me."

Devious eyes look back, ready to sprint to the edge of the precipice. Warnings offered a million times reflect on a child that fell and cried out across a meadow, but they are swallowed as the child's eyes watch back – no longer a child: Presiding over the edge of their experience. Instead of warning, they're given trust, and it feels like a falling body – launched from the apex of the monument, falling past smooth rockface to the bottom of the world, waiting for the impact that is certain.

There is a sound that cracks against consciousness, but it is sung away by the starlight washing down and filled with laughter. Althrae races with other children while their younger sibling cradles a parent and utters warning, "You have to be focused. You have to be locked in." Castigating an immature parent for leaping before they're ready.

The elder joins, and they are strong and capably rights the fallen parent, but they don't hold the build of the younger sibling: Always in motion, always pushing their body -always climbing. They are kind and well liked, but they are not the force of nature Axael naturally carries. They are not the unending, effervescent personality that draws others. They calculate risks and hold awareness that is more attuned to the larger world.

Axael climbs ahead of dozens of others, fearless with the knowledge of a parent's gift that allows compulsion the space to stretch without the fear of death. The body scrambles across the rockface as if it were a well-stepped rise: Fluid and unstopping.

Muddled words carve out of a dysphoria, another trait inherited but not one that gains accolades and recognition. They simmer over as their sibling is watched rising quickly, followed by others that wish they could match the speed. The words are, "Failure," and, "I'm not good at anything."

It is inaccurate and against most others, skills across the rocks are considered excellent. But Axael is naturally inclined and their destiny is determined.

"You," wavers from a bog of disillusion that sees the advantages given a second child. A child that has another hand to lift, to offer shortcuts and insights that fall from the dead-ends and failures experienced in the few years before the other arrived. But the words that follow fall empty and are muddled beneath the surface of the water.

Clarity focuses against the helpless stab into the chest: "You are good at coordinating. Others look to you – you lead others. You bring out the best of those around you. That is not insignificant, Althrae. Those are traits that will serve you well."

The words fall away as an echo against the walls of the surrounding stone. They fall like the shattered glass of memories lost but form a landscape of crystals that's still remembered. That's still pulled upon when doubts fall and lead to the valleys of disillusion. That glint against darkness and pull sadness, but feel the love and belief within words spoken. A light that illuminates a validity of what was heard and cleaves doubts that threaten shadows over the mind.

Children are watched: One climbs methodically, the other as if adhered against the surface, but both rise to higher land. Both find success and reach with sureness.

"It seems like ours was just yesterday." It is discovered that Aedra says this when eyes turn to find a typical ceremony underway. The mind scratches to make sense of the change in scenery – half-way up a mountain, to betrothed. There is a flash against the consciousness as images collide, and silver threads begin to sail away, teased free from memories sealed behind closed eyes.

Eyes squint open to a sea of bodies sleeping on the floor, an enclosed space in the hollowed catacombs of stone beneath the surface. There is a moment of reconciliation, where reality and the imagined, experience and dreams hold together with equal stature and sorting them apart finds pieces shared. Finds eyes closed against reality to try and visualize a moment left, that fell from nowhere and disturbed the mind to consciousness.

Aedra had spoken the words and leaned in closer – took a hand and clasped it firmly; arms entwined. It had been a moment that was more unsettling than expected. The beginning of sudden quiet. Evenings where meals were had with only two and the constant conversation that had filled the home for sixteen years was abruptly gone. Only echoes remained, that stretched from infancy to the dawn of a career: Following a parent's footsteps and playing roukta. The enthusiasm and excitement that led up to the moment had not forewarned of what would follow.

The transition was not easily adapted, but two hands that'd come together years before, did so again to forge a future that was only focused on each other. It had not been better, but it had been good: Rewarding – fulfilling. A rediscovery between two that found what drew them still remained. Change, but renewed appreciation was found for one another, and there'd been a return to nights shared beside the old columbrum.

Less chaos, but it had offered room to build. Quieter, but not silent, and the absence of other voices allowed for resonance.

The thin sheet is tossed aside and feet are taken. There's an urge to throw the blanket violently. There is a scream that's stifled. There's a strong desire to punch the wall. But all of it would be pointless: The blanket would fall softly, the scream would just disturb others just as disturbed, and the stone walls are unyielding and would only bring injury to the fist that's thrown.

The field of sleeping bodies is navigated but escape is only to more stone – passageways and spaces – and departure ends before the exit. Eyes look back to those sleeping with jealousy, as they still have a chance to dream of families. Peaceful, and momentarily unaware of their current circumstance. A collection of bodies buried beneath the surface and every one of them sleeps alone. They are looked back upon with sympathy, because it is understood that every one of them shares the silence. The notes that filled their lives with music have been stolen.

PART 3

Chapter one:

A burst of steam erupts from the edges of the press. It is a momentary cloud that quickly dissipates in the chilled air. A burst of heat and filter over bodies pressing uniforms, a hiss of water vapor that kisses thoughts in memory: The best of memories. Of sunny days with heavy air in Marphy. Of cool and quiet atop upcrops where sometime clouds were close enough to touch. A uniform is pressed and hung with others on a rack, each one assigned a specific destination.

The operation was an insight. An understanding of the bodies behind the walls. Of the unseen operations that are conducted in every city – of the cry for help that was passed, once, through a drawer. Most pressed into service have a checkered past and have been forced into contributing out of sight, and under tightly controlled conditions. At least, they were intended to be controlled.

There was no way to retrofit what has been created, and that's been demonstrated by the repeat efforts in the northeast sector of Greater Nespia. Time and again, even the most disruptive efforts cannot completely annihilate the adaptations and secrets built over millennia, and more walls, more digging, and more oversight still fail to uncover the disruptive elements known to exist, because the only thing those forced beneath the surface, those moving behind the walls in every city still find a will to live for, is the faintest, flickering spark of hope that runs through those that walk amongst them. A hope that rests in the hands of the underground, those that have planned and plotted since before the revolution.

They are the only ones that abide by the agreements made after the uprising of Januk. They are the only ones that share the most menial duties and do so without complaint. They are the only ones that bring food, and news, and glimpses of sunshine from the outside world. They are the ones that hunt down long-lost members of the family and report their circumstance.

It is a contract between those thrown away and those that intend to relieve them. That give rest to those that are meant to have none. That were thrown into assignments intended to grind them down until they surrendered to hopelessness and to the futility of their fate. A fate that can be saved by providing information to those that watch, however those walking amongst discarded as equal citizens are given esteem and cover, despite the hopelessness and pointlessness of their efforts – the many failings.

"Ready for release," is a cynical offer to replace another at a press – elsewhere, the many other duties undertaken by an invisible workforce that has become unmanageable, yet remains crucial to order and the function of society.

Water drips from the face, and it's as much intentional as unavoidable.

"Unless you need to," Antru says. It is a process that helps alleviate the stress. It helps wash away worry for a lost child – a parent disappeared days later. It is a flash into the past of hard work under sedated state making deliveries, as well, the thoughts to a prior life in other cities, as a child, and raising a family: "I don't mind another shift."

There is conversation that filters through the corridors. There is cynicism rampant, and it's well earned. There is yet another person making promises, that claims to enjoy trite work, and offers to take another shift feel like the greatest betrayals life has ever delivered. There is an underlying current that flows, that it is just another ploy meant to manipulate those viewed with zero value.

However, there was also the walk from a mountain in Alvel. There was a utilization of the net that was unprecedented, and that is enough to end the conversations. It is enough to ignite the hope that the speeches broadcast were more than just manipulation, more false promises – more attempts to infiltrate the underground.

The orations broadcast were uneven, somewhat awkward, and uninspiring. Most overhead had simply viewed them as an irritating interruption to their distractions.

"It takes me back," Antru says. "It reminds me of where I grew up, and where I raised my family." A smile forms as eyes look inward and remember, "The air in Marphy. I almost choked when I first got there, but that's where I'd go if I got to choose. You ever been?"

"No," the other answers: "I was always Alvel."

Antru shares, "My heart's split between Capriot and Marphy, but I think Marphy gets the edge: That's what I think of first when I think of family."

The other motions, and says, "If it's all the same."

"Yeah." It's agreed: "It's satisfying. It relaxes my thoughts to where I can think."

The other says, "It's my assignment."

"There's two to fill the rack. You want," is answered by a grunt. The other moves in and pulls a suit, and it's briefly squashed between the plates. It's slipped on a hanger and hooked beside the rest. "It's important," Antru claims: "What we do here. At the institute, when

I was working – it was appreciated. It's a huge help when you've got time constraints."

It's asked, "You believe it? The words you say – you really believe it? 'Cause I don't think it's appreciated, and I don't think it's needed. You're not the first walked through that had a lot to say. Won't be the last."

"Yeah," says Antru: "I just wanted to find my family. But how the net reached out – how I walked away: They thought people would listen." There's a smirk – a nod the other physically displays to demonstrate confirmation of opinion, but it's stressed, "Yeah: I believe in the promises they gave us when we were children. I believe everyone should contribute, and I believe at the end of the day we should go home to our families. I believe what we do here's important, and I believe everyone in the world should participate. That's what I believe."

The other mocks, "Yeah," in return, and asks with dripping doubt, "You're gonna make that happen?"

"I'm just a face," Antru answers. "I'll start the fires. I'll call: But what happens after that is up to you."

There's less certainty how to respond. Cynicism and doubt are dug deeper than the useful investigative tools that give them merit, but there's also a willingness observed that's different. There's shared suffering that's not always apparent from those of the movement – often callous and uncaring towards others. Often wielding an air of superiority and overtly infatuated with themselves. There is a sickness carried that's not unfamiliar, and it's one that comes from memories, as well as years held in captivity.

The rack is pulled away without another word, and the press remains idle as Antru's watched. As heavy feet pull the uniforms and head towards passages where they'll be slipped into a cabinet behind closed doors. Where the sedated will slip them on before plodding off for another day of servitude.

The design of passages beneath the surface and behind the walls of housing units was intended to have safeguards to prevent malcontents from using them. There are checkpoints where scans are made at several points, however, there was no foresight given for how to directly intervene should that ever become needed – and it's long, and widely agreed it is. There are ways to punish and eliminate, but like embedded scanners, those controls were overridden over time. Those that commit crimes, and those that need to disappear can be sent below, but control is only maintained through managed resources and rewards for those that contribute - especially those that work as moles.

Rewards are food and water, and the ability to sleep, controls that have been offset by the presence of the underground. However, they also insist on maintaining the appearance of order and continued contribution. That they have communication with the outside world is the leverage they maintain, but it is also the source of resentment held towards them: Access is kept exclusively for themselves.

The arrangement of cooperation was born from hope, thousands of years before, but it's continuation rests mostly on the existence of a common enemy. An arrangement that is somewhat antagonistic, but viewed as agreeable to all with shared eyes looking to Nespia. It is a delicate balance that has been undermined thousands of times, and that has benefitted no one, neither below, nor above the surface.

The current below is slightly elevated enthusiasm, and above, slight trepidation. There is uncertainty for everyone as the words that were widely broadcast have not made demands as in the past, and have only spoken about loved ones and wanting their return. It is a message that has struck through the omnipresent sedatives that are laced within the food, the water, and the air. It is a message that reminds the world that people are missing.

The first uniform is slid into the dark recess of a cabinet. A fresh-pressed uniform that appears each morning and is adorned without question. Present, just like nutrients and hydration capsules. A second uniform is placed, and feet move on to the next in darkened passages.

There had once been an effort to automate the process and some consideration had been given to reconstructing what was built, but those efforts are the continued failings in northeastern Greater Nespia, where the confined population breathes open air and not only plots underground with simple aims, but also riots with continuity, finding ways beneath, or over, or through the walls intended to confine them. The ones beneath the surface at least are kept free from eyes and out of mind. They are kept buried under stone and the weakest points – the cubicles, remain designed to eliminate a second from departure before they ever make the exit. For the most part, those beneath the surface continue to serve a purpose and deliver a needed service to society.

However, new worries grow with a blasted mountain and recent reticence to coordinate from Capriot and Marphy. Concerns rise as whispers are amplified overhead of a brewing plot.

"You'll do it," is questioned — contravening protocol and risking exposure. To make sure it's clear, the question is, "You'll bring the fire down on them?"

Every interaction is a risk — especially in the halls. One compromised individual given promise of freedom, or more likely, freedom for a partner or their child, and the chosen face to lead assault against the clans is gone: Soon enough, from memory.

The person's answered, "No," and it's clarified, "We bring the fire. We will burn down their fortresses. The net is our protection while that happens. Think about it while we attack their castles." Another attempt to glean information's given, "No. Do what you have to here. No conversation."

The misconception is the greatest impediment to the plan: Just like the clans, those underground believe the net can become a weapon. Just like security in Capriot, there is a belief that a person can control it — bend it's will to wreak violence and destruction.

It is not misguided, as both have been wrought since its inception, but the misunderstanding arises from the belief that a person controls the action, rather than the truth that sometimes, extreme measures are taken to protect a person. It is a subtle distinction, but ultimately, one that's necessary to share for what's planned to have success: The more protected, the more likely they are to have it.

Feet walk the dark halls in near silence, with padded slip-ons muting scuffs as well as scurries of which both serve different interests. Quiet footsteps pass in the confinement of near darkness and a sharp jab is sent into the shoulder.

The other continues. It is not clear if the collision was intent, or another unaware, in the midst of some sort of movement. They continue on without a word and without pause, just as orders that were delivered have required. Feet walk on in near complete darkness, in near complete silence, with nothing known of one, but one moving on with growing dissolution: Every person becomes suspect. Suspicion falls everywhere, and plans continue to demand patience. There is too much to do, too much to share, and too many to turn. Every passing shadow is one more darkening of the passage towards success, and another reminder of how unlikely it is that any involved will see it, or even tomorrow.

Another panel's grasped, but it remains. It is the third, already, that finds the resident inside and it is one more point that speaks against success: Everyone needs to continue in their roles and present a sense of normalcy. The sooner action is taken against behavior, the less likely the plans of attack will find success: Discontent needs to be harbored yet licked at with an infected tongue to keep wounds in the forefront of the mind. It is a hopelessly fragile balance that is continuously finding failure at every end.

A panel's grasped, and it remains still. It is the seventh of twenty-five, already, and an alarming strike against common order. By the end of the run there are nine, and that number is non-anomalous.

"I have a plan," says Antru. The materials are not unattainable, though, they aren't ideal, but it's agreed to sacrifice emergency ventilation, to create an apparent automated system. That will alleviate the potential for contact. It will also be an opportunity to deliver messages, and that will also be done through contacts that have been established. For Antru, that connection is bittersweet, as despite an agreement to forego the pills, Aedra's memories still remain out of reach – only wisps of glimpses into the past. "I have a plan," Antru repeats into the protest that arises, and the plan's explained, considered, and adopted.

There had been insistence that Antru of Capriot, the bludgeoner of Marphy, and the salvation of Elite, the person that blasted a massive hole through tons upon tons of rock, and then blasted out of the side of it – that person was held up as the face of the resistance. As the person that would restore the agreements promised to Januk. That the person would no longer allow families to be pulled apart: Partners lost, parents disappeared; children forgotten. "They still remember you," it had been said. "You're the one person we have that can inspire the people."

Ripped from a partner, a parent stolen, and a child that can't be located. Stuffed into the menial labor that was meant to be shared, and then forgotten.

"The hero," says a dissenter, of the contrivance. An explanation: "All we've got's emergency evac. You rip it down – we're helpless against them. Who's side are you really on?"

"Mine," is the answer: Fighting for Aedra, for Axael, and even Éayren. Someone that gave up everything for the people: Career, family, and potentially their life. The answer is, "I'm here like everyone: They wanted me gone. They've ripped my family apart, and that's whose side I'm on: My family. I'm going to set the hills on fire – for them. And, I hope you'll join me. Because I won't walk away from this world – like it is – for my children. They deserve better."

There was applause, which wasn't wanted, nor expected. The interaction was recorded and released to the general public, which was considered inappropriate, and also, premature. There was a growing push towards isolation, which was considered counterproductive and unnecessary.

However, in Capriot and Marphy there was a day held to celebrate the accomplishments of Antru from those cities, of a storied family with success in roukta, and otherwise. Of a parent joined with the net that had likely passed that to their offspring, and a re-consideration voiced about what had ever been accomplished. The brief speech about fighting for children followed, and the first protests began with any numbers in the northeastern section of Greater Nespia.

Protests remain mild and are a distraction to put eyes on that location, to further the suspicion that the underground is centered there, and remains intact, despite yet another attempt to eliminate entirely.

"When is it happening," is a question that's asked too frequently, and the answer's always disappointing:

"I wish it already happened, but there's so much we have to put in place. We have to raise awareness. We need to have eyes focused on the hills. And we need to build weaponry and supply the caches. It feels like it's taking forever, but when the day comes – it will feel like we should have waited."

Chapter two:

"Something interesting?"

It's a question asked of the rough map graphed of the nation. The island is central, and cities are adjacent in more detail. The deep, orange circles have been increasingly filled with neon purple, indications caches have been filled. Of note are three in the proximity to\ northeast Nespia.

"We're ready to move in?"

The other says, "Just looking for volunteers," which earns: "I'm the volunteer."

"Ah," is returned. "I don't – I don't," is stammered before more salient words find ground: "I don't think they'll let you do that."

Antru insists, "I am."

There is no more argument as the other observes the statement's believed – as if it would happen. As if the increasingly familiar face of the Borrean Underground would be allowed to risk their life to pass a message. To deliver instructions to those confined within the walls they'd also delivered. The walls believed to confine members of the family and why no argument will succeed: A child's life at stake is worth the chance of sacrifice.

The other leaves with nothing more said, but noting opinions and ideas grow more entrenched. That a sense of progression towards an end is narrowing: There is a real, and growing sense, below, and overhead, that significant undertakings are underfoot.

It brought a convening of the co-ology: Clans come together to discuss the disruptive violence that's increasingly anticipated. Efforts to flood intoxicants across the population and significantly underground have found those efforts have not lessened discontent.

More worrisome, that discontent was openly aired by the Emperor of Capriot and given support and uninhibited applause by the cohort out of Marphy. Even the Rims communities and Minaut have not expressed unwavering support for the status quo, and opting to abstain from votes brings a consensus approach to move forward at a stalemate. There has also been express demand for the safety of southern citizens.

It is an upheaval and show of defiance unrecognized by any living, but it is also a callback to the stories shared from history, of Januk's courageous sacrifices for the nation. Antru is claimed by Capriot and Marphy, and increasingly hailed as the modern visionary that sees through the deceptions indoctrinated through society. That clans have begun to openly support the movement is viewed by the north as a worrisome threat to national security. Unfortunately, the simplest action of eliminating the problematic, is also viewed as a move that would be unreconcilable with the rest of the county.

Especially after the last message aired by the Borreans: Not just of Antru, but dozens with lost partners, parents, and children. Executing all of those that have been cleverly, and emotionally linked to the broader population is recognized as a recipe for disaster. A move that would bring an emotional uprising that would not easily be dispensed.

The latest, intercepted order from Nespia, is to let emotions settle before taking any further action. Unfortunately, the greatest challenge to that is the ability to control the net, and to eliminate further messaging: Counter-messaging speaks to common ground, common heritage, and common interests. It has at least shaved the sharpest edges from the nation's angst, but the discontent still roils through society, and increasingly there is a breakdown of expected function:

Uniforms are missing. Streets remain dirty. Syphons clog and back into living quarters. Transports remain idle with deliveries stranded. Pleas for calm and patience find eyes increasingly looking back at failing leadership.

Except in Marphy – not in Capriot. There are failings in both, but they are not the force behind the program designed to avoid conscription to the vilest of services. That blame falls where it's deserved: On Alvel, but mostly upon Nespia.

Ire focuses on the Nespian clan, and that is where forces are coalesced, prepared to destroy anticipated attempts of rebellion. However, despite the failing order, there is an eerie calm and the slightest disruptions have led to several unintended casualties. It has only added to the growing distrust in the population, but days tick by without even the usual protests from behind the walls of the Borrean northeast: Three circles are filled with purple on the map, nearby.

"Checking on the progress," interrupts just that.

The voice is of one familiar, and the one behind the plan. That's questioned, "How is this going to work?"

It's admitted, "No matter what the plan is, we're going to need luck. They feel the heat – we hope that brings them into conversation. That's the best shot we've got."

Shot is the word that reverberates in mind at scenes envisioned of masses swarming against the steep slopes of the Nespian fortress: A highly defensible position with forces dug in and prepared for months. Throngs against well-known terrain are seen as bodies that will be left scattered across it.

Says Mash, "You have a plan, bring it up at the next round-table. But we're spread too thin to split our resources. Focusing on a single point's our best chance."

"I've seen," Antru says, but protest's doused:

"I think – you have better things to think about – right now." Mash says, "Go see Aedra. You can share your ideas, but everyone that's agreed to move forward knows what's being volunteered. They're gonna want to stick together." Mash says, "Later," as another attempt is made to press the point – and their point is made as they exit for other places.

It's a moment claimed as the best chance to force change in generations, at a moment where the underground is near its weakest. Where infiltration has eliminated most units, and at best, the majority of those that live will have to be sprung from cages. It is the perfect alignment and coincidence of circumstances with the worst possible timing. A point where public awareness is at its highest, and those that would lead the charge against the status quo are the fewest – possibly ever – weakest, and possibly compromised. There is suspicion with the plans in place, that comes from the top.

The sound of a foot digging at the floor, followed by the sound of two posts staging position brings eyes to another, familiar face.

It is a face that is grizzled by time and experience, and one that will never be suspected of being compromised. They are a person that is the epitome of the resistance, and one willing to sacrifice everything to salvage the lives of the person or persons they've lost.

Their desperation has been seen, and it's understood. Their rash actions are the same as the rash insistence to enter the northeast prison of Nespia.

"You trust Mash," brings a cloud of darkness that suggests that trust should never be questioned:

"You," says Onton, "Got no idea what you just said."

"You broke rank:"

"Not trust," says Onton. "And, case you forgot: I should've listened. You call Mash a pompous nit I'll let it slip, but they'll be front-n-center in the trenches."

"In case you forgot," is shot back bitterly, because, "I got volunteered to be front and center. I don't feel like being there if it's pointless."

A finger pokes into the shoulder, and Onton says, "You got a better plan, then tell 'em. Otherwise, that's what we're gonna do."

A smirk follows, as nothing else is said, but it's not because a point was made, nor that there was anything valuable in what was offered – outside of a shared sense of commitment: A demonstration of loyalty. But deference for the movement's leader remains missing. It's one more part of an equation that fails to resolve.

A plan that looks like another that ended with disaster. Like ignoring orders then, warnings about failure are overridden because the chance of opportunity. A moment where a swell of support is felt and caches have been filled. But a plan to storm a well-defended fortress built on upcrops is not one devised upon the lessons of experience. It is the same, rash decision that's driven by the taste of opportunity, that left a transport overturned at the entrance to the quarry.

"Not too many," says Onton, and the words are openly derisive: "Get half the troops involved so they can see their partner. Must be nice to have that kind of leverage."

They're answered, "Yes. It is." However, that leverage is limited, and it's more of what fails to settle comfortably.

There's no sense of inclusivity. Most that survived the raids to eliminate the underground were overhead when that went down. There is little connection between the members of the units. There is shared purpose and experience that's similar but social connections are limited to small sub-groups. Elements that move the same direction, with shared purpose, but without cohesiveness. And the underground's public face is the epitome of that disconnect: A forgotten hero resurrected in the public consciousness to stand as the face and voice of a resistance that has always left most uneasy. However, that voice is almost entirely disregarded by those that are supposedly represented.

But there is leverage, as noted by the efforts undertaken to provide security. The voice and face are the trigger for a population's memory and thoughts to those that have disappeared without an explanation. There is leverage, because without the voice and face, the slim chance the general population will rise against the clans is close to none. By the time the trolley reaches its destination, a spark has grown to a full idea to use the little leverage that there is to alter the approach that will be taken.

"It's secure," is answered, "As close as we're gonna get."

"Because if anything happens," Antru begins, but it's paused: "We got eyes outside. We've got position.

403

As far as we can tell, the room's clear. Just make it quick."

Instructions are passed, but they're unnecessary. The cube is the fifth from the end, and it opens to disappointment: It opens, indicating no one's present.

The small opening is more difficult to clamber through, than remembered. Shoulders barely pass, and the waddle into the cabinet on hands is awkward and far from quiet. There is a point where arms leave the near surface for the floor, and the discomfort from the position wasn't remembered. However, there was a quick push to reach the bunk that's re-enacted, and anything that can be grabbed is used as aid to fall into the room. That the door doesn't burst open with waves of black-clad members of security indicates that the efforts to secure the space were initially successful.

The panel is closed, and cabinet doors follow, and the room is breathed in and accepted: Dark and quiet. Slightly cool for the person that will return from a day of labor. There is a sound that fills the ears as the space is taken, and it remembers the sounds of memory. Of voices that sang with cheer – of laughter. Three that melded together in perfect harmony, and the memory swims in the atmosphere, but the chord is minor and the feeling is only despair. Hopelessness for what the future holds.

Even with changes to plans, there is a sense there's no return. That the battle begins where it ends for one. That the only hope is that others take the lead, filled with inspiration from one that is willing to sacrifice everything to save their family.

And, it is a sacrifice that is willing. But it is achingly painful to think of the loss – time within the song. Moments to hear the harmony and create new memories. Tears fall at the thought that there will never be another moment beside the columbrum.

The door opens after how much time has passed is uncertain, but it's not been inconsequential. Aedra enters and only pauses momentarily to process the situation.

Their first words are, "I saw you."

"Yes," says Antru.

"I didn't know if you'd come back." Aedra moves for the sanitation station and removes clothes as they walk. They are tossed at the syphon and the chamber closes. There is only a momentary hiss, and then the whirl of wind that follows, and Aedra emerges and moves for the drawers and evening clothes.

"I want to share – what's happening," Antru starts.

Aedra sits and hits the bunk, and says, "Come. Sit with me."

It's an invitation that's taken immediately. The song remains sour, but as much as it's heartbreaking, the overture finds triumphant notes in an ocean of dissolution. Those sparkle more brilliantly as a hand is taken at arrival and eyes meet others that hint at recognition.

It is prematurely presumed a point's been overtaken, and the invitation, "You can leave with me," dampens what was hoped a grand finale:

"No," Aedra says: "Not yet. I've started seeing things a different way and, I think I understand some of what you said. But I need some time. Can you give me that?"

Antru says, "Yes," however, "I don't think I have much time. Can I tell you what's happening?"

"You can," says Aedra, "But I want to know, am I who you lost?"

A hand reaches across the shoulder and pulls the other close, and there's no resistance. There's familiarity found in both, and comfort to be close, but still bitterness and sickness that the efforts have affected, as intended: There are hints at memories nipping at the consciousness, that remember feelings, and warmth, and the sound of the symphony that was built through years together. They hold together, and both are falling into the well of despair as children are remembered.

"I'm going to Capriot," Antru says. It is soft – almost whispered. Words are daggers that bite the tongue, and every iota of those shared leaves a trail of blood: "I need to meet with Dalune, and Althrae is there with their family." There is a pause – a breath held momentarily – before offering, "You can join me."

Silence follows.

The hand grips tighter, and the shoulder leans into familiarity. But, "I can't," is the answer given.

There's regret, and a feeling of failure, but Antru says, "I know. I get it: I've been where you are. It isn't easy – just keep trying."

Aedra replies, "Okay."

More is shared, but it isn't quickly. There are long pauses that rest between the ability to speak. To share of plans, and caches, and the need to bring more into the fold. For the first time in a long time, what's shared is listened to attentively, and there's an understanding that lies beneath the question, "How do you fit into all of this?"

The answer to the question is from where the underlying sickness that has existed for all eternity finds its origin. It is threads pulled together since the start of time to paint a picture, to give knowledge and understanding, training and experience that fulfill abilities that are necessary for a revolution to find success.

"I just wanted to live my life with you," says Antru: "And our children; visit the parents when we could. That's all I wanted."

Wonders Aedra, "So, why don't you?"

"That leaves you here," is answered, and worse, "With Axael still missing. I don't have a choice, and I don't think I ever did. Come with me, Aedra: You don't have to stay here."

"And what happens," is asked, "When this fails? Then I'm left with nothing: Without you; without our children. I'd rather forget everything again."

"You heard that," Antru asks – regret that anything was said. It was presumed it would likely be forgotten – for a moment guard was lost and the hopelessness seeped through. "I have to find Axael. But otherwise, I can walk away."

"Would you," is definitively answered, "Yes." Because, "Sometimes I want to. I feel like a fool being used like a puppet. I have an idea that might actually work but no one will listen. Come with me and I'll walk away after I find Axael."

But Aedra's head is found low, and slowly shaking: "You can't." Pleas otherwise are brushed aside because, "I heard you talking – when you were talking. With the people. When you weren't just reading what they wrote for you. Just say what you feel, because that's what's breaking through. That – is what broke through."

Antru swears, "I would," but is answered, "Make them listen. Make them listen – for me. I don't want to lose you: Promise you'll make them listen."

"Come with me," Antru begs.

But Aedra answers, "No. I'm not ready. Make them listen. Come back once they agree, and then you can tell me your plan. But I don't want to leave until I know there's at least a chance."

A smile is shared as eyes meet, but they're not well. They are ailing with the memories that were nearly lost, and the heaviness of a future that weighs uncertainly.

But the words are what was always held, from early days as children, to quiet conversations beside the columbrum, to later years and raising children. It is the trust that was always there and belief in one another. Of knowing a plan devised keeps another one in mind and holds a chance, at least, that the future might still survive. The press to impress a better plan and faith it is better than another lies in the shared experience they'd grown together.

The fog has lifted, but the future remains shrouded, and there is fear.

"I promise you," Antru says. Feet are taken, the cabinet door is opened, and one last offer's given, "Last chance."

"Stay with me," rebuts the offer, and it's repeated, "Stay with me until I have to leave."

Sirens warn of impending danger. Shadows impinge against the tender moments of intimacy bared, and there's a pounding drum that thrubs within the cranium that are the words ignored that everything should move quickly.

However, those clouds are unable to extinguish the light that shines. They cannot tarnish the naked, earnest honesty that shared the fears and reasons for the reticence to leave. They break like shards of glass across the floor as eyes are met, and they are watering – a face that's strained and the smile is brought as much from sorrow as the hope that another moment can be shared.

If there was duplicity – and there's no question that it isn't – there would have been no resistance. Antru says, "Okay," and the door is pressed gently closed against the cabinet.

A hand reaches forward, and it's taken. "Pretend I have my columbrum," is the opening to share the bunk, and an evening of quiet conversation. It is the veil lifted from the past and memories settling, and the need for comfort and quietude with the most trusted person of existence. A person that is finally whole in memory and the only anchor to the scattered thoughts that continue fragmenting the foundation searched to set upon. It is the reunion of the past in the uncertain present, with a future that remains unclear. Arms hold together for stability and hope, but hopelessness is near and an equal motivator.

Chapter three:

When the cabinet is opened another time, after the cubicle's been abandoned the next morning, immediate hostility is encountered. There is anger and castigation. There are warnings of compromise and recounts of dangers brought to others.

There is no relief to the angst that's being shared, as the response that's offered, is simply, "I know."

No apology, no regret; no sympathy for others. An admission that acknowledges the dangers, but it was not intended, and that's not shared. It is part of a larger conversation that can turn the outcome. An example to be held as argument for other options.

Arrival back at the central compound is met with more hostility and angered words, and, "Where's Mash," is not received with positivity.

"I'm walking unless we talk," finally brings movement, though it's preceded with profanity and further accusations, and motion's only taken after, "Where're you going," is asked, but not answered: Motion made to exit the underground.

Empty threats fall, and they're exemplar of the lacking cohesion that threatens to undermine any operation, regardless. It is the same undercurrent that brought the promise to abandon everyone, to concentrate on searching solely for one's child, and if Aedra had accepted, it would have happened.

Progress is blockaded by a phalanx that fills the passageway. They are uncertain, but weapons are displayed, though, held down. It is evident that orders have been passed but the lack of connection is still displayed: Uncertainty of how to act and what should happen – the degree to which authority should be laid.

It results in none and a success only because the hall is narrow and the several present straddle it many deep.

Antru asks, "Why are you here?"

"You can't," one person says. Their thoughts drift off as an afterthought as eyes look upward. As there's a cringe away – as if there was a threat amongst them.

"The net," Antru questions: "That's for you. That's to protect you." And it's clarified, because it is apparently needed, "I'm also not a threat to you: I'm just walking. I thought I'd go see starlight."

"That," another says, "Is why they sent us here: You can't go out."

Antru muses, "The underground." The mysterious organization fighting the good fight out of sight within the shadows. The last stalwart against the practices that were supposedly eliminated millennia, before. "The Borrean Underground," says Antru: The mystique tarnished by the literal existence – burrowed beneath the surface and frightened to come out. Hiding underground and forcing anyone that joins to remain buried. Antru says, "I'm not part of an underground. I am Borrean, and this is my land. I will walk on it, under starlight and without fear. If they want to kill me because of it, then they can kill me, but I won't hide from who I am. This is my planet, my country, my land, and my people. We are not subjects of the Nespian cult that has subjugated us throughout history. We have our own - our own history: In the austere stone of Capriot, and the warm embrace of Marphy. We don't hide or bow our heads to anyone. Step aside," Antru orders, "Let me see the starlight."

Eyes look back for guidance, and another says, "Antru." It is the voice that was called for, and eyes turn back find its body's surrounded by dozens more:

There are hundreds present under the ostensible pretense to prevent a single person from exiting an underground fortress that is supposedly plotting to overthrow the world's governance. There are so many flaws in the narrative that it's impossible to begin the outline of the story.

But Mash avers, "You are continuing to put our operations at risk."

Antru says, "I could say the same," and it's angrily rebutted:

"You played – roukta? A game? We're trying to end a history of abuses: This is not a game. This is a small militia trying to end the tyranny of the Nespian clan. Everything we do is carefully planned, and you're compromising – possibly – the best opportunity we've had in several lifetimes. If you don't want to represent us, that's fine. We can find something better than a former roukta player."

It is a strangely personal attack, and it leads to an offramp from the planned angle to address the failings of the accepted strategy. The concept of unity and working together for shared objectives is abandoned with the accusation, as a light shines down on the failures of the approach, like the net's own vision. There is an opening that finds clarity with the statement:

"You played," asks Antru.

"Sure," Mash answers – cool, dismissive; derogatorily said, "When I was a child."

It plays into the road that fell into vision, and Antru says, "Yeah:" Humored, reflective – bemused. Because, "We all used to race the upcrops – that's what you did?"

Mash answers, "Yeah," without understanding it's exactly what was hoped for.

"Right up the upcrops," Antru says – still reflectively. Still, as if, the conversation is trite and only thinking back to memories. But the question, "The first one up's the winner, right," is the hook setting up the takedown to the strategy that's been held up as the best, possible approach to ending the enmired practices of society. Practices that remain pervasive, even in the country's south – despite claims made to the contrary. "Race up – who's the winner," Antru asks."

"The first one," Mash answers, "That gets there. What's your point?"

The question earns a smile – a sick, twisted smile that looks back to the understanding that there is one: "Everyone attacks at once, and the first one to the top's the winner. But you never see that in the league, and there's a reason. Do you know why?"

"You need to come back down," Mash answers. "Everyone knows you don't like our plan, but Nespia's the head of everything. If we decapitate the head, then we win."

"Agreed," says Antru. "However, no team rushes the whole squad at once straight up the rocks. Because – the defense – has the advantage. It would be a losing strategy, every time. Nespia's upcrops are tall and well defended. Access points will be traps for anyone that enters, and aerial vehicles will scrape anyone off that's trying to climb. No one would watch our matches if we took that approach, because they wouldn't last ten minutes. Like you said, it's just a game, and everyone knows what the other team is doing: Climbing up rocks, gathering stones, and then running the gauntlet.

It's a simple game, but it's the strategy that makes it interesting. Without one, it will be a slaughter, and no one watching will be inspired. They'll turn away, turn within and reach back for the comfort and familiarity of the known. To get the general population to follow us, we need to demonstrate not only that we have a winning strategy – just as importantly – that we have staying power. Our effort needs to be ongoing and build to the finale. That's how we gain the rest of the world's support, and that's how we get the southern clans to openly voice it."

"Hear, hear," is called the instant there's a hint of silence. A foot stabs against the cool, stone surface with more force than necessary and two posts jab and rattle as they land, as Onton moves with the same approach taken towards everything: Harder than necessary, with more force, more rashly, and ready to fight to the last. But the truth was spoken: "I ain't climbing, and like Capriot said, they got the A.V.'s. They've been reinforcing those roads since that mountain got blasted. They know we're coming and I can't wait until we do, but we see the same thing: We're gettin' wasted. I think you oughtta let the team captain share the plan. Respect," Mash is offered, "But I wanna be around to see what happens next."

Eyes turn as it's a sentiment that's widely shared: Ready to act, but unwilling to be a sacrifice. The entirety of the plan rests on a public willing to act after watching the horrific. Hearing doubt openly spoken gives words to what had been felt, a growing sickness that the ultimate sacrifice will be for nothing.

Mash asks, as if unlikely, "You got something?"

"Yes," says Antru, and the plan is shared:

"It begins when I go to the northeast sector. I'll deliver the when, how, and what we need from them. Despite efforts to prevent it, I will be taken into custody. I know where they'll take me, and I know how I'll get away, but I'll remain for several days. That's when you become the face, Mash: You will need to formally air our grievances and file formal protests through Capriot and Marphy – Minaut, as well, but they're not as important. Keep them in the loop, but concentrate on the conversation with the southern clans, and broadcast updates to share what is happening with the public. When I re-appear, I will share that the Nespian Clan is holding my child and parent, forcing them into service against their will, and keeping them separated from their family. You will then need to deliver our demands to the Nespian Clan. They will probably refuse to even acknowledge them, and we will escalate the rhetoric – against the clan. We will need to beseech the Greater Nespian people to work with us. They are subjugated just like everyone.

"All of this will raise the alarm of the Nespian clan and their security will further reinforce their positions and be on alert. And this is when we will give them our feint: We will attack, but it won't be against Nespia – we attack Alvel."

Mash protests, "Alvel's not going to change anything. Everything runs through Nespia, and if that's not addressed, then nothing changes."

"That's the feint," Antru says again. "That's why we have the ongoing conversation, and if we're lucky – support – with Capriot and Marphy. We take Alvel with the hinted intent to isolate Nespia. If the southern cities support, or even don't speak out against our assault, it will draw the public's imagination. They will see us fighting for what they want."

"That's the feint," Mash acknowledges, and truly curious, inquires, "What's the plan?"

"The Alvel clan is much smaller, their security force is small, and the terrain is much more approachable. We'll start with lightning attacks and destroy what we can, but the point will be to keep fires burning. Let the people below see smoke rising from the compound in the hills, for days. That will further inspire the wider public's imagination, as they will see an ongoing assault on Nespia's closest ally. If we can get even one single clan to throw their support behind us, those watching will know this is bigger than the attempts that have been made before."

"And then," Mash surmises, "They rise up and force the Nespian clan to meet our demands. You really think that's going to happen?"

Antru answers, "No."

The odds of overthrowing even the smaller Alvel clan are slim, but a sustained attack could result in significant damage. "If we chase the clan out of the compound, we will have to re-assess our next plan of action, but I don't think we'll get to that point before they call for help. At that point, Nespia will have to act to demonstrate they still hold control and can support those that have been most loyal to them. If they do not take action, they will look weak and cowardly, but when they do, that is when we move for Nespia.

"They move south, we move north, and we open the northeast sector of the city. As hundreds of thousands of very motivated people begin moving across the city, we will formally begin our assault against Nespia. What was done to Alvel will be done to Nespia, and we will then call on the public to support us, to rise up against the Nespian clan. I believe, at that point, at least some will."

"Where do you fit in," Mash questions.

"I will launch the first strike." It is a role that a lifetime has prepared for: Climb the highest upcrop above the city, stand at its apex and call the people to rise against the oppression of the clan. "I will light the stone on fire as a beacon, calling on everyone to join us."

Fairly, Mash questions, "What happened to getting wiped-out by the av's? You got a plan for that?"

"Yes," says Antru: "I can pull the net to defend against them, and I'll need others to do the same. I can train you well-enough that you can establish contact with it – enough you can pull defensive cover. I would like to ask Onton's crew to join me for that initial attack, to hold off any assault on the ground. If I may, and if you will, Onton: I will need people like you with me."

Said proudly, "It will be my honor," as posts rattle against the stone for emphasis.

Eyes look back to Mash and find a new severity is worn. There has been a change of expectation. A chance and hope, and wishful thinking are removed by possibilities, and grounding. There's a real chance a real war might break out and the thought's terrifying: "You think that has a chance?"

"Yes," Antru answers, though, admits, "A lot will have to go right for us. A lot of what I think they might do has to happen. But if we stay in the public eye for days, or weeks, with an assault that grows and with continued smoke rising over Alvel, I think the flame over Nespia will ignite the emotions of our people. I

417

think it will earn an outpouring of support as people remember those that are gone. They will not accept the excuses for why that happens any longer and they will – want – to join us. But I think that's why we start with Alvel. We have to build for that moment."

Mash says, "Onton," and it's an order: "Work with Antru. Learn the net thing, and I'll organize divisions. How long to train about two-hundred people to do this?"

"Two days," says Antru: "It isn't hard. They won't be able to control it, but they'll be able to let it find them and make it aware of imminent danger. It's very simple, and it will protect them."

Chapter four:

"Moboti," falls across eternity like drops of rain against the threads of time. Filaments that, for an instant, appear to have cohesion, seem to have substance; are felt to hold meaning. Emboldened by the song that sprung from voices melded, they were considered to hold solidity that was never real. There were only threads together that reflected the light of stars to paint a picture but it's only an illusion, and with the song grown wilted with the fraud known more, they shatter at the slightest perturbation.

A word ripples across trillions of threads and the real and existence are shredded into tangles that warp vision. A word that was a song becomes condemnation as eyes no longer look for hope, or help, or answers. Eyes look back as equals and the threads no longer conceal a reality that was suspended in a bubble of delusion. That relied upon the untenable to warp the comprehension of the one that called, of the voice that wondered, and a note that was one that made a symphony.

Threads hang loose and uneven, ribbons of a painting of which the essence, only, remains. There is an impression. A breath against an entire universe that still clings in the afterthought of the emptiness that is seen behind the remnants of liquid silver threads that were once believed – led to believe – they were constant and eternal. That tomorrows follow and voices will never leave.

"Moboti," wonders, and innocence is shattered. The solid world falls to pieces in an instant. Disbelief throttles the mind with numbing incomprehension. The world turns black, and the negligent threads of existence are seen, thin and always slicing at the flesh, spilling blood that flows into a void, below, that fills a pool with liquid that is blackened by the vacancy of starlight.

It is where innocence is drained. It is where the dewy eyes that looked up with trust upon those eyes fell upon, bring the greatest injury of disappointment. Where the deepest failing lies as the bubble bursts and the birth of understanding begins to grow. Where omniscience falters, and the solidity of knowledge, protection and provision blows through the window in tattered threads that bare the sense of helplessness experienced, is a shared condition. Soft eyes sharpen as the solid ground of existence begins to blow away as nothing more than an illusion painted on the poison threads of a flowing liquid that is unsustainable.

Condemnation echoes in that poured on prior generations, from eyes that saw beyond the window and found exactly the same thoughts that cross the child's mind. That wonder why and question lessons taught, but moreso, everything that's not. That watch the remnant threads of all existence slowly drip away into an endless future that holds no starlight to reflect it. That see through feigned solidity to the narrow bands which are momentarily strung together in a woven web that once deceived as resolute, but it is liquid and was never lasting.

The atmosphere weighs heavily with the despair from promises that were levied, vows that were never more than fairy tales. Ideas, ideals, and truths deployed within the guise of offering serenity and safeguard, but the sophistry always leant a dissonance that shadowed starlight even on completely cloudless days. A shadow cast by words that lack provision. Storm clouds built from questions left unanswered, by words that worm around the corners of square replies.

A dark cloud in thoughts for children wondering, but a weight that grows for the source of discontent. A weight shouldered before awareness had arisen, as an infant's cradled, slowly swaying in the arms that vowed protection: Security and comfort - nourishment and health. But they are powerless against the arms of time and can only hope to mold a moment to enjoy: Offer words and direction that fall as empty as they are spoken; seen inadequate when eventually they are realized.

Weight pulls tired legs beneath the surface as all the liquid silver flowing in the universe and all the stars combined are inadequate to overcome the obliterating darkness that arises from complete inadequacy and failure as a child's eyes look back with accusation.

The body falls and light fades quickly. Lungs ache against stale air that was long ago consumed, kept only as a reminder of incapacity. To remember words that were spoken that skirted truth, and arms that were promised as salves despite a flesh of shattered crystals.

The body falls and shadows pass to commemorate a brief moment where starlight caught a spill of liquid silver, and for a moment, it appeared as if it wasn't poison. For one small instant, starlight reflected, and it appeared the world was whole and everything was beautiful.

Axael asserts, "You were looking for me."

They are a shadow that washes away in currents before they're even seen. They are an impression within the water that escapes from fists that grasp desperately to uphold a promise. But all that's left is ash that slips between the fingers to the darkened seabed in a grossly futile effort to manage the ocean. Currents wash them to oblivion as Althrae rows a tiny boat that's sinking, overhead.

The oar stabs against the surface to ignite starlight against the broken waters. There is no progression, but despite the flood that swamps the hull, the dinghy manages to remain just even with the surface.

The oar stabs, and light shimmers down, sharing the beauty and warmth of a burning orb with the desecrated creatures that roam, below. But it is that glint that catches in the eye, that springs the thought that there are fires that can burn in the vastness of the waters that spurs the arms to hold, to heal, and to offer promises that are known will not be realized. They are sparks that are desperately tended, in an ocean filled with water that cannot sustain them, and they were only an illusion, regardless.

A cherished moment of insignificance is taken to claw for the existence of an evanescent spark that blinks away at nearly the precise instant the moment started. An aberration of the nothing that remains, that is just a molecule of floating silver in an endless vacuum. An insignificant speck that is irrelevant but not forgotten because there is nothing that could remember.

Descent falls deeper and the shimmering surface decays into silver threads that flow downward to a blackened pool that rests at the bottom of an upcrop. They slither down within the water, still with a sense of connectivity – still as if the shredded threads of life were pieces that held existence – and not merely coincidence in proximity with a certain mass and density. They fall into the dark and slip away until there's no delineation of direction, of space, nor time, nor presence. There's no surface, nor within – there is nothing. There is no passage of time. There is no imagination. There are no thoughts, and existence isn't present. It is dark but not because it's lightless – it is where everything is swallowed.

It is nothing, and it's only understood because silver flecks lick back against it. They seep free and wend through oceans, turning on unseen waves in search of starlight to give reflection. There are strands that stretch in length for the random chance they can catch a passing star and bask in its reflection. That light can be shared and redirected to bring visions, and voices, and experience.

They call from the shadow of darkness, from the bottom of a well that's filled with black liquid that throttles the call. Words are muffled and voices only evoke a reminisce of another person. They round in sound that almost finds footing and feels as if there's meaning involved, but there's no clarity. There's no person, no event; no place. They are echoes that punch against nothing to ring in the sparkling warmth of starlight and remember those cared about and moments shared together. They break free, abruptly, and find visions fill in almost instantly.

Confusion and dark is erased as, "Antru," is spoken by Dalune. They are standing above. They are displeased, and wonder, "Why are you in the water?"

There is a desperate message to share, but it's caught in the throat and the failing effort only brings greater disapproval. The water is lost and there is no way to share the immense failing that's taken place, because Axael is a word that means nothing at that age. The word is spoken into gale force winds that swallow the sound and a message is sent that what's most important is to, "Live."

Axael washes in the sound despite the best efforts from Althrae to save a sibling. They fish from a failing raft and wave a net through the waters with a hand that's attached to nothing. It is inappropriate, but, "Enjoy," is shouted from the shore.

The storm rages as Althrae grasps the edges of the sinking raft as it's tossed across the waves, while still fishing for the other. Rain pelts down, the wind howls; ice pellets rake against the skin.

"Enjoy," Antru calls from shattered shards of glass that litter the seashore: "Enjoy," is yelled with a menacing laugh – that it could ever have been believed to be so easy.

"Just live your life," Dalune says. They are at a table, and there is calm. They speak as if the words hold substance and have meaning. They claim, "Enjoy your life," as if it was ever a reasonable expectation.

"Enjoy your life," Antru says. Axael is in tears and wondering why blood is spilling from their arm. They had been whole and had expected that to remain. It is promised, "We can fix this," but the liquid draining has never made those promises.

It springs from the obsidian void beside a pile of broken rocks in the shadow of a massive upcrop. They are threads that stole away from the infinity of nothing to spend an infinitesimally small moment of glory in the spotlight of a star. Voices shriek in violent protest to the unfairness of the balance, as quicksilver slips away just as it finds its glorious reflection.

Words fall into threads; fall into darkness. Hope fails, and the architecture built around it begins to crumble from the moment it was erected. Impassioned wishes shared as reality and truths fall like the ashes that slip through fingers that grasped, as if capable of offering an iota of protection.

Waves lash against the broken shoreline glass and rinse the blood from slivered flesh back to the pool that waits, below. They are the waters of generations that found failures, that vowed to amend the worst and did everything they could – and found that others rose as a single one was counteracted.

Waves fall against the shoreline as a sigh of disappointment and despair, as the failures of generations are infectious, and the forces of existence and in the world find every effort to evade the inexorable are entirely ineffective.

Waters crash as Axael is washed away, as Althrae paddles helplessly in a sinking boat – as Antru falls across a rockface, with fate sealed before a first breath was ever taken.

"Listen," is demanded. Dalune is informed, "I want to know." Water still drips, and the failings of the future already tick threads away. But Antru says, and insists, "I know what Éayren's doing."

"Be happy," rings with faulty hope that never truly found roots. "Live your life," was offered with a shadow that never shared the other half, of while you can.

Axael questions, "Why were you looking for me?"

"Because I have to," Antru pleads. Hands reach for the child but the body falls away as ash, and a dirty hand rinses in the ocean – a delusional thought that the slightest, remnant fragment of solidity could have even the slightest effect on the vast mass of an entire ocean.

"Axael," is called desperately, and the ocean lashes back and rocks the shoulder.

The shoulder rocks, and, "Hey: Hey," is spoke, increasingly aggressively.

There is pressure against a shoulder, and eyes fight the forces to keep them sealed to squint into a dim-lit room of stone and people. A hand grips the shoulder and firmly moves it, and that's accompanied, by, "Hey," again.

"Hey," is said, and the person explains the unnecessary: "You were having dreams again."

Threads of confusion shake away the clouds as eyes blink against the intrusion of the dimmest light. They ache at the sight of stone walls and floor, and the dozens sleeping, thereon: Muscles ache from a night upon them.

Cool air is breathed in deeply and chills the lungs, a chill that spreads across the shoulders, through the spine, and then, over the entire body.

"Sorry," is offered, however, "You were really goin'."

An arm cringes against the effort to rise, but the visions still swirl in memory, and while most are miserable, there are still the children, and still – Dalune.

Feet taken, a hand reciprocates the gesture and brings pressure against a shoulder. It is an expression of understanding. It is forgiveness, and appreciation of the disturbance. But the feet taken take an exit from the room finding increasing coolness preferable to the coolness that finds absence of wide eyes watching from a doorway, or the warmth of conversation and the empathy that was shared, for a moment that was far too brief, far too infrequent, and far too limited.

Passages are taken into increasing darkness, until only fingertips guide the way against smooth stone. The excursion ends as an opening is met that leads in multiple directions. It is an empty void considered for many moments before another empty vow is offered, just like the many others that never had a chance to find fruition.

Emptiness and dark are told, "I'll find you." Silent thoughts speak more, and to others, and the return is only to where light is barely shown. To where there is just a hint that there are others present, but still in the shadows. Away from strangers, alone with thoughts, and eyes that look into a future and only see more failure.

Chapter five:

A cool breeze cuts through channels cut millennia before as foundations for ancient architecture, buildings that remain in significant number only in the farthest, southeast corner of the nation. Modern constructs of that city are still required to use the stone and to reflect techniques and style that have stood through the passing drift of time.

The stone city of Capriot remains an outlier in many ways: From its architecture, to governance; to culture. It is still built almost entirely of stone and recent introduction of other material is allowed solely as ornamental. It is the last empire that stands, an Emporer and Clan that continue holding broad support from the city's residents.

"The opinion," Antru tells those gathered: "That you've heard, that they are propped up by the underground – is false."

It is considered, elsewhere, a cult that remains unfortunately tolerated – even protected, within the city's border. That is not entirely by choice, and there have always been concerns, and fear that have led to efforts to infiltrate, influence, or coopt. All of those efforts failed.

"Just like," Antru says, "The efforts to get rid of us throughout the country."

Outside of Capriot, arms of the underground have been and continue to be targeted for eradication, and there's been success. Recent assaults successfully eliminated tens of thousands. However, "We won't disappear." Antru swears, "We will bring your children home."

As soon as one cell's down, another rises to cause more problems somewhere else. The latest, a long-time target that was temporarily neutralized, that somehow walked away after the defensive net apparently vaporized tons of solid stone. However, the greatest concerns over the connection with the net grow allayed, as over time – nothing else has happened.

Rumors have filtered out there were connections that were complicit to create the spectacle. That opinion is denied, however there has been a greater call for help from the city where it happened: Demand for security, assistance to upgrade, and increasingly, requests for resources. Rumors filtered to the street and an unexpected complication was discovered: Many had come to believe that Antru was just a ploy to get attention. Even in Alvel that opinion is strong, as it's implausible the net could drill through an entire mountain.

Meanwhile, Nespia watches: There is blatant disregard for security. A figurehead walks undaunted and is observed recruiting in the open. Nearby, observations become more complicated, but it is known that gatherings are being held in ancient quarries. Besides concerns about the net, the old ruins and caverns are filled with passageways that can be well-defended. It has been incorrectly deemed the operation center, and time and patience are taken for reconnaissance, and to form a plan. The foremost intercepted is a plan to flood the mine when expected forces gather to attack, but that effort would fail because no one will be meeting there.

A zap turns eye to ashes falling from the sky like those through fingers in a nightmare. They are all that remain of an object that was only known as present at the sound.

"It protects you," Antru says. "It sees those as a threat."

It is a useful lie. It is a demonstration meant to emphasize, "It will protect you."

To support the claim, "It's easy."

To offer visuals to a lecture shared, repeatedly: "Focus on the threat, your fear, and the net. It will find you."

"You believe that," a person asks, and further, "You really believe you have any chance?"

Antru says, "Yes," and that's the truth. "As long as we have you. We can start the fight, but success depends on you."

They are words that have been heard, and they're appealing. There is a hole in the chest that all gathered share, and it was found by invoking family: Family was not imagined, nor just a dream. Experience is shared with those who ask, but end of day, with family in thought, each person finds their cubicle is empty. It is a track that has found success in energizing minds and planting seeds to follow: Up the slopes in a rain of fire to finally rattle loose the grip held on the country by Nespia's clan. It will require at least tacit support from other cities, and the presence of many people. Overwhelming numbers that cannot simply be eliminated without consequence: Agreements in place have always been fragile and are closer to a shallow inhalation: Ready to exhale. Ready to shout back against long-held disagreement.

The familiar words are for the first time followed by the ominous, "It will be soon." It is the order to dissipate as observed by the departure of the one that spoke.

Antru is openly of Capriot, and that's noted in quiet conversations between those gaining clarity of mind, because those of Capriot are said to be hostile and reserved. They are opinions that misunderstand behavior and that everything's related.

The lack of interaction observed, the unwillingness to engage, the seeming lack of social contacts are the products of eons of effort by northern clans. Efforts to infiltrate, manipulate, and eliminate. Cold shoulders turned are from warnings to avoid a pinch and even those seen interacting. Quick strides through city streets with no greeting to others passing comes from knowing there are towers with someone watching.

Those towers were once believed to be the city's clan's, however time, experience, and information have tilted opinion towards Nespia: Part of an agreement to end hostilities, to allow for observation, but that is also believed to have exceeded what has been agreed upon.

However, no one wants another war. No one wants the disruptions of the past. Posts abandoned for the streets and subjects taken can be looked past with justification: Intervention against a crime, a scoundrel; anyone not societally aligned. Streets kept clean and removal of potential problems becomes tacitly agreed upon with no good argument, otherwise.

However, there is a line, and political targets are well across: The visit to Capriot was more than personal – it was an appeal to the emperor and found a sympathetic ear:

"This is where they went wrong with Januk," rasped an ancient voice. However, the most granted was, "We will watch."

It was more than expected by most, but Antru remembered to a miserable time when the future was interrupted. When plans were subverted and desperation drove young feet to beg a conference. What had been met was not the emperor, but neither was it dismissal. Pains were taken to explain the why, and who was behind the challenge. It had been devastating, but in retrospect – enlightening: Regarding parents, the clan, and the world.

That memory argued for a hearing with the belief that Capriot might at least withhold their condemnation as the assault began. The promise to watch spoke to failures of the past and an unwillingness to commit to potential tumult. It also left the door open for greater support.

"I can't," punctures into the sea of brewing thoughts as passages are taken. There is a person being goaded forward by several others that are unwilling to take burden of the task. They demand and physically attempt to move the person forward, but it is clear they are staggered by fear and willing to die by hands that are known if it is necessary, rather than face what threatens them beyond. They are approached and Antru lifts them and feels the terror that shudders through their body.

It's noted, "You're afraid," and there is no attempt to deny it. There is frailty of soul that wears failure and a wish there was more to be offered, but the fight is over. They have surrendered to the suffocating fear that overwhelms them. And, "I know," is offered: "Fear."

It is rational. It is reasonable. And as time ticks by with the threat of action ever closer, "I am more afraid than I've ever been." That the plan is already known. That the forces are infiltrated and being guided by baited information. That the move against Alvel was anticipated and they will walk into a trap:

"It is important to acknowledge our fear. There is a day coming when we will need to move through it, but that doesn't happen by pretending it isn't there. We have to focus on it. Focus on the fear, and when we see an object that's a threat – another person, a vehicle, or something in the air – we focus on that. Focus – fear, target; net. The more of us that focus on our fears, on targets, and put thoughts out to the net – the safer we will all be when that day comes."

There is a whimper that comes from the complete collapse of spirit. From a person that hears words and wants to believe them, but is failing in the moment and incapable of moving forward. They're given a warm embrace, and left with, "Where does this get delivered?"

It is reckoning. There is a sickness that drains from the shoulders, that descends into the body as another's watched that walks with no encumbrance. They watch as an argument ensues but it's not engaged – information's gathered: Antru exits with the cart to fill a cache that will be necessary for what's planned to follow.

It is not entirely without worry. The net's violent response to thoughts while buried beneath stone was unexpected, and there's no certainty that can be called again. Nonetheless, there are hundreds of thousands that are being asked to risk their skin, and if the person that was a face and has slowly begun to be accepted as a leader was unwilling to share the risk, they would be unworthy. Against protest by all, the cart is taken.

It is not a brief diversion, and three days find proximity to the prospective plan's origination.

It is where Éayren is confined amongst three-hundred thousand others. It is hoped to be where Axael will be found, and if they aren't connected, hope will be lost: If Axael's not there, then they are nowhere, and the wrath that will unleash is already felt, scarcely kept in control – a thin bubble that somehow restrains an explosion.

The passage is cool, and dark, and the sound of water dripping into a shallow pool reverberates within the stone. It evokes calls of young children that once held innocence, that looked to parents as authorities and as forces that could protect them. Forces that failed and now find one is lost, and the other has retreated back to Capriot under the purview of a more capable grandparent.

They are all captives to a system of exploitation. One being attacked across open airwaves, but the calls have also prevailed for service and cooperation – a mixed message that brings confusion, though history could clarify the intent.

It is near the endpoint of the passage where access will be taken, and the cart is left behind to explore ahead. To ensure the stash is safely placed.

Feet step quietly, the final hundred meters, as they approach the ladder that ascends to the surface access. It is met, and raised, and there is surprise that it's the middle of the day – bright starlight shines brilliantly. Like all others, it is an access point that is away from the main thoroughfare but it is not unobvious, and the disk is quietly re-set.

With the passage cleared, there is just a need to secure the cache and then return. However, the memory of a planned escape stops motion – a hazy shadow filled with duplicity. Steps are retraced nearly to the access, and a light is struck:

Wide eyes look back from within a recess, a person frozen in fear, their body trembling from terror. A hand raises and rests against their cheek – cool: A sentry standing in place for hours.

Antru suspects, "Didn't expect me?"

Their head turns with halting motion to indicate that is precisely right – eyes unblinking and never leave their subject.

"You're okay," Antru says. "We don't want to hurt you. But you made an enemy where you didn't need to – I was not bothering you. I didn't want to be a part of this. But you stole my Aedra – my children. You can end this without anyone getting hurt."

Their voice is choked, but they manage, "How?"

They are offered a smile: It is sorrowful and filled with regret because the answer's easy. It is known and it's been requested many times before – part of a nation's celebrated history.

Yet history finds that history remains intact. That vows and promises have fallen empty, and the great permutations flaunted have done little to alter anything.

Still, Antru hopes, "Speak with our Emperor," can prevent the worst from happening. "You know what we want," is a given because it's been taught to every child since they were young. "We don't want violence," Antru begs, "But you will meet our demands." And they are given a threat to carry back: "This time is going to be different. I think you've seen that."

Eyes focus on the person. They are a threat, a danger invoking fear, and the net is tested: Ear-shattering blast erupts from overhead, and the sub-surface access is opened to the sky. Rubble settles as dust carries with ringing in the ears, and a terrified person reels against the wall.

They are told – arm waving towards the path that's been created, "Let them know."

There is a moment of hesitation before instinct sets in. They flee with unsteady footing, slipping several times as they scramble to the surface.

They will report their experience. They will share what they have seen, and the concerns that opened with a mountain will erupt again, as it will be clear that the net is being used with precision: It is targeting near objects to the assets it protects without harm to them. It is on demand and being used like it was always promised that it couldn't – as a weapon.

It is also news to the person left below the surface, uncertain how strong the connection was, and exactly how it could be used.

The unexpected encounter will be a blow to opinions that had grown and likely bring calls for greater action, but it will also reinforce the message that has been given: The net is watching, and with proper mindfulness, it will protect those it was intended to protect.

The cache is secured as planned as it's supposed there will be little interest in exploration. Initial examination will find that the passage remains as it always was: A small space that was previously buried that gave access to utilities. It will be found to have no access other than the disk that still remains set within the surface. At least no access other than that and the hole that was blasted just adjacent.

It's a chance taken, like everything else that's chance: There is risk with everything. But for anything to go right – some things will have to: The encounter might invoke fear and confusion. Understanding how the face of the underground might suddenly appear there might be explained away as a slight of hand, a bit of trickery – after all, the access was momentarily lifted.

There's hope that curiosity is not too great, and the sub-surface access is not explored too carefully: That what's seen is just accepted for what it is.

Hope is a dangerous intoxicant, but it's one that's taken when there's no solid ground to stand on, when everything that's planned rests on tenuous bones, where the discovery of a cache might bring widespread search and then awareness, and all that's worked for to collapse in abject failure.

The sense of doldrums is gone to urgency. There is a sense of the impending action, and it brings fear, but also enthusiasm. Excitement to finally bring action. To finally fight for children and parents; to fight for Aedra.

The return trip is much quicker without the cumbersome attachment, but the anxiety of the moment also fed adrenaline, and time was not counted as it had been.

Return finds a much more solemn mood than expected. Eyes fall with disapproval, and it's explained, "They're talking with Capriot."

"It doesn't matter," Antru swears: "They won't agree to anything. Capriot is after what we want – that's where this started. They won't agree to work against us."

"Not," Onton says: A foot stabs at floor and two posts shout anger that reverberates against the stone: "What we heard."

Chapter six:

The door opens, but this time there isn't any hesitation – the opposite: The door's quickly closed, and concern is shared, "Do they know you're here?"

The answer is, "Probably." But it doesn't matter. Because there's an attachment that's been recognized. There is a target being protected by a weapon that acts autonomously. A move against will certainly earn response, and how to overcome that and the risk have yet to be determined.

That had been offered as a possibility more than a year before, but had largely been dismissed as millennia of evidence rightfully earned complacence. However, there is concern the net is looking in again, and at the least, there is one or more that is directly interfacing. It is an escalation not believed a possibility – an ancient solution to a problem that had been resolved during the Astrasian altercation.

"Everyone's scared," Aedra shares. They walk forward like they always do – for the sanitation station – but clothes discarded are thrown with anger at the syphon.

Familiar sounds follow that indicate a cleanse and dry, but there is no exit from the machine.

There is a heaviness that is new to the encounters. It is one that's brought from memories and understanding – from awareness and comprehension of what's happening. It is clear that Aedra's mind's no longer fogged and the distress from that experience is well remembered – understood that what's been shared across the airwaves is a significant contribution.

Knuckles tap against the translucent glass, and a soul that aches suggests, "Come with me."

The door slides open and it's pushed with a violence that has no effect. The entreaty goes ignored as Aedra brushes past, to adorn the usual uniform that's pointlessly worn for a night alone in a cubicle that no one else will – should – ever enter.

Antru begs, "Come with me, Aedra – for what," is shouted back.

It's suggested, "We can work together."

"You're not walking away," Aedra says, and it's through tears that are unavoidable: "They are not going to let you walk away from this, so what will I have?"

It's a sorrow that's inconsolable because where they've come to stand is impossible to comprehend by either one of them. They look to each other, and Antru can only repeat the words that were previously spoken, because the mind is broken, and they are the last fragment held before thoughts float away.

"So," says Aedra: "Where does that leave me? I don't want to lose you, Antru, but they won't let you walk away from this. So, what do I do? Hide back in Capriot? You should have helped me first," Aedra says, and the regret is crushing: "You should have found me before you started this."

However, "They have Axael," is why that narrative is crushed. "I had to do something – do you know how long it's taken to get to this point? Did you want me to wait?"

"No. I don't, okay," is yelled: "I don't."

Antru reaches, and tries, "Aedra," but the entreaty's brushed aside:

"I don't understand why we're not dead, already. Because everywhere I go there are people watching. I'm constantly being asked questions and so far I've been able to answer honestly: I don't know. I don't know where you are; I don't know what you're doing. I don't want to go with you because I feel like I'm just going to lose you, and I can't handle that."

"I made up our plan in two minutes," does not engender confidence, but it's suggested, "Come with me and we'll work up something better."

"Attack Nespia," Aedra says bitterly: "They literally have security stationed on every corner. They are embedded twenty-deep going up into the hills. I don't think you'll get close enough to scare them."

"Entrenched," Antru questions, and it's questioned back, "Like that's a good thing?"

"Yes," is answered: "It's exactly what we want. Come with me, Aedra. We'll find Axael together, and then we'll disappear. We can make that happen."

"No," Aedra says, "You can't. Everyone's talking about what's happening. Everyone's asking about families and if they remember who they are. People get on the transports and ask, who are you in your dreams? Everybody – security, the people in the city – are waiting for you to do something. You'll never be able to just walk away."

"Then, join me," Antru quietly suggests. "Or, go to Capriot and stay with Althrae. You don't need to stay here, anymore."

"That," supposes Aedra, "Is probably why we're still alive."

"Could be," is considered.

The numerous interventions mentioned would have certainly noted the clouds had blown away. That there was clarity of mind and a fear response to questions asked. There is no doubt at all that would be seen as the result of contact and persuasion, and it is likely Aedra walks and action's yet taken against the most public mark because there is a larger plot at play: "We have ways to compensate."

Ways to scan for any trace, a bug, an implant that might monitor in some manner, or another. There are ways to detect, and ways to erase transponders without immediately giving notice. Objects surreptitiously planted to listen in or trace, with the latter the likely reason that death's delayed. An opportunity that was almost inevitable after Antru stumbled across Aedra: There was always going to be an attempt to restore their memory, and eventually, they would leave together for the heart of operations.

It's why there's been patience, and while certainly preparation, why no attempt's been made against the most significant problem in several, thousand years. It is an opportunity to discover where operations are centered, and it's worth the irritation to finally put a missile through its heart.

"Tell me," Antru urges, "What to do. I'm listening: Tell me what you want me to do."

"I don't know," is the answer because every one has failures: A lost child, or a partner that won't return. "Build a time machine," Aedra suggests: "Take us back to Marphy."

"If I could, I would," Antru says, and it's regrettably, because the wish remains that everything was different. That nothing changed, and life continued like it was: "The last thing I remember is teaching at the institute. I don't even know what happened."

"You were gone," Aedra recalls. "We were all going back to Capriot. That's the last thing I can remember."

"Tell me what to do," Antru says again. "Tell me what you think is the best for us – you, me, and the children – moving forward."

Aedra hopes, "You found Axael?"

Hopes are dashed with, "No." There is no clue to whereabouts, but that hints, "Nespia's the most likely location." It is a sentence that's not completed, but the same thought is held by both that ends it, that is the same as the one that wonders why they're still alive. Still, hope is given rope, "I'm almost positive that's where Éayren is. If Axael is there, then they're together. At least someone's there for them."

"You know I can't tell you what to do," Aedra returns, and the regret felt earlier only deepens and fills them both.

There is no walking away from a lost child. There's no slipping away and hiding with Axael gone. But the alternative is the risk of losing the future together and it feels to both there's no escape in that direction.

"A hundred years tracking Januk," Aedra marvels: At the petulance. The persistence. At the depths of manipulation and control over even Capriot.

"It's a hundred years," Antu offers, and more: "We can work together. You can help us devise a better plan."

But the suggestion's shaken away: "People are talking. Antru: Do you understand what I'm telling you? People are talking. That stupid line is how everyone greets each other. It's turned into some kind of idiotic metric. You did what you wanted: There's no going back and starting over."

"We can try," but that hope sailed visits ago and began the trip back into memories.

It was where an unwanted burden was taken on the shoulders. Where the weight was taken and carried to the point they'd risen: At the point where history rolls, one way or another. Either back, or moving forward.

Softly, Aedra asks, "How do we find Axael?"

The world falls away as the path determined is raked from the cover of distractions. There is a line that extends, that arrived by lightning strike, and nothing that's strived to change it since, has found an alternative that's better:

"It sets everything in motion."

It is the initiation of events intended to upend the world. Meant to set fire to the planet until that extends to the Nespian hills. Force the clan to finally face their reckoning, face consequence, and finally, legitimately lift the grip they've held over the population for all known history. It is a monumental undertaking that sees failure at every step. That sees it quashed from the outset if the net is not as connected as well as thought – as hoped. There is always the chance that Alvel falls and Nespia does not react. A chance Nespia finds mass extermination preferable to losing power – the chance they won't need to, because no one will follow. It is a plan that's ripe for failure, but there's a chance, and that's better than the plan that didn't have one, but it offers no one consolation.

"That was always part of the plan," is said quietly. As both reflect and they see nothing left but moving forward. There is a common goal, and that's finding a child, and neither finds a way to do so without the disruption to what they've known. Without losing a future that was always expected, and years to share together. Eyes meet, and agreement's found as objective aligns with understanding of the consequence. That violence will follow and it might well spell disaster. In one of any of several ways.

"It can protect you," Aedra suggests – clarified, and asked, "The net?"

Antru answers, "It does." But the answer's recognized as imperfect and incomplete. There is more beyond it, and as eyes meet and share that's understood, a secret held but known, regardless, is given words: "I've dreamed about my death since I was born. I've watched myself fall ten-thousand times. I've heard my body crushed against the rubble at the bottom. I'm not going to pretend that's not what I see as the end result, because I think I've told you that before – if you remember. I'll call the net, but I know they've planned something."

"Antru," Aedra says. Tears fall, but arms extend and reach for the other – reach out for touch, for connectedness, for the warmth that's been missed, and longed for. They come together, and hold together in miserable hopelessness that sees clearly there is no resolution that meets everything that's wanted. Not without loss. Not without sacrifice. Not without the loss of life – of many.

There will be battles that will see the loss of lives. The best scenario will find thousands slaughtered as they storm the hills. As anger drives them into the fire of the enemy, as planned defenses utilize every strategy developed to push back protest, and maintain the power of those that have controlled society, forever.

It begs, "Why," from Aedra: "What's even the point?"

"What is," Antru agrees, and pleads, again, "Come with me."

"Stay," Aedra counters. "Spend one more night with me. In the morning, you can send me to Capriot, but I need one last night with you. Promise you'll do everything you can to protect yourself."

"Okay," is answered to everything.

If it is an evening heard, what's heard is love shared. Memories are shared, and there is laughter – there are tears. There is a walk through the history of experience from the earliest days of cognizance. There is a shared experience that was regrettably broken in years that followed, but the connection never faltered. They were born together and stayed together their entire lives – until those lives were ripped apart and left them separated.

It is not the first night spent together since reunion, but it is the first night where they're together as they've been. Where they hold together a last time as forever slips away into the absence of light, where even the brilliant, silver, liquid strands of life are indistinguishable from anything, because they are draining away to nothing.

There is little sleep because every second shared is held desperately. There is little said, but what is tells everything. There is a calm that falls across them both that accepts that fate has never offered an even journey. Not for anyone – not for Éayren: An understanding finally settles. Not only Éayren, but of parents: Everything done is for the future. For children. To build a legacy that leaves behind a better world, and a chance to live freely. For them to live their lives with those they love, until the end.

There is not a surprise, the next morning, when Aedra is first to exit. The order given is taught, and thin: "Decontamination, then Capriot. Make it happen as quickly as you can."

It's asked, "Did something happen?"

Antru shares with the dozen gathered, "Contact central: Initiate lightning strike."

It is a message that's sent that's known will be intercepted. It will bring forces to pull in to protect the capitol, and they will be tightly collected in mass confusion as nothing happens. At least, nothing particularly threatening, and not what is expected.

"This gets us somewhere?"

It isn't the first time the question's been asked in some manner or another over the days of the complicated journey. There's enthusiasm to do something and support has grown, but going to prison strikes all as an uninspired way to start the process. More like a wet blanket on fires that were stoked.

It's answered like it's been answered every time: "It's the first step in the process." One step of many that need to pass a checkpoint for another one to follow. Step one is gauging support in the Nespian prison. Step two is getting out. As with every step, success depends on the reactions to events.

"Luck – hope," Antru says: "The further we get in, the more likely we'll find success, but that absolutely needs this end of it to work. I think the odds are pretty good."

The mind shoots fireworks at blood-stained failure, and the mental images of bodies scraped from the hills of Greater Nespia. It shuts down the cacophony of drums that pound futility – that crash symbols against the ear to press the point that every aspect of the plan is rife with plot-holes, and ripe for failure. There is a rock-face envisioned as the last thing ever seen before unceremonious obliteration across the rockpile at the bottom – and it's just one body of thousands mowed down during the ill-advised assault against the compound. The sight for success is narrowed to a sliver, just a small thread of silver that still reflects starlight before succumbing to inevitable dissolution. Still hanging on by a thread, but even hope that will stay together, fails.

"I appreciate you helping me get there," Antru says: "I know there's a lot of tension, but we still need a few more days of patience. Once it's underway, everything's going to move very quickly." And it's offered, sincerely, "I appreciate you trusting us. We've had the same doubts you do."

"This is happening," is a revelation: Words are words, and everyone encountered's always had some: Something to say, claims of the brave, and oaths of action that have always held the taint of fantastic notions. But there's a clive away of the emptiness, and a spark let in: "This is happening," repeated, as a statement. As understanding, and belief, "We're doing this. Okay," is said, and it's followed, with heartbeat rising, "We are doing this. We are really doing this – you're going in. Okay – okay."

"Easy," says Antru, and again, "Patience."

"Got it," is answered. But a moment is taken for another oath: "I'm with you. Hundred percent. We're gonna do this, then I am a hundred percent there with you. I've been waiting for this, forever."

Again, "Patience," is given: "There are a series of steps we need to take to find success. I need you to be a voice for patience, because it might not always look like what we're doing is getting us what we want, but I can promise you it is. Be a voice around others you know to let this work."

"I hear you," gives comfort that at least a few more might have a voice that keeps the messaging alive, because days, to weeks in the best scenarios will lose the one that's become familiar. "You want me to stay?"

It is the destination arrived at that precedes the final leg: The upcrops where the road turns in for northeastern Nespia. For the tall walls and open prison where those taken are housed, and who need to be aware enough to give their support for what will follow. Considering memory and experience, there is deeply held concern.

"Head back," Antru says, and stresses: "Be safe: We need you."

"Same to you," is offered back, with skepticism, that, "They'll let you in?"

With knowing confidence, it's shared, "I'll get in. It's getting out that's tough." There's a wink, and with well-disguised doubt, it's confidently claimed, "We can do this."

It's questioned, "Yeah," and the veneer remains, still glowing brightly as the other shares, "Good luck." As they watch the odd positioning in upcrops. As the face of dissent is observed wedging into the underbrush in a move that is badly misinterpreted, that will bring report of forces that surround the entire city, and of secret passages and outposts where there are none.

It is just a position taken because of experience, of bringing materials across the city, and knowing vehicles will slow as they make the turn. It's a position taken because it's the safest place along the route to the northeast section of the city to jump onto a transport – with hope, without detection. Imaginations are let to fill in what isn't stated, because if the fragility of the enterprise was truly known, not a person would be inspired.

It is just the first of many potential points of failure: Getting on without notice, and the same for getting off. And there's – if – the vehicle will even pass one of the few locations determined safe to exit.

The wind blows cool as indecision lets the few that pass continue. Light fades over transports holding people that return after their day of labor. But as it does, an idea grows – to camp down for the night – but it already feels like the effort's drawn: That the opportunity is slipping. That anxiety spurs a chance that those inside will not be swayed by the sound of a body landing, a launch that finds the terminus at once – both resounding, but quiet and brief enough that minds sedated might not be pulled to investigate. Position's taken with another chance that fading light won't make a stow-away acutely evident.

It is a naked journey: Fully exposed after days of snaking passageways and careful progress over land. If anything flew over, or if anyone was looking, the grand uprising would be over.

The vehicle travels steadily; no interruptions. Northeast gates open with minimal inspection, and the city's entered – the first point of failure sailed over. Bridged as planned – crossed without a problem. The transport continues slowly through city streets, a city much different than remembered.

More complete. More inescapable. Better guarded and more restrictive. Gates are not used solely in times of crises but implemented to control movement within the territory. It is appalling, but also brings hope that those within will be motivated to push back against their isolation. That they will follow willingly across the city to force the hand of the Nespian clan.

The brief cover of an overhanging fabric that waggles in the breeze gives legs to another whimsical decision: Nothing is recognized, and so the opportunity is taken to disembark, landing with a prayer that any enterprise that's near will still be open.

Chance finds fortune at the first door tried, and the building's quickly entered, and door, re-sealed. Three heads turn in unison at the interruption, and one stands abruptly on recognition.

They had been sitting casually around a table. There are teacups in front of each of them, and assorted foods are spread between them.

The calm is lost as the one that stood inquires, "What are you doing here?"

"Looking for Eayren," Antru explains. "I was hoping you could help me."

"Quick:" Another stands. Another asks, "Do they know you're here?"

"You know," Antru says: "That's all I know."

"We have to get you underground," is stated urgently, as another moves quickly to an adjacent counter where a series of actions are initiated, and the third one echos, "Quick. Quick," is repeated, and Antru is guided over as the cabinet tips.

Beneath, there is a gaping hole of darkness, but there is urgency, and hands encourage the body forward towards the stairs that descend into the pool of black.

It's promised, "Someone will get you."

"Stay where you are," is ordered.

The last asks quietly, "Is it starting?"

"Soon," Antru says, "But not quite yet."

There is a nod of understanding that is the last thing seen before the ceiling falls and seals the space in total darkness; complete silence.

If conversation continues overhead, it is entirely sealed away: No sound of voices, no footsteps – nothing: Completely silent, and completely lightless. The air is dry and dusty and brings memories to a strange back room that was lined with flour sacks. Where the first kink in the security of youth was felt and a dark shadow first cast over reality: Awareness given with warnings of pinches and towers. Somehow, those warnings failed on at least two occasions.

It is a small room: Height, and footprint. Not tall enough to extend arms fully overhead, and fingers tracing walls slide over paces that paint an image that's not quite square. It would be shelter for a dozen in an emergency – much more would quickly grow uncomfortable.

Alone, the room is comfortable. The temperature is just warm enough there is no chill. It is dry, but it stirs memories of lessons learned from parents. Not only that day, but a scent that evokes the ancient books that were lessons from the dawn of memory. Lessons shared almost exclusively with Dalune, however the few with Éayren are also remembered fondly: There was always a desire for affirmation – part of why roukta was not entirely rejected.

Despite a trajectory it interrupted. Despite plans that never gained traction – because of it and Marphy. There was still Éayren, proud to watch their only child follow in their footsteps, and even in latter years, that helped fill the void created by a parent's absence.

Circling footsteps slow as memories fill in for senses that are deprived. They come to a stop with a sigh that arrives in the center of many trains of thought. It is a breath that leaves with expectations that events will be put in motion quickly, and the days of travel finally admit to tired bones, and the solid floor is stretched across with appreciation for the rare moment of quiet, and a chance to reflect on thoughts – as well, experience.

They intermingle as breaths grow softer. As memories swirl in a sea of worries about the future. Eyes flicker with amusement it doesn't matter: There isn't the slightest hint of light. It is not just black, it is absence. Without tactile input, the room dissolves into an endless sea of dark – of nothingness.

Even the surface begins to fade as the body numbs against it: It is a board, carried across an ocean of obsidian, beneath a sky of nothing, within a vacuum. Only the sense of smell continues to give attachment to existence – as if the room was designed to deprive the senses: Perfect temperature, impenetrable insulation, and completely dark.

The trajectory of passage is imperceptible. It is impossible to determine, but there is no doubt there's distance crossed. Time moves forward, regardless if it is sensed, and that movement pushes a crude ship across the ocean waters.

Neither are seen, but they are evident because time passes. They are there as an explanation to explain the lack of sensory information. There is a ship, and there's no need for light because the layout is well-known: Steps and hallways travelled ten-thousand times, and even under daylight, feet guide their own, with interruption to the unconscious, only for others passing.

Unseen passes across a surface that can't be seen, for a destination that isn't mapped, and can't be read. But the direction is determined and moves quickly – skating across a surface that is just beginning to surrender threads of silver to reflect greater reality.

But they are faltering. Infinitesimal tendrils make the surface where they disintegrate almost instantly. It brings only the faintest gray soil across the surface. A slick of mar like a sanded patch on basalt columns. A discoloration out of the corner of the eye that can't be seen when it's focused on, directly.

The ship sails, but it cuts the waves in silence. Waves spray against the sides and give only the slightest indication they are present – slight tapping. Slight scratching: A patter against the deck as droplets land.

The stack rattles warning in the fog to warn the unseen that are near that another's passing. The sound repeats, but it goes unheeded – the ship rolls as another hits: The sound grows harsher – movement grows more violent.

One shoulder crashes against a wall as the ship grows compromised, rocking wildly against the shoulder; pushing harder. The waves roar as they rise against the sinking vessel and seem to call, "Antru," as if the end result was inevitable.

The shoulder rolls, and, "Antru," is called, and, "Antru," is said again, more succinctly. More clearly, words are firmly stated, "Antru: Wake up."

"Antru – Antru," is said by a voice that echoes out of memories. A voice that has always brought mixed feelings – a space of longing, and despair. One for whom effort was always made to be the best with the hope for even the slightest acknowledgment or approval.

Éayren says, again, "Wake up, Antru," and eyes open to a face that is stone as the floor.

"Moboti," initiates a scramble to embrace, heart racing with sight of a long-lost parent, but it's an act that's not reciprocated, and arms separate under dim illumination as eyes stare back with unexpected condemnation:

"This ends, here," Éayren demands: "This is over. Do you understand?"

Truly, that is answered, "No," quietly, and feeling the hurt so often felt when together. That expectations were never met; that effort was never good enough – decisions looked back on with disapproval. It is a hurt that has always been centered on the failing of a relationship, one built at one end seeking affirmation, and the other - unilateral decisions that made no sense without the context for them. It falls out weakly, "I thought this is what you wanted."

"No," Éayren whispers harshly: "This is the exact opposite of what I want. I need you to listen – I need you to understand: You are in extreme danger. You have made yourself Nespia's greatest enemy. If there is a chance to make you disappear – they will take it. They will take it in broad daylight, in the presence of everyone; even if you are recording. The only thing they want right now, is for you to disappear. Do you understand that, Antru?"

"I was," says Antru, and a calm restores within the waters of the last words said to Aedra, as both looked into the clouds of eternity and saw only ruin in their wake, as the legacy brought on children, and their own. It begs the question, "Did you know that?"

"Don't you dare ask me that." There is anger: "My entire life has been dedicated to protecting you. I gave up everything to protect you."

"And still," says Antru.

"You are alive." It is the point, and what sacrifice was intended to protect, and what remains the sole objective: "What you have done is over. I need you to listen: You will be taken to Capriot. You will be taken into protective custody until we negotiate a settlement.

What you won't do, is interact with the net, and – especially – you will not use it to communicate with the population. Is that understood? Antru?"

Says Antru, "No," because, "I've been there. I've been a prisoner for crimes I didn't commit, after I was a prisoner but didn't know it. I might as well be dead if that's the life I have to lead."

"You will be," Éayren promises, "If you try to approach the fortress. You, and anyone with you, will be killed and there will be ample justification. There is no reasonable argument to invoke violence."

"I'm confused," is admitted. Because it was always believed that a missing parent wasn't there because they fought with the resistance. That they were fighting back against towers and pinches. That they were the front against forced labor. It was always believed, "I thought you were part of the underground."

"Underground," questions Éayren: "I work for Capriot – I have always worked for Capriot. I have nothing to do with any sort of underground."

Antru says, "I'm more confused – they said they worked with you."

"Who," is answered, "Mash – Onton: The Borrean underground."

The words, "That's who you're with," is said derisively. It's claimed, "Worked, in the loosest sense of the word. They are a collection of misfits and criminals. They're using you just like everyone wants to use you. They're a few hundred people looking for angles to gain advantage for themselves."

But, "Hundreds," is questioned with dubiety. Hundreds were observed on first contact, and crowds were seen in the largest gatherings – thousands, at least. It's entirely possible that claims of numbers are exaggerated, but they've proceeded as if they're accurate. However, that is not the most concerning claim that was made. That was, "Why would people want to use me?"

"Antru," says Éayren, and there is softening. There is sadness, and there is something that wasn't always obvious – there's love. Says Éayren, "That miserable roukta net."

There had been a day where a child had led another for the acme of an upcrop: Concerns were raised by other parents. There were concerns from the child's parents. And from that moment, a child too young to understand the technicals of the implement, proposed a way to use the overseeing net to protect those climbing.

"We were young," Éayren reflects: "We were so proud of you: We pushed the idea forward. But we should have understood the consequences. We should have realized what it meant."

A connection – a capacity not seen since the lore of ancient history. An ability considered hyperbolized by the majority. A connection with the net that could pull it to drill through mountains, to connect through airwaves, and to turn it into a weapon. The last person that had fielded that capability was the hero of the nation, heroics that remained in ruins, as nothing they fought for seemed to ever have found a footing.

"I'm not going quietly," says Antru, "And I don't believe most of what you've told me." Because there was no recognition on introduction: The hijack wasn't simply an angle to gain profit – it was for the materials to make weapons. There was passion behind it and while promotion was unquestionably opportunistic, the conversation had developed from both ends. There

457

might be criminals and misfits, as assigned for whatever reason, but there is no question to dedication: Those met are willing to sacrifice life or limb for what they believe in. "And so am I," is given: "We have a plan that we think can work, but we need your help."

"I am not," Éayren answers, "Going to be any part of this. I cannot do anything more to help you unless you do exactly what I've told you. Go to Capriot and stay there until things quiet."

"We need numbers," Antru says: "The more we have, the better the odds."

"I need you safe," is the desperate plea that answers. "You are my only child. I have given up everything for you, Antru. I am begging you: Do not do this."

"My child is missing," is the counter-argument. As well, "They took Aedra, and you. And – your child. How can I leave this as the world my children live in?"

"You won't have a chance," sees the vision of failure: "There are hundreds of thousands in their forces and they know you're coming. Anyone that approaches that compound will be slaughtered."

"We have a plan," Antru offers: "Those forces are spread around the country, and we plan to pull more away."

"And what will you do," is questioned. "What is your role in all of this?"

The question ends at the part of the plan that is it's greatest weakness: It relies entirely upon potentialities. On inspiring the public and motivating them to follow into the hills. It is at once unnecessary, but also seen as vital to have a beacon that will draw them. To see a sign attack is underway and finding at least nominal success.

It will be futile, and, "You will be scraped off that rock before you're half-way up," sees as much.

"Wherever I am, that's where the flames will start. It will be something."

Éayren insists, "I will not let that happen," but that adamancy's struck:

"I'd hoped you'd help. But we're not going back if you won't. Everything is already set in motion."

"Antru," is said firmly. "Do you understand," is questioned: "You will not survive this."

It is an understanding already reconciled: "Aedra and I have already said goodbye. Do you know if Axael is here?"

"I can send them with you," takes the opening: "You can leave together. You can all be safe in Capriot."

But the offer's countered, "Take them with you. Ask Capriot not to publicly condemn what's happening. And Marphy, if you have contacts."

"Antru," it's stressed, "They'll know something's happening as soon as they realize we're both missing," but it's argued back, "They'll know something's happening as soon as they see me walking in the streets," and it's explained, "That sets everything in motion."

Éayren begs, "Explain."

It is admitted – a plan that's far from perfect. "But Aedra says people are talking." Awareness raised and verboten conversation aired in public discourse: "When will we ever have a better chance?"

"You have done a good job with that," is recognized. Admitted, "Everyone is talking. Everyone expects you to attack. But your numbers are much smaller than you've been told. You have a few thousand at the most."

"Our numbers don't matter," Antru answers, "What matters is how many people join us. That's where I need you."

"My verdict remains, I'm not convinced." It is the turning point angled for a lifetime. A moment in time where the opportunity for change looks promising, however, "You're my only child. You will not climb the upcrop and just throw your life away. That will not be part of any plan, moving forward. Give me your word on that and I'll get Axael safely to Capriot. Give me your word."

"Find me an alternative and you have it."

"No promises, Antru. But I'll present your ideas to council. You will need to stay underground until I'm back – it will become very active, very quickly. Promise you will not do anything until I'm back."

"I told them to start," Antru shares, "If they don't hear from me in ten days. That's seven from the day I entered."

"You've never made anything easy," is not so much complaint as admission to failure: "We only wanted to keep you safe."

It is a concession: "I understand that. But I think I was going to get to this point no matter what you did."

"You never listen," acknowledges that was feared. It was the force behind actions and decisions. A fear that what was dreamt was somehow prescient: "The net seemed like the solution to your nightmares. But it's become the source of the ones that I envision. Promise you'll stay here until I'm back."

"Okay," Antru agrees: "Six days, and can I ask? If you're with Capriot, you knew I got pulled in when I was younger – didn't you?"

Sad laughter's stifled as a child's taken in the arms, again. A gentle nod as arms strive to hold a life that always felt like it would slip away. There is sadness in the words, admonishment that repeats, "You never listen."

"Why," Antru asks. "Why would you tell me to disconnect when you knew I couldn't? What was the point?"

"Because I am trying to keep you alive," Fayren answers, and there's more emotion in the words than any ever spoken in their child's presence, prior. But that mission is seeing the effort muted by the subject, and fear that it's already too late: "I thought it might scare you. That you'd forget about the net and move on with life. That's all we ever wanted: A chance for you to enjoy your life."

Antru says, "I tried. They wouldn't let me." But there's something else sour in the formula. It is a paean said repeatedly by parents, that their hope and wish was for their child to find fulfillment. However, "You never had that chance, yourself," and worse, "And neither has my child. The more we have working together, the better odds for the many to have that opportunity. Work with me, and we can find a way to make that happen." And a last word is added, "Please."

A plea. An entreaty that raises the curtain on the impossibility always shadowing the lives of almost everyone: That someone known – a friend, a child, and most often parents – would disappear, never to be heard from, thereafter.

"Antru," says Éayren, and it's softer. It is reminiscent of the voice infrequently heard at night, after the terrors of the mind woke everyone in the home. It's shared, quietly, "I have been working to end the practice – so does Dalune. I have tried working with your friends, but they were a catastrophe. I don't know what the solution is to where we are right now, but I desperately need you to trust me. Let me bring the situation to Capriot: I will share your ideas with them and listen to what they think is the best way forward."

A child is taken by the shoulders. They are still innocent, but naïve no longer holds. They look back with the big round eyes that are just like their other parent's – they are a wisp that will blow away when wind rises:

"Promise you will stay here while I'm gone." The light is shone more fully across their child's face, and the sight only grows more urgency to the mission: "I promise, we will find a way through this, together. We will work together, okay? But I am going to do everything I can to make sure nothing happens to you. That has been my promise since the day you were born. Do we have agreement?"

It is agreed, and Antru says, "Okay," but new worries wonder, "Can you do this in six days?"

The answer's a repeated warning: "They will know we're gone by morning. You will have to stay here and remain quiet, and still. They can give you the provisions you'll need, but you have to stay here. You have to be silent."

"When I sleep," says Antru, and the back half of the statement's unneeded. Moboti says,

"Part of the provisions: Your voice will be hoarse, and your throat will probably be a little sore. But you will be quiet enough they won't hear you. Do this for me, Antru."

"Okay," solidifies agreement, as well – cooperation. The light is offered, but rejected: "I don't mind the dark."

Chapter eight:

Two stars shine brilliantly in the dark, night sky. They watch from overhead, beacons of light that reach despite position – millions of light-years in the distance. They burn unseen, even when the sky is bright, when starlight shines brilliantly across the planet and washes out their visage. They still remain, adding their own irradiation even if its presence is so dilute it isn't felt. Just an afterthought in mind that passes on occasion, or a nod given to the familiar when skies are dark. They remain, regardless. Always reaching across the universe to subtly wield a difference. To make infinitesimal changes to an existence that is blunt and brutal. To a timeline that was always on a path that it could not turn from.

Stars shine and plead against the dark, always impinging. Always sapping threads away to steal the opportunity for stars to reflect upon.

The light and heat is unrelenting, seeking the slightest glimmer to grasp and hold. Looking for any fragment of a thread that might sustain another moment before futility. Giving light to dark when starlight fades and the cool winds of evening begin to blow.

They hold a beauty that is not always given recognition. A motif that laid the groundwork for everything that would follow – the origin for the fanfare that would overwhelm them. A melody so different it could be forgotten there was one already present from the dawning of existence. But it's always present. Always shining, and always watching – always pushing.

The stars shine down and burn fire into existence. They burn with urgency while knowing the flames will bring destruction – why distance given. The edges singe as daylight obliterates the heavens and the surrounding world becomes blanketed by the wash of light. It is the opposite of absence – it is everything – but the end result is a world left overwhelmed by flames.

The edges singe, and flames erupt, spreading fire across the landscape while the stars watch helplessly at the destruction for which they're blamed – knowing their influence was nominal, weak consolation. They watch with desperate helplessness as the world begins to burn, lost and forgotten in the sky above, distant, but still beside two moons that rest softly.

Moon eyes look down. Moon eyes pull at the waters that have been lapping at the shore, and pull them closer with the tides. They bring calm within the fires that are raging. They give comfort that is absent from distant stars. They are only stone and give no heat to fuel the fires – only absorb: A balance to the universe. Equilibrium restored within their presence. They are the constant, and even in daylight they are often evident, overhead in the sky, above. The moons look down as the bass line for all existence. They are restorative and constant. They are consistency that brings thoughts that life is more than a chance thread stumbled over in the starlight.

The moons are compassion when the world goes up in flames, when everything ever wanted and expected falls away. When the path that was always followed is nudged aside by distance stars, into a forest where the destination finds no conclusion.

A warm blanket is pulled across the shoulders to offer comfort. It is a blanket that is protective, that is the story of existence and eternity. It is always waiting

– it is always watching – and when the cold sends brittle thoughts across the mind and down the spine, it will be waiting to implement its orders. It will wrap cold shoulders and calm the soul. It offers protection from anyone or thing that might bring harm. It is the tomes of dusty keepsakes passed through families for generations that tell a history and give a knowledge that is only held by those that have the seeds implanted early.

Moon eyes look down into the confusion of innocence, and offer kindness that melts away any chance that words will meet rejection or go ignored. They are words that hold stories within the story. Side notes that pull curiosity and amusement. Small treats held in the iron fist with razor claws. A caricature that becomes familiar and feels like the comfort of a blanket pulled over shoulders.

A small creature stands on tip-toes to complain about the gravitational gradients across collators. The creature scuttles over the pages, scurrying through the millions of calculations that are impossible to understand. Tork questions, "Do you understand this?"

"Yes," Antru answers, but the interruption is found to be extremely irritating.

There is a moment where darkness slips around the edges, but the creature remains, and with it, starlight finds enough to reflect upon that the emptiness is forgotten.

It is a bright day with no clouds in the sky, and the temperature is perfect. There had been flames that had begun to ignite fires in the forest, but as it did, the tide came in, and the starlight only brings a welcome warmth.

Waves lap against the shoreline as pages of ancient writing pile in layers over the shore where a small creature is complaining about a tilting tower. Of unmatched values that bring a spin in search of equilibrium, but that's countered by particles that revert against it: An unending cycle that grows to maximal spin, extremely quickly.

"You think I'm small," Tork says with multiple exclamation points.

The creature stands on a pile of the paper, and it's a mountain. It is the largest upcrop on the planet. Vision pulls away and the mound is magnificent, but the one that questioned cannot be seen – too small: Too insignificant.

"One point," drifts from the fog to find Dalune emerges. The memory of the explanation changes so that it's heard as it should have been: Dalune saying, "One point."

One point out of many, one of countless zillions that collect as thread and catch the starlight.

Silver threads fall out of oblivion and with their totality, they are able to reflect the starlight that brings existence. They are able to hold imagined stars and planets. They envision breath and life. The give rise to imagination and creativity, and full civilizations rise from quadrillions of points of insignificance.

"Do you understand," Dalune questions.

The irritation is felt even beyond consciousness, and, "Yes," rasps in an echo that falls like sand as life grows complicated and the shoreline becomes distorted by interruptions.

"Do you understand," Tork asks.

There is a song that falls amongst twisted laughter. There are flashes of petulance and regret, but another

467

moment slides into frame where the words are sung together. Where a creature is imagined and voiced together, and an idea of a blanket fell as the solution to concerns that had been raised.

Words fall like concrete bricks – the sound of them breaking – as lights flash on monitors, as formulas fall over them, as voices speak nonsensically with great gravity: Talking of gravity.

The creature crawls over the monitors, and a chase begins, running through parents and adults, crashing through the instruments; smashing the wall: Bringing destruction to everything that was built and leaving it scattered across the planet.

"Problem," says Antru.

Problem is stated as an angle's seen that had never, previously been understood: An opening. Insight, and more information than should be shared: A lesson learned from a small creature on the corner of a page.

"Dalune," is not moboti, and the first time the name was ever said.

It brings shadows, and sadness. It is a crack against existence. It is the first shoulder of responsibility, and it comes, far, far too soon.

The world floats apart as stars retreat to distant heavens. Arms reach down and the satellites of care put space between exposure and reprobation. A creature sulks away and is never focused upon again.

Only content and formulas. Only the piles of paper that rot in the waters that rock against them as the starlight casts fire down to burn them.

They work together – their purpose is the same. But the water is inadequate to destroy what's written, and the fire can't burn them in their saturated state. They come together and find an equilibrium: An imperfect state where the weather's fine, however storms are always threatening.

The tempest in the waters sends waves crashing against the shore with violent thrashing. The essence of the stars lights the world on fire, and they meet in the middle with a sludge of ashen pages washing in the tide. It was never perfect, and the end result's scratched forward with thought in mind that it was always going to fail.

"Moboti," echoes, and there's a chorus softly singing in the background.

It is an echo that calls through generations and towards the future. The song is one that carries across the threads of time and is the one constant that holds them together. It is the pull of gravity and warmth of starlight that fold in layers to protect an evanescent shard of essence, that wrap around the note that calls like the layers around rocks to protect children.

They are one and the same. Forces that work together to band quicksilver shreds of time for the brief instant they are sustainable. An objective that is critical, that saps the gravity of moons and fuel of stars but it will always be unrelenting. It is not a question, but an honor worn, for an immaterial fleck of time that was always going to be forgotten, yet grasped as if there was ever any substance. The particles of time are fleeting, and they're poison. They shine brilliantly, only to disappear.

The gentle wind blows a blanket from a child's shoulders, but the air is pleasant and the starlight beats down warmly across the back.

The blanket grows as it rises, flying higher but never appearing smaller as it does. It flies into the atmosphere, getting larger until it has entirely encircled the entire planet, invisibly wrapping the world in the ionosphere. A blanket to keep the planet safe, and warm, and to offer its protection. It is a distance where the well is of little significance to a particle that is not large enough to measure. Where the gradient measured over distance is negligible.

"It is one point," Dalune lectures, and a small creature speaks up to remind the tomes once served as entertainment:

"You can't count the number of points there are. There are – *too* – many."

Thunder rolls from the clouds as a blanket's pulled around the upcrops were children play. Folds brought down in the mind of a child from an object spoken of as if it's tactile. As if a woven object surrounded the planet to protect it. A novel solution conjectured and tested to see if it was possible – an idea that should have been dismissed as childish, and silly.

Until it was discovered it could be done.

Thunder rumbles as fat raindrops splatter against the ground. As eyes look up and see nothing but what was always there. Up through folds of time that react against ingress. That are a novelty for everyone that uses them, but recognized as a threat to those that understand the implications.

The wet rock is climbed at a pace that's much slower than necessary. It is a climb towards the inevitable. It is the race for the top towards the ever-nearing ending. The climb is soggy as the weather and arms and legs are noodles on their grips. They lash and pull, but they're unsteady – always ready to slip.

It is an arduous climb, as it's a climb that's not wanted. There is no joy, nor goal – only duty. Only the honor worn to have the opportunity.

When the acme's finally reached it is disappointing. It is a unremarkable surface: Flat, small, and covered with rain. But there is an image that slides from memories in the mountains, where the other side, another rise stood higher. There is a step – all that's needed to reach the other end – but misstep in the water brings a loss of balance, and any chance to react is thwarted as flames erupt from the upcrops' surface.

The smooth wall passes in vision. The wall pours with waterfalls of retreating silver. There is a strong smell of acrid smoke and it begins to blacken out the atmosphere.

It is a terror so familiar, it's simply accepted. It has been seen so many times, so many ways, that the end is simply waited: Waiting below is a pile of debris that will shatter bones and sponge the blood that follows.

It calls, and the voice is that of a siren – inescapable. It is a voice that is distance but familiar. It says, "I'm with – Capriot."

Smoke vanishes as a parent slides into vision. Éayren explains, "I'm with Capriot."

Smoke disappears and there's only a sunny day with pleasant weather, but one is falling while the other climbs down rockface.

There is a disturbance to the atmosphere, as words are spoken, but they don't make sense. "I'm with Capriot," is incoherent. It does not fit in the world that's known. It a schism that questions, "Aren't you?"

"Antru." A boot toe stabs into the shoulder as threads fall away into darkness. "Antru of Capriot," is questioned.

"You are Antru," is questioned, and it is finally noted that the dimmest light is being held, adjacent.

They are answered, "What do you want?"

It's questioned, "Can you walk?"

Antru questions back, "Why would I?"

The voice is stern, stating back in harsh whisper, "Your moboti said to cooperate. The answer to the question you're supposed to ask is Tork."

Antru rises immediately. The other takes a hand and leads them from the cell, travelling in complete darkness down the hallway. They pause, momentarily, while hands are pulled behind and binds are loosely draped around them. Shortly after, the sound of a familiar door slides open to reveal the room of doors that lead to several rooms and connecting hallways.

There is little interest shown by the few apparently waiting. They watch, but nothing is said as another door opens, as guard and prisoner head down a hallway that is known for certain measures – taken against those that are problematic or refuse to disclose needed information. No suspicion is raised, because it's a direction that's been taken on multiple occasions. However, bindings were never loose, those prior times, nor do they follow the same path.

They move quickly, following numerous passageways. They reach a barrier that is physically slid to give passage. It leads to a long channel that is observed as ancient by the narrowness and the crude manner it was cut. A door is reached, leading to a room through which they walk, and it becomes one of many. They follow halls and traverse rooms until they finally come to one with windows. At its opening, alarms immediately begin to wail.

There is no need for words as the other quickly scrambles through and motions towards a waiting vehicle. They accelerate quickly away as aerial vehicles begin arriving – some holding members of security, but most without. Their attention is initially turned to the broken opening, one that is not adjacent to anything particularly interesting. However, if a person attained the proper knowledge, it is understood that the maze of caverns mined throughout millennia could get a person from one place to anywhere. The breach is seen and the concern is observed to elevate in strained words shouted and frantic action – scrambling to secure the scene and initiate a search.

The vehicle speeds away across the open meadow which would seem to make it an easy target. However, only cursory searches are made in that direction as nothing goes detected in the open space.

Ideas float that might be pertinent, but they go unquestioned, because detection often relies on anomalous sounds or conversation, so the travel continues in silence.

It is not long before the forest's entered. Travel slows and the vehicle is steered from the usual, traveled road, through underbrush that had been cleared for the evening's purpose.

One exits, and the other follows. A tablet's pulled, there's brief instruction entered, and a wave of distortion seems to follow: A ripple of fog passes vision. As soon as it has, the vehicle begins trampling through the forest, moving loudly and crushing the plants it travels over.

A quick nod, and the duo begin moving the opposite direction, at first cautiously, but that soon become a full sprint as it's observed that Antru remains capable.

They run for only a minute before being pushed to move faster by the sound of an explosion. Further violence erupts as efforts are made to fully extinguish any trace of brain function that might be present as instantly as possible. It gives the pounding footsteps cover as leaves crinkle and twigs crack beneath feet. They continue as sounds begin abating because this stretch of the plan was another that was prone to failure. Avoiding detection is nearly impossible.

There is finally an end-point reached as the familiar hum of av's can be heard in the near distance. They have already recognized the vehicle a distraction, but they won't know if that was for a local move, or to pull them the wrong direction. The parameters for the search will be wide, and will buy a few more seconds – every last one needed as the sound of airborne scanners hum near as entry's made.

It is not the end of the frantic scramble. The lead continues into much cruder corridors, still running, still looking to escape detection. That chance comes, finally, at a giant pit that glows with a mineral the resistance would have found very useful: If only they had known how near it was, much might have been averted. At least, it would have been a battle others shouldered.

A rope and anchor are handed over, and like the other, the rope's dropped in the hole and the anchor's secured.

"Ready," is asked, and that is demonstrated by testing the hold, and both begin descent into the chasm.

It is a considerable drop, and after weeks of starvation and dehydration arms are not as equipped as typical for the effort. Only part way down, a strategy turns to twisting feet within the rope to give support. It slows the effort, but Antru methodically lowers down to meet the other. They immediately douse the rope with a liquid that burns the material away, rising with only a putrid plume remaining.

"Half-way home," is given, and a hand extends: "Endreeus: It's nice to finally meet you. Can you continue?"

Emphatically, that is answered, "Yes."

A canteen is pulled from the waist and handed over, with instruction, "Drink while we walk. I'll update you when we get to safety." There is an eyeball as choices solidify, and a decision is finalized as one of the many implements hanging from the waist is handed over. Another order passes, "Stay alert. Anything that moves down here needs to be killed. Hesitate, and it's over."

They begin a more complicated travel. Most of what's navigated was created through natural forces, with only interconnecting openings crudely cut.

It is a beautiful and surreal trek, through glowing rocks that cast an eerie blue. They give comfort to have sight, but give just enough light to cast shadows at every corner and in their absence. The terrain is rough and uneven, and travel is arduous. It is not quiet and moving quickly through it is impossible. But neither is deterred – one desperate to move forward, and the other desperate to protect what matters most: Most of both ends fall into the same category.

The walk finally concludes at a point well past exhaustion. A stone wall is met, and it is the final barrier that delineates fleeing from defense.

The tablet's pulled free, again, and there's more information entered. It does not initiate the immediate action as with the vehicle and there are numerous benchmarks that were unexpected.

Both answer questions and have their faces scanned. Both are required to place both hands on the surface of the tablet, and both are required to repeat specific phrases.

If there had been someone following that was close, they would have had ample time to find their targets, and there is a history that found most were. Most that attempted escape through the storied passage were executed at the divider between the Empire of Nespia and the southern states. Few ever made it through the impenetrable wall.

There is a scraping as a portion of the floor begins to descend. It is an archaic artifact from ancient times that has never been updated – rarely used and for most, considered to be a legend. A mechanical device that can give access to defectors, but more often to spies and those engaged in subterfuge or special operations.

The floor lowers, and the dim light that acclimated eyes can use finds stairs that descend into darkness.

Endreeus moves instantly, and Antru follows. They walk the stairs as light fades away in the sound of rocks scraping together.

There is hesitance to bring light, and whispers agree to follow the passage with fingers against the walls, and with feet carefully testing their progression.

Several minutes pass that seem much longer, as steps continue down to a plateau, where feet find more rise, the other side: Rising, and curving sharply on precariously angled steps. A circling tower staircase that would be a formidable obstacle to attack – position severely compromised and unstable. It leads to a solid wall for which no prior instructions were passed.

"Now what," is frustration that escapes, but Antru questions, "Knock?"

Novel, but exhausted, the suggestion's followed.

The wall slides open, and it reveals a more formal passageway. It is clearly designed to meet an enemy with advantage, with a small area beneath steep stairs that lead to a larger space. If there was an adversary approaching, they would be severely disadvantaged: Emerging single file, drawn forward to a bottleneck, and likely facing hundreds of hostiles that were only the first line against invasion. The whole of the construct makes that prospect extraordinarily unlikely. The methods employed to counteract bring two in awe of the depths of historical concern as they enter.

"Welcome home," is offered by a single person. They are older than the vision kept in memory, but they were a person that showed empathy and kindness for a child facing a world filled with confusion and distress. They were a person put in the unfortunate position to explain the decision made was parents'. A decision made with the hope to prevent the present circumstance.

Antru says, "Nice to see you," and it's sincere. However, "Where do we stand," is for the need to understand what the present circumstance delivers: "Tell me Alvel's in flames."

"Tell me you can protect my family," is Endreeus' response: "Our necks are on the line as a favor to your parents, but I need that favor returned."

Antru answers: "I'm not magic. No one's safety or freedom's guaranteed until this is over. But I can get you to Capriot. We can look out for you on the way there, and I'm pretty sure they'll take you in – that's the best I can do. I can't know if that returns the favor until we see what happens."

Chapter nine:

Another exhausting journey comes to an end. Unlike others, it was only days, and most of that was spent waiting. Idle while the world was going up in flames at the request of the person sitting in a room and doing nothing. But just as with an extraction that was managed more carefully than known, there are new orders in place that formalize actions and give the safety of personnel highest priority.

That fell across the theatre, and while effective, the theater that was planned had been less effective consequently. It is intended that will change very quickly.

The final incline is taken on the only leg of the journey that moves underground. It is the opening to a mine that once meant to exploit resources of the planet, locally. That operation ended shortly after opening, shut down after a partial collapse that fouled the landscape – no longer even recognizable after thousands of years. The entrance was permanently sealed and the caverns were flooded with water, which seeped out over the millennia and even began the work to create further passages.

The chasms stumbled on were claimed by the Alvel underground at the time Januk was forcing change, and they'd been maintained and expanded since, becoming space for less of an opposing force, than a society: A place where voices of dissent could speak openly. No one recently engaged ever intended to upend society, but their presence known was exploited by Capriot intelligence. Their support was given for the operation, but their observations were, that was a failing effort. That opinion was universally shelved as word spread: Antru was still alive and would join the effort.

A space is entered that is packed with people. They are subdued, but that gradually changes as eyes fall upon the person that joins them. As, "Antru," is called with surprise, but welcome, and the end of the name rises with the same enthusiasm growing throughout the room.

"Welcome back," a person says. They greet with familiarity. Hand is taken and they move in for embrace. It is firm and warm, and they release and look back with emotion washing over them.

"Tell me where we are," Antru requests.

"Waiting for you," says a voice of life across the room: Eyes target, and two that weren't supposed to be there are found smiling.

Space closes in an instant. The younger of the two is gripped in shaking arms, only released to demand from both:

"Why," asks Antru, "Are you here," and Éayren question back, "Why are you?"

"You're supposed to be in Capriot," Antru swears in anger: "I told you to take Axael back."

"I told you to go back," Éayren answers back: "What argument do I have?"

"No," is answered, but the question's undeniably valid: The two that square are asking for the same thing – asking for the safety of a child. "I can't walk away," Antru explains.

It leaves no room for push-back, when Axael says, "We won't walk away from you."

There is regret with acceptance that drips with, "Where do we stand?" A question that chinks commitment for the first time, and the answer's complicated.

"We have not had a lot of success," supersedes the concern of finding family: Fires had been set but they were quickly doused. Smoke had risen over the prior, several weeks, but it was inconsistent. The most positive development is that the net has come to identify a.v.'s as a threat and they are consequently vaporized upon detection. Spotters have easily kept them at bay.

It has allowed the raids that send incendiaries against the walls, but that effort has been stymied by the altered rules that have been insisted by the emperor of Capriot.

"There are orders," Éayren explains. They alter the plans that were never solid to begin with, but what they were would at least have provided a better demonstration. However, tacit support is traded for, "Minimizing casualties: Theirs, and ours. This has to move forward as non-violently as we can. They want you to make efforts to negotiate."

"We have been," Antru says, but it's pressed:

"They will oppose you if you do not minimize the loss of life. We can make noise, but the conversation has to remain open. Can I tell them you agree to that?"

"Loss of life," Antru ponders: It's an opening and mass casualties were never the objective. There is a nod; thoughts turn to the net, turn to bringing calm and the need to broadcast. It is not understood why Antru begins talking:

"This is Antru of Capriot. I have left Greater Nespia to join forces with those putting pressure on Alvel. To be clear, we do not want anyone harmed. Up until now, our approach has been to make a point, and that point is that the agreement you signed thousands of years ago, has to be honored. There is no need to negotiate, because you have already agreed to the terms on that document and those terms are all we're asking. We are asking you — Alvel clan — honor that commitment. Publicly state you will abide by the agreement that you negotiated thousands of years ago. Speak with us against the use of forced medication and labor, and let all of Nespia reunite with their children, their parents, and their friends. Help us transition through what will be a difficult time, one that should have happened long ago. Help us make this happen peacefully — Alvel clan; Nespia: Live up to the promises you proudly teach us when we're children. Make this planet the world all of us deserve. Because all of us deserve to return to that person remembered in our dreams. All of us deserve to come back home to family. We're begging you — Nespian Clan; Alvel Clan — honor the commitments you made and help us move towards that ideal that you promise the children of this world is in their future. We'll give you to the end of this day to respond, but if we don't hear from you, we will be forced to escalate. Because stealing our children and our parents, that — will — come to an end. By whatever means necessary. If you refuse to stand by the commitments you already made, if we do not hear from you, we will begin our full assault. That will begin from the western end of the Alvel compound. If you don't intend to cooperate, we strongly recommend that you evacuate that area, for your protection: We won't be setting small fires, going forward. Thank you for listening, and I hope to hear from you."

"That's it," Éayren wonders: The stunned reaction questioned; explained, "You just talk."

"I have to concentrate," Antru says.

But a parent wonders, "What did we teach you?"

"I don't think you did," and an idea that was once amorphous finds body with reflection: "I think I'm part of the net. Maybe, a barometer for what's happening. But I think it watches through me."

There is regret, as Éayren says, "I don't want to hear that."

"I know," is a sentiment understood because a child not seen for years has hardly been acknowledged. Proper greeting was delayed because the urgency of what's seeped into existence took priority. Eyes turn to find the child smiling: Grown, but always holding history that continuously plays: "It's good to see you."

The smile grows as they come together, and another follows. The heaviness and formality melts away as a reunion finally has the chance to spill, as experience is shared. As questions of, "How," and what they've been through mostly go unanswered.

There is time of respite as tales are told and laughter finds a hold amongst the solemn. Details fall out at a misplaced thought of the effort and magnitude of an extraction that seemed capricious and poorly planned.

Éayren quips, "Usually things don't go that well: We were ready if they didn't."

It is a reminder of the efforts taken over the years to secure continued life for an only child, and those thoughts filter down through generations to do the same for the youngest in the conversation: The idea of careful plotting and minimizing risks gains weight. Protecting lives and harming as few as possible becomes a priority that isn't thought, specifically, but one submitted by Capriot and cemented with thoughts of a future for a child.

When, "It's gettin' late," serves as reminder of a deadline, it is pre-eminent in thought for what will follow.

The noise of the conversation had veiled an approach usually announced by the rattle of metal posts, usually the result of using them incorrectly – of stabbing them at the floor. Onton arrives to deliver the announcement with no preamble, but with concern weeks of effort have been pointless: Not insignificant despite their limited result. Not without effort, and not without losses – especially early on with av's attacking freely. The meager returns were gained by unyielding effort and refusing to back down. Continued with the trust that one person saw something others couldn't. That Antru was going to be able to move them forward:

"Nice speech, but they're quiet. We gonna do something, or it's all talk, now?"

"Onton," Antru explains, and introductions follow.

"Nice and all," is returned, and they're reminded, "We're at the deadline. If you're done fighting – I'll go it alone."

"No," is answered curtly, but a smile follows, of warmth and appreciation – an ill-advised attempt to rise and embrace to demonstrate the sentiments, is battled back by a post that threatens harm. Antru promises, "Not 'til we're done."

"Okay," says Onton – and there's relief: Words were shared that spoke with authority though they still were uncertain. Motivation to continue held one as an example, willing to sacrifice everything. With the evening unfolding the way it had, anger grew with ideas building – the battle's done, now that the one had found their own. Anger drains, and determination assumes it's place within the question, "What's the plan?"

"Well," says Antru: "If they won't talk with us, we have to act. I want to consult with Mash, and,"

"Mash is dead."

"Oh," says Antru, and the reality of the enterprise encounters its first body. Eyes lock, and the weeks of brutal imprisonment no longer seem like a tremendous hardship compared to what was happening beyond the walls. Antru says, "We're going to begin destroying the compound, but we've been asked to minimize loss of life. That's how we get the support of the southern clans. I was going to discuss that with – Mash – and Éayren. How we approach that."

Steel eyes look back over frosted words that state, "You're who everybody's lookin' at."

Eyes fall to a parent and every atom of cheer has left them. They make no motion, nor say a word, and Antru asks:

"Can you coordinate the plan?"

Onton gives, "Whatever you want."

"I warned them," Antru decides: "Everyone on the planet knows that."

"My advice," is interjected. Onton suggests, "Give them five."

Children and parents remain unaccounted – potential for use to turn the conversation, or worse, for retribution – and a plan like every plan comes together in an instant:

"I'm a face," Antru says, however, to Onton, "You're the general. I'll be at the front to lead the charge, but I need you to coordinate the action:"

To broadcast warning and arrange the sorties that will follow, that will illuminate the night air and show sporadic smoke was just a warning. Waves upon waves will be thrown against the compound until there is no capacity to drench the fire. The clan will be forced into retreat, into a space they can reinforce, where they can prevent the fire's spread, and defend themselves more capably.

Onton asks, but it's a demand, "You're gonna use the net?"

"Remind everyone to use it," Antru instructs: "The more pulling, the better protection we'll have."

Preparations begin with Onton shouting newly given authority – responsibility and custody of many's safety. It is an authority that fits comfortably, despite the weight, for a person that wasn't always great in battle but always understood in any moment what was needed to field a win. Standing in concert with the one force that didn't let that happen anneals a confidence barked in orders and stabbed against the stone with the chatter of steel posts.

"Whenever you want," is delivered to their captain. It is a loyalty and commitment never felt for prior leadership, and despite the feelings of loss and camaraderie through years, orders from a prior leader went ignored because they'd never seemed completely serious, nor capable of delivering on their promises. Whenever you want is the offer to follow into battle, and it's an offer that's spread through many.

A hand reaches out to take another that leaves a post, and Antru says, "You were always capable. You have my complete trust."

"I've been trustin' you a long time," says Onton, and there's a sparkle. There's a twitch that pulls at the face, and eyes gleam glossed by tears that will never fall, and humor, with, "'Bout time you did."

Eyes move to a parent and a child, and, "I know you're probably coming with me, but I wish you wouldn't," is a plea that's been made before, but by another, and it's expected wishes, like Éayren's, will go ignored.

Complete control of the attack is handed over, and the first to attack sit in wait as preparations are made to give them cover.

It will be unlike any of the prior attacks – crude assaults made on foot or using vehicles. The tacit support from southern cities includes forces nearby and the use of airborne vehicles – for transportation. With many softly pulling at the net and eyes on everything, the order's passed, and Onton sends the one hope still remaining for reunion into battle.

It is three – and twenty. A single unit that's been forward since the beginning that already has suffered significant losses. Twenty follow with newfound duty and purpose, engaging with the one that leads the mission – the face of the mission. The voice of the world: Antru of Capriot – a suggestion that became reality.

Flying machines are strapped to backs and there's a temptation to fly directly over, except, "I don't know how to use these," worries Antru.

There's a coughing laugh as a steel post slabs into the stone: Onton shares, "Plan's the wall – we'll get you there. Just be ready to get pulled out."

Twenty-three march from the shelter with packs on backs and for the first time that day breathe fresh air. They walk out beneath a sky brightly lit by one full moon, and the waning crescent of the other. Those without experience are quickly lifted, while twenty-one others guide themselves forward to the start of the mission they'd signed up for: The start of the war to bring the Nespian clan to its knees. Some degree of that desire is held in all of them, with only two holding any concern for them at all, and the same antipathy is felt for Alvel's clan – complicit, and the front-line of the assault.

At landing, Antru immediately begins: "Good evening, Alvel clan. I am not happy to be here," and a view scans across the screens of every tablet in the world, of those gathered, and then the wall of the Alvel castle. Antru says, "We've asked you to respect the commitments you made. We asked you to hold a conversation with us. But you have done neither."

A quiet hum rises, and dozens think of danger – dozens identify threats: There are screams of agony as av's explode in fire and the people that they carry fall to the ground.

"You're killing your own," Antru observes: "The net acts autonomously: They won't get to us."

It is a warning spoken desperately – desperate to hold support of Capriot and Marphy. It is a call against the pointless loss of life and explanation that any airborne vehicles approaching will be a sacrifice, uncontrolled by those outside the walls – it is autonomous and will attack any threat perceived: An understanding that should have been inured.

But there's another test. There is a crackle as the second wave is obliterated: Remote, aerial vehicles raised in a massive wave to attack, and simply destroyed. There is a warning flashing in the brain that there's more behind it, as if a test against the limits and capacity of the net. To see how it responds and if there's a way to overwhelm it.

That thought's chocked away as Antru says, "I wish you would have worked with us," and the broadcast sees the flames that erupt against the compound.

It is pulled away, for Antru to continue, "We are three generations of my family. All of us were kidnapped and forced into labor. Moboti – Éayren – my child – Axael – and, myself. All of us were stolen from our families, and we stand, here, with hundreds of thousands that have experienced the same. Talk to us now, or we will change our world, however we have to."

Explosions erupt overhead as the net intercepts the missiles thrown against those standing at the burning walls of the Alvel fortress.

It should have been understood a pointless effort if lessons had been learned from history, as the Astrasian assault was much larger, and with munitions that were more advanced: Weapons have little effect on time and gravity, but there are few that truly understand.

It is the point where the first assailants will be withdrawn until the fires begin to dwindle. The intent is to bring wave, after wave against the compound, to create fires that will burn for days and destruction that is palpable. But like every plan, a quirk is thrown against it: An explosion is thrown against it.

An eruption not expected blows out of the Alvel walls and sends debris towards those attacking. It is a destructive move, intended to take off the head of the insurrection, however, the head was already actively engaged, and so was another in proximity.

There is a violent thrash that falls from the heavens. What appears a blast rakes down against the fire and debris, and explodes the nearby structure.

Flames erupt and fill the sky so fully that those awake would think they walked in daylight. The thunder that roars across the city shakes buildings from their foundations and shatters nearby windows. If anyone had remained in the western portion of the compound, they were eviscerated like the rest of it.

Shock is quickly brushed off as the destruction brings an opening never expected. It opens the door to actual victory – a chance to defeat the Alvel clan, quickly and decidedly.

Antru orders, "Bring everyone, but remember: Prisoners, not bodies." Urgently, those in proximity – child, and parent – are told, "Go back. Go back to the caves, and get to Capriot."

"Antru," Éayren questions, "What did you do?"

"I didn't," and, "You both need to leave," is said understanding what follows is crucial, yet also carries the greatest risk of the operation.

But Axael says, "I won't leave you," and that's doubled down by Éayren: "I'm not leaving," however, that's followed by the question, "How did you get the net to do that?"

Desperately, Antru says, "I was calling – everyone was calling: I trained dozens to reach it. Please go, because this is not going to be safe for you."

But Éayren says, "No," and, "No one else can do that," is given emphasis, with, "Antru: No one else is calling the net. You are."

A momentary pause slumps the pressing need to move, and it's recalled, "I told you that: I am the net. It's working through me."

"Moboti," Axael says: "We are with you. Every step you take – we take with you. You are not alone – whatever happens."

"I don't want that," is countered by, "Neither do we."

"I can't guarantee anything," Antru warns: "I don't know why it does what it does – I don't know how safe I can keep us."

"We know," Éayren says, and Axael confirms, "We're sticking with you."

Ticking time brings only a shaken head and no more argument, and three generations begin leading a single, forward unit past massive destruction, against the heat that presses them away and for the middle of the compound. They move with weakened confidence, walking in the open as easy targets if any had the notion.

But it's not the first time one's been let to walk without assault, and like the first time, there is significant concern that taking action will lead to more destruction. Twenty-three breach the Alvel compound and are greeted by a line of unwilling security – security that is less a force than an imposition, as instructions have been quickly passed to make every effort not to appear that they're a threat.

They are greeted softly, with, "I'm sorry," that is unexpected. But admonition follows: "The net reacts to threats. Don't you know that?" The voice rises, as, "Don't you," is questioned with a rise of anger, and Antru stabs a finger against their shoulder, to emphasize, "I – am – the net. If you destroy the net, you put all of us in danger. Do you understand that?"

Words are stammered that have no meaning – still incapable of comprehending everything that happened: The violence and the level of destruction; the person standing within the fortress with impunity, even demanding:

"I need to talk with the emperor."

Confusion remains, but, "Keep weapons down," is certain, even as a familiar hum begins to rise:

Eyes turn, but even in the darkness, the metal poles that hang can be identified.

Onton is the first to land, but the sound of hundreds, even thousands of approaching aerial vehicles is unmistakable.

Onton arrives with the message, "You are not gonna believe this."

It's met by, "I have to go." Antru says, "Make the emperor put it in writing that Alvel will follow the world constitution. Occupy the compound and take prisoners if you have to, but no one gets hurt."

"So long," Onton says: "They try nothin'. But you got to hear this: We got Marphy comin' from the south, and Capriot's holding the southern demarcation." A fist pumps to rouse those falling in behind and it's declared, "We're gonna do this."

"It's not over," Antru warns. "Occupy the compound and hold the ground. We'll try to finish it."

Chapter ten:

Stars and moons align to stem the fate quicksilver pulls, a momentary pause to dissolution. Sorrow still carries in uncertainty, but there are tones of hope within the symphony even if the tune wends minor. It is still the music known and longed for, still the company that completes the chord – prelude present, as well as the finale: A song that brings all together to secure the future where the final becomes the first to lead, anew.

It crescendos in the small room where reunion plays, a room filled instantly as an unbreakable bond is drawn together and holds so close and tight that bodies share a heart-rate, and not a word is needed to understand what is held between them.

All arguments against the presence of any gathered are lost by the chance considered lost. By the opportunity to hold the other in arms, again. To feel the warmth of body and hold the deep emotions that live between them.

Quiet had fallen, but the moment slowly grew into the music, as those watching knew the passion that they saw, knew the emotions behind the desire to meet the impossible. Willing to risk everything for that opportunity:

To see a child, again. To find a parent. To reunite with their lost partners.

It is what brought every one to commit to what could never be accomplished: To join raids, to plan attacks; to take on those that are better armed, better trained, with significantly more and better weaponry. It is the last glimmer of hope, a tiny fleck that catches starlight and holds to it the longest, the strongest, and that will die only once every, last effort has been expended. It will die as the body dies in the effort.

Two hold each other while others in their presence steel their commitment to the mission. See two together and taste blood to find that for themselves. Remember notes that have long been absent – broken chords that sing hollow – remember laughter, and see memories built together.

Two came together, and silence fell, but that fell into the ocean as others felt their missions find new breath. The ocean's roar flooded through the room, but the waters receded with the tide as two remained together as it left, and the muted room is again matched by quiet conversation.

Two come together and not a person in their presence wants to interrupt them, except one, a child whose own have whispered, "Why are they doing that?"

"Hey," shutters the orchestra that is willing to play for all eternity. It brings the curtain down and shunts the light that had become the only focus. Center stage is brought awareness of the applause that surrounds, by a child that moves forward, gently reaches, and awkwardly interrupts the moment with a hand, and by saying, "Hey."

A hand touches a parent's shoulder, and it's a syphon for the feelings that are between them. It brings eyes to focus. It brings thoughts to the present, and it brings memory to why everyone is gathered. There's an effort to greet the child not seen for several months, and they attempt to break the deep emotions:

"Half hug: See where I rank."

There's some forced laughter, but the intensity of the force between the two is felt by everyone in the room. The desire is strong to find that memory for themselves. There is laughter, but it's mostly to respect the effort. There is no levity in any one of them.

"Althrae," says Antru: "No. You are not going to be a part of this." A finger points to the other child, and also answers, "No." It is said again, against Dalune: "No. None of you are going to be part of this. And especially," Antru insists to Aedra, "Not you."

Éayren says, "I won't let you walk alone."

And Axael suggests, "You'll need someone else pulling on the net."

"I'll be here," Dalune says. "Just in case: I'll make sure everyone here is safe."

It is a waterfall of thoughts as the person that was most instrumental in bringing the moment stands as the guardian against its failure. Someone always associated with the far-east, southern city of Capriot, and someone long known as a guardian of the net, yet their origins are in Bitor:

The strange, small city of the northeastern-most peninsula. The city of spongy ground and secret agents in the sewers. There is an answer to questions in that connection – an anomalous behavior observed, once, as a prisoner – but it isn't the time to travel down those roads: Alvel is compromised at the minimum, and Nespian forces have finally begun a move as news of trouble traveled. It is the moment hoped for, planned for; that was never expected to be met: Too many opportunities for failure, however, those points of weakness had found strength as others interceded to provide support.

It changed everything, but also nothing. Points of failure had been redirected, however, the greatest of them was the – hope – that hundreds of thousands would storm across Greater Nespia to support a small cast that would never have success, if left to their own.

Reunion and joy are abandoned, and Antru shares, "Alvel's down. Marphy's moving this way, and Capriot's on the border." It's declared, "This is our moment." There's a look to Aedra – a look to Dalune: Looks follow to children, to Éayren, and grandchildren. Eyes remain focused on them, as Antru says, "Tonight, we will bring an end to the practices of the Nespian clan, and we will begin reuniting with those we've lost."

It was not intended that the moment should be broadcast: It was spontaneous. It was heartfelt for those that had lost members of their families, or friends. However, an autonomous blanket of particles that work together calculates the outcomes of what's unfolding, and finds the moment matches against a particular algorithm. Shortly after, the entirety of the world hears the emotion spoken in the words.

The entire world hears, "Tonight, we will rise up. We will take back our lives. Who are we," Antru yells, "In our dreams?" Tears fall, as that memory falls, of a time where those dearest were forgotten. It is bitter, that it's observed, "That's what Januk meant: We are who we remember in our dreams – what the people in our dreams are calling us. That's who we are," Antru says: "And we – will – bring back the people that we've lost. We will help them remember who they are – we will help them remember they are who they see in their dreams." It is a battle cry, as Antru calls, "Who are you in your dreams?"

The room erupts in cheers, and emotion. Those present would throw their bodies at a missile if there was a chance it would move the moment forward.

It is the moment that life has been moving towards since birth – since the dawning of existence. It is the words shared to quiet a troubled mind; the words of a creature on the corner of a page.

It is the end that always seemed inevitable: Whether in dreams, beside the columbrum, or when helping a distressed pedestrian. It is a moment that always felt like it was lurking around the corner, and its presence was always felt by everyone: Parents, partner, and even children – Nespia. And when the time came that meant to intercept it, there was always something that prevented that from happening, whether dissent, pressure, or interjection from outside forces. The moment was always lurking in the waters – a bassoon in the symphony with a wilted reed.

Hands slip away from love, and into uncertainty. Focus moves from family to others that are seeking to be with the same. They are gunned and ready to explode, and that desire is not wilted, despite effort to drain the thirst.

There is fervor.

News brought brings fire to the sparks. However, the numbers are in the thousands, and despite the drain of forces towards Alvel, they remain outnumbered by more than ten to one. Hope remains there's inspiration across the city but it's only hope. Alvel down and southern states in tow, the numbers remain disadvantageous, and it's been shown that loyalties flow where advantage grows, regardless of best interests.

Antru says, "It's time to see what happens."

Complete silence falls as the words snap all that are present into action. They are buried not far from the citadel that will be lit on fire as the beacon that calls citizens across the city. It will be the flames that were intended to rise over Alvel, that became intermittent smoke, and if a random attack had not brought the net's reaction, there is no doubt by anyone that none of them would be in the position to move the mission forward: To send it towards conclusion – one way, or the other.

Multiple units emerge into the darkness. From across the city, the rumble of explosions is heard as the massive, restrictive walls are reduced to rubble in several places.

It is the point of no return. It is the one chance to accomplish anything, and with the sound, the units slip into pre-determined shadows where they will wait for light, and then for the throngs they hope will follow: To serve as the example, to lead them forward for the assault against the grandiose compound of the Nespian clan.

Thunder rumbles from the distance, and the most challenging aspect of the plan is left to a vehicle that will fly incendiaries to the tallest upcrop. It is sent low and moves nearly silently, powering fans just enough to keep it afloat. Behind, a small unit with three generations of a family follows, to guide, to monitor, and to protect. Two pull the net while spotters scan the skies and streets. Others guide the vehicle, and more train weapons on everything approached, and everything that's passed.

They reach the edge of the open space they have to cross to meet the rise of rock that is their target, before the first sign of problems begins emerging: There is a hum that is familiar. It is the sound of a plan put in place to quash any effort to assault the palace, and like those skulking towards it, those looking to push them back remain in cover.

"Sound, Axael," is said as both warning and instruction and as quietly as possible, but it's the giveaway.

The hum becomes a rush, and with cover lost, spotters begin shouting out, and pointing at positions.

Minds focus on dangers and lean into the net as flying machines emerge en mass from everywhere. There is instant crackling across the skies and fire falls as the net strikes back, trails of flames lighting the earth, below.

The net destroys machines, but they're relentless. It is the worry that crossed the mind during the assault at Alvel, that something had been seen and was being tested. As wave after wave of av's fall from the sky, it's seen for what it is – a distraction.

"Get it up there," is screamed frantically. Antru points above and shouts, "Now. Get it up there, now."

The machine roars to life and moves without regard to subtlety, moving in a line for the top of the upcrop. It is then that counterplan begins to reveal itself, as new tactics emerge that seem to show that plans were intercepted: The initial target is the vehicle carrying explosives:

Antru yells, "Protect the av: Focus on what's moving differently." That there are thousands, meets, "They aren't weapons. They're going for the av."

Spotters focus turns to anomalous movement and it isn't insignificant, and it isn't easy to find: All move together and those attacking break free abruptly.

It is a game of eyes and net against machine, and it's one that's losing ground with altitude – they grow closer and numerous strikes are taken, still, the machine continues.

A cry gives light to the next assault, as a body falls, and a tablet tumbles across the ground. It is grabbed almost instantly, but there's sudden assault, and those trying to land the vehicle are forced to seek better cover – forced to retreat, to crash through windows into buildings.

"Ilek," Antru shouts.

"Alive," is answered, but they're questioned, "Position?"

The answer, "It's up there, but not responsive."

Eyes peer out as plinks rattle against the window frames. It won't be long before more effective weaponry is brought to the field, and desperate hope looks up for signs of fire.

There is none.

The seven that share the space watch as Antru's eyes fall shut and head falls back, as they see defeat already upon them.

However, it's a known space. It is a city that's well-known and the layout of roads and buildings was a knowledge that was once necessary for the sake of efficiency. Eyes roll back into the mind to envision a path and pockets where assailants are hiding. There are folds of gravity and time imagined as blankets of particles, that are capable of wrapping a person in protection as they climb. They are imagined as a blanket that extends further, a necessity to protect the child that's wrapped in them: A person that is an element of the fabric of time.

Antru bolts, and cries follow, but focus necessitates concentration on the vision. Voices cry and they drip like a river of wax off the side of a broken candle:

Weeping at the mind. Seeping against the mission, and nearly breaking focus from where it's needed.

They are notes of a song that has brought the moment. They are inverted and cold because that same wax falls against them.

They remain as the space is crossed. They follow and refuse to be ignored, but there's a single mission: Reach the av and start the fire.

Explosions rain out of the skies above as ground is crossed. The ever-present hum ebbs and flows as the crackle of their demise succeeds in waves: Burning debris rains down in trails so thick that the moons and stars become obliterated. Smoke grows so heavy, so quickly, that despite the light that's generated, everything is cloudy.

"Antru," is the last, desperate word heard before the wall is met. It breaks concentration just enough to give an opening to the attempt at preventing the effort: Projectiles crash and splinter stone, and something more significant impacts, above.

Whether the net, or sheer luck, injury is avoided, and concentration resumes focus where it's needed: On the security blanket that surrounds the world. The fabric of time that protects children and roukta players. A fold into existence that never should have happened, except a child that didn't quite understand the concepts wanted to climb.

Antru climbs at a pace that is fueled by terror and adrenaline. The explosions of missiles have grown distant, and they're no longer a threat. The av's flying are plucked apart without effort, and those below fire pointlessly at a target no longer within their reach. Antru climbs against arms that ache and legs that no longer have the strength from younger years. But they move regardless. They dig against imperfections with a vision that sees holds and footstops as if they're the grand staircase leading into the castle. The body moves against time and age, but with a fuel that moves for the apex, with an urgency that's never been felt before.

There are explosions above, and fire heard below: It is clear there is direct engagement, and it makes the moment all that more important.

The top is finally reached, and the av is found resting, idly upon it. There is no hesitation. No concern for personal perseverance, and the shadows that arrive haven't registered in mind as an arm is raised, and a shot is fired.

It is direct, and perfect. The tank explodes, and fire erupts immediately.

Flames erupt and rise high into the sky, and instantly, cheers can be heard rising with them: Inspiration is rising with them. It is the culmination of the mission – culmination of a lifetime: Culmination of existence.

This is thought as the flames are watched, as they rise further, and further above. As a body falls after an eruption that sent it falling.

Hands reach out to grip the stone that rises, smooth and cold, and they fall away as sand as they claw as if reaching for a failing friend.

There is dark as the body falls. It is cold, and there is just a whisper of the silver that was flowing before the moons were gone. Harsh rock rakes against the body as descent accelerates. The wind is cold and howls like a starving creature begging for a bowl of food before it dies from exposure or starvation. There is growing apprehension as the fall grows darker and knowing certainty of how it ends.

It is an absolute that was always coming. It was pre-ordained before consciousness emerged. It is the end result for a life that was always circumstance – always precariously allowed.

It will end, as it always ends. There is a pile of debris at the bottom, and bones will be shattered against it. Blood will flow through it. Life will end upon it.

The thought drops conclusion on the plummet and time is frozen for an instant. For one, brief breath of time, the jolt holds, knowing that following will find noise and pain, and certainly death. It is black except one finger of mercury that reflects light – only enough – to imagine Aedra leaning across a broken body, one lying in a crumpled heap on a pile of rubble, and covered in blood: Lying with blood across the fabric of their clothing and bathed in tears.

The jolt rips eyes open, and a shiver shakes violently through the shoulders – already tears are falling. Distant memories float away of sunny days, and joy in fields, sand, and rocks with nothing to grip to prevent a fall. Shadows from the dark except for the last. Except for the instant that was frozen and the vision of Aedra.

It is quiet. It is a vision that has been lived a thousand times. It is a future forecast before existence – one passed through generations, and regrettably, to the next. To another child – unaware.

It is where the end was always expected – expectation that life would always end in violence, whether accidental, or by intent. But those dreams, and that end had never called, "Antru." And more alarmingly, they'd never cried, "Moboti."

Eyes turn to eyes that look back desperately, to a person falling with no ability to alter what will follow.

Axael still looks with the eyes of a child, looking to one that has always been relied upon, who their life was dedicated to find, and who still expects the person they call to have the answers. That person had found acceptance, but that is not an option any longer: Nothing is acceptable, except protecting what's most important.

Eyes focus: The plummet is nearly done. There's a pause in time that gives the mind a moment to evaluate, and it calculates that the landing will be fatal. And even if it's not – the security forces of Nespia are waiting.

There is no good solution, but ideas matriculate, and outcomes are instantly assessed: It brings a pounding against the rubble below that explodes as a cloud of shrapnel.

It brings screams of agony as flesh is torn and bones are broken, and the force awaiting is left completely compromised. They are left to watch as three bodies fall with a gentle caress against the planet's surface: Set gently down as a fire rages overhead and the sound of a frantic mob can be heard in the near distance.

"Antru," Éayren says, and there's much behind it: Disparagement, disapproval, anger – relief.

All that's doused, by, "I have an idea."

It is just the beginning of the end. It is just the start to what will fall: Efforts to the moment have been successful, but a trip through memory and the layout of the city brings one more recollection of a moment where the compound was once compromised, where there is the potential to truly break through the defenses of the fortress.

Antru shouts to the moaning injured, "We're not your enemy. We're just trying to find our children – our parents." They're called, "You don't have to do this –

join us. We want to work together." They are forgotten, as Éayren's told, "I need a vehicle. Can you hijack one?"

It is a request for which Éayren is the perfect subject after a lifetime of subterfuge and covert missions: "Follow," is ordered as a sprint for a nearby neighborhood begins.

It isn't evident what the plans are beyond what's been seen, as most forces are not focused on the field, though it is likely their greater concern is the mob moving across the city. However, they either overestimated the success they'd have with av's and missiles, considered the threat of the few that would ascend the rock to be minimal, or thought the unit that had awaited at the bottom to be adequate, because the three running were momentarily an easy target. They become more complicated as city streets are reached.

Éayren shatters the glass of the first vehicle they reach, and motions the others in as work begins to override security. It is already moving before the other two have steadied feet, however, "Where am I going," is still unknown.

Antru motions – points to the soaring rock – and shares the thought: "Follow around to the side. I'll tell you when to turn: Get to the rock, and then I'll have to climb."

Axael says, "We'll climb."

The one at the helm looks briefly over and the look passed holds the same thought as the one between them: A wish for the safety of those loved, and a wish to carry the mission alone. But words are held by everyone, as all recognize commitment's already given. Argument would only waste time and effort.

"Here," Antru says.

They turn left on a road that leads from a mine. One driven hundreds of times – perhaps thousands – and one sprinted down on foot one time with the intent to prevent what was currently occurring.

They meet the rock, and all exit. Exertion brings, "We'll have to scale the edge," haltingly, as all three climb as quickly as their bodies allow. It's shared, "There's a recess in the mountain where they'll be hiding." Fingers grab at tiny imperfections, and feet dig at rock seeking anything at all that will propel a body upward. "We'll have to take them out," is an order that's unexpected and unwelcome, but hope is lit by, "Unless we can," is added: "Convince them to let us pass."

The edge of the winding road is reached, but it's avoided, unlike the prior time. Three bodies move through the trees and underbrush meant to obscure the grandiosity of the compound from the streets, but it serves the purpose to give cover from anyone that might be watching.

Where the road snakes into a pass and where the rise on the outside lifts, the three climb to the apex to assess the situation: Only one person can be seen. One standing at the opening of the recess and it appears likely that no one saw the three escape – at least, not the direction they ran – because the person is leaning against the opening, standing casually, and engaged in conversation. It should be a welcome sign but alarms are screaming: They are not concerned.

"Stay," is whispered, and it's insisted: "Let me talk to them."

Antru slips down, and two others follow, making the effort to be as quiet, and keeping slight distance to prevent communication. They are ignored as descent is made to the road, as it's quietly tip-toed across, and Antru slips against the rise and towards the opening.

"We arent' your enemy," brings a start, and cry, and there's a moment where an idea sees tremendous miscalculation: The cavern is much deeper than expected, and the numbers are significantly higher. It's quickly added, "You'll be obliterated if you try to harm us." It's emphasized, "The whole mountain. The net will pummel it to oblivion. You realize that by now – right?"

There are words passed that can't be heard – it's conversation. It's conversation that could be local, or could be relaying their position.

Antru steps to the opening and faces the hundreds that are present: "We're just trying to find our children. We're looking for parents and our partners. Do you think that's wrong? It's not just for us," Antru emphasizes, "It's for everyone: I know they take people from anywhere in the world, and I'm sure some of you've lost parents, or children, or partners. Tell me," Antru asks, "Do you go home after this to your families, or do you go home to an empty box, alone. Because we're just trying to end that. We're just trying to help people remember who they are, and the words Januk said, who are you in your dreams, wasn't asking about aspirations, it was telling you that you are that person that people call you in your dreams. Remember," Antru says, "And join us. We're fighting for you just as much as everyone. Let us go back home to our families."

That no action was taken gives hope a stand, and, "You think you have a chance," builds it further.

Antru answers, "Yes: We have Marphy closing in and Capriot's following behind them. Alvel's down, and the other cities are waiting to see what happens. It doesn't matter if I'm here or not. It's over."

For the first time, there's a flash across the face of the person addressed. There's some quiet words shared throughout those gathered, and it remains unclear it it's between them, only, or passed to others. But something said triggers conversation.

"They're in the rotunda." A person steps forward, and shares, "The emperor retreats there to reflect."

"Thank you," is offered, but there's another alarm that rings – a ring of red that foretells the words are given with duplicity.

Few more words are shared with a force that is more than capable of overwhelming just three that stand in their presence. They might be uncertain of capabilities, but any true defense would make attempt to decapitate the threat against them. Instead, they stood idly. They reacted calmly. There was no attempt to eliminate the face of the assault against authority.

It is why Antru says to Axael, "Pull hard on the net. This is going to be a set up."

They climb into the hills that are the highest most have ascended, but it is a place of familiarity to Antru. A place where deliveries were made with regularity, where unexpected kindness and consideration was always shown, and where breaks were taken despite desire to conclude obligations quickly. A place where sandwiches were shared and tea was given, in a space and time where both were given for an older person that always offered the impression they were lonely. They had never offered the impression they were an emperor, or, at least, the figurehead of the clan. It is, nevertheless, unsurprising.

"I'm first," insists Éayren.

There's no chance to argue as feet smash through a window and enter the dome. They are followed instantly. First their child, and then their child's own. They land, and they are already cringing as they do, as another explosion erupts around them:

The stone ceiling they've entered beneath implodes and rains down against a ring of soldiers that stood ready to eliminate the infiltrators. But their reaction was insufficient against an eye that was always expecting problems. An eye that didn't even register the danger before the roof caved in and any threat was eliminated before feet had met the surface within the building.

One stands against the three that entered, amongst the destruction and violence rendered, and hears a cry:

Antru calls, "Pull the rocks off them." There's a desperate plea called to the person standing, "Get help. Get people in here." And it's said, as the move to help them's started: "Help me get the rocks off."

One watches as three frantically pull the collapsed ceiling away, an attempt to salvage as many as possible. It's an observation that's superseded calls for elimination as there's always been a sense much could be offered: There was a belief that a connection to something that wasn't understood could be exploited. As that person's watched desperately pulling rocks off bodies, it's considered that the tangent adopted did not connect.

"They're alive," Antru cries after three were dead.

It is not long after that others begin to enter. Their order is, "Help find survivors."

It is there that thoughts finally break and Antru demands, "Why would you do that?" Bewildered, and

508

wondering, "What did you think was going to happen?"

That's answered, "It was a contingency we didn't think we'd need."

A last hurrah suggested on the chance, said humorously, at the time, as if there was any possibility that defenses might be breached. It is still a point where orders could be leveled, where those desperately striving to save the few that survived the stone collapsing, could be assailed, and the voice and face of a movement could be eliminated.

But the fire burns. It can be seen from where they stand, and the sounds of anger and violence make their way to the haughty heights. It is considered that a point's been reached where death might be more a motivator than deterrence. That a bulwark's passed and the tide will flood, regardless.

Eyes fall on a person that was always viewed sympathetically. First on an excited child with grand ideas – ideas that were then considered planted, but since then, a belief they are innate. They were a person watched as they found success on the roukta field, and one always invited for conversation when they brought deliveries.

At many points there had been discussions about threats posed by ideas, and eventually the person, but what was always remembered of them was their kindness.

First as a child that enthusiastically extolled the benefits of something incomprehensible, and still present as their first instinct after attempted assassination was to save as many as possible from the injuries that resulted.

They stand, looking back with anger. They look back with hurt that after everything, instinct is to attack with no room for conversation.

The fire burns and the sound of violence rises up the mountain.

"We've tried this," is the answer given – and the question's asked, "Are you aware of how that went?"

It is the history of the nation, and, "I am not Januk," refutes the implication.

"What will be different," is asked, and further, "What will stop our world from descending into chaos?"

"Us," says Antru. "I'm not hiding in Capriot. But you have to let us walk freely. We work together and it can work."

Doubt remains. Head shakes, but Antru insists, "We can use your system that's in place. We need to work together and show unity – show everyone that we participate, just like them." It's emphasized, "There will be accountability."

"You've made a mess," Antru's told, then questioned, "Do you remember coming up here?"

It's answered, "Yes."

"I think you were breaking through, back then – there was concern about that. Some even argued for your release, but I wouldn't let them. I kept you in the program. I ordered them to bring in every member of your family – including the youngest children. Do you really think you can work with someone like that?"

"Yes," Antru says, because, "I've seen a side of you that cares. You showed me kindness, and I think you've tried to act in the best interests of the people. Can you see that's different than you thought?"

There's a slight chuckle at the volley returned. Amusement found where it had been observed before: From a child lobbying to pull the net so they could climb without parental interference. Of a player with unchecked confidence and determination, that stated honestly that Elite could match their name. Of a transport operator always willing to go above the necessary, to arrange furnishing, build shelves, or just remain for unnecessary conversation.

After silence, "I've always liked you," is admitted. There was always a soft spot warned against – always a threat identified since birth: Of parents that were somewhat problematic, but managed. Concern had long been held the child could be an issue – there was something different. There had been warnings about the mythical connection: "Maybe that's important."

"This is Antru of Capriot," is stated to the air. Words shared, "I am standing in the ruins of the great rotunda of the Nespian clan's compound. We have agreed to work together. The opening created will serve as the opening for change, and this will be made into a public garden to represent that cooperation. Put down arms and celebrate with everyone in your presence. This is a night for celebration. Enjoy the day, knowing tomorrow, hard work begins. We will reunite all families and put in place the agreement of our ancestors. Nespia will be the brightest star in the entire universe."

"You just talk," is realized: "We are actually seeing through your eyes: I never would have believed it."

Antru approaches and extends a hand, and, "Thank you." The hand is taken with acknowledgement, "This won't be easy. But if we work together, we can do it."

There is doubt, and, "We'll have to have enforcement," speaks to the forces that brought failure to prior efforts.

It's not unintentional that the moment's shared, as Antru agrees: "It's our duty to take care of our children. No one wants to see them struggle while they're at the institutes. No one wants to see them struggle for food or not have clothes to wear, and that extends to all of us. We all want to eat, we all want to contribute to a functional society, because at the end of the day, we all want to come home to our families."

There are mixed feelings. There are doubts and alarms ringing, but, "Okay," is agreed, and an unseen face that has stayed in shadows is given order: "High alert, but we are coordinating with Capriot and Marphy. The next week will be used to celebrate," and eyes turn. Look to Antru, and question, "Antru of Capriot? Something about the Borrean Nation and their success?"

But Antru says, "Nespia. We celebrate ourselves."

It is an invitation that solidifies cooperation. It is a handshake that leads to an embrace – to understanding that what will follow will not be easy, and that forces of chaos will always tug at the social fabric. But it is also with the intoxicating poison that fuels every effort to change anything, to do anything, and that is hope: A poisonous liquid that slips through time with a glimmer that blinds the eye to the realization it is only a reflection. Silver that melts away from stars that burn incessantly, even when they're surrounded by only darkness.

End.

Unisource database

Open ticket: Nespia

☒ Revision   ☒ Entry

Details

See attached files: Numerous updates are needed

- Accuracy of historical record needs review
- Add sub-section - Borrean Culture and Influence.
    - Related: Borrean movement of resistance
- See: Culture - history of forced labor and cultural impact
- Add sub-section - Second civil uprising
    - Note constitutional revisions
    - Influence of Antru of Capriot
    - Aedra of Capriot
    - Axael of Marphy
- See: Nespian Defensive Net - Reference file, Gravitational anomalies in the Nespian region.
    - Add sub-section - Temporal particulate and adaptation
- New entry: Antru of Capriot - Resistance leader
- New entry: Althrae of Marphy - First reformation steward